THE
MARTIAN
CONTINGENCY

THE
MARTIAN
CONTINGENCY

MARY ROBINETTE KOWAL

TOR

TOR PUBLISHING GROUP ✳ NEW YORK

THE MARTIAN CONTINGENCY

Copyright © 2025 by Mary Robinette Kowal

Map by Mary Robinette Kowal

A Tor Book
Published by Tom Doherty Associates / Tor Publishing Group
120 Broadway
New York, NY 10271

www.torpublishinggroup.com

Tor® is a registered trademark of Macmillan Publishing Group, LLC.

The Library of Congress Cataloging-in-Publication Data
is available upon request.

ISBN 978-1-250-23705-7 (trade paperback)
ISBN 978-1-250-23704-0 (hardcover)
ISBN 978-1-250-23703-3 (ebook)

Our books may be purchased in bulk for promotional,
educational, or business use. Please contact your local bookseller
or the Macmillan Corporate and Premium Sales Department
at 1-800-221-7945, extension 5442, or by email at
MacmillanSpecialMarkets@macmillan.com.

First Edition: 2025

Printed in the United States of America

0 9 8 7 6 5 4 3 2 1

For the members of the Lady Astronaut Club.
Thank you for being the kindest corner of the internet.

Tell me how you see my role—
To stay, to wait, yet yearn to go.
Where is the comfort for my soul?
You, my love, have helped me know.

Patricia Collins

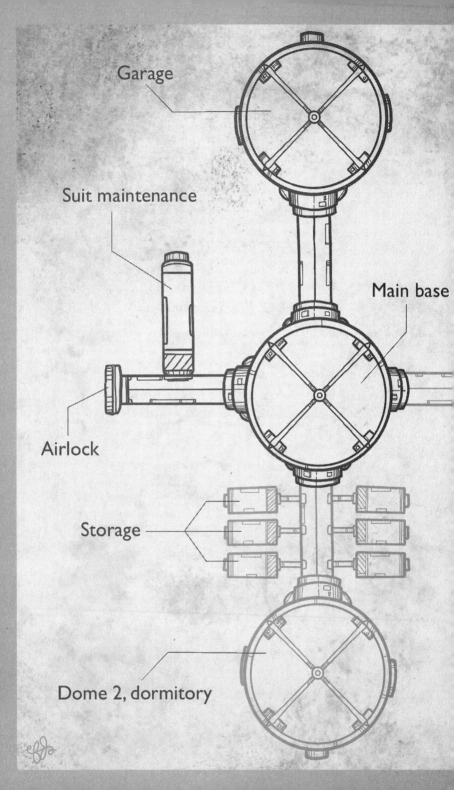

Garage

Suit maintenance

Main base

Airlock

Storage

Dome 2, dormitory

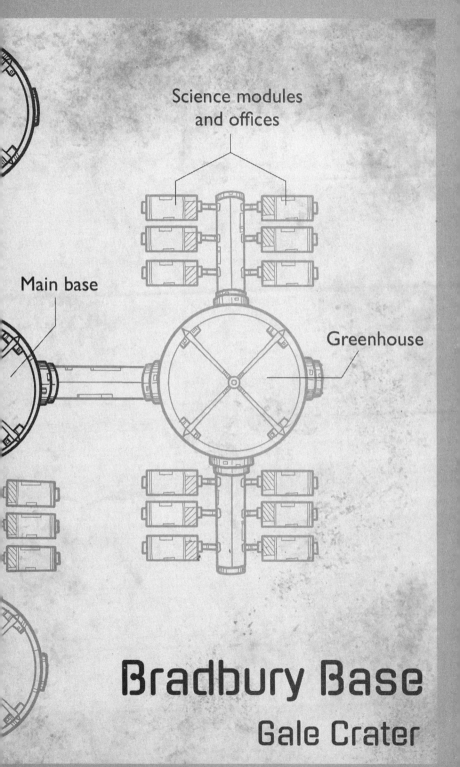

Science modules
and offices

Main base

Greenhouse

Bradbury Base
Gale Crater

PART I

ONE

A NEW ELLINGTON SCORE MARKING
THE RETURN TO MARS

Special to The National Times

KANSAS CITY, February 5, 1970—Duke Ellington
has been commissioned to compose and perform an original score to celebrate man's return to Mars. The Ellington composition takes about ten minutes to perform: It
includes vocal music entitled "Mars Maid," to be sung by
Ella Fitzgerald.

President Wargin and Ellington watched together as
the Marswalkers left their spacecraft this morning. "This
is a tremendous day," the president said, "as we take our
next step to establishing a permanent presence on Mars to
create a new safe haven for humanity."

The performance will be staged in the New White
House in Kansas City in mid-August when the second
dome at Bradbury Base will be opened and the colonists
now in orbit descend to their new home on Mars. The performance will be transmitted to the Red Planet for the enjoyment of the one hundred men and women living there.

Fem 50, Mars Year 5, Frisol, 1900 hours—Landing + 0 sols

Do you remember where you were when the stars came out? I
was with my husband, on Mars.

So many pivotal moments in my life had involved stargazing before the Meteor. I hadn't seen a clear night sky from the
surface of a planet since it struck Washington, D.C., on March

3, 1952. Twenty-six million dead. Numbers have shape and texture in my head, and this one was dense and pitted and worn smooth from seventeen years of grief.

Seventeen years since the Meteor and here we were on Mars.

Above the undulating horizon of Gale Crater, the Martian night twinkled. The stars did not blaze in crystalline perfection the way they did in space. They sparkled through the atmosphere. Blue and red, silver and gold, danced against a deep purple.

The stars that had been our navigational aids on the voyage here drew my eye like old friends.

I wanted to linger on the surface of Mars and stargaze with Nathaniel, not knowing when I'd be suited up and outside at night again. But it was a selfish waste of consumables.

I needed to head into Bradbury Base, where the rest of the team was, but as soon as I did . . . as soon as I finished that last item on my checklist, I would stop being a pilot and switch to my other role as second-in-command on the mission.

Nathaniel leaned his helmet against mine. "What's going on?"

"Hm?" I blinked and turned my head to smile brightly at him. We were on Mars! After years of working to get off Earth, we were here as part of the Second Mars Expedition. We were the next step in creating a new permanent home for humanity. I should be happy. I was happy. "Just enjoying the stars."

"Uh-huh . . . For the record, how long have we been married?" He raised an eyebrow.

"Twenty years."

"Twenty years! And none of this gear hides your fretting face."

"Fretting face?" I rolled my eyes, but I could feel the line between my brows relax. "Fine. I'm fretting because I'm about to have to go inside and be in charge. Why did I let Nicole talk me into this?"

"Well, I mean, she is the president of the United States." He gave a rueful chuckle. "And very persuasive."

The bean counters back on Earth had wanted me—no, they'd

wanted the famous Lady Astronaut of Mars in a visible command position to lend credibility to the mission. That should have come from the actual mission commander, but Leonard Flannery was Black. He was also eminently more qualified to be mission commander than I was. He'd landed on the planet on the first mission. I hadn't. But I was very good at being a pretty face for publicity.

Thank God we were past the days where we had to avoid mentioning that I was Jewish. Mostly past.

"All right. Let me finish this checklist and we'll go in."

I walked around our landing craft, the *Esther,* one last time to check the tie-down straps. The landing pad was the same familiar shape as the one on the Moon, but a soft salmon instead of lunar gray. Everything felt different from training. I'd experienced spacesuits and Moon suits, both were stiffer than a Mars suit. Training on Earth, it was heavier. Training on the centrifugal ring of the *Goddard,* we always fought the Coriolis effect. Training on the Moon, you couldn't hear the whisper of wind outside your helmet.

Wind. Just wind. Not the sound of a spacesuit failing.

The hours after landing had been a focused series of checklists and supervising the off-loading while other members of the team got the habitat up and running. Then I'd turned to making sure that the *Esther* was locked down since it would be a month, at best, before I launched again. And Martian months were fifty-five sols long, so beyond the checklists, I wanted to make sure my ship was tucked in snug and secure.

And she was. There was nothing left to do. The last box was checked on my list.

"Elma, come look." Nathaniel stood between the *Esther* and the arched doorway into the base. "The *Goddard* is transiting."

I didn't run, because that's a good way to fall and damage your suit. But I looked up as I walked to him. Across the dancing backdrop of the evening sky, the clear bright light of the *Goddard,* the ship that had brought us here, traced an arc across the heavens.

"Oh—" My breath caught at the sight of an evening star. We weren't displaced enough in the galactic disc to make a difference, so we had the same stars and the same constellations. Except for one significant difference. "It's Earth."

Small and the palest blue, if you thought about the color blue while looking at it, our home planet sat low on the horizon to the west where the sun had set.

Nathaniel was silent as we leaned against each other in an embrace. I could feel his weight against me, but the details of his body were lost to the pressurized surfaces of our suits. He shifted. "Where?"

"See Orion? Follow the belt and then . . . it's the one that's bright like Venus."

His helmet rested against mine and I could hear the telltale snuffle of an astronaut whose nose is running. You can't wipe them in a spacesuit. It was good to know that the sheer joy of having made it here—to Mars—was making him cry, too.

When the *Goddard* passed below the horizon, I sighed and turned to look at Nathaniel. The one exterior light at Bradbury Base cast his face into yellow and gray relief.

My piloting work was truly done for tonight and I could feel the fatigue starting to catch up.

I squeezed Nathaniel's hands. "How are things inside?"

"Starting to wind down for the night." He nodded toward the dome, which cast a warm glow up through the bit of translucent curve that peeked above the regolith. "A couple of annoyances but nothing we didn't plan for."

"I can't believe you suited up again to come back out for me." And not just because putting on a Mars suit was tedious, but because he had voluntarily walked away from ongoing work.

"I wanted to be here when you looked up."

Holding his hand, I took one last look at the night sky before walking back to the base. I could stare at the stars forever.

Ahead of us, the entrance to Bradbury Base waited to guide us into our new home. The First Mars Expedition landing team had built it in 1963 as part of the long process to create another habitat for humanity. Nathaniel's engineering team had blueprints and plans for expanding the base, but for now it was comfortably cozy for twenty. Our first order of business would be to build the second dome so that the eighty colonists still aboard the *Goddard* could start coming down to join us.

I paused at the entrance to check the pressure gauge and then looked through the porthole to confirm that the interior door was shut. I pumped the ratchet handle to open it and Nathaniel followed me in, pulling the hatch shut. I was proud of him as he went through the process of latching it. He'd had training, yes, but this was his first long-duration mission in space.

When the hatch was secured, I activated the suction fans that pulled the worst of the Martian dust off our suits. Our suit techs would get the rest. Suit techs. A luxury we hadn't had when I'd started going into space.

When the cleaning cycle ended, the airlock automatically began to pressurize.

A part of me had expected Bradbury to be as rustic as the original lunar base, but on the First Expedition, my teammates had spent thirteen months working on the surface and had built this habitat to be ready for shirtsleeve levels of casual living. Assuming that nothing went wrong.

If I knew anything about space, it was that something always went wrong.

The green light lit, and I checked the gauge anyway. Pressure normalized, I released the valve on the side of my suit, feeling the slight pop as the pressure inflating it relaxed and fabric settled against my undergarments. Hands aching from a sol in the suit, I pulled off my gloves and tucked them under my right arm in a way I absolutely could not while it was pressurized. I had my helmet off while Nathaniel was still fidgeting with his left glove.

"Need help?" I reached for the latch to open the interior airlock.

"I can get it." His words echoed, coming through the comm earpiece and muffled by the glass of his helmet.

Nodding, I inhaled and stopped. A scent of sulfur with a chalky sweet overtone filled the airlock, in a combination unlike anything I'd smelled before. On the Moon, when you came back in, you got a scent of gunpowder and old campfire that was the weird but unmistakable smell of lunar regolith.

This was Mars.

This was what Mars smelled like. I let go of the handle and turned back to Nathaniel, waiting for the moment when he had his helmet off. The second glove was clear. Grinning, I bounded over to him, so that I was directly in front of him when he removed his helmet.

"Breathe in." I bounced on my toes.

His nose wrinkled. "I know. It smells like rotten eggs."

"That's Mars." I grinned at him. "The folks who got to go down to the surface during the First Mars Expedition said it smelled like rotten eggs. That's Mars. We're smelling Mars."

"You are very excited about rotten eggs."

I leaned forward and kissed him. "I am." I kissed him again. "It's a whole new planet."

The door to the airlock gave plenty of warning that it was opening, as the fifteen latches released in their distinctive ripplebang and Leonard poked his head in. "Are we already going to have to have a conversation about appropriate use of airlocks?"

"We can smell Mars!" I beckoned to our mission commander before remembering that he'd been here before as one of the geologists on the First Mars Expedition. "Oh. I guess . . . I guess that's old hat for you."

Leonard grinned. "True story. When we were back on Earth, my mom cracked an egg that was rotten. Stunk up the house but the first thought that went through my head was, 'home.'"

A little flush of excited reality went through my body because until I heard him say "home" it hadn't really sunk in that we were here to stay. Every mission before this had been a stepping stone making sure that humanity wasn't trapped on a single dying planet. But every mission before this had also been finite. Establishing a permanent colony was why I was here, and also . . . Earth was still home to me.

I think Leonard must have seen some of that on my face, because he pulled the airlock door wider and stepped back. "You get used to it."

I squinted at our mission commander. My hands and shoulders ached from being in the suit all sol. I wanted to relish the memory of flying in a red-hot slice through the atmosphere, but also, Leonard shouldn't be meeting us at the door. I wanted to retreat to the ship so I didn't have to shift to my administrative duties so fast.

I followed him out of the airlock into the long hallway that connected to the main dome. "Aren't you scheduled to be in comms now? What's up?"

"The engineering team needs Nathaniel." He held up his hands. "Nothing urgent. Everything is under control. It's just that Reynard has questions about the defaults on the life support."

Nathaniel looked down at his suit as if he wanted to run straight there. "Be there as soon as I change."

I raised my eyebrows at Leonard. "I thought you said everything was under control?"

"Wouldn't be space without contingency planning." Leonard's voice was relaxed, but I could see the alertness that straightened his neck.

"What's going on with life support?"

"It's stable." Nathaniel ran his hand through his hair and grimaced. "I mean, stable enough. One of the secondary redundant flow sensors for the scrubbers isn't coming online the way I'd like, which we'd expected might be the case after being shut down for four years."

"So it's nothing outside of mission parameters?"

"Nothing we don't have contingency plans for." Nathaniel took a step away from us. "I should really . . ."

"Go." Leonard made a shooing motion. As my husband awkwardly bounded toward the donning station, Leonard looked back to me. "I would remind you that you're scheduled for a rest period but I know you well enough to recognize the urge to stress bake when I see it."

"Baking is resting." I stuck my tongue out at him. "And there's no way the kitchen is set up enough to be able to bake in yet."

He laughed and that felt good. During the first expedition, I had been a replacement crew member due to political pressures. The rest of the team had resented me. I was part of the crew but also outside of it.

This time, I was here from the start. I was a part of the team.

After I dropped my suit off with our techs and changed into a clean flight suit, I went down the corridor to the airlock that led to the main dome. I'd opened airlocks hundreds of times while living and working on the lunar base but on the other side of this one, the sense of the familiar and strange intertwined.

Just like Artemis Base, Bradbury Base was a broad hemisphere about sixteen meters across, half buried with ten meters of regolith mounded over it save for a large translucent skylight to let in natural light. The "buildings" were large packing containers lining "streets." The staircase down to the two lower floors curved from the same spot near the outer wall.

Where they had offices, we had a large open area along the north wall that doubled as a recreation area and as a large project assembly area. I imagine this is what Dorothy felt like stepping out the farmhouse door. It's the familiar door, but strangeness awaits on the other side of the threshold.

Waving at crewmates, who were all following their own checklists, I walked across the dome toward the kitchen area, but my path curved to one of the imprints left by the First Expedition.

Along the north wall, behind the large project assembly area, was a gorgeous mural in sapphires and umbers. I stopped in front of it, staring in wonder at the brilliant color amid all the white and gray and aluminum of the dome. I hadn't seen anything like it in the other habitats. If Nicole had been here, she would have told me what style it was, but all I knew was that what had at first seemed like abstract shapes resolved into an organic cityscape.

"What are you staring at?" Wilburt Schnöhaus, one of our mechanics, looked up from the case he was unpacking and followed my gaze. His brow creased for a moment.

"The mural. It's amazing. Who did it?"

The line between his brows vanished and his shoulders relaxed. He opened his mouth, then gave a little head shake as if changing his mind about what he was going to say. "Dawn's work. The city of tomorrow."

"I didn't know she painted." We'd had two ships on the First Expedition. Dawn and Wilburt had been on the *Pinta*, so we hadn't had much interaction until ours was disabled, and then . . . well, then we were focused on other things.

"Very good, too." He stood, stretching. "I have a joke about paint drying. It's a bit boring and takes too long to tell."

I snorted. "Does it feel good to be back?"

"It does. I had expected that cobwebs and dust would cover all, but everything is flawless as if we had yestersol departed."

I blinked, looking at everything again. My crewmates on the First Expedition had been on the surface for 380 sols, about 13 months by the Earth calendar, and had left signs of wear but it was as if they had left yestersol. "That is . . . surprising."

"This was my thinking as well. Kam took great delight in informing me that most dust in a house comes from human skin. So . . ." He gestured at the dome. "No inhabitants for four years means no dust. And also there are no spiders to make webs."

Would there ever be? We were supposed to be making another home for humanity here. Would future generations of Martian children recite "Little Miss Muffet" and be as baffled by spiders as I was by tuffets?

Wilburt's checklist sat open on the floor next to where he'd been kneeling with only a few items marked off. I was supposed to be in a command role, not distracting him with chitchat. "Well, I'll let you get back to it."

He sighed and knelt again as I headed to the kitchen.

At the moment, it was a large rectangular packing module with built-in rehydrator taps and heating units. We'd be stuck with rehydrated food until we got the greenhouse up and running. We wouldn't get a full kitchen until sometime after that. The moment it was open, I intended to bake a pie.

When I stepped into the kitchen module, two of the newer crew members were stowing supplies. Jaidev Kamal looked up from a checklist. Jaidev had been a chemist working on the lunar colony and jumped at the chance to come to Mars, where he'd oversee the processes that converted in situ resources to consumables. "Oh, good. The inventory, it shows the kitchen shears in cabinet A7, but I cannot find them. Where did you keep them?"

"Um . . ." I looked around as if I could help out in some way, but I was still in the land of the familiar and strange. The kitchen was the same basic module as the one we had started with on the Moon, but with a decorative border of rusty diamonds painted at the top of the ceiling. That was probably also Dawn's work, since she'd been down. "I don't know. This is the first time I've been in the module."

Across from Jaidev, his wife Aahana smiled at me apologetically and rested a hand on his arm. "Elma wasn't allowed to land because she was too important as a computer on the First Expedition."

"Sort of . . ." That made it sound like it had been about me, but it had just been practical. Terrorists from the group Earth First had taken out the Deep Space Network, and that meant we hadn't been able to rely on Earth for navigation. "Mission Control kept the NavComps aboard. It's the first time down for me and for Heidi, too, when she lands."

"But you did the calculations." They were both from the India contingent, and Aahana had a British accent that was as plummy as the Queen's. Her specialty was geology and she'd worked on identifying lava tubes that could be used for habitation on the Moon.

"We both did. Redundancies." My smile felt too tight. She was making it out as if I was something special. NavComps did navigation and computing. Doing that math had been my job. Nothing more. "Do you want me to find Dawn? She might remember where things are."

"That's all right." Jaidev shook his head. "It's a get-ahead, so I can ask her when I see her. Did you need anything?"

Aahana's eyes widened. "Oh, I'm sorry. You probably came in for dinner." She stood and moved away from the water tap. "We're ahead of schedule but we still don't have everything unpacked."

"I actually came in to see if I could be helpful."

Jaidev consulted his list. "No . . . no, unless you have a way to improve freeze-dried meals."

"Beats the astronaut kibble."

Aahana laughed. "Nicole told us about that in training. I can't believe that was a real thing."

"Oh, we never flew with it." I looked at the bins stacked along one wall. It was so tempting to open one and start unpacking it, but they had a method and me jumping in to help would throw their plan off. "When it got damp, it was like glue."

"What did it taste like?" Aahana's eyes were bright with curiosity.

"Meat-flavored cardboard."

She laughed again just a little too loud and watched me just a little too intently. I'd managed to forget that Aahana had been fourteen when the Meteor struck. She literally went into this field because of me. I know that because she told me when we met. She had shown me a copy of her Lady Astronaut Club membership card.

During training and on the trip out, with a hundred people on the *Goddard,* her . . . her *interest* in my career hadn't been obvious. It was now. But she was a brilliant geologist who had done good work on the Moon.

She would settle down again. It was just because we were in a new place. I turned my attention to Jaidev, who had probably joined because of Stetson Parker, the First Man in Space. We got paired all the time in people's minds even though he'd hated me for more than a decade.

"Sol 1 dinners are stacked on the outside wall." Jaidev consulted his clipboard. "Bin 1632-A."

Aahana leaned in as if she were confiding a secret. "I knew you would want it—this being Frisol—so I made sure your kosher meals were accessible when we were bringing things in from the ship."

"Great." I did not have the energy to explain that keeping Shabbat was not a deciding factor in keeping kosher. "Thanks."

I extracted myself and went in search of the bin.

On Earth, Nathaniel and I were casually kosher, didn't mix meat and dairy when I was cooking but did if we were at a friend's house. But for the first time, I wasn't the only Jew on the mission, and I'd advocated for others in ways that I wouldn't have for myself. So there were kosher meals on this mission.

My first Shabbat on Mars. Don't ask me if I started crying when I pulled those vacuum packs out.

TWO

Dear Aunt Elma,

Look at me using Mars dates! Because you're on Mars! How was your *sol*?

I had the funniest experience yester*day*. I was on a training run with the Berkeley track team and really lagging. One of the girls teased me about the fact that I kept yawning and I joked, "I was up late watching my aunt go to her new job." And she joked back, "I don't think I want to know what your aunt does."

And I said, "Just wanders around on Mars, I guess."

And then I realized that she wasn't running next to me anymore so I stopped and she was standing in the middle of the track with her mouth hanging open. "Your aunt Elma is *Elma York*?!?"

Apparently, I'd talked about you a lot but had only said that you were a pilot. Because, honestly, sometimes people get so weird about it. Anyway, she's swell and we've known each other long enough that it doesn't change anything but I just thought it was hilarious. I wish you could have seen her face it was soooooo funny.

Write back when you get a chance although I know you'll be horrifically busy so it's okay if it takes a while.

Love,
Rachel

P.S. Mars months are ridiculous. 55 sols? Really? And why didn't they come up with new months instead of just tacking an *M* on to everything? Fem? Aprim? Maym! It sounds like the month could hurt someone.

Fem 51, Year 5, Satursol–Landing + 1 sol

My first Shabbat on Mars was *not* going to be a day of rest. The light through the translucent part of the dome had shifted since I got up. That was going to take some getting used to. On the Moon, a day lasted two weeks, so the light change was as slow as molasses in winter.

Leonard stood in front of the whiteboard that had been on Mars since the First Expedition. They'd left it wiped clean, ready for us to arrive. With his hands clasped behind him, he looked professorial somehow.

Compared to me, who had curlers in my hair for the news-reel we had to record later.

He smiled at our small contingent of astronauts. "Good morning, everyone."

"Good morning, Dr. Flannery," Lance called in a singsong, so apparently I wasn't the only one who saw the geology professor that Leonard used to be.

He smiled, one corner of his mouth going up at an angle to twist his crooked nose even farther. "All right, class . . . welcome to your first sol on Mars. Let's go over your assignments for to-sol, but—" He glanced at the one empty chair and sighed. "Can someone go fetch Nathaniel?"

I started to stand, but Lance was on his feet first. "I know where he is."

"While we're waiting, let me bump something forward on the agenda. Helen, Howard, and Nuan Su?"

Helen stood up, picking up a carry bag I hadn't noticed. Howard and Nuan Su Tang, from the Singapore and US contingents, respectively, stood to join her. Howard was in the engineering department and had such cheekbones. I mean, I love my husband, but Howard Tang was worth looking at. He was also married and had met his wife, Nuan Su, in L.A., where they'd both studied at CalTech.

On the Moon, Howard had often worn soft sweaters and

looked like someone's idealized idea of a boyfriend. "Hi, folks. It's . . . um . . . it's Lunar New Year back home."

Helen said, "It seems appropriate that it is also the beginning of our time here on Mars. I know we all have to work, but I hope you'll indulge us in a little bit of celebration." Helen unzipped the carry bag and held it so that Nuan Su could reach in.

Nuan Su pulled out a handful of red envelopes. "We are wishing you great happiness and prosperity here."

Florence grinned at Howard when he handed her one. "*Gong xi fa cai.*"

His face lit up and he winked.

By the time Helen reached me, I'd managed to pull the Hokkien phrase out of the part of my brain that had learned it years ago. "*Kiong hee huat tsai.*"

Her eyes sparkled as she gave me the envelope with both hands. We'd been training together for years, so this wasn't our first Lunar New Year as a team, but Helen, Howard, and Nuan Su were the only crew members on Mars who had grown up celebrating the holiday.

The envelope had a dog perched atop a stylized "1970" and had a little bit of a heft to it. More than I expected. Around me, I could hear other people making surprised exclamations, but I paused before opening mine as Nathaniel and Lance emerged from the stairs. They jogged over in a less extreme version of the forward bounding run that we'd learned on the Moon.

Nathaniel skidded to a stop, looking at Aahana sitting next to me, and then settled in the remaining empty chair. I shrugged a little apology to him, but also, he could have been on time.

I opened my envelope and slid out a gold coin. "Hanukkah gelt?"

Beside me, Aahana said, "Are you okay?"

"Yes. It's just . . ." A surprised laugh bubbled out of me looking at the menorah on the back of the gold coin. "Why?"

Helen blushed a little. "We're supposed to give money but it didn't make any sense here. Chocolate, on the other hand . . ."

From his seat, Howard said, "It was shaped like money so it seemed to fit symbolically. I didn't . . ." He faltered. "Is it okay?"

"I think it's great." I tucked it back into the envelope and a happy glow filled me. The thoughtfulness of everyone on this team was just . . . I loved all of these people.

Leonard tucked his envelope into one of the pockets of his flight suit. "Now that we're all here . . . Each department will begin confirming the inventory of equipment left behind."

"That's what we were doing downstairs, in fact." Nathaniel's hands were clasped tightly in front of him in the way that he did when he was annoyed at being interrupted by something. "Sorry to keep you waiting."

"With the curlers in your hair, I thought you two had just overslept." Catalina swung around in her chair and raised her eyebrows, grinning at me. "You two were 'firing all thrusters' pretty late last night."

My cheeks flared so hot that I thought I'd probably gone through the red of a blush into an incandescent white. I was a modern woman and Nathaniel and I were a healthy, married couple. And yet . . . there was a part of my brain that immediately thought about how my mother would be so appalled that anyone had heard us. *What would people think?*

Aahana hissed through her teeth. "Catalina! Don't be rude."

She said it as if teasing me was like teasing someone's mom. As if I were old and a prude. The curlers did not help this image. While it was true that Nathaniel and I were the oldest people on the mission, we were still all peers. I was not a prude.

In a voice I usually reserved for the bedroom, I said to Catalina, "I'm a pilot. We fire thrusters, prepare for launch, and prime engines as needed. What do planetary ecologists do?"

The crew burst into laughter. Lance's booming laugh bounced off the curve of the dome. Shaking his head, he leaned forward and slapped Catalina on the back. "She got you."

"Rocketry is all fine, but come to me if you want to talk about pollination."

"How does pollination compare with orbital insertion?"

It was like we had unleashed a tide of innuendo. "I'm fond of second stage, myself." "Buddy, my main engine don't ever cut off." "Who's going to light your candle?"

Leonard cleared his throat.

"Sorry." Wilburt grinned. "We're being astronaughty."

Groaning, Leonard clapped his hands together. "People. We have work to do. Try to hold it together."

Someone muttered "between the sheets" and a chuckle rippled through the group. We probably needed the tension release—such as it was—but I had not intended to derail the meeting. I was supposed to be supporting Leonard, not making things more difficult. If I tried to help him restore order, it would look like I was using my position to protect myself. The only thing I could do to help was to just shut up.

As I jogged over from finishing an inventory of CO_2 scrubbers, Dawn and Florence were setting up for what we affectionately called the "Elma and Leonard Show" to be broadcast back to Earth. Publicity was . . . not my favorite part of my job.

But it was necessary because there were constantly people who thought that the Earth was not really warming after the Meteor strike of '52. That all of the money spent on the space program was due to a hoax. They were convinced that after the three years of Meteor Winter, the planet had healed. They ignored the fact the Chesapeake Bay had been ejected into the upper atmosphere and all that water had stayed up there. Turns out, the greenhouse effect was very real. So, I had the lovely job of trying to make space seem "exciting" and "for everyone."

Dawn had one of the camera tripods unpacked already and was gesturing toward the kitchen module. ". . . show everyone how we are settling in, then the kitchen, it seems, is an appropriate choice."

I stopped by the women, tucking my lipstick into one of the pockets of my flight suit. "Sorry I'm late. There was a discrepancy."

Florence lifted her head from the audio gear and gave me a once-over, taking in the curlers in my hair. And yes, the IAC had sent a checklist for how to do my hair. She sniffed and turned back to the console. "You saying we couldn't count?"

"No, no, I'm sure it was probably just a transposition error back at Mission Control." Florence and I had always had an uneasy relationship and I did not want to annoy her by implying anything negative about the First Expedition folks. She and Dawn had landed. I hadn't. I started pulling curlers out, irritated that I had to pay attention to my appearance even here. "Anyway, thanks for getting started. Catch me up?"

Florence tilted her head away from me and nodded at the kitchen module. "Looking at the list of choices, we're thinking the most interesting backdrop will be the kitchen. If we turn off the water heater, the audio shouldn't be too bad."

"What about in front of the mural Dawn painted?" It would be unexpected and get right to the idea of culture that Nicole was always going on about. The curler snagged and I slowed down, unwinding it carefully.

"No." Florence shot a glance at Dawn and shook her head. "Mission Control sent a list of possible locations and we're going to go with one of those."

"But they didn't know about the mural." I drew the curler in my bangs out, looking through the soft brown curls at Dawn. "I hadn't known you painted anything down here until we arrived."

Her face heated and she shared a glance with Florence. "It did not fit in the reports."

"Well . . . all right. But we know about it now, so why not? It's pretty and it gets away from the whole 'woman's place is in the kitchen' thing." Which would have seemed more compelling if I weren't stowing curlers in my pockets.

Dawn held out her hand, beckoning for me to hand her the curlers as I removed them. Then she glanced at the mural, shaking her head. "I'd rather not." She set the curlers on a case and turned her attention to cleaning the lens of the camera.

I would wonder why she didn't want anyone knowing she

painted, but I have my own demons about being in the spot-light. "We don't have to mention that you painted it."

"Kitchen." Florence picked up her audio gear and looked pointedly over my shoulder at Leonard. "Right, boss?"

I kept my face placid, even though it felt like a slap. I was the deputy administrator and she'd just cut me right out.

I turned to hide the sting behind a smile at Leonard. My hair was half down and half in curlers and it was really not the image of authority I wanted to convey. "I would really like to avoid the implication that a woman's place is in the kitchen. The mural is beautiful and showing art created on Mars would be a powerful statement about what we're building here."

"Let's stick with the preapproved locations. And if we're *both* there, no one will assume that a kitchen is a woman's place." Leonard put his hands on his hips. "We need to hop to it to get ready for this cockamamie scheme."

They didn't leave me a lot of choice but to go along with it. I pulled another IAC-approved curler out of my hair and broad-ened my smile, because I was a team player, after all. "Right, kitchen it is."

Leonard sighed. "Don't be mad, Elma."

"I'm not." I knew that my voice was level and my face was happy. I winked at him as I reached for another curler. "I'm just disappointed."

"Ouch!" He laughed, moving us toward the kitchen, and handed me the script we were supposed to use for this "live" broadcast to Earth. The paper was lightweight onionskin and rattled against itself. "Mission Control sent updated pages."

I took them, skimming over the pages, which were filled with platitudes. "Wait. We're talking to Clemons? What happened to the UN Secretary General?"

"Apparently he's reading to his son's kindergarten class, so they're delegating the task of speaking to us to the IAC."

"Wow." Kansas was nearly six hours behind us now, so this was scheduled to air during their morning news. "I knew space-flight was becoming routine, but . . ."

"But it burns." Leonard nodded, stopping next to the kitchen module. "May as well have prerecorded the whole thing."

"It would have been a better image, that's for sure." Florence set her audio gear down and knelt next to it. "First time we were here, the idea of sending video back was laughable. Even still photos felt like a miracle."

"Mechanical computers." I dramatically rolled my eyes, even though I didn't mind not having to do grunt computation anymore. I patted my hair, feeling for lingering curlers or pins. "Pretty soon I'm going to be out of a job."

"You're here as a pilot anyway." Dawn set up her tripod and camera next to the kitchen module. "Stand there and let me frame this. Both of you."

Here as a pilot. No. I had been a pilot. Now I was supposed to be the deputy administrator. In name, at any rate. Restraining a sigh, I moved to stand where indicated, still holding one of the curlers in my left hand. This, at least, was familiar. The entire time we'd been on Earth, the two of us had pounded the publicity pavement doing the "Elma and Leonard Show" in order to drum up support for the Mars program. I stood on his left, just the way I had on Earth, except that instead of wearing a pencil skirt I was in a flight suit.

For the next hour, I was able to slip into the routine of rehearsing for an event. Dawn and Florence both had PhDs in telecommunications engineering and were probably overqualified for filming this segment. They adjusted angles and put dry-erase marks on the floor so we'd know where we should be. I patted my hair and checked my lipstick one more time. Leonard just adjusted the cuffs of his flight suit.

And then Dawn was saying, "Five minutes."

"Thank you, five minutes." I'd learned some of the rituals of theater over the years of being the public face of the space program. The five-minute warning triggered my own ritual inside my head. *0, 1, 1, 2, 3, 5, 8, 13 . . .*

Around us, the work of our colleagues slowed to a halt as everyone came to watch us "talk" to Earth. We had a script that told us what Clemons would say, and when Florence gave us the mark, we would begin speaking as if we'd heard him. In reality, his words wouldn't get to us until sixteen minutes after he'd said them.

The entire thing was a stupid idea, but someone had gotten it into their head that a "live" broadcast would be more compelling than sending video. And who was I to tell them no?

Florence watched her gear and raised her hand into the air. A moment later, she dropped her hand and pointed at us. I smiled at the camera, imagining that I'd just heard the posh British vowels of Norman Clemons, director of the International Aerospace Coalition. He would be sitting at his desk with his fingers steepled over his belly and contrails of cigar smoke around his head.

Leonard nodded, smiling with the calm of someone who lectures to geology students and ambassadors with equal ease, and launched in as if we'd actually heard the man. "Thank you for those kind words, Director Clemons. We are proud to create this new homestead for humanity. We have spent the last sol waking up the base that we established on the First Mars Expedition."

I cut in, as scripted. "We should explain what a sol is, don't you think, Leonard?"

"Yes, Elma, that's a swell idea." Leonard smiled at the camera. "We've been living on Mars time since before we left the Earth and it's just become second nature to say 'sol' instead of 'day.' I don't even notice it anymore."

"Same here. You see, folks, a Martian day is thirty-nine minutes longer than one on Earth. To help our engineers back home know if they are talking about something that's happening tomorrow on Earth or 'next sol' out here, we've got different words."

"Yestersol, next sol, tosol . . ."

"My favorite sol is Frisol!" I quipped with a gee-whiz grin, facing the mural with its strong lines and vibrant blues. It really was a shame we hadn't set up in front of that. It had a depth and texture—it had texture.

It had texture because it was painted over something else.

"Yestersol," said Leonard, with a matching grin that he faded into earnestness as scripted, "we began the work of creating a colony. It is our great honor and privilege to be here representing people of peaceable nations with a vision for the future." He turned a little toward me, yielding the floor almost invisibly.

I dragged my attention away from the mural and smiled wider at the camera, imagining my niece watching with her college roommates. Most of those young people wouldn't remember life before the Meteor. "Yes, I think we are all looking forward to creating a place of safety and refuge." Anyone under twenty would only know a planet that was sliding down the slope of a runaway greenhouse effect. I wanted my family to come here so badly and hoped that would show in my face as a welcome to the rest of the world. Then, because it was my job to "humanize the experience," I had to continue to be warm and folksy. "I'm already planning what pie I can bake to greet the next group of colonists."

Then came the awkward silence. Sixteen minutes there and sixteen minutes back. If we timed it right, Director Clemons would have finished his remarks right before we started talking. He would be able to react to us in "real time," while we would have thirty-two minutes before we could hear his response. We'd practiced this on Earth with a timer. They would play a retrospective after his response, but no one was going to wait for us to reply to the director.

No wonder the UN Secretary General was reading to kindergarteners.

After we finished our respective Night Two checklists, Nathaniel and I walked to the cubicle along the outer wall that held our berth. This small space would be our home until we built the second dome.

He pulled open the plastic door and held it for me. Inside, light from the larger dome filtered through the translucent "skylight" at the top of the cubby and cast blue-gray shadows over us. This cubby had belonged to Rafael Avelino on the First Expedition, and he had taped pale blue tissue paper over the skylight. I missed him.

On the other hand, his absence was part of why I got to pilot this time. It would have made sense to have the ship piloted by someone who had already flown in Martian atmosphere. Instead, he had trained me and stayed home.

Home. He had stayed on Earth.

Nathaniel pulled the door shut, securing it with the flimsy latch. I leaned against one wall, feeling it give slightly at my weight, and tugged the zipper of my flight suit down very, very slowly. "Well, Dr. York . . ."

"Yes, Dr. York?"

"It's occurred to me that it would be a good idea to make sure the thrusters receive regular maintenance."

His dimple appeared, and he lowered his head to mine. At contact with his warm lips, my entire body lit up with delight. Slight stubble dusted his chin where his windup razor didn't give as close a shave as a safety razor. The sacrifices we make to conserve water. I didn't mind. The stubble added a delightful buzz, like feeling the hum of a plane's engine through your seat.

I slid my arm around Nathaniel's waist, running my other hand up the back of his neck to draw circles at the base of his skull. His hands skimmed down my back, one resting on my buttock to pull me closer. Through the thin walls, a single, unmistakable cry told me that one of the other married couples was having the same urges we were.

From the other direction, someone shouted, "Get a Busy-Bee!"

Nathaniel and I broke apart, laughing. I was glad that tonight someone else was getting teased for thruster maintenance. On the way out, the small shuttles had been one of the few places where one could have complete privacy. Here, the cost of shipping things to Mars meant that our walls were thin plastic panels. We could hear laughter all around us, joyful and not mocking. We were here. On Mars. And with a handful of exceptions due to expertise, most of us were married couples. Of course a lot of people were having sex.

Nathaniel and I found each other again in the dim light. Tonight we would—I pulled back. "Do you have the condoms?"

He opened his mouth and paused, frowning. "In the luggage." He meant our personal allowance, which was in one of the larger crates, not the small personal bag we'd had on the *Esther*. "I . . . sorry. I don't know why I didn't put them in my carry bag."

I grimaced and dug out the calendar I carried in my pocket. We generally used the rhythm method, so I kept careful track, but with the workload it was easy for me to lose whole sols, and the Martian calendar did not align neatly with my cycle. There was no good pattern for mapping the twenty-eight days of my cycle to the fifty-five or fifty-six sols of a Martian month.

Nathaniel tilted his head, trying to make sense of the circles and stars on the calendar. "Is there a launch window?"

I slid the calendar back in to my pocket. "Indeed there is, Dr. York, and I'm happy to report that we are Go for launch."

THREE

73 DEAD, 200 HURT IN BOMBAY RIOTING

Special to The National Times

NEW DELHI, February 12, 1970—The toll in Bombay rose to seventy-three today after three days of the worst rioting that a major Indian city has seen in recent years. The disturbances started Friday night with agitation over a long-standing boundary dispute between the states of Maharashtra and Mysore that was led by the Shiv Sena, a Marathi revivalist movement that has flourished in Bombay in the last two years after receiving funding from Earth First.

Earth First, a terrorist movement that began in the United States, believes that humanity should concentrate on preserving life on Earth. Prime Minister Indira Gandhi and other Indian leaders have denounced the movement as fascist.

Marm 1, Year 5, Frisol-Landing + 7 sols

Dark tire marks scuffed the floor of the base's garage. On the other side of the Mars Surface Rover, Wilburt decoupled the MSR geology pallet mounting post and checked it for wear. "Here, I have one now. Okay. An old lady for the first time drinks whiskey. She looks at the glass with some surprise and says, 'How odd, this tastes like exactly the medicine my late husband for twenty years had to take.'"

I laughed and moved on to step nineteen of my checklist,

the rear fender extension. "That actually sounds like my aunt, except that the whiskey would be for *her* rheumatism."

He laughed, slapping a hand on his knee. "I would have liked your aunt."

"Aunt Esther was a hoot."

"Ah . . . the aunt you named our landing craft after."

"Yeah." I concentrated on verifying that the rear fender extension was still secured to the vehicle. Sometimes work helps push away the grief. Sometimes it doesn't. She'd passed on our way home from Mars after the First Expedition. I hadn't gotten to say goodbye. She had always been delicate in build and in the last year before we left, she seemed like paper and glass, but in her lucid moments still had the wryest wit. Aunt Esther would have loved Mars.

Heck, my whole family would. My niece and nephew might get to come someday, but my brother wouldn't. As a polio survivor, he couldn't meet the flight-readiness qualifications. My chest burned with tightness and I had to swallow against the ball in my throat.

We hadn't even lived in the same time zone at ho—on Earth. It wasn't as if I had gotten to see Herschel regularly.

But I could have.

At least we had enough gravity on Mars that tears didn't form bubbles over your eyes. I swiped my thumb under my eye before I reinserted the hinge pin and moved to the next item on my checklist.

Wilburt cleared his throat. "You know, my last vacation before we left was terrible."

"Oh?" I glanced across the rover to where he was checking the rear steering decouple ring.

"Yes. In the hotel, I had room number one hundred." He paused dramatically. "And the one fell off the sign!"

"Um . . . sorry to hear that?"

He sat up. "It's a joke."

I stared at him, turning the sentence over in my head. "Did you go to the wrong room?"

He sighed. "At home in Germany, the bathrooms are marked with two zeros. See? Without the one, it looked like my room—only not my room, because it is a joke, but for the purposes of the joke my room would then look like a bathroom and people would be coming to it at all hours of the night."

"Got it . . . Very funny."

He snorted. "It is."

"I believe you." I released the inboard handheld tie-down. As it dropped, I straightened, cracking my back, and my gaze went to the wall of the dome. There was a patch there and it kept drawing my gaze in between steps.

The wall was multiple layers thick, but it was still unnerving to see a potential breach. The patch was chest high and only about the size of a glove, so the hole under it couldn't be very large. Still. This dome was aboveground. I could hear sand hissing across the outside. At some point, I'd get used to the sound of wind, but a decade spent working in airless places made me keep thinking that air was hissing out of the dome.

I nodded at the patch. I couldn't remember anything in the reports from the surface about an event that would have caused that. "So what happened there?"

"What do you mean?" Wilburt did a pull/twist test of the mounting bracket, checking that it was secure.

"The patch in the wall."

"Oh." He didn't turn to look at it.

How do you describe feelings like this? Wilburt and I have worked together for years, so I know the way that the skin around his eyes tightens when he is having a thought he doesn't want to say.

I know how his mouth twists a little to the side as he chews on the inside corner of his lip when he's working a problem. What problem was he working now?

His thumb drummed the top of the bracket. "It was dinged by the rover."

This was like when I'd been forced onto the First Mars Expedition team. The way they'd have conversations that didn't include me because I was an outsider. But I wasn't an outsider this time. Although I suppose you could argue that being in the command structure as deputy administrator did make me something of an outsider.

But he was lying to me. Why was he lying?

"How deep is it?"

"I don't know."

It was inconceivable to me that as one of two mechanics on the previous expedition he wouldn't know exactly how bad the damage was. "Did Rafael do the repair?"

There was that tightening around the eyes again and then Wilburt shook his head decisively. "No, it was I." Wilburt grabbed his clipboard and studied it for the first time since we'd come into the garage. "Where are you in process now?"

"Just finished nineteen."

"Nineteen? Only there?"

I knew he was changing the subject, but a little blush of panic sent a quick spike through my heart anyway. I checked my Marswatch against the list of procedures. "We're not behind."

"No, no . . ." He waved his hands and leaned back from the rover. "Only you are so meticulous that you are quite slow. It is like working with a rookie."

"Slow is fast." On my first trip, I'd had to play so much catch-up that I was mostly a pretty face who did math in her head. I was not going to let that happen again. "Also, this is the way we practiced it on Earth."

"Yes, because Mission Control was watching." He flipped the pages of his procedure manual, then looked up and pointed to my tool bag. "Ah! That is why you brought all of that gear. I thought you knew better."

I gaped at him a little. We had practiced this in multiple simulations and gone out for drinks afterward. There had been so many opportunities for him to revise the procedure. "The checklist says—"

"Yes. Yes. The checklist has everything that ground thinks we might possibly need at some point for every contingency."

He held up a hex wrench in one hand and a pair of pliers in the other. "You really only need these."

"You can't know that."

"No, but I *can* know that this is all I needed when I did the rover maintenance on our first trip." He shrugged and set them down. "Take your time."

I had been taking my time. Not going slowly, mind you, but I was being meticulous because that was the point of checklists. They kept you from making stupid mistakes.

Like driving a rover into the wall.

After I finished prepping the rover with Wilburt, the light through the dome had deepened to the cool blue of Martian sunset. I wanted to ask Nathaniel about the patch because asking Wilburt anything else had seemed like a fool's errand. Not when he was actively lying to me. I needed to talk to Leonard, too, but first I wanted more information.

On the other hand, it was almost Shabbat. If Nathaniel got too interested in the question, I could wind up making him work even later.

I took the stairs down to the administration level and followed the curve along the hall toward the engineering department. That took me past the comms center and what would one sol become our flight center.

The engineering area where Nathaniel managed his team of people was just past the spiral staircase and took up most of that hemisphere. The murmur of voices bubbled out into the hall, mingling with the hum of the ventilation system. When I ducked through the hatch, my husband wasn't in sight.

Reynard looked up from the schematic he was bending over and saw me first. The tall French man was probably Nathaniel's best friend—well, I guess on Mars he definitely was. He smiled. "He is downstairs with Lance."

"Thanks." I nodded and took the stairs to the bottom floor of the habitat. The hum of the life-support systems was louder here.

The entire bottom floor had been given over to the equipment room. Since the habitats were constructed from inflatable bubbles, the bottom floor was the smallest. I'd come down the spiral stairs into the middle, where four aisles made spokes to a walkway around the perimeter. Batteries, dehumidifier, oxygen, CO_2 scrubbers. They were all self-contained in the crates they'd been shipped in and installed in neat quadrants. The original plan had been to have central processing for things like power and water reclamation, but after the sabotage on the Moon, they'd decided to make each habitat self-contained with distributed battery backups.

Nathaniel and his team had to make changes to the equipment the First Expedition had installed in order to add the backups. My husband was crouched next to Lance, who was on his back with only his legs visible. One knee was hiked up and his other foot was rotating in slow circles.

Nathaniel looked around at the sound of my footsteps and grinned at me. His hair was mussed and he had that electric vibrancy he got when he was working. It sent out a current, lighting me up.

I bent to kiss him on the cheek. "Sun's nearly down. Finished soon?"

His brow furrowed as he looked at his watch. "Another fifteen minutes? I just want to see this assem—"

Lance's foot jerked. "Damn it. Ah. Shit."

"You okay?" Nathaniel spun back. He ducked his head lower, trying to see in.

"The head of the screw just sheared off." From inside the backup O_2 generator, Lance sighed heavily. "I'll have to drill it out. Or . . . actually, hang on . . . Yeah. There's enough of a stub that I can do the hacksaw trick and back it out by hand."

Nathaniel turned to a red toolbox and was opening it as Lance wriggled out of the access hatch. He was a jolly white American and had the largest hands of anyone I'd ever met. In the low gravity his sandy curls stood out as if he had a permanent static charge. He saw me and waved. "Hey, Elma." Squinting, he glanced at his watch. "Wow. It got late fast."

"Having trouble?" I stepped back out of his way.

Lance jerked a thumb at the access hatch. "Trying to track down why the backup O_2 generator is performing under capacity."

"The hacksaw is upstairs. Be right back." Nathaniel stood up, dusting off his hands and glanced at me. "You don't mind, do you?"

I did mind and also I knew why we were here. Two things can be true. At some point we would get to prioritize our own needs, but right now the safety of the crew came first. But there was also the question of the patch and the fact that Wilburt had lied to me. Catastrophic failures fluttered at the edges of my mind, urging me to think about what would happen if Wilburt was part of Earth First.

But the patch had been placed four years ago. It was out in the open. If Wilburt had been involved in Earth First, then the others wouldn't have let him come back. Unless, unbelievably, Leonard, Kam, Florence, Dawn, Graeham, and Heidi all were involved.

There was some perfectly reasonable explanation. Like Wilburt being distracted by prepping the rover. I mentally folded my question up and put it to the side for later. Nathaniel didn't know any of this. All he knew was that I wanted him to come up for dinner and Shabbat.

I brought a smile up from somewhere. "Sure. I understand."

He hesitated, eyes moving around my face, and I'm not sure how he measures what he sees there, but he can often tell when I'm not happy, even when I know I'm smiling and my voice is cheerful.

Nathaniel's lips compressed in the smallest of winces. "I won't be long."

This was clearly not true. Because what was about to happen was that he would help Lance get the screw backed out and then

he would want to see the assembly and then he would want to
test just one more thing and then he would come in and apologize and tell me that I knew when I married him that he was a
bad Jew.

And I would have had Shabbat dinner on my own.

Upstairs, Florence sat across the table from me and gestured
with a noodle dangling from the end of her fork. "No. No.
Nothing about that is right. Mm-mm. No."

Laughing, Opal Woolen leaned across the table toward her
and waggled her fingers. "Bees. Full of bees. Beeeeeeeeeees."

"So here's my question." Florence ate the noodle and shook
her head. "Why did you stay in it?"

Opal hesitated, tucking a strand of her straight dark hair behind her ear before shrugging. "The rent was cheap. And—oh,
hi, Nathaniel. I was wondering if you'd ever be finished with
my husband."

"Sorry." Behind me, my husband cleared his throat. "Just . . .
just got caught up in something."

I slid over to make room for him on the bench and he set his
meal pack down on the table. "Figure it out?"

"Not a clue!" Lance laughed and came around the end of the
table to squeeze in beside Opal. "But, the good news is that the
assembly is nominal so it's not that."

Lowering his voice, Nathaniel leaned into me. "I'm sorry.
You know how—"

"I do."

"You knew when you married me that I was a bad Jew."

It was a frequent joke between us, but this time I tensed to
keep from slamming my drink pack down. "Right now, we're
the only two Jews on Mars, so whatever you decide to do is how
Judaism is observed here."

He stopped with his hand on the seal of his vacuum meal kit.
"We have a whole minyan on orbit."

"Yes." There were, in fact, more than the quorum of ten adult

Jews required for a minyan, but that wasn't the point. "Do you think Isaac Abenrey, for instance, is going to be happy if we establish a precedent of working through Shabbat when it's not necessary?"

He sighed, lowering his head. "It's not . . . I've never been observant. He knows that. No one is going to take what I do as a model."

"Okay." I ate the last bite of cookie. Around us, the conversation had moved on to that TV show with a character inspired by Florence. I'd heard the story about her getting to visit the set and meet the actress, but it was clearly new to Opal and Lance.

Nathaniel put his hand over mine. "Hey. I'm sorry."

"Thank you." He was right. I did know who I married and I knew that he would work too long and too late and that changing that would change him. I loved him deeply because of his flaws, not in spite of them. I leaned over to kiss him on the cheek.

Nathaniel turned his head to meet me. His lips were warm and he tasted of coffee. My cheeks heated and I tightened my fingers in his.

Opal whistled and my cheeks got even hotter.

Straightening, I tucked my hair behind my ear as if being slightly tidier would help.

Beneath his bright blue eyes, his cheeks were rosier than usual. He cleared his throat as he fumbled peeling the plastic back on his meal. Steam rose from what looked like the meatloaf and beans dinner.

Nathaniel stirred the beans with his fork. "So. How was the rest of your sol?"

"Oh, fine." I folded the plastic that had covered my dinner. "There was one thing I wanted to talk to you about, though. Do you know about the patch in the garage wall?"

"Patch?" Frowning, he used the edge of his fork to cut the meatloaf. "No, but there are small changes that didn't get documented."

"A patch on an outer wall is not a small change." I brushed

crumbs from my cookie off the table into my other hand. "And there was also this weird moment with Wilburt—"

"Hey, Elma." Florence pushed back from the table. "I think you and I are on cleanup duty tonight, right?"

"Um." I looked around and everyone except Nathaniel and Lance was finished eating. "Yes. Coming."

Everyone bussed their own meals, and cleanup duty involved starting the processing for our composting and recycling. We all took turns, but Florence had complained every time she had cleaning duty.

I tried telling myself that it was good that she wasn't complaining now. But my brain kept spinning out catastrophes. I was primed to see problems where there weren't any because there'd been a terrorist on the Moon. *0, 1, 1, 2, 3, 5, 8* . . . It was only a coincidence that she had interrupted us.

This wasn't the Moon. Mars had to be different.

FOUR

February 16, 1970

Our dearest Kamilah,

How are you getting on? We have not heard from you in some time and your mother is worried. We are naturally reading the reports from Mars with much interest. We see your picture in newsreels and this causes her some anxiety.

Daughter, we understood that you were being very modern when you chose not to wear ḥijāb so I must tell you our concern is not that. But it allows us to see the way you have cut your hair. I must tell you that for a moment we thought somehow your brother Bachir, may Allah bless his soul, was on Mars. Our concern is that we remember you cutting your hair like this after your brothers died. We remember how you became so quiet. We are worried for you, beloved.

Please write to us and tell us your heart.

Yours in peace,
Baba and Yemma

Marm 5, Year 5, Tuesol-Landing + 11 sols

I barked my knee on the leg of Leonard's desk as I slid into place next to it with the pages I'd brought from comms with Mission Control's most recent schedules and procedures. "They bumped up the first supply drop pickup."

The first page had the brief overview of assignments.

Survey Dome 2 site—Aahana Kamal, Jaidev Kamal, Helen Carmouche (driver)
Engineering cable prep—Nathaniel York, Reynard Carmouche, Opal Woolen, Bolívar Gallego

Hopper flight prep—Lance Woolen, Graeham Stewman
Comms—Dawn Schnöhaus, Florence Grey
Suit maintenance—Zainabu Tatu, Mosi Mohammed Tatu
Greenhouse prep—Catalina Suarez Gallego, Nuan Su Tang
Floats—Kam Shamoun, Howard Tang, Leonard Flannery
Cargo retrieval run—Elma York, Wilburt Schnöhaus

He took the sheets from me. "Why the schedule change?"

"Weather. Apparently we're getting dust storms later." I shook my head in wonder. I had never, in all my years in space, had to worry about the weather except for launch and landing on Earth. But we were working on the surface of Mars. It had weather. So when we were talking about driving an hour away from the dome to pick up supplies that had been hurled to Mars from Earth months before we got here . . . yeah, weather would be a concern. Not rain, but dust storms.

Leonard flipped some pages and grimaced. "Will you and Wilburt be ready to go?"

"Yes?"

"That sounds like a question, which I don't like."

Gnawing on my lower lip, I scribbled a note on the duty roster. "Can I ask a question that's going to sound like a change of subject, but I swear is related?"

He studied me, then nodded. "Go ahead."

"Why wasn't the patch in the garage reported?"

The hum of the habitat's fans filled the silence. After a moment, Leonard shifted in his chair. "That was on Benkoski's watch. I was just a geologist on the first mission."

"What happened?" It was hard to tell how much of my desire to know was just wanting to feel included versus genuine concern that something was wrong. "Wilburt said it was a rover impact, but . . ."

But how did I explain that I thought he was lying?

"That's right." Leonard grabbed the schedule and started running his pencil down it.

"I checked the logs from the First Expedition and there's nothing in there."

"You know how it is . . . Benkoski sometimes wasn't the best at logging things."

That had never been true. I'd known Benkoski since before either of us were astronauts. The reports might be brief but he always completed them.

"Leonard—" I rolled my pencil under the palm of my hand. "Leonard, what is going on?"

He lifted his head, mouth a little pursed. "I'm not following."

My skin tightened at the back of my neck. The part of me that had been taught not to make waves wanted to back down. I swallowed and sat up straighter in my chair, pressing my hand flat on the pencil as if that would anchor me. "As your deputy administrator, it seems like something that I should know about."

He cocked his head to the side. "You do know about it. There was a rover impact. There's a patch . . . How is this related to the supply run?"

It was just that feeling again of being on the outside. I was supposed to be his teammate. We were supposed to work together. I shook my head, trying to find a concrete problem to point at besides "why are y'all lying to me," which wasn't going to get me anywhere. "I guess I'm just unsettled because Wilburt was skipping checklist steps when we were prepping the rover. I want to know if this is going to be a problem. He said that he did the repair. Was it done correctly?"

Leonard frowned, leaning back in his chair. "Did you talk to him about skipping checklist steps?"

"Yes, and he said it was okay because it worked before. He hadn't wanted to have meetings about changes."

"That's not a good answer."

"I know!" I picked the pencil up and flopped back as far as I could in my own chair. "That's one of the reasons I'm worried about the patch and why I have questions about if we're ready."

"Did you make him go back and finish the steps he missed?"

"I—no."

"Elma . . ." Leonard leaned forward in his seat again with full professorial face on. "I know you don't like being in charge but I do need you to help enforce discipline."

"Sorry." My body wanted to curl in on itself for having disappointed him, but I kept my spine straight out of long habit. "I'll talk to him after this."

"No, I'll take it. And don't worry about that patch anymore." Leonard picked up the duty roster again, flipping deeper into the procedure lists. "Now . . . let's see what other ways Mission Control has decided to mess with us."

He had given every appearance of supporting me. Yet somehow, I felt like I was on the outside again, because I didn't think that the patch was just a patch.

The next sol, I was inside the rover with Wilburt, and Leonard must have talked to him, because he was meticulous about his checklists. I was glad of that because we were going out on the surface of Mars. Mars. I wiggled in my seat and tried to clamp down on my excitement. I had a job to do. I needed to remember that this wasn't glamorous or exciting.

It was cramped, like the old lunar landers back in the day, but the grit caught in the edges of panels was reddish instead of the gray of lunar regolith. Reddish because it was Mars. We were going out on the surface of Mars.

Wilburt rolled the rover into the vehicular airlock and stopped it neatly in the middle.

In the hangar behind us, Graeham pushed the airlock door shut. His voice came over the speaker in our cabin. "Airlock secure."

"Copy, airlock secure." Wilburt set the hand brake. "Rover secured. Begin depress sequence at will."

"Depress sequence beginning." Graeham could have left that unsaid, as the sound of a train began outside the rover as the compressors pumped the airlock's atmosphere into storage tanks for our return.

On the airlock wall beside us, someone had hand-lettered a speed limit sign. *0.40 meters per second.*

Laughing, I nodded at it as I flipped to the next sheet on the checklist. "Think you were going a little over the limit there."

"I do not want to miss Eid al-Adha tonight, so perhaps I was speeding. A little." He grinned. "So, a police stops a woman driver and says, 'When I saw you coming round that corner, thought I, "At least forty-five."' And the lady says, 'Well, always this hat makes me look old.'"

Despite myself, I chuckled and at the same time winced because I was nearly forty-eight. "BUS A, BUS B, BUS C, BUS D circuit breakers—closed."

"Nav power CB—closed." The rover's electric engine hummed underneath us.

"Note, do not torque gyro or move the MSR for a minute and a half."

"I know, Elma. I have driven this before. And besides, the airlock doors are closed."

"Just reading the checklist. The one we're supposed to do all the steps of . . ." I didn't actually see him roll his eyes at me in response, but I could feel it. Outside the rover, the sound of rushing wind had begun to quiet.

"So did y'all put the speed limit sign in place after the rover accident?"

"Sorry, I am following the checklist, which does not give time for idle chatter. +15 VDC Switch—PRIM. Depress sequence sounds like it is finished." Wilburt leaned forward and looked out the window at the pressure gauge mounted in the outer airlock door. "Ah—and so it is."

The way he kept dodging the topic was deeply aggravating. But also, he wasn't wrong about needing to do our jobs. I toggled the mic. "Bradbury, can you confirm depress sequence is complete?"

Over our comms, Florence's voice crackled into the rover cabin. "Affirmative, Rover One."

Wilburt put one hand on the parking brake and the other on the right-hand controller. "Bradbury. We are prepped and request permission to drive to the nav alignment site."

"You are clear to proceed when the garage door is fully open."

On the one hand, this was just like a sim. I'd been in a model of this rover in a model of this garage more times than I could count.

On the other hand, as the door rolled up, Martian sunlight preceded a swirl of salmon dust. Mars!

Through the frame of the door, a ruddy landscape rolled away from us, bounded by the sheer wall of Gale Crater. It was almost like the training ground in Hawaii but the sky was a pale yellow instead of the silver blue we'd had there.

Wilburt rolled the MRV forward through the outer airlock door and it sounded different. Even being in the rover's pocket of Earth atmosphere, the Martian air transmitted sounds differently, so that when the crunch of the wheels on the compressed regolith reached us it was a thinner, higher sound. Despite everything, I was grinning.

We rolled into the sunlight, which was at once dimmer than on Earth and sharper. The sky was a clear, vivid butterscotch with the sun casting long morning shadows. Not the way they were on the Moon, where the shadows were a deep black without an atmosphere to diffract the light. These had sharp edges but still transferred a glow to their centers.

Since the Meteor, we so rarely got a day without clouds back on Earth that seeing shadows in an atmosphere was bittersweet. Familiar and strange, tugging at my heart and tying it up into knots.

A little dust devil swirled across the landscape, reminding me, again, that this was a planet with weather. "Wow . . ." I shook my head, watching it dance. "Wind."

During our landing, all I'd had time to pay attention to was the horizon. A sudden desire to take a plane up surged over me and then crashed back down. There wasn't enough atmosphere here for a plane. Not really. Not unless the wings were absurdly, unsustainably long. They'd come up with a "hopper," which Lance and Graeham were unpacking tosol, but the flight would be radically different than the soaring flight of a plane.

Pulling my gaze away from that beautiful strange and familiar landscape, I said, "Good job not scraping the wall."

"Why did the wall go to school?"

I rolled my eyes. "I don't know, Wilburt, why *did* the wall go to school?"

"To get a little plastered." He grinned. "See? Plastered can also mean drunk."

What I wanted was a teammate who would explain what had happened. What I got was a teammate who explained jokes.

That evening, when we got back after spending a sol on the Martian surface, I should have been exhausted. Maybe I was and I'd feel it next sol, but right now, instrumental Middle Eastern music full of ouds and goblet drums played over the base's speakers as crew members on the *Goddard* played a small concert for everyone on or around Mars to celebrate Eid al-Adha. A decade ago I wouldn't have known what any of those instruments were, and now I could recognize the players. Wangari Ogot, from the Kenyan contingent, played the ney with a round sweetness of tone that almost sounded like a human voice.

The smells of turmeric and savory fried samosas filled the dome. I sat at a table with Nathaniel and the Carmouches, holding an aluminum plate brimming with biryani, tagine, and curry.

My shoulders still ached from a sol spent in a Mars suit, but that seemed to fade away as I lifted one of the samosas. When I bit through the tender crust into the warm, savory interior, I closed my eyes and moaned a little.

"Should I be jealous?" Nathaniel laughed.

I grinned around the mouthful of samosa and nodded.

"Woe!" He clutched his hand to his heart dramatically and his fork spun out of his grasp. He fumbled for it as we all dissolved into the sort of exhausted laughter that comes at the end of a long sol of manual labor.

"Listen, you should know that as a Southern woman, I cannot resist anything fried." There's some magical alchemy that happens to dough when you fry it. The full kitchen was months away from installation, but Zainabu Tatu and her husband Mosi had done wonders with an induction burner.

Lance's sudden laugh boomed through the conversation. "Look! Fireworks."

Over his head, he held a balloon with a starburst drawn in marker. He clapped his hands together and the balloon popped. Confetti fluttered down. In the lighter gravity, it spread out in a wider arc, swirling in the draft from our fans. The laughter of our group bounced off the parabola of the dome and it seemed as if Bradbury Base was filled with more than just the twenty of us.

"Hooboy . . . That is going to be a pain to clean up." I pushed back from the table "Excuse me before he sets off more 'fireworks' and clogs the air filters."

I made my way across the dome to Lance, who was in a small cluster of folks.

Dawn was saying, ". . . let me get my camera and do it again."

I hated being the one to spoil fun. "Friends . . . two words. Air filters."

Lance winced, looking at the confetti still fluttering in the light Martian gravity. "I'll take care of it. Sorry."

"I'm not mad!" I patted him on the shoulder. "Just thinking ahead."

"We'll all help!" Zainabu beamed at me, wearing a headscarf spangled with mirrors and sequins. She held out a basket woven from strips of the foil pouches our freeze-dried food came in. It was filled with small round cookies. "Have a ma'amoul?"

I grinned because I recognized the filled shortbread cookie from years of working with Halim. Purim and Eid al-Adha both involved gifts of food, and that had involved more than one meeting when we'd been discussing stores for the trip. "Eid Mubarak!"

"Thank you!" She passed the basket to Dawn. "Now, what were you saying about blue before *someone* decided to set off fireworks?"

"Oh." Dawn took a ma'amoul and shrugged. "Right. The planet has blues here, but everyone focuses on the reds when they paint it back on Earth. There's this gorgeous deep purple-blue wash across the *chapéu de bruxa*."

I tilted my head. "Excuse me?"

"That's what Rafael called the . . . Come on, I'll show you."

She and I headed toward the mural for a closer look, which I should have already done, but we'd just been so busy. Mission Control had every minute of every sol scheduled. The mural had swaths of broad rough strokes. Looking at it, I realized that the squares weren't just a geometric abstraction but a rectangular habitat in front of the wall of Gale Crater. Dawn pointed to an outcropping.

"It looks like a witch's hat, so that's how you say it in Portuguese." She almost glared at it and then sighed. "I had only brought small brushes, so I had to use a rag to paint."

"I like the roughness." And I did. The painting had a sort of energy to it, as if the future couldn't arrive fast enough.

"I'll probably paint over it now that I brought the right brushes." She nibbled on her cookie while the party swirled on. "It looks clumsy to me."

I didn't know enough about painting to know if she was right or not. My own crafts tended to be paper. I could sew, of course, but I didn't take enjoyment from it the same way that I did with math or with the crispness of folding paper.

"What's this version painted over?"

"Nothing." Dawn swallowed, smiling, but her eyes darted to the spot where the paint was thickest.

"Oh." I wandered to the area that had caught my attention earlier. "It's just that there's this rough spot."

"That's . . . that's just adhesive from a leftover sticker." She looked down at her empty hand. "I'm going to get another ma'amoul. You?"

"I still have one. Thanks." I smiled and held up one of my remaining extremely delicious cookies. "I'm going slow because I want them to last longer."

After she left, I stayed in front of the mural, looking at Dawn's vision of our future. It was an awe-inspiring thought that someday there would be cities here. If everything went well. There were still so many things that could go wrong.

But for the moment, this was as convivial as any dinner party at home, even if the drinks were apple juice in bags. As I turned to go, my pattern-seeking brain saw a pair of vertical lines. Then a crosspiece.

In the area that had the most roughness, there was an *N*.

Interesting. Squinting my eyes, I found an *I*. Dawn had worked them into the structure of her city. Beneath a pair of curved windows, I saw two *G*s.

I stopped, suddenly cold. Now that I knew what to look for, I could see the rest of the word hidden under paint but still there. Who would have written that word on the wall of the—

No, I knew who it was. Vanderbilt DeBeer. On the First Expedition, the South African had been a constant problem to the brown members of our crew.

So, the question wasn't really "who had done this" or "why had it been painted over" but "why hadn't I known about it?"

FIVE

INDIAN SCHOOLING IN U.S. IS ASSAILED

New Agency Is Called for at a Senate Hearing

By E. W. KENWORTHY
Special to The National Times

KANSAS CITY, February 18, 1970—For nearly five hours today a series of witnesses told a Senate subcommittee on Indian affairs that, in their view, the only good Bureau of Indian Affairs would be a dismantled Bureau of Indian Affairs. The most prominent witness today was Ralph Nader, whose interest in Indians predates by many years his interest in auto safety.

The Indian child, Mr. Nader said, is dependent for his education "upon an archaic and unresponsive bureaucracy" in Kansas City and the field. Despite disclaimers to the contrary, Mr. Nader said, this bureaucracy is motivated by an "assimilation policy" and visualizes the objective of Indian education as teaching Indians "the superiority of white ways."

Marm 7, Year 5, Thursol—Landing + 13 sols

As distressing as the vulgar slur buried in the mural was, there didn't seem to be a good way to bring it up—or rather, there didn't seem to be a good way to ask about why no one had told me about it. I think what actually troubled me most was that it was just one of several things that hadn't made it into the reports. It reminded me all over again about how much of an outsider I'd been on the First Expedition.

At least the slur was the action of someone who wasn't even on the current mission. It was bad, but it was also in the past.

My work on the base now was divided into paperwork with Leonard, which seemed unending, trips out on the surface with Wilburt, which would be fun if I weren't feeling like I constantly had to follow up on him, and general maintenance tasks.

Of those, the one I enjoyed most was the general maintenance because the goals were concrete and very often I was not the person in charge. Like tosol, when I was assigned to helping the suit maintenance techs.

Even when I was cleaning dust out of the seams of a Mars suit, there was a delightful conviviality to working with the suit maintenance team. Zainabu and Mosi had brought a fortune of cassettes with them and Algerian pop music filled the suit maintenance area. It was a cramped room off the side of the tunnel that led from the outer airlock to the main dome airlock. The room and the corridor had exactly the same dimensions because they'd both once been fuel tanks.

Next to me, Opal Woolen inspected the threads that gathered near each finger joint. They took a lot of wear and you did *not* want a glove to fail when you were on a Marswalk.

Zainabu lifted a helmet over her head as if she were an Olympic athlete. "Finished!" Pushing her stool back, she stood and grinned at her husband. "I beat you."

He sucked air through his teeth and shook his head. "Only because I paused to help our helpers."

Shaking her head, she laughed at him. "You will take any excuse to not do the work and claim kindness as your reason. Every time."

"You admit that I stopped working to help someone." He buffed one final spot on the helmet visor and set aside his polishing cloth. "And now I, too, am finished. So I would have finished first if I had not stopped to help Elma and Opal."

"Did you need his help?" Zainabu turned to me, with her helmet propped on her hip.

"Uh-uh. No, I am not getting pulled into this." I held up my hands as if I could ward them off. "I'm going to come in last as it is. I swear I'm the slowest person in this colony."

"Could we not—" Opal Woolen cut herself off and bent her head back to the table.

I waited for her to keep going and she acted as if she had never started speaking. This pattern of people omitting things around me was getting exhausting. I set my brush down on the counter and spun to face her. "What is going on?"

"Nothing. I was just going to ask . . ." The younger astronaut looked genuinely frightened, the way one does when they've said something they didn't intend to. She ducked her head. "It's not important."

This was like Leonard's omissions but clumsier. Was it related? I didn't know, but I did know that it was getting very old very fast. I was tired of playing games.

Leonard thought that I should act more like I was in charge? I could do that—or at least I could pretend that I was Nicole, who could quiet you to death. I straightened my back and said, very quietly, "Would you like to reconsider that answer?"

The entire room got quiet, which honestly was more reaction than I had expected.

Opal looked as if she wanted to crawl under the table. "It's just . . ." She looked to Mosi and Zainabu for support. Honestly, was everyone in on this except me? "Um . . . could we not call this a colony?"

I frowned, trying to draw a connection between that request and the patch and the mural. "What else are we supposed to call it?"

"A habitat? A base? A town? Almost anything, really."

Zainabu cut in and her usual cheer was flattened beneath serious intent. "Not a settlement, either."

"I need some help understanding why 'colony' is bad."

"It's . . . it's not got a good history for my people."

"Or ours." Zainabu folded her arms.

"Okay . . ." I tried to find the connection. Opal had said "my people" but I didn't know what she meant by that because she was a white American. And Zainabu and Mosi were from the Algerian contingent. "I don't have a problem with changing the words, I just feel like I'm still missing something."

Opal stared at her knees for a moment, before she blew out her breath. She inhaled and straightened, meeting my gaze for the first time since I'd used my Nicole voice on her. Opal lifted her chin. "I'm Potawatomi."

"I'm . . . I'm still lost."

"I'm Native—I'm an Indian."

I caught myself before I voiced that I thought she was white. People had said that sort of thing to me all the time when they found out that I was Jewish. I didn't ask her if she knew Deana Whitney, who was the only other Native American person I knew, because it never, ever felt good when people assumed that I knew all Jews. Besides, Deana was Choctaw, and if that was anything like Sephardic and Ashkenazi Jews, there would be differences. "All right . . . And 'colony' is bad because?"

"To us . . . to me 'colony' means that a bunch of people came to my home and killed my ancestors and forced my family from their lands and—" She caught herself visibly with her hands clenched on her knees.

Zainabu rested a hand on her shoulder and squeezed gently. "And to us . . . I think you know that nothing good came of being colonized."

I bit my lips, nodding. I could see the problem, now that they had pointed it out. If the IAC had called this a ghetto, it might have been accurate in the strictest sense—a small, insular community surrounded by walls—but all of the emotion of it would be completely wrong. "I can start calling it a habitat, sure."

Opal's shoulders relaxed and her spine sagged a little as if she had been braced to fight me. "Thank you."

"Why didn't you bring it up during training? We could have rewritten the manuals."

Mosi picked up a glove and started unstitching it. "I was going to say something, but my wife told me not to."

"As if you ever listen to that!"

Opal shrugged. "I wanted to get here, and I was afraid that if I rocked the boat, I wouldn't."

That was an all-too-familiar sensation. "Well, I promise that I'll change the way I talk about it."

"Can you . . ." Opal picked up her magnifying glass and focused on it. "Can you ask Mission Control to make the change, too?"

People kept thinking that I had some sort of power. Yes, as deputy administrator, I could message MC at any time, but Clemons would do whatever he wanted as the director of the IAC. "I'll run it past Leonard, but I've got to warn you that the final decision will be up to Clemons."

"Sure . . ." She nodded, rolling the handle of the magnifying glass between her fingers. "But you're the Lady Astronaut of Mars."

I winced. She wasn't even thinking of me in the command chain. Just my fame. The title "The Lady Astronaut" was nothing but a PR moniker. It might have power outside the IAC, but inside, as soon as they decided that my smiles for the camera weren't useful, any power I had would vanish. I felt queasy and the room was too hot.

It wasn't that I wanted power. I didn't like being in charge of anything. But having responsibilities without the power to make change was worse.

SIX

TRANSCRIPT OF PRESIDENT WARGIN'S
ADDRESS TO THE NATION—March 3, 1970

On March third, the world remembers all those who were lost when the Meteor struck eighteen years ago today. Of the 26 million people who died, two million were lost instantly with the impact into the Chesapeake Bay. On that day, the nature of the planet changed, as massive tsunamis and rains of fire affected every corner of the globe. Those changes continue as the climate of our fragile planet keeps shifting in response to that massive blow.

But this day is different, not only because of the efforts to rebuild here on Earth, but because we now have people living and working on a planet outside of Earth's orbit. Today we set aside the distinction between countries and creeds to see ourselves as one. With the people who live on the Moon and on Mars, with the scientists building habitats deep under mountains on Earth, and with the farmers who grow our food, we inevitably honor the millions who died on March third. And we have hope.

Marm 20, Year 5, Wednesol, 0900—Landing + 26 sols

March third. We all stood in a circle, in the middle of the dome. Leonard looked around our group and nodded to us. Like the rest of us, he wore a felt cherry blossom pinned to his flight suit. He lifted the small pair of finger cymbals that had somehow become a part of every remembrance ceremony around the world. They were small and dark, and—even without looking—I knew that they were embossed with a cherry blossom for the cherry trees that were lost when the Meteor struck Washington, D.C.

At 0953 local time, the chime's high, clear tone rang through the dome. "Today, we remember the Meteor."

"We remember."

"We remember those lost to the Meteor."

"We remember."

I remembered begging Daddy to do barrel rolls in his plane when I was tiny. I remembered Mama working on her giant cross-stitched bedspread while tutoring me on biology.

"All of us remember the time before the Meteor. We are building now, together, toward a home for the future. As you go through your sol, think about what parts of Earth you want remembered here. We are on Mars to add to the worlds where humanity lives and thrives. Remember the Meteor."

"We remember."

He chimed the cymbals again and the small ceremony was finished.

Tears threatened to burst out of me as I suddenly, violently, missed Earth. I missed the smell of rain. I missed grass. I missed the clear blue sky of Before. I missed being able to pick up the phone and call my parents.

I've had a lot of practice hiding tears, so I swallowed that salt in a trail that burned down my throat. Nathaniel took my hand and squeezed it. He wasn't even trying to hide his tears. I leaned against him as that day bubbled up in my memory. We had been in the mountains on vacation and then there had been a light . . . A light. That does nothing to describe it.

If you were anywhere within five hundred miles of Washington, D.C., at 9:53 a.m. on March 3rd, 1952, and facing a window, then you remember that light. Briefly red, and then so violently white that it washed out even the shadows.

Aahana and her husband Jaidev had paused next to us. He was rubbing her arms and speaking to her in a low voice. She swallowed, and nodded. Blinking tears back, she looked up and saw me watching her.

"Sorry, it's just . . . I don't remember." She wrapped her arms around herself. "I was fourteen when it hit and I was sick with cholera. My whole family was. When I got better, my parents had . . . not."

"I'm so sorry. I didn't know." How had I not known?

How? Because after the Meteor, we stopped asking about people's families. So many people had lost everyone. The other Meteor Remembrances at the IAC had been large, formal affairs. We left Earth after the last one, so this was the first we'd marked as a small group.

She compressed her lips and nodded. "Do you remember where you were when the Meteor hit?"

I'd never understood why people phrased it like a question. Now I did. Among other things, it was a way to find out if people's families had lived. "Nathaniel and I were in the mountains—the Poconos. He had inherited this cabin from his father and we used to go up there for stargazing."

"The Poconos." Jaidev's eyes widened. "So you . . . you saw it."

Nathaniel squeezed my hand harder, because the Meteor was not the only thing we saw that day. We saw a terrifying amount of death. "We did."

Across the circle, Wilburt rested his hand on Dawn's shoulder before he walked over to me. His eyes were red and he sniffled. "We should go, if we're to get to the drop site with enough light."

Light. I *remembered* the light of the Meteor. Yes, I remembered where I was when the Meteor struck.

Marm 29, Year 5, Frisol—Landing + 35 sols

Another sol, another cargo run. Hefting the bags containing my helmet and gloves, I stepped onto the floor of the garage. After the confines of the rover, the air in the garage cooled the sweat beneath my LCVG. Theoretically, the Liquid Cooling and Ventilation Garment did just that, kept you cool inside a

Mars suit. But a sol of hard labor still worked up a sweat. I was going to head straight to the shower after this. Two showers. I had skipped yestersol so that I could have five glorious minutes standing under water tosol.

Leonard waited with Mosi, each ready to help us unload.

Behind me, I heard Wilburt clamber out of the rover. "Thank God. Have any of you a beer?"

"Good luck." Leonard wheeled a hand truck to the back of the rover. "Go on and get out of your LCVGs. We've got this."

"Roger, wilco." I hauled my helmet and gloves to the donning station. Mosi and Zainabu would bag the Mars suits to clean later so I didn't drag regolith through the base.

When I walked into the suit room, the music was loud and cheerful. Zainabu came around the table to take my helmet and gloves, already starting to inspect them before they were out of my hands. "Thank you . . . What happened to your glove?"

I froze, hand still outstretched. "What?"

She held up my right glove, which had a laceration through at least two layers where my little finger joined the palm. There were eleven layers in most of the suit, but the gloves had to be thinnest for dexterity. Three more layers and I would have been exposed to Mars.

And I'd made work for our suit techs. I hadn't even known that it had happened and I was supposed to do regular glove checks. What had I been doing instead? Gawking at a dust devil, probably. "I . . . I'll write it up in my report."

She made a *tsk*ing sound through her teeth. "I'm glad it was nothing more. And that you wear a standard size so we can swap it."

"I'm sorry."

"This is why we are here. The First Expedition was hard on their suits and had to do the repairs themselves. Patience is the key to paradise." She winked at me. "Go. Leave me to work."

After I left her, I changed into a flight suit. God, I wanted those showers, but I still had work to do. I caught up with Leonard at the airlock that was designated as overflow storage for the gear coming off this load. Eventually, this airlock would lead to the dormitory. For now, it was a nice, secure, and unused location.

I grabbed one of the smaller bins from the hand truck and carried it into the airlock. Leonard looked around, grinning when he saw me. "How was it outside?"

"The weather or the cargo drop?"

"Mars." He took the bin and stacked it atop a pile along the sidewall of the airlock. "I'm stuck at my desk half the time and haven't gotten to see the surface since we landed."

"I'll bring you a rock next time." I headed out to get another load and Lance met me at the door.

He thrust out a crate. "Bucket brigade?"

"Works for me." Grabbing it, I turned back to Leonard.

He nodded in appreciation as he took it. "So, Mars?"

"So, Mars was pretty spectacular." Guilt gnawed at me. "Although . . . I put a pretty big gash in my glove."

Leonard set the crate down and turned to give me his full attention as I did a quick debrief. It didn't take long, but by the time I had finished, Lance had set two other crates by the door. Leonard put a hand on my shoulder and made strong eye contact.

"Before we left Earth, I said this would be a no-fault mission? That includes you. An accident happened and we learn from them, but that does not mean that you are guilty." He held up a finger to stop my protest before I'd gotten a good breath in. "I know you. I've seen you beat yourself up for things that are not your fault more than once. Mars is brutal and this isn't the first compromised suit. We learn and we move on."

I ducked my head. "Yes, sir."

He laughed and I swear for a moment I thought he was going to ruffle my hair, but he turned and grabbed one of the cases. "Bring me two rocks as penance and make sure they're interesting rocks."

"So you want a *gneiss* rock?" I grabbed the other crate.

He groaned. "I don't want schist."

"Of quartz you don't. The finest rocks for my commander."
As I handed him the crate, the light caught on a roughness just
visible behind the wall of boxes he was stacking. On the curve
of the airlock a series of hashmarks had been scratched into the
surface. The sort that you use for tracking dates, and there were
a lot of them. "Leonard . . . what's that?"

He peered over my shoulder. "Oh, we were tracking how
long we were down here."

"In the airlock no one used?"

"Yeah. It made sense at the time." He turned back to the entrance. "Looks like Lance has more boxes for us."

I stared at what I could see of the hashmarks. It looked like
something was written beside them. As I took a step closer,
wanting to count them, Leonard walked between me and the
wall and set another crate in place.

He turned around. "You've had a long sol. Why don't you let
me take it from here?"

"Sure." Sweating as if the environmental controls had failed,
I took a step backward, split between wanting a closer look and
wanting to be out of the airlock. Long practice at hiding panic
gave me the ability to say, "I've had a rough sol, but I don't want
to *chalk* about it."

He laughed and I think that, at least, was real. "You've been
hanging out with Wilburt too much."

"Blame Mission Control."

I walked straight from there to the shower and shut myself
into the tiny closet. I was so discombobulated that I almost
turned the tap while I still had my clothes on. *0, 1, 1, 2, 3, 5,
8 . . .*

Something had happened on the First Expedition. Something
bad. Something that I absolutely should have known about and
didn't.

Had Parker known? Or was this a secret just from me?

Unzipping my flight suit, I made a list in my head. Mural,
patch, hashmarks. I soaped myself down, still turning the problem over. No matter which way I reoriented things, I couldn't

find any pattern except that it was something they felt they needed to keep from me. DeBeer being a racist asshole was common knowledge. I turned the tap on and leaned into the water.

But what had caused them to patch the garage wall?

And why keep it from me?

I rinsed and shut the water off. I didn't have any answers and I wasn't going to waste my shower ration trying to figure out why people were lying to me.

One of the things I remember from our days setting up the Lunar colo—base was that every moment was scheduled. Now Mission Control had a slightly better understanding that we needed downtime.

The problem was that you had to actually take it.

Nathaniel was not good at that. I had tried to catch him after my conversation with Leonard, but he was in the middle of something and then there were other folks about. So I had finally gone to bed and was drifting in and out of sleep when the door to our cubicle opened. Dim light from the main dome fell across the bed as Nathaniel slipped in. I rolled onto my back. "I'm awake."

"Lower bunk." He pushed the door shut. "That holds promise."

I snorted. "Do I want to know what time it is?"

"You do not." He put one knee on the bed and leaned down to kiss me. His hand ran through my hair and the caress dragged me back down toward sleep.

I forced my eyes open and sat up, scooching a little away from him. "I need to talk to you."

"Do you want me to turn the light on?" The shadow of my husband shifted to sit down on the bed, one foot drawn up and tucked under his other leg. The dim glow from our "skylight" silvered his shoulders.

"No." I knotted my hands together and dropped my voice to a whisper. Our walls were thin plastic. Wilburt and Dawn were on one side of us. Leonard was on the other. "When we were loading the supplies into the number two airlock, I noticed hashmarks scratched on one wall. Like someone was counting sols."

"How many?"

"I don't know. Leonard was stacking the crates in front of the marks so I couldn't see them all."

"Did you ask—"

"Yes. Leonard said that they had just been keeping track of the remaining mission sols."

"Huh." Nathaniel bent down and pulled his shoes off as if our mission commander weren't trying to hide something. "In the number two airlock. Which is a dead end until we set up the second dome."

"That was my reaction!" I winced as my voice rose and brought it back down to a whisper. "Have you found out anything about the patch?"

He nodded, digging his thumb into the ball of his foot. "I sent a list of inquiries to Rafael and included that. He said it was from a rover accident and told me how he'd patched it."

I had expected Rafael to not answer because no one else was answering questions. "But . . . but Wilburt said that *he'd* patched it."

"Maybe they worked together?"

Maybe. Or maybe it was all just part of the same pattern that I could feel but couldn't sort. "Did he say who was driving?"

"I didn't ask." Nathaniel's hand stilled. "Do you want me to?"

I flopped back on the bed, staring at the shadowed upper bunk where I usually slept. "I don't know what I would do with the information."

He sighed and unzipped his flight suit. "Let's approach it a different way. What are you afraid of?"

I chewed on the inside of my lip. Filtering out the everyday fears from this specific area was hard. I was afraid that I was an outsider again. But that was a personal fear. "Did Rafael answer about the other undocumented changes?"

"Some." Nathaniel shrugged out of his suit. "Others he said he didn't remember and that he'd have to check his notes."

"I just . . ." I was good at patterns. Show me a set of numbers and it took on shape and texture in my head. I could feel a pattern here, but people were messy. I couldn't get the pieces to come together into a neat answer. "It's just not like any of them to forget to log things. Well, Wilburt might not. But Rafael was meticulous with his documentation."

Especially after Terrazas had died. I'm not sure he ever stopped blaming himself for that faulty valve.

Nathaniel slid into bed beside me. "Well, maybe Wilburt doesn't remember because the repair was five years ago. Do you remember where you were on the morning of May 25, 1965, Dr. York?"

I laughed and rolled on top of him. "Yes. I was on orbit around Mars, ready to go home to my husband."

The rest of the night we had other sorts of questions and answers to keep us occupied.

But when I woke up, I was still wondering how I had become an outsider again.

SEVEN

FATAL DISASTERS ON THE RISE

Increased Peril Attributed to
Meteor-Induced Climate Change

By Erik Eckholm

March 19, 1970—The death toll caused by the world's
natural disasters—floods, droughts, earthquakes, hur-
ricanes and volcanic eruptions—is on the rise as global
temperatures continue to increase. A new report, analyz-
ing data from the United States government and the international Red Cross, found that in the 1960s the average
number of natural disasters recorded per year was 75, a
50 percent increase over the previous decade. But comparing the same two decades, the estimated deaths caused
by these events climbed fivefold, to 114,000 per year.
During the average year of the 1960s, disasters caused
disruptions, often costly and wrenching, in the lives of
an estimated 44 million people. Many relief officials are
beginning to feel that emergency assistance today is "like
trying to bandage a wound that is constantly growing,"
as expressed by Anders Wijkman, Secretary General of
the Swedish Red Cross, which sponsored the study.

Marm 35, Year 5, Thursol–Landing + 41 sols

As I went into suit maintenance, a cascade of drums and wind
instruments backing a throaty voice poured out of the room to

greet me. As I walked in, Zainabu saw me and shoved something under a cloth. "Mosi—look who is here. It is Elma!"

He jumped and flipped cloth over something at his work station. "Elma. Hi. Nothing to see here."

"Well, that is not at all suspicious." Zainabu *tsk*ed at him. "That is the best you can do?"

I stopped in the hatch. "What's going on?"

She sighed, straightening the cloth. "Well. Since you have caught us, I will tell you that we have made Purim costumes, but I will not show you until tomorrow."

"Can't wait to see them." My eyes watered and I grinned all at the same time. We'd all started sharing holidays during the planning of the mission. But it's one thing to have told people about your holy days and plans and another entirely to have folks joining in willingly.

On the other hand, Purim is really a big ole costume party. We're very much "They tried to kill us, we survived! Let's eat!" which isn't a bad philosophy for space, really.

"Meanwhile . . ." Zainabu held up my glove. "It is fixed!"

"You're amazing." When I took the glove, the side panel that I'd torn was startlingly fresh. I winced. "You had to unstitch this, didn't you?"

"I made Mosi do it." She winked. "We save my work for the precision of sewing."

What I had not talked about in the group meeting was the Fast of Esther. It's not as commonly observed as Yom Kippur—I mean outside the Orthodox world—but it begins at dawn and ends at dusk when Purim begins, except on years when Purim begins on Shabbat, which it did this year. My aunt Esther always did the fasts because it centered around her namesake, and so when our visits to Charleston overlapped with Purim, I'd sometimes join her. I mean, the way a kid does, skipping one meal and feeling like you'd done a thing.

My mouth salivated, remembering the tables groaning with food—schnitzel, chicken 'n' dumplings, jeweled rice, collards, cornbread, and hamantaschen cookies. My throat tightened and suddenly all I could taste was salt. I missed my family so much. My aunts and my mom and dad.

Biting my lips, I kept my back to Zainabu until I was able to sniffle the grief back down. I wanted to tell my family that I remembered them. Every day. Every sol.

"What are we listening to tosol?" I stripped out of my flight suit.

"Cheikha Habiba el Abassia. Just came out." She waggled her hand. "I mean before we left."

Wiggling into the LCVG, I kept turning the question of the fast over in my head. To fast or not to fast, that is the question.

I'd landed us on Mars in a ship named for Aunt Esther, so it felt right to try it. I had already skipped breakfast but kept second-guessing that decision because I had a physically strenuous sol ahead of me.

I wanted to. But I'd had long conversations with my rabbi before I left for Mars the first time and he had stressed that I—all of the astronauts—needed to remember to measure our jobs against the principle of pikuach nefesh. I was going on a Marswalk, and the preservation of life overruled any other religious obligation, so I shouldn't fast. On the other hand, would fasting really endanger me or Wilburt? I had done enough of these cargo drops by now to know how much energy it took. I'm not a fainter, so it would make the sol harder for me, but it wouldn't affect him. Probably.

I had a lunch packed for when we were in the pressurized cabin, but if I skipped that and was wrong about my energy levels I ran the risk of another mistake. And on a Marswalk any mistake could be fatal. It wasn't as if I could just leave Wilburt working on the surface while I went into the cabin to eat. Nothing about getting in or out of a pressurized space was quick. "Hey, could I have a pull-up fruit bar for my suit?"

"Eh, yes, of course." Zainabu spun away and grabbed one from the supply rack.

The pull-up sleeves were a partial solution to the "how do you eat" problem of a spacesuit, if you can call a compressed bar of vaguely fruit-flavored paste "eating."

Velcroed to the inside of my hard upper torso was a plastic sleeve angled so that the top just peeked up into the helmet with me. Zainabu tucked the fruit bar inside and made sure that a bite-sized portion was above the sleeve. If I needed the energy, I'd bite it, and use my teeth to pull it up. The last little bit inevitably fell out of the sleeve and rattled around inside the suit.

They used to issue cherry pull-ups until a medic almost had a heart attack thinking that an astronaut's foot was covered in blood. Now we got apricot.

"You ready to go?" Zainabu looked up from securing the fruit bar.

"I am." I felt lighter and more eager than I had on other trips. Maybe it was because we'd had to take a little bit of a break due to weather. Maybe it was fasting. Or maybe it was because I was excited about Purim.

Because it wasn't just me this time. The folks up on the *Goddard* had a whole radio play Purimspiel planned to share with us. We'd packed hamantaschen, and we had little packages of food to give out to friends.

Purim is easily the most fun of the Jewish holidays. It's all about feasting and drinking—well, we couldn't do the drinking part on Mars. Yet. But we could do the sharing of stories and the gifts of food. One of my earliest memories is listening to the megillah being read and wanting to be as strong as Queen Esther had been when she saved the Jewish people from Haman. I can remember being that little girl, but I can't remember what it was like to be without fear.

But I still loved the story and the holiday. And the costumes! Mosi and Zainabu had made costumes. I grinned as I hoisted the bag with my Mars suit, which was its own sort of costume. In it, I was clearly an astronaut. I'd always loved the costumes at Purim.

THE MARTIAN CONTINGENCY * 65

It was a chance to wear my mask on the outside. I could be with people and not be me.

The rover bounced over the Martian landscape no matter how carefully I tried to avoid rocks. After a particularly vigorous jarring, Wilburt braced himself on the dashboard in an overly dramatic pose.

"Before we left Earth, whenever I saw a bus with a woman driver, I smiled and I thought about how far the society has come." He glanced at me and I could feel the punch line starting to bubble out of him. "And then I waited to take the next one."

I groaned and shook my head. "You need a better class of jokes."

"It is not a joke, it is a fact on account of how easily women drivers are distracted."

"So you're trying to demonstrate that by deliberately distracting me while I'm driving?" I had factored in the fatigue of fasting, but I'd forgotten to account for the fact that I get a little sharp when I'm hungry.

"Piece of faring on your right."

"I see it." I would normally have logged it, but Wilburt was in the passenger seat. "Let me know if you need help with the notation. You know, since men are so easily distracted."

"Speaking of distraction, yestersol I was distracted while reading an anatomy textbook of our library." He waited with the obvious pause that had come to let me know a punch line was inbound. "Someone had ripped out the appendix."

"Where do you find these?" A flash of metal caught my eye. "Another piece of faring on the left at about ten o'clock."

"Where—ah, I see it. Noted." He marked it on the map. "And I have a book. I have read that jokes are a way to bond with teammates, and so I acquired a book."

"Soooo many things become clearer." I steered the rover around a rocky outcropping. "Faring."

"What do you call an elephant with—faring."

The next piece of faring was closer and it was charred. Then there was another. We came over a small rise and the rusty plain ahead of us was littered with debris. Too much of it to be the faring and all of it scorched.

I slowed the rover and brought it to a stop as a singed piece of parachute nylon swirled in a dust devil. We were where the cargo drop should be and all that was here was blackened rubble scattered across the Martian landscape.

The shock of the explosion shatters the car windows. It roars on and on, vibrating through my chest like a rocket leaving a launchpad. The oscillations press against my skin, filling every part of my consciousness with roaring waves and then secondary and tertiary explosions. I cling to Nathaniel, and he clings to the steering wheel, as the car bucks and slides across the road.

The world groans and roars and wind howls through the empty—

"*Scheiße . . .*" Wilburt breathed out.

I shook my head. That was eighteen years ago. *3.14159265 . . .* I swallowed the panic rising in my empty stomach.

. . . 358979323 . . .

We had redundancies built in. We were professionals. We would work the problem.

And also . . . and also, I looked at that field of debris and I *remembered* the Meteor.

I turned my head and bit off a piece of the pull-up in my suit. It stuck to the inside of my mouth as I stared at the landscape and reached for the mic. "Bradbury Base, Rover One. We have a problem."

EIGHT

Thursday, March 19, 1970

Dear Leonard,

Good to hear from you, man. Myrtle says to say "hi" before I forget about it. My second term is going well but I don't think I'm going to run again. I'm trying to encourage Guillermo to run for lunar mayor because he has a good organizational head on his shoulders and people like him. I think it would be good to have someone who isn't a native English speaker in charge.

Not that I object to the circumstances that got me here, but Clemons has a slight prejudice against non-English speakers in command roles. I brought this up, and he pointed to Halim and Otto as signs that I'm wrong. I countered with Parker, Benkoski, me, Elma, Nathaniel, you, etc., and then I let it drop. Figure I'll do what I can, where I can.

Speaking of "do what I can," if there's anything we can do for you from the Moon, you let me know. We're just a teletype away.

Also . . . I have some good news. We are sending you our first-born child. Phillip just got rotated onto the Third Expedition. He was backup, but his prime got polio. Devastating, but fortunately one of the milder varieties, so she's expected to make a full recovery, just not be declared flight ready. Phillip has these ideas that he and "Doc Flannery" are going to get to do a bunch of fieldwork on Mars. I didn't have the heart to tell him that you haven't even gone outside yet.

Listen, Leonard . . . just a reminder that you can ask for a replacement on the next expedition. You don't have to keep being the mission commander. You got there. Your name is in the books. You made a path for someone else. It's okay to stand down and go back to doing geology. It's the thing that you love.

All the best,
Eugene

Marm 35, Year 5, Thursol-Landing + 41 sols

Leonard met us at the airlock. His face was calm and focused, but it looked like someone had starched his spine. Nathaniel was just behind him, a crease between his brows.

I shifted the bag off my shoulder and held it out to him. "We collected more in the cargo bay of the rover, if you want it."

Nathaniel reached for the bag, cracking it open. He whistled. "Tell me that there were pieces bigger than this."

I nodded. "We saw the faring."

"Did you find the black box?"

Wilburt held out his duffel. "Yes, for all the good it will do."

"Hey." Leonard slashed his hand through the conversation. "None of that. We're going to work the problem. I've got the full team waiting for you in the dome."

Nathaniel pulled a scorched piece of steel out of my bag. "What was the scatter range of the debris field?"

"Hold until we're with the rest of the team." Leonard jerked his thumb toward the dome. "The *Goddard* is standing by, so join us ASAP."

"Now is fine." Still sweaty and in my LCVG, as if this were a sim and I was heading for a debrief, I went with the others straight to the main dome.

Kam met us and handed ice packs to Wilburt and me. Fun fact about being an astronaut. If you didn't have problems with your shoulders before you joined the corps, you do now. I slid the ice pack under my LCVG to nestle the focused cold on the ball of my right shoulder.

As I sat down, Helen put a vacuum-sealed meal in front of me. I had given up on fasting the moment I saw the debris field but I'd skipped breakfast this morning and was ravenous now. She slid another across to Wilburt. Aahana and Jaidev handed us both waters.

I nodded my thanks and sipped the room-temperature liquid with relief.

Leonard turned from conferring with Dawn and Florence.

He saw us sitting down and clapped his hands. "All right. Let's dive in. Elma, Wilburt, the floor is yours."

I swallowed my water and set it down. "When we arrived at the site of Cargo Drop Four, we encountered a debris field. The faring appeared to have separated as intended, but we saw pieces of parachute. It either failed to deploy or ripped apart on impact. We found the black box and the telemetry package where the entire cargo pod should have been. We did not find any intact cargo cases. Everything had scorching. The transponder was still sending us a signal that it was in a nominal state. It was not." I reseated the ice pack on my shoulder. "Do we know why the *Goddard* or one of the satellites didn't spot this as a crash site?"

"No." Leonard's face was tight with concern. "We'll find out."

As we talked, describing the size of the debris field and the impact depth of the remains of the heat shield, Florence was transcribing everything we said. She'd send it, encrypted, back to Mission Control on Earth. When we finished, the speakers buzzed.

"Bradbury, *Goddard*." Halim Malouf's voice joined us from the ship orbiting Mars. "We'll set up our cameras to survey the site on our next pass."

"What happened to that craft is a secondary concern." Nathaniel bent his head, looking at the plans spread on the table. "The main HVAC system for the second dome was on that drop."

My stomach clenched more than it had already. I'd had the manifest of what was supposed to be on the cargo drop so we could inventory it as we unloaded. And yet we'd been so focused on the disaster in front of us that I hadn't looked ahead to the impending one. Without the HVAC, we couldn't open the second dome. Without the second dome, the other folks couldn't come down from the *Goddard*. Without them down here, we couldn't get the greenhouse up, which led to a long list of cascading failures that would mean the Third Expedition might not launch.

It was supposed to include the children that my teammates had left behind until it was safe. Safer.

My brain immediately started calculating supply lists, pulling up figures about the amount of cable and trying to cross-reference that with the heat indexes on Mars for a dome without a working HVAC. Nathaniel sometimes teases me about trying to math every problem, but this was something that we could answer with math. The problem was that I didn't have a full inventory.

Because right now, we didn't know if there were other cargo drops that had also failed. The telemetry had said that this one landed safely. "We'll need to check the other cargo drop sites ASAP."

Slowly, Leonard nodded and I felt the room shift as they all followed where my thoughts had gone. Leonard swung around to the whiteboard and wrote "Action items." Underneath it, "Inventory."

As he wrote, he said, "We're going to work the problem in parallel with Mission Control. Right now, we'll capture all the actions that we think we need to take, and when we hear back from them, we'll set a priority list."

There's nothing like facing an emergency with a room full of competent people to make you feel energized and focused.

And also, selfishly, sad. I had wanted to share Purim with everyone next sol. It wouldn't be the first time I had missed it because I was in space, but this time I wasn't the only Jew. This time other people had made costumes.

Aahana raised her hand. "Do you think they'll tell us to abort?"

"I don't think we'll need to." Nathaniel shook his head. "If we haven't lost any other cargo drops."

The IAC believes in redundancies, but there are payload limits to what they can send, and we were 330 million kilometers from the nearest replacement.

The comms center was on subfloor 1, the same as the engineering department, which was handy because engineering would be steering the brunt of the work ahead of us. A murmur of conversation filled the hallway as people lingered, waiting for Mission Control to respond. I kept hearing snatches as people tried to work the problem.

"COPV tanks particularly susceptible . . ."

". . . don't expect things to blow away or get covered up by dust . . ."

". . . any sign of buckling?"

We'd sent our report off through our encrypted channel immediately after the meeting and had been waiting for a response. Thirty-seven minutes would have been the fastest we could have expected to hear back from them. We'd long passed that.

Nathaniel was flipping through a manual, cross-referencing some detail about some part of the dome. He was hunched forward, face intent on his work. When he worked, there was a light that filled his whole being. Yes, even in a time like this, I was admiring my husband.

Across the small room, Leonard leaned on the console next to Florence and checked his watch. "It's been an hour."

"They're four and a half hours behind us now." Florence checked the wall clock, which had two dials, one for Mars Time at Bradbury Base and one for Earth GMT. The gears were apparently an engineering marvel to be able to adjust for the thirty-nine-minute difference between days and sols. "It's just after fourteen hundred hours at Sunflower Base in Kansas City."

Wilburt poked his head into the room, with a carryall in his left hand. "I have brought for you some coffee."

"They haven't replied yet." Florence peered at him from her console because of course, we all had coffee so this was an obvious excuse to be in the room instead of milling about in the hall with everyone else.

He looked offended and guilty at the same time, face going red and brows coming down. "I was simply bringing coffee as a way to be helpf—"

The console pinged and text began appearing on the screen.

It seemed to develop its own gravitational pull, drawing us all closer. Behind us, the light from the hallway dimmed as everyone crowded around the door.

Leonard looked back at the crowd and hesitated, then read the message aloud. "'From Mission Control, Kansas City, White Team, CAPCOM Rafael Avelino. Thank you for the clear report. In answer to your question, a review of imaging taken of the site was obscured by cloud cover. We are looking at why a second attempt to image the site wasn't made. We are conferring with the backrooms on next steps. While we do, we'd like you to send teams out to recover debris so that we have an understanding of why the cargo drop failed. Following are instructions for recovery procedures.' And then there's a procedure list, which we'll get distributed to your department leaders."

"Recovery procedures?" Nathaniel leaned closer, as if he could reach through the screen and talk directly to any of the "backrooms" of subject matter experts who were standing by to consult on each piece of the enormously complex system that made up the Mars Expedition. "What about how to work around the missing HVAC? That's a tad more important than what happened to the craft."

"Given that they are getting ready to launch more supplies our way, I can understand their concerns," Leonard said.

"Yes, again, I think it's good information to have, but determining mission viability is more important."

"Unless they are planning to have us abort and have not yet told us." Wilburt still held the bag of coffee in one hand. "Then gathering the information would become the priority while we have boots on the ground."

Scowling, Nathaniel looked at Leonard. "Do *not* let them abort the mission."

Leonard's eyebrows rose. "We'll proceed with the best possible infor—"

"Leonard . . ." Florence touched Leonard's arm and pointed to a line on the console after the instructions. None of us read it aloud.

Is it possible that an explosion occurred after it reached the ground?

Leonard inhaled sharply. I half turned, ready to shut the door to comms, which would only make things worse. They were all distracted now. Some were splitting off to build lists. As awful as it was, there was a part of us that had been trained through simulations to thrive in a crisis. We understood how to handle equipment failures.

But an explosion after it reached the ground? They were asking if there had been a bomb.

I looked at Wilburt, remembering the field of debris and the scorching.

The sky to the east is a long dark wall of dust and smoke, lit from beneath by an inferno. The fire stretches to the curvature of the Earth, as if someone has peeled back the mantle and opened a gateway into Hell itself. Streaks of fire light the sky as ejecta continues to fall to the Earth.

I took a slow breath through my nose and let it out through my mouth. *0, 1, 1, 2, 3, 5, 8, 13 . . .*

"Well?" Leonard looked at Wilburt and me, and nodded at the screen, his voice low. "You saw it. Any indication?"

Wilburt shook his head. "I don't think so."

"The spread was wide." I scrunched up my nose, tracing the patterns encoded in the field of debris with my mind. As much as I hate that I know this, years of rocket tests gave me a pretty clear idea of what happened when a spacecraft experienced rapid unplanned disassembly. "I think it failed in atmosphere."

"Good. We'll let them know that." Leonard rested one hand on the back of Florence's chair as he stared at the console. "Right now, I'm praying that there's not a specific reason they think there might have been an explosion."

"Why send a bomb all the way to Mars?" Wilburt said, and it was as if his question had carved a silence into the hallway. "If you want to blow something up, do it en route."

From the doorway, Bolí started listing things. "You might want it to explode when the capsule is opened. Or after something is carried into the main habitat. Maybe it was supposed to have gone off en route. Maybe you want people to think that it's here safely so you need the telemetry to be completed."

"Bolí." Leonard cut in. "Not helping. We need to focus on what we *can* do and leave the what-ifs to Mission Control."

He was absolutely right. The only problem was that everyone on the mission remembered what Earth First had done before. Some of us had been on the way to Mars and been without contact for a terrifying month. Others had been trapped on the Moon. Some had been in Mission Control when Earth First had bombed it.

We had our work to do, but that wouldn't stop people from wondering if somehow, impossibly, terrorists had reached all the way to Mars.

NINE

DISASTER IN SPACE

KANSAS CITY, March 20, 1970—Reports have reached Earth of a disaster at the Bradbury Base on Mars, only one month into its multiyear mission. At least one of the twelve automated supply drops crashed upon the Martian surface leaving the crew without vital supplies. Three of these supply caches have been retrieved and it is not known how many others have also failed to reach the surface.

When queried about why the failure occurred, Director Norman Clemons of the International Aerospace Coalition said, "It is too early to tell. Perhaps the main parachute lines tangled and the parachute failed to deploy or the shock from explosive separation charges on the faring might have ruptured a seal on the spacecraft." However, an anonymous source on the UN advisory board to the IAC said that the agency was also looking at whether it might be due to possible sabotage by the Earth First movement.

Marm 36, Year 5, Frisol-Landing + 42 sols

After the meeting yestersol, I'd dropped into my role as a computer next to Helen as if I'd never left it, but we kept having to wait for Earth to verify our calculations before we could move on. I'd been chased to bed after I fell asleep the second time at the table.

Couldn't stay awake at the table. Couldn't sleep in bed. I

spent the night waking up with my brain frantically trying to calculate useless things like the amount of room our food would occupy if we hydrated all of it. Or the wingspan necessary to allow a plane that could fly in the thin atmosphere of Mars because somehow *that* would solve our problem.

I stared at the ceiling where the skylight had begun to lighten. *If we could fly . . .* Maybe we could. Not with an airplane, but we did have a way to fly. This wasn't the planned use, but maybe flying was the answer. Stifling a groan because I was still tired but definitely awake, I climbed down from the top bunk.

Nathaniel had come to bed at some point and was sacked out on the lower bunk. I could not wait for us to expand the base so we could sleep in the same bed again.

I got dressed as quietly as I could, but he still woke up with a start. "What time is it?"

"Seven a.m. You can sleep for another hour."

He grunted and closed his eyes. But then he dragged them open again and reached for my hand. When I gave it to him, he brought it to his lips and kissed the back of my knuckles. "Love you."

I squeezed his hand and then gave in to the gravitational pull of my husband. Crawling onto the lower bunk, I curled onto my side as he scooted over to make room. His right arm came around me and he pulled me close against him.

I sighed into his embrace, letting tension ebb into the mattress. I still ached from the run yestersol where we'd found the shattered cargo drop. There hadn't been any crates to schlep, but we'd spent a heck of a lot of time clambering over uneven terrain and cataloging random pieces of debris. The warmth of Nathaniel pressing against the length of my body was a comfort.

When we were young, we had sex at every available opportunity. As much as I had loved that, I relished these moments of quiet intimacy. Our breathing slowed and matched pace. It was tempting to stay there and pretend that our world hadn't changed yestersol with that crashed supply drop.

But as deputy administrator, I didn't want anyone to think I was shirking. I wanted to be up and cheerful to help set the tone for the sol. Patting his arm, I sighed and pushed myself up to sit on the edge of the bed.

Twisting, I bent down and kissed his cheek. "Love you."

He smiled, but his eyes stayed closed and his breathing was even. I ached, wanting to stay with him. But I had work to do.

When I was outside of our cubicle, I took a moment to stretch. Later, I could break out the hamantaschen we'd brought from Earth. Each triangular pastry was packed in individual wrappers by IAC's food technicians so that we could share the buttery cookies with our friends as part of the celebration. They were still in a bin, carefully cataloged and stacked by the kitchen. It would be a little early for Purim, but sharing a treat now could be a much needed morale boost.

The door three cubicles down opened and Florence stepped out. She saw me and nodded. "Glad I'm not the only one up."

"Have to prep for the meeting." I rolled my wrists, feeling the burn deep in my forearms. "You?"

"Gotta relieve Dawn." She stifled a yawn. "We're splitting shifts while this is . . ."

"Yeah . . ." I walked with her to the kitchen, where Leonard was already rehydrating some coffee. He'd clearly been up for a while, because he had a clipboard tucked under one arm. Normally, we went off duty during our night because Earth could set off an alarm if there was an emergency. Their Mission Control stayed staffed, but they had more people.

He pulled the drink bag off the spigot and nodded. "Morning, ladies."

"Morning." I pulled a vacuum pack out of the supply drawer and attached it to the spigot, glancing at Florence. "Make you a cup? Bag? Whatever?"

"I will murder someone for coffee in any form."

"That would slow things down." I made an exaggerated face. "So much extra paperwork."

"Listen, if coffee is on the line, that paperwork would be

worth it." She looked sharply at Leonard. "Tell me our coffee wasn't on that cargo drop."

He chuckled and shook his head. "We have multiple redundancies for coffee. Mission Control knows what actually runs the program."

She sagged with mock relief. Or maybe real relief, I don't know. At some point, the runaway greenhouse effect caused by the Meteor would warm the Earth to the point where we'd stop being able to get coffee, which is why there were trials of coffee plants growing in the greenhouse caves on the Moon now. Regardless, I handed her the vacuum pack and she lifted it in a salute. "I'll go relieve Dawn. Catch you later."

"She'll be happy to see you," he said.

"No, because I'm not sharing my coffee."

Leonard laughed and swung his leg over one of the benches, sitting down. "I already talked to Dawn and got the update from Earth. Want to talk through the sol's business before the meeting?"

"The sol's business," as if this were an entirely ordinary sol.

"What's the big picture?" I attached my drink bag to the spigot. My love of coffee was not an exaggeration, even when freeze-dried and served in a vacuum pack.

"Spinning in circles, and still not generating any gravity." Leonard shook his head. "We're in a holding pattern as they try to decide how they want you and Wilburt to use our one rover. Confirm the satellite survey of the other supply drops or go out and look at the crash site."

I nodded and watched the bag fill. "I've been thinking about this overnight. What if we power up the hopper early?"

The hopper was a suborbital craft that was a little conical thing, which used compressed oxygen and carbon monoxide from the Mars atmosphere to allow us to do short "hops" covering up to seventy kilometers in a go. It had been intended for exploration when we began surveying for water ice because it could go farther than the rover.

"Interesting..." Leonard rubbed his chin and I could see the shadow of stubble. "As long as it's not picking up cargo, it'll be able to visit three supply drop sites in a sol... Have the crew camp overnight to give the compressor time to refill the tanks and we can probably get it done in three sols. Plus having answers will make your husband calm down."

"Sorry about him."

Leonard waved his hand, snorting. "I tease. But back to the hopper. Yeah, I like this idea."

The urge to raise my hand to pilot the hopper was so strong. I wanted to tell him that we should assign me to the flights, but I couldn't tell if that was a conflict of interest to take the "fun" job or if it was the correct choice because I was currently the most qualified pilot on Mars.

"What about Helen? To pilot the hopper, I mean."

He didn't even hesitate. "You're the only one on the planet who has flown in Martian atmo. If we do this, it's you."

I didn't try to fight him. Just nodded and sipped my coffee as if this were not a big deal. I had missed flying so much. Yes, I had landed the *Esther* just a month ago, but that was the first time—the only time—I'd flown in Martian atmosphere. Before that, it had been over a year since I'd flown. Piloted, yes, but somehow *flying* to me still required atmosphere.

He gnawed his lower lip, scribbled some notes on his clipboard and slid it across to me. "What about this task list?"

Flight—Elma York, Wilburt Schnöhaus

Crash site survey—Graeham Stewman, Helen Carmouche, Aahana Kamal, Jaidev Kamal

Engineering planning—Nathaniel York, Reynard Carmouche, Lance Woolen, Opal Woolen, Bolívar Gallego

Comms—Dawn Schnöhaus, Florence Grey

Suit maintenance—Zainabu Tatu, Mosi Mohammed Tatu

Floaters—Kam Shamoun, Catalina Suarez Gallego, Leonard Flannery, Howard Tang, Nuan Su Tang

I tapped the list. "Put Jaidev on kitchen, which isn't on your list. He's a good cook. And then Catalina on the outside crew. She's our planetary ecologist. Plus she aced the navigation tests in survival training."

"Sounds reasonable."

"Although I'm pretty sure Mission Control will say no to the hopper. Or at least 'not now.'" I sighed. It was a good idea; it was just that they would want to do a test back on Earth and would feel like it was too radical a change in plan.

"Maybe . . ." He fiddled with the cap of his pen. "And maybe we don't tell them that you're going. Forgiveness rather than permission."

I opened my mouth to ask if this was what had happened with the patch in the garage wall. Leonard hadn't been the one in charge, but had the whole crew decided to opt for forgiveness instead of permission? I didn't, though. We had more pressing things to worry about.

"They would know. The telemetry from the hopper goes straight to Mission Control."

Leonard waved a hand to brush the suggestion away. "I'm kidding. I'll put the suggestion through normal channels and we'll see what happens."

To my shock, when he asked them they responded quickly and with an affirmative. We were Go to take the hopper out next sol. As much as I was looking forward to flying a brand-new aircraft, it also drove home how much urgency we were facing.

Losing one supply drop was bad. If we had lost more than that, it could be fatal.

Marm 37, Year 5, Satursol—Landing + 43 sols

Next sol, I stood in the pilot's station of the hopper. Like the early lunar landers, they had saved weight by eliminating chairs. And by "they" I meant Nathaniel. This was a craft he had designed.

It was intended for exploration and none of the flights would be long. Wilburt stood on my right. The cabin was pressurized, but we stayed in our suits, per procedure, as if that would protect us if I crashed the thing.

Wilburt and I had our checklists. I moved down each step with my thick, gloved finger on the list. "Bat 5&6: NORM—on tb-gray. BAT 1&3—off and reset tb-bp."

"DES 820—close." Wilburt confirmed from his side of the crowded gray console. Labels with raised letters named every conceivable part of the ship.

Through the small triangular windows below our console, I caught glimpses of our ground crew as they stowed the tarp that had covered our small craft. Their bright green suits were easy to see against the ruddy ground as they worked. Eventually there would be a pressurized docking tunnel that would lead out to the hopper, but it hadn't been built yet. For now, it lived under a tarp on a small landing pad and we walked out to it in Mars suits.

"Hopper One, ground crew." Lance's voice crackled over the speakers in my helmet. "We have cleared the area."

"Thank you, ground crew." I confirmed the next steps on my checklist, moving through methodically. Slow was fast and especially when flying. I rested my hands on the flight controllers. Even though I'd never flown this particular craft, they felt so familiar from all the sims we'd done.

Wilburt flipped a switch on his side of the dashboard. "ECS: glycol pump sec-open."

"Engine armed."

I wasn't scared or anxious, but just so eager to be *up*. To see Mars spread out below me like a tapestry. "Bradbury Base, Hopper One. We've completed our checklist and are ready for takeoff."

Dawn's voice answered. "Hopper One, Bradbury. You are Go for takeoff with flight path heading 320."

I glanced at Wilburt who was writing it down as my copilot. "Copy heading 320."

My suit's fans hummed as I glanced one last time at the checklist. "All right. Here we go, off into the wild red yonder."

I fired the engines and the little hopper lived up to its name, hopping into the air like a jackrabbit on his second cup of coffee. Sudden gravity pulled at my suit, trying to hold me on the surface. But we were up and flying.

My speakers crackled as Wilburt gave a long, delighted roll of giggles. I had a matching set trapped in my throat and leaking out through the enormous grin I wore. Through the long sliver of a window over the dashboard, I could see Mars. It was beautiful.

More colors unveiled themselves the longer I looked. Mars was not just red. It had broad swatches of blue-gray dust or rocks. The horizon was so close. I knew that Mars was smaller than the Earth, but until I got into the air and saw how close the horizon was, it hadn't hit home.

I turned my gaze back to my instrument panel and fired thrusters to align our direction with the heading that Dawn had given us. The pop-pop-pop of them pressed the hard ridges of my Mars suit into my bruised shoulders.

I've never minded the strain of flight. The only thing that caused me to fret was knowing that the reason I was getting to use the hopper tosol was because for us—for the habitat—this was a bad sol.

I didn't have much time to look at the scenery on the way to the first site, because I was so focused on not crashing this weird ship. When we'd gotten there, that cargo drop had been in good shape and the hatch seal was intact.

The transit to our second site took us up over Aeolis Mons, the mountain at the center of Gale Crater. I was starting to get the feel of the hopper now. Flying her felt a little like using a lunar lander. She had no lift and started dropping the moment acceleration stopped.

The slopes of Aeolis Mons lay beneath us with deceptively

smooth sides, sweeping up to a soft peak like a child's mound of sand before they build a castle. It was a burnished orange with dark pops of shadows made by boulders sticking up through its dusty flanks.

"Throttling back."

"Copy."

I eased off the throttle, letting the hopper arc back down toward the ground before "hopping" back up for another arc. As we glided down, I could feel the small resistances of the Mars atmosphere. This was so different from bringing the *Esther* in. We had screamed down through the atmosphere with her, cutting the thin air with the white-hot blade of our heat shield. It had been a wild and glorious ride.

And too short.

This . . . When we had started the sol, each drop had caused me to tense because it made all of my terrestrial pilot instincts tell me that we were stalling and that I needed to regain control of the craft. But I had control.

"Why are you laughing?" Wilburt kept his eyes on the instruments.

"I was just thinking that at least there aren't any birds."

"You do not like birds?"

"Not when I'm flying . . ." I watched my instruments because distances were still hard to judge here. There were no trees or anything else to give scale so I might as well be flying a toy plane over a sandbox. "Applying thrust."

"Copy that."

For a moment, the gravity of Mars reached into the cabin and tried to pull us back down. The rush and hiss of compressed gas propelling us up and forward made me want to giggle all over again. It wasn't a plane, but by all that was holy, it felt good to be flying again.

Everything in my body hurt. At the end of the first sol, I sat on the floor of the hopper with our first aid kit open as Wilburt taped a bandage around the end of my left index finger. I hated delaminating nails. The cotton liner glove was stiff with my blood.

The gloves of every spacesuit I've ever worn are so stiff when they're pressurized that it's like working against a spring. The only way you can tell you have something in your hand is to overgrip it. The little caps on the ends of our gloves provide protection and traction, and sometimes, sometimes they can peel a nail right off.

"Sorry about this."

"Why sorry?" Finished, Wilburt put the tape back in its sleeve in the kit and snapped the spring-loaded cover shut.

"Because it slows us down."

"I thought being slow was a virtue." He stowed the med kit and dropped back to sit on his rear, leaning against the side of the hopper's cabin. "Sorry for any discomfort I caused."

I waved my good hand. "My own fault. We're moving faster than I'd like and I have to keep reminding myself that slow is fast."

"And the good news is that here we are and we have only two sols more until we go home." He had a red mark on his cheek where his mic had pressed into the skin. "Good flying tosol."

"Thank you." Leaning back, I grabbed my checklist which I was profoundly grateful for because it freed up more of my brain for doing my job. "Okay . . . Oh, thank God. Dinner."

He gave a little groan. "I am so hungry."

"Same." I scrubbed my face with my hands, wincing as the nail bed protested. I just wanted to hang up the hammocks and go straight to sleep. I yawned so wide that my jaw cracked. "Excuse me."

"It is catching." Wilburt yawned back. "What is a tired dragon's favorite dinner?"

"I don't know, Wilburt. What *is* a tired dragon's favorite dinner?"

"Flamin' yawn."

I groaned and opened my carry bag to pull out one of the

meal kits. A piece of plastic rustled in the bag. Frowning, I fished it out.

It was a package of hamantaschen.

Specifically, my bag held two of the packages that Nathaniel and I had brought to Mars so that we could celebrate Purim. The triangular cookies were a little banged up but still recognizably that wonderful blend of shortbread and poppy seed.

When had Nathaniel had time to put these in my bag?

Everything caught up with me all at once and I just started crying like a boy over his first puppy. I clapped my hands over my mouth, as if muffling the sobs would somehow make them less noticeable.

I closed my eyes so I wouldn't have to see Wilburt staring at me and buried my face in my knees. My shoulders shook and all I could taste was salt and snot.

Nathaniel had remembered and we were here and they were just cookies. That's all. Just cookies.

So why was I crying?

Sniffling, I tried to wipe my face on my sleeve, but it was covered in tubes so all I did was scrape my nose. At least that made me laugh a little. "Sorry."

Wilburt sat in front of me, concern creasing his brow. He held out a piece of medical gauze. "I don't have a handkerchief."

Which set me off again. Only a little this time, but still. I took the gauze and blew my nose into it and it was disgusting. Gauze, just to be clear, is very permeable. I didn't complain to Wilburt, though. "Thank you."

"Your finger did not make you cry, but . . . something else?" He pointed to the bag. "Are you all right?"

I swallowed bitter salt and nodded, turning the crumpled packet over so he could see it better. "Nathaniel packed these."

"They are not too broken, surely?"

"No—no, it's not that. These are hamantaschen." I held out one of the packets. "This is for you."

He pulled back a little. "I can't take a gift that your husband packed for you."

"They're part of how we celebrate Purim." I held it out again, seeing the confusion and hesitation in his gaze. "It's this holiday celebrating when Esther saved us from Haman. There's feasting and costumes and we're supposed to exchange gifts of food. He put two packets in here. I promise that this is for you."

He started to reach for it and paused. "If it will not make you cry?"

"It might, but these are happy tears. It's okay."

"Good." He took the packet and looked at it. "And . . . Esther. Is that where your aunt gets her name?"

I nodded, peeling the package open as carefully as I could to avoid spilling crumbs everywhere. Should I have eaten dinner first? No, in fact, these cookies were the most important thing in that bag. "So, there was this king who had a wicked vizier—"

"Sorry. 'Vizier'? I do not know this word."

"'Vizier' means . . ." I swallowed, but not because I had trouble defining it but because it reminded me that English was not his first language. "Sorry, I—I'd forgotten that you were German. 'Vizier' means a sort of high official."

We'd worked together for years and I had deliberately never asked him what he did during the war. Because when you work in rocketry, there's a very limited range of things that you did during the war. And if you were German all of them would have been for the Nazis.

The cabin seemed suddenly cramped. It had seemed cozy before. How had I forgotten that he was German? I had just given hamantaschen to a German.

I swallowed again and looked at the floor, playing with the edges of the package. Did I continue to open it or did I fold it up and put it away?

Wilburt cleared his throat. "I was a child. During the war."

Startled, I looked up. Wilburt's face was stricken and he was looking out one of our small triangular windows at the Martian dusk. I don't know if the fifteen years of difference in our ages wasn't noticeable or if I were just in denial that I was almost forty-eight.

He would have been two years old when the war started.

Wilburt drew his knees up, wrapping his arm around them to hug his legs to his chest. His other hand still held the hamantaschen as he stared out at Mars. His jaw worked and it seemed as if he were almost about to speak.

"I'm . . . I'm sorry. That's not what I was—" That was absolutely what I had been thinking. "I thought I was probably boring you is all."

Lips compressing, he nodded. "It is not the first time someone has thought I was a Nazi. Blond. German. Blue eyes. An atheist. A scientist. What else could I be?"

"Wilburt, I—"

"It is all right, Elma." He frowned, still staring out the window. "Because, in truth, if I had been an adult or even a teenager, I likely would have been. Not because I believed in any of their hatred but because my own family would have . . ." His voice broke and he lowered his head.

A moment later he lifted it and looked at me. The rims of his eyes were red. "Here is something that I have never told you. Do you know what my mother said when I told her that you had been added to the First Mars Expedition?"

My mouth was utterly dry. I shook my head, unable to speak as I braced myself.

"She told me . . . she told me that she was Jewish." His voice went high and thin as he fought through the next sentence. "I was an adult. My whole life, she had hidden this part of herself. I had been raised to be an atheist and taught to never, ever talk about religion. And you—your existence on that ship meant that for the first time my mother could tell me about this essential part of her."

"Why didn't you say something before?"

His face twisted and he looked down at the hamantaschen. "What was I to say? Hallo, my name is Wilburt and you are the famous Lady Astronaut and by the way, I have just learned that my mother is Jewish and therefore—therefore so am I."

He started to cry.

I did not know what to say. He had been holding this in for years. Just like his mother had. "It would have been okay if you had told me that." I grabbed the medical kit and fished inside for a piece of gauze. "Did you know . . . did you know that Parker's wife was Jewish?"

His head came up, shock written across his face. "But he was always so awful to you."

"He disliked me for my own attributes. Not my religion. We had a history before the Meteor." I handed him the gauze. "I have to warn you that all of your snot will go straight through this, but it's the best choice available."

"I appreciate the warning." He blew his nose and made a disgusted face, looking at his hand. "*Ach du Scheiße,* you are not kidding."

"I was not."

"Do you know how astronauts blow their noses?"

"I do not." I smiled, relieved to see him starting to steady out again.

"Easy, it's snot rocket science." He folded the gauze looking for a clean spot.

I shifted to my knees and slid a few centimeters closer to him. "You aren't alone, you know. There are a bunch of us on this mission and more will come on the Third Expedition."

"My mother will be very relieved." He frowned at the gauze and tucked it into the waste bag that would eventually be composted. Then he picked up the cookies. "Thank you."

"Sure." My throat was tight.

He turned and reached for his carry bag. "Now, you said that it is a night for feasting and sharing of gifts of food . . . Butterscotch pudding. For you."

"Freilichin Purim." I smiled at him. The butterscotch pudding was absolutely one of the best things to come out of the space food labs. On the early Moon missions we used to fight for it. Just a little.

Wilburt pulled a hamantasch out of the wrapper, a few

crumbs dropping away. He took a bite of the triangular cookie and his face did weird things. He made a muffled sound.

The poppy seed filling is, to me, delightful, but the crackle of the seeds could be surprising if you weren't used to it. "You don't have to eat it if you don't like it."

He shook his head. "It is . . . I remember these, I think . . . I think my mother used to make these when I was very little."

If you were trying to hide the fact that you were Jewish, the food could give you away. It's why my parents never kept kosher, because they were trying to protect my dad's career in the military. I pulled out my own hamantaschen and carefully extracted a single cookie.

The shortbread-like dough was a year stale and the poppy seeds had the metallic overlay of freezer burn, but that first mouthful was one of the most delicious things I had ever tasted.

"So . . ." Wilburt cleared his throat. "I understand that there was an evil vizier."

My smile grew wider. "Let me tell it to you properly. Now, every time you hear me say 'Haman,' you need to stomp your feet and hiss to drown out his name . . ."

TEN

50,000 SAID TO FLEE FLOODS IN VIETNAM

DANANG, Vietnam, March 22, 1970—(AP)—Officials estimated today that the heaviest floods in six years in three northern provinces of Vietnam had left 50,000 people homeless.

The Saigon government flew relief supplies here, and a transport ship loaded with food docked at Danang Harbor. Dr. Tran Nguyen Phieu, the Minister of Social Welfare, flew here for an investigation.

Marm 38, Year 5, Sunsol-Landing + 44 sols

At the first site that sol—which had been our fourth overall—the cargo drop had come down in one of those beautiful landings where everything was so level that it looked like a human had landed it. Now, I stared out of my helmet at the fifth of our sites, which was a mess.

Oh, it had landed successfully and on target, but it was on a hill. As best as I could tell, the upslope leg had crumpled after landing causing the cargo pallet to tip over, slide off the lander, and embed the hatch in the side of the hill.

Beside me, Wilburt said, "I don't suppose we can say that this one is fine?"

"And if the hatch seal is broken under all that?" If the hatch seal had failed, we could be looking at anything from a charred interior due to the heat of entry to a compartment filled with sand. Plus, extended contact with the surface would also mean the cargo would have been cold soaked at a much lower temperature than if it had been sitting "high and dry."

Wilburt sighed, his breath hissing over our comms. "I'll get the shovel. You take photos of the site for reference."

My hands preemptively ached and that delaminated nail throbbed just thinking about digging. I was simultaneously grateful to him for taking the unpleasant gig and annoyed that he was issuing orders. "We should check in with Bradbury Base to see what we need to do."

"You do not need to always ask permission, Elma." Wilburt stumped back to the hopper. "You can tell just them what your decision is."

What was it with people from the First Expedition and not talking to Mission Control? "We have the resource of smart people back at the base who can identify if we're missing something. Why wouldn't I call them?"

His back was to me but his voice still sounded right next to me. "You argued with Parker about everything you did not agree with, why is this different? You are in the command structure now and yet you are so cautious."

"It's not different." I had not argued with Parker about most things. Most of the time, I had bit my tongue and hunkered down, hoping he wouldn't notice me. "Maybe, for instance, they'll tell us that we don't need to dig this cargo drop out. I'm just following protocol the way we're supposed to."

Wilburt snorted.

I flipped the switch on my suit to the big loop. Wilburt would still be on hot mic in my ear, but he wouldn't be able to hear me as I talked to the base.

"Bradbury Base, York." I plodded around the cargo drop and lined up a photo of the heat shield, not sure what they would be looking for once it was scanned and transmitted back to Earth. Given everything, you would think that they would have trained us to look for sabotage, but they hadn't.

"York, Bradbury." Florence's voice filled my speakers. "You aren't due to check in for another hour. Everything okay?"

"I just wanted to do an update. This cargo drop came down on a hill and one of the legs crumpled. The pallet slipped off so the door is pretty well covered over with regolith. We're digging it out to see if the door seal is intact." Wilburt was digging now, but I was not going to let him do all the hard work, delaminated fingernail or no.

"Copy that. Any sense of how that will affect your overall schedule?"

"I suspect we won't get to the last supply drop of tosol." Lowering the camera, I backed away from the craft so I could get a better picture of it in situ.

"Keep us posted—hang on. Leonard wants to talk to you."

The microphone shifted and his voice joined me on the Martian surface. "Would you be up to doing an interview when you come back? Publicity is asking."

Sweat prickled across my whole body. This was not something the LCVG could compensate for. "I don't know . . . We've got a lot—"

Wilburt made a sound. It was the kind of sound you make when something hurts and you know you're on a hot mic. He dropped the shovel and staggered down the hill.

"I have to go." Slogging forward, I flipped back to our private loop.

The static was a little louder than usual, but Wilburt was completely quiet. He left the shovel on the ground, turned, and started walking toward the lander. No. He was limping.

No.

"Wilburt?"

"Suit puncture." He moved with purpose but didn't run. Running increased the chances that he would fall. "Not bad."

The suit designers on Earth had been proud of telling us that you could punch up to a quarter-inch hole in your suit and still have half an hour to get inside. We practiced that. But the only person I knew whose suit had actually been breached had died.

That hole had been a massive gash, but right now, Wilburt was limping. I didn't know how big the hole in his suit was.

"I'll start the repress sequence as soon as you're inside." Ten meters to our craft and safety.

"Copy." His voice was as calm as if this were a sim.

Five meters.

He stumbled. I grabbed his arm and steadied him. I wanted to see the gauges on his suit but there was no way to do that without slowing him down.

Ladder.

I practically pushed him ahead of me up into the hopper. As soon as I was through the hatch, I slammed it shut and went into the emergency ingress sequence. We'd run it so many times that I didn't need to consult a checklist. Muscle memory just took over.

Wilburt sat on the floor, hands pressed over his foot, which might even help.

I got the final latch secured and glanced at the checklist, confirming that I'd run through everything before I started the repress sequence.

Air roared into the cabin. It sounded as if a train were trying to run through the ship. Wilburt visibly relaxed, but kept holding his foot. I watched him and there was nothing I could do to help.

But he was breathing and oxygen levels were rising.

"What happened?" I crouched as best I could in front of him.

He squinted at the gauge on the wall, then nodded. "The sand slipped as I was driving the shovel down. And now . . . here we have the salad."

When the pressure stabilized, I gave a sigh of relief and released the valve in my suit. As the suit depressurized around me, it became more flexible. Opening the seal of my left glove, I winced as I pulled it off my wounded hand. As soon as I had both gloves off, I knelt to give Wilburt some assistance.

He waved me off. His hands were shaking. "I have hurt my foot. Also my ego and this Mars suit. Still, I can myself remove it."

"Sure." I took my helmet off. "Oh shit. I was talking to Bradbury when—"

The moment I toggled back to the big loop, the ear pieces in my Snoopy cap filled with Florence's voice. "—ou copy. Repeat. Hopper One, Bradbury. Do you copy? Hopper One, Bradbury—"

"We're here." I cut in to save her as much panic as I could. "We're okay."

"What the hell is going on?" Leonard's voice was farther from the mic but no less present for that.

"We had a suit malfunction, but we're both back in the hopper and it's repressurized." That tame version would suffice until we were more sorted.

Wilburt had his helmet off and looked green. Sweat stood out in beads under his Snoopy cap. I grabbed an emesis bag from the med kit and handed it to him. He took it and stared blankly at the bright blue plastic.

With his hands away, I could see where the shovel had broken the seal where beta cloth connected to the outsized sole, the one that was supposed to prevent any rocks from compromising the suit. The shovel had hit and scraped forward until it was stopped by the thick rim and all its motion translated downward. It was unlucky. The kind of breach you couldn't predict because it was built of cascading failures. Buried cargo pallet leads to sand leads to shovel leads to slipping leads to accidental impact leads to force applied directly on a seam.

I flipped my mic to mute and knelt in front of him. "You're all right."

Wilburt nodded but it looked more like a puppet being poorly manipulated. "I'm all right."

He was lucky because it had happened close to the hopper. He was lucky because it had happened early during that Marswalk, while his consumables were still high. He was lucky because he was alive.

I toggled my mic back on. "Bradbury, we're going to need to come back ASAP."

We couldn't finish this site with a breach in his suit. The hopper didn't have an airlock. It's one of those compromises the engineers had to make to get the hopper light enough to fly on compressed gas. The hatch just opened straight to Mars. No big deal, if you assume that both astronauts will be in Mars suits.

But if you've got a hole in the suit . . . To be sure, his suit could handle about a half hour of losses. But that wasn't enough because in order to keep O_2 losses to a minimum, the depress procedure took about forty-five minutes as the air inside the cabin got crammed back into oxygen tanks.

"Understood." Florence's voice was an absolute rock. "What assistance will you require?"

"Let us finish assessing and I'll report back in ten minutes."

"Copy. Bradbury Base standing by."

I toggled my mic out of the big loop and focused Wilburt. "All right, let's get that boot off so we can patch it." I leaned over and grabbed my bag, which had a suit repair kit in it. "You'll be happy to know that one of us brings all the items on the checklist."

That made him laugh, which I was grateful for. As he decoupled the boot connector, I scraped my brain for a joke, any joke, that would make him laugh.

"So this Southern lady moved into a new neighborhood and met her neighbor for the first time. It was an old money neighborhood and she was trying to fit in so she wore her new fur coat. 'My husband gave me this mink coat.'

"Her neighbor said, 'That's nice.'"

I pulled the boot off as Wilburt dragged his foot out, wincing.

"'And my pearls, he gave me those, too.' And her neighbor sipped her tea and said, 'That's nice.'"

I'd braced myself for his sock to be bloody and thank God, it wasn't.

"'And he bought me a yacht, too. You should come sometime.' Her neighbor said, 'That's nice.'"

As he worked the other boot off, I set the damaged one to the side. "She was real frustrated that none of this appeared to impress her neighbor. 'Well, what did your husband give you?'"

Wilburt was watching me and his color looked better. His hands weren't shaking as much.

I pulled out the flat beta cloth repair kit and set it next to the boot. "The neighbor said, 'He gave me etiquette lessons, where . . .' She sipped her tea. 'I learned to say "That's nice" instead of "Fuck you."'"

Wilburt burst into laughter, slapping his hand on his knee. "Aha! That is very good!" He laughed much longer than the joke merited. "I did not know you were so funny."

"That's nice."

He laughed harder and I let him. Because I was looking at the breach and I was looking at the repair kit. It was designed to fix a hole in the internal bladder. Flat surface to flat surface. The damage he'd done? I didn't think we could fix that. Not with what we had on the hopper.

And that led to the next problem. When we got back . . . the hopper parked on a landing pad. Eventually, there would be a docking tunnel that we could attach the hopper to, but right now, the only way for Wilburt to get back to the base was to walk outside.

ELEVEN

**SUBORBITAL UNITÉ AIRLINER SUCCESSFUL
IN 38-MINUTE MAIDEN FLIGHT**

TOULOUSE, France, March 22, 1970—The French-Brazilian Unité, the Western world's first suborbital airliner, made its maiden flight today. Though the test flight was only a limited initial step, it was an impressive success going from Nice, France, to Rio de Janeiro in only thirty-eight minutes.

Marm 38, Year 5, Sunsol—Landing + 44 sols

When we finally got back, the light had a golden-honey character that made me think it was later than it was. With quick bursts from my thrusters, I ignored the landing pad and maneuvered the hopper to set down as close to the main entrance to Bradbury as I could. We didn't want to subject the suit to any more strain than necessary.

Double tap to correct away from the *Esther* and another to confirm height. I released the right-hand controller and the hopper dropped the last few centimeters to settle on the surface. "We have contact."

As soon as we'd shut down the hopper, I toggled up the mic. "All right, folks, what do you have for us?"

Zainabu answered. "We're going to bring a good boot out to you."

"We can't depressurize, though."

"We've got a plan that will hold air long enough for you to depressurize, we'll fling the boot in to you and that will suffice to get him inside." Her voice had a slight smirk to it. "I feel that I need to stress that we did mock this up and it works."

"Copy. And also the fact that you have to stress that is a little concerning."

"First tool will tell you why." Zainabu's pause felt like one of Wilburt's jokes. "Do you have any apricot pull-up bars left?"

"Um . . . Yes." I looked out the window at the Martian regolith mounded around the dome as if I could see into Bradbury. "Are you serious?"

"I am."

Wilburt and I stared at each other for a moment, with our mouths open like we were trying to catch flies. If there were flies to catch on Mars. Anyway, after a minute, he shrugged, shook his head, and grabbed the bag the kitchen had packed for us.

He held up one of the chewy fruit pull-up bars as if it were an Olympic torch. "I have here an apricot bar."

"Good. Keeping the bar inside its wrapper, one of you should remove your gloves and hold the bar between both hands."

Brow creased with incredulity, Wilburt wrapped his hands around the pull-up bar. I was as confused as he was.

"What are . . ." It was hard to imagine where this was going. "May we ask for the big picture?"

"You're going to soften the bar as much as you can, shove it into the gap, and tape the hell out of it. It will slow the leak to acceptable levels."

That was the most absurd thing I had ever heard. "Well, at least 'the hell out of' is a clearly defined metric."

"The goal is to slow the leak, not eliminate it, and to also leave the boot repairable. The other solution would have been permanent and rendered the boot unusable for future missions." Zainabu's voice was cheerfully matter-of-fact.

"And apricot is the best tool for this?" This felt like we were being hazed, but they wouldn't play jokes with a suit breach.

"The glucose in the paste is pliable, sticky, and won't blow up like a balloon. It'll be easy to clean off and leave no residue afterwards—I was also dubious and have to give Jaidev credit for the suggestion."

"Roger, wilco." I checked in with Wilburt who was still holding the pull-up bar. "Wilburt is warming the bar. What should I be doing?"

"Cut four strips of medical tape approximately ten centimeters long and one that is twenty-five centimeters."

"On it."

For the next ten minutes, Wilburt and I followed the instructions coming out of Bradbury Mission Control, and I have to say, once we started working with the apricot paste, it made sense. I knelt in front of Wilburt, shoving the gooey stuff into the crack in the boot. I kept my injured finger lifted away so that it didn't get sticky with paste.

Then I ran tape over the area to hold everything in place with a cross-hatching pattern that wrapped around the edges of the boot.

I stood up, looking down at my work. "Everything is installed."

Wilburt stood with his arms out a little, afraid to move, and acted as if keeping his arms away from his sides would somehow help.

"Handing you back to Florence now." Zainabu signed off from the mic, I assume because the suit-repair portion of the procedure was accomplished and we were back to regular CAPCOM stuff. I say "regular" because as weird as this situation was, the fact that we had all trained together and trusted each other's expertise made everything feel normal. Or at least retained enough of the trappings that I was reasonably calm.

"As soon as you're both suited up the rest of the way, the next step will be depressing the hopper." Florence's calm working diction was a welcome comfort. "Start with step twelve B on the EVA egress checklist, but we recommend that Wilburt tries to move his feet as little as possible."

"*Toe*riffic."

I groaned as I turned to the checklist pasted to the hull of the hopper. Twelve B put us after donning boots, which we'd both already done. I grabbed Wilburt's helmet and gloves from stowage and handed the helmet to him first. He put it on with the ease of someone who has done a lot of EVAs.

Honestly, neither of us needed the checklist for this but I still followed it step-by-step and he didn't object at all. The only place I deviated was making sure that his suit was holding pressure before I finished donning my own.

"Will you look at that . . ." I stared at the gauge in wonder. "I'm going to think twice about eating a pull-up bar in the future knowing that it's this good of a glue."

Wilburt raised his arm to use his wrist mirror to look at the gauges on his suit. "Is there a reason then that I cannot simply walk into Bradbury?"

"Yes." Florence was fast on the response. "That would be the weather. The high tosol is negative thirty-five degrees Celsius. The paste will freeze and crack if you try to walk."

I snugged my helmet into place and then tightened my jaw as I pulled my gloves on. It meant shoving my delaminated nail into the tight confines of the glove bladder. I wrinkled my nose and compressed my lips, but didn't make a sound.

As I flipped the switch to power up my PLSS, the familiar tension stiffened my suit. And the gloves. I hated delaminating nails so, so much.

Lifting my wrist mirror, I checked my own gauges. "We're suited up and ready to depress the hopper."

"When it is depressed, open the hatch. Graeham will be standing outside and patched in on the big loop. He will be holding the boot at six o'clock."

"All right . . ." I walked to the hatch and checked the pressure gauges. "Depressing now. See you soon, Graeham."

"Looking forward to it." His posh British baritone had that faint confined echo of someone talking inside a helmet.

I glanced at Wilburt one more time and he gave me a thumbs-up. I pushed the depress button.

Some part of me honestly expected something to fail with

THE MARTIAN CONTINGENCY * 101

that. But it began the train engine whooshing of cramming all of our oxygen back into the reserve tanks. Or rather, most of it. We'd lose about 8 percent of the O_2 in the craft when we opened the door, because on Mars, it didn't make sense to depress to a vacuum. Not when we had to match the atmospheric pressure of the planet.

Thank God they'd figured out how to resupply oxygen from Mars without needing it to come from Earth. That wouldn't have been sustainable over the long haul.

I watched the gauge as the pressure came down over the next forty-five minutes. "How's your suit holding, Wilburt?"

"Super." He paused and I could almost hear him searching his internal joke book. "Do you know why the IAC has trouble recruiting suit repair techs?"

"No, Wilburt. Why *does* the IAC have trouble recruiting suit repair techs?"

"They can't handle the pressure."

The mic crackled and Zainabu said, "I resent that." But you could hear the laughter in her voice.

The time crawled by. Wilburt kept clenching and unclenching his jaw. Partly to distract him and partly because I thought the tension might make him tell me, I switched to our private channel and asked, "You want to tell me what really happened in the garage?"

Wilburt stared straight ahead. "What do you mean?"

"The hole. The place where the 'rover dinged it' on the First Expedition."

"Oh, yes." The Mars suit obscured his body language so all I could see was a flat calm. "I had all of that forgotten. We were carrying out a repair on the antennas and, when moving the vehicle, bumped one of the struts, which impacted the wall. It was a very small hole that we nearly did not notice. But the patches come only in one size, therefore it seems worse than it is."

Plausible. Barely. And of course, there was no way for me to check the size of that hole without peeling the patch back, which would create unnecessary risk.

Finally, the pressure gauge equalized with outside. "I'm opening the hatch."

The ripple-bang of fifteen latches releasing out here was higher pitched than those in the airlock leading into the base. Same mechanism. Different atmosphere.

It was harder to pull the hatch open from a kneeling position, but it put me close enough to be able to shove my hand out the door.

Graeham put the boot into my outstretched hand. "You have the boot."

I clutched it until I could feel the hard O-ring through my glove. "I have the boot."

Pulling it inside, I set it on the floor of the hopper. Using both hands, I pushed the hatch back into place and snugged it closed. Clambering to my feet, I double-checked the seal.

"Repressurizing the cabin." I hit the repress button and air rushed into the cabin.

This process is faster and louder than depressurizing. I picked up the boot again to take it to Wilburt. Inside, it had the name patch of the astronaut for whom it had first been made. Vanderbilt DeBeer.

It also had a dark, reddish-brown stain where it looked as if something had dripped down inside. It wasn't a lot. Just a smeared dribble. My own suit probably had bloodstains in the fingertips.

But still, it stopped me because I kept seeing these patterns.

"Something wrong, Elma?" Wilburt's voice was in my earphones and on the big loop.

"Nope." Because no one would answer my question if I asked why DeBeer had been bleeding. "Just realizing that I don't need to get out of my suit while you put this on. We're all good to proceed."

They would feed me some line about how it was paint or coolant fluid or a normal injury. I've spent more than a decade living and working in spacesuits. I had bled inside my suit quite a bit. Hands. Upper arms against the hard upper torso. Rough seams. But the blood was always absorbed by all the underlayers we wore.

There's no injury that I could think of that would cause blood to drip down into a boot without being catastrophic.

I knew for a fact that DeBeer had returned from Mars. What had happened to him while he was on the surface?

TWELVE

Marm 38, Year 5, Sunsol-Landing + 44 sols

I was honestly surprised that Nathaniel hadn't greeted us, which made me suspect that no one had told him about our misadventure. That was going to be a fun conversation.

Wilburt was talking to Kam now, who was looking at his foot. Thankfully, it was only bruised. A deep muscle bruise, probably, but the initial assessment was that nothing was broken. Not that we had an X-ray machine to confirm that. Yet.

I handed the film I'd taken off to Howard Tang to be developed and then scanned and sent back to Earth via radio transmission.

With our logbook of the sites tucked under one arm, I entered the main dome planning to find Leonard for a debriefing. Then I would need to find Nathaniel for an entirely different debriefing.

Catalina was kneeling near the wall over to my right, working on assembling the frame of what would eventually be a greenwall. The botanists and farmers had developed this beautiful gardening system that could turn vertical surfaces into living walls of greenery.

Pausing by her, I asked, "Have you seen Leonard?"

"Downstairs in his office." She wrinkled her nose and nodded at my hand. "Are you okay?"

"Frankly, I'm exhausted, but otherwise fine." I ignored the hand. I'd only radioed in about it because Wilburt would have given me grief about being a hypocrite by ignoring procedure if I hadn't. Best course was to change the subject. I nodded at the greenwall. "That's exciting to see."

"I thought I might as well try to stay on schedule while we're in a holding pattern." She consulted her checklist and grabbed a piece of wall grid.

"Elma!" Kam's voice preceded our doctor, who was jogging across the dome to me, carrying a med kit. "You are not escaping me that easily."

I waved the unbandaged hand, conscious of the fact that the dressing on the other had soaked through a little. "It's fine. It's just a delaminated nail."

"And I'd like for it to not get infected, so you're going to let me clean it before you go anywhere else." Kam pointed to the kitchen area with the tables. "No arguing."

"I didn't argue! I just clarified that it's not a serious injury." I looked toward the stairs to the lower level and glanced at my watch. It was just coming up on dinnertime. What were the chances that someone else had made Nathaniel eat while I'd been gone?

"Pilots are the worst patients and I'm reminding myself that you've just flown." Kam made a comically aggrieved sigh and looked heavenward. "This is me, forgiving you for being stubborn, but I will also become deeply annoying if you don't follow me right now."

"I'm following, I'm following." I could check on Nathaniel and debrief with Leonard as soon as I had my hand attended to. As we walked, I said, "You know after sims they let us go home with just a Band-Aid."

"And they also had hospitals if things got infected." Kam set the battered white med kit on a table in front of the kitchen and pulled on a pair of latex gloves from the medical bag. I got a classic "show me" gesture.

Sighing, I settled on a bench and put the logbook on the table. I held out my hand and listened to Kam's *tsk* of annoyance. When the bandages were clear, the aggrieved sigh from our resident doctor made me look down at my hand. All right. That was maybe a little more than just a torn fingernail.

I'd managed to peel the whole thing off since last night.

"I suppose you are going to tell me that it doesn't hurt." Kam fished in the bag and pulled out a pair of scissors.

"It doesn't."

"Are you sure?" That was a very wicked grin. "Because then I can proceed without numbing."

"It hurts. Yes. Definitely."

"Good." Kam mimed writing in a logbook. "Miracle occurred. Pilot admitted to pain."

"But listen . . . I need to debrief with Leonard. Give me half an hour?"

"And have to chase you down again? Ha!" Kam pulled out a curved needle. "It'll take me less time than that to address this nail situation. Now, be quiet and let me work."

At least I was good at being quiet.

Kam was very fast, and also, as if it were a form of punishment, the wrapping on my extremely minor wound was twice as big as it had been. A Band-Aid would have been fine. I looked at it in some disbelief. "So we aren't worried about conserving resources?"

"Listen . . . the one thing I have plenty of is gauze. We stuck it in every available crevice as additional packing material."

"And how am I supposed to get it into a glove?"

I have never had such a dismissive look turned on me. With the same hand that had beckoned me, Kam now shooed me away. "Go on. Go find Leonard."

"Thank you." Grabbing my logbook, I stood up and started to

walk away, because I know better than to argue with a flight surgeon right after they've treated you. I could take up the topic later.

"And keep that elevated!"

My mother would have been appalled, but I was a pilot, so I
flipped Kam the bird as I walked.

"Wrong finger."

The laughter helped revive me a little. I headed to the stairs
and turned away from the gravitational pull of engineering to
head to Leonard's office. I could see my husband after I finished my work.

But as I went around the curve, the timbre of Nathaniel's
voice came from ahead of me. I couldn't make out the substance
of it until I arrived at Leonard's office, where my husband sat
opposite him in the cramped chair that I usually occupied.

"Right, right . . . So a heat sink can take advantage of the
amount of CO_2 in the atmosphere here and turn that into a
coolant by pumping it into the ground and—" Nathaniel broke
off as I came into the room and his face lit up. "Welcome home."

As distracted as he could get when he was working, whenever
I came back from a flight, I got his whole attention. Seeing him
light up gave me a glow of my own. And that full attention might
also be why I tucked my bandaged hand behind me a little bit.

I smiled back at him and leaned past the small desk to give
him a kiss on the cheek. "Don't let me interrupt." I glanced over
at Leonard. "Ready to debrief when you're finished here."

"We're just recapping. How's Wilburt?" Leonard looked like
he'd slept about as much as we had.

"Just bruised. Thankfully."

"And your hand?"

"Hand?" Nathaniel's brow furrowed as he spotted Kam's
ridiculously oversized dressing, and he turned back to our mission commander. "You said they were okay."

"We are, sweetie." I shrugged it off as if it weren't a big
deal and then backtracked in my own mind. As much as I
was complaining about other people withholding information from me, I wasn't going to start doing that to Nathaniel.

"Wilburt's suit breach was scary, but he's fine. And I just de-laminated a nail."

I could see the fear rising in Nathaniel. I'd been an astronaut for thirteen years and he was mostly inured at this point, but sometimes he would remember that every single day of my job was a day that I could possibly die. Being here, inside Bradbury Base all the time, I think he'd started to forget that. And the thing is there were so many possible ways for all of us to die on this planet.

"Elma, I bet you're probably famished." Leonard gestured toward the door. "While I read through your logs, why don't you go up and take a meal break."

"I am, in fact, and would love to eat something that's been heated." I shouldn't take him up on that. I should stay and de-brief but I was also exhausted and the adrenaline that had kept me going had turned into shaky fatigue. So I handed him the logbook. "We'll be at the kitchen when you're ready for me."

Nathaniel followed me into the hall. "Oh—wait. Do you mind if I grab a report?"

"Go right ahead." I loved him because of his flaws and I was also going to follow him to the engineering office or we'd prob-ably never get him out of there. I squeezed his hand with my good one. "Thank you for slipping the hamantaschen in."

The corner of his mouth drew up in a smile and brought out one of his dimples. "I was a little worried they'd get crushed."

"A little crumbly, but I think the poppy seed filling held them together. And thank you for sending enough for Wilburt."

"Of course. You needed enough for mishloach manot." He pushed the door to the engineering department open on the smell of solder and pencil lead. Lance was bent over a work-bench wiring something and Helen sat at a table doing calcula-tions. Nathaniel veered toward his desk. "I handed the rest out here."

"Oh good!" Because it meant that he had taken a break, how-ever small, while I was gone. And he had done something to celebrate Purim. I wanted to tell him about Wilburt's mother, but not in the middle of the engineering department. I'd only asked him if I could tell Nathaniel.

It was still a private place in Wilburt and I didn't want him to have to navigate that in front of his crewmates unless he wanted to.

Before Nathaniel got to his desk, Lance beckoned him. I sighed and wandered over to Helen. She looked up from her slide rule and spotted the bandage. "What happened to your finger?"

"Attacked by a kitten." I settled at the table across from her, the way we had in the old days back in the computer department of the IAC. "Need any help?"

Mission Control had whole backrooms of people to run calculations, but Nathaniel wanted to present his own data to them so they didn't get caught up in quibbles about small errors.

Helen slid a report and a sheet of graph paper across to me. "Check me?"

"That sounds like a chess invitation." I leaned forward and ran my pencil down her tidy handwriting.

"I have been thinking about running a chess tournament once the rest of the colonists are down." She tidied her slide rule, setting the cursor and slide back to zero. The quiet hiss of the cursor across plastic made a comfortable underscore to the conversations that the engineers were having a few feet away.

Across the room, Opal was bent over her desk drafting something or other. Biting my lower lip, I remembered our conversation about history. Did I want to bring this up with Helen? Yes. I swallowed before saying, "There's been some talk about finding another word for us than 'colonists.'"

Helen tilted her head. "Why?"

"Because . . . well, when you look at the history of the United States, colonies were real bad for the Indians. And Britain with . . . well, basically everyone." I was aware of Opal's head coming up, but I kept my gaze on Helen.

"Mm . . . Taiwan as well. China continues to think that we are a colony."

"I—right, exactly. And we're an international group. It made sense to use English for the training manuals, but we could use different languages for other things, right? Like . . . what would you call us?"

"*Quántǐ rényuán* or maybe *tuántǐ*." She pronounced the second word almost like "twenty."

"We could call ourselves the Twenties since we come down in groups of twenty on the *Esther.* Although I guess I should know what that means first."

"Just 'group.'" She frowned again. "It's not a very good fit for what we're doing, though."

I flipped through the report, skimming the text as I looked for the next set of numbers she referenced.

". . . looking for redundancies that can be sacrificed without affecting the overall mission, the main engines of the *Goddard* are one such example of . . ."

I backed up to see if I understood what Nathaniel was proposing and then read forward again to make sure I was reading the thing that I thought I was. Indeed, I was.

My husband was proposing a workaround for the missing HVAC system that involved cannibalizing one of the *Goddard*'s engines for parts. That ship was our path home if things really went sideways.

I was supposed to be second-in-command and somehow Nathaniel just hadn't mentioned that he wanted to pull an engine out of my ship. Why the hell was I finding out about this while reading a report? Goddamn it. If I were going to have this role, I wanted to do it well. I wanted to be more than just a pretty face for the IAC.

Biting the inside of my lip, I did not immediately get up to confront him. I confirmed Helen's numbers and slid the pages back to her. "Looks good."

"Thank you."

I put the slide rule on the table, set perpendicular to the edge. "I need to double-check with Nathaniel about something."

She started to nod and then did a double take. "What did he do?"

The corner of my mouth twisted into something midway between a grimace and a grin. "It's a very 'bless his heart' kind of thing."

"That bad?" Helen raised her eyebrows and glanced to the door. "Should I prime the fire suppression system?"

"I'm certain we can come to an understanding." I pushed my chair back from the table and stood. It was a good reminder to put my game face on so I didn't disturb our fellow crew members.

I crossed the room to where Nathaniel was still talking to Lance.

My husband turned around as if he felt me approaching and his face softened. "Hello, beautiful."

It was hard to be mad at him when he loved me so much. And yet. "May I borrow you for a moment?"

"Oh! Right. I'm so sorry." He stepped away from Lance. "We were going to get you fed. I just . . ."

"I understand." That part I did. Even before we got married, the way his work enveloped him and lit him afire was one of the things that attracted me to him. But not talking to me about his plans for the *Goddard* was a different thing entirely. "I was just helping Helen confirm some numbers and I find that I have some questions for you."

His gaze flicked across the room to Helen and tension came into his body with the recognition of what I had been reading. "Ah. Yes, but—"

"Let's step into the hallway." I smiled at him as sweetly as I could for the benefit of the people we worked with. "Please."

As Nathaniel followed me, Reynard made eye contact with him with a sort of wince and eyebrow raise as if he already knew what the problem was going to be. Because of course Nathaniel would have discussed it with his fellow engineers. But

Reynard's face made it seem as if he had known that it would be a surprise to me. As if . . . as if Nathaniel had *not* discussed it with Leonard.

Had he planned to present this to Mission Control without talking to Leonard first—I grabbed my anger again because I was borrowing trouble from a future that might not be true.

Nathaniel followed me into the hall, and as soon as we were clear of the room, he said, "Look, it's the easiest option."

"I need to know something." I shoved my hands into the pockets of my flight suit and caught the bandage on the edge, which hurt and was annoying, and so I had to stand there with my hands awkwardly by my sides. I huffed a little with aggravation. "Have you talked to Leonard?"

"Of course." He shook his head. "Not the details, but the general outline of scavenging parts from the *Goddard*."

"Does he know you are taking an engine apart?"

"There are five of them. In case one fails, the other four—"

"That's not the point. It doesn't matter if that is ultimately what we have to do. It's still something that should be discussed." My voice was rising with each sentence.

"I have been discussing it!"

"Not with me. Not with the people who have to—"

"It is *redundant*!"

"It involves spacewalks. It involves taking apart an engine that was built under gravity. It involves dismantling part of our safety net—"

"I know that. Who do you think was in charge of getting the thing built?"

"The point. The actual point is that you are *not* in charge anymore."

Nathaniel pulled his head back as if I'd slapped him.

"I'm sorry." I took a step toward him. "I'm sorry, I shouldn't have said that."

"No. No, it's true. I'm not in charge anymore. I run a department that's all of five people on a fucking inhospitable planet beca—" He stopped, holding a finger in the air. Drawing in a slow breath, he looked at the wall and then back at me as he exhaled. "I'm angry. Give me a minute."

"Sure." I nodded. "I'm mad, too. I should cool down."

"Walk?"

I nodded and joined him as we walked down the long, curving corridor. Even if I hadn't been exhausted and hungry, I would have been angry. But those were fanning the fires of my rage. I vibrated with all of the other things that I wanted to say. Heat radiated off of Nathaniel as we walked. When we passed the door to the engineering room, I did not look in so I didn't have to see if anyone was staring at us. I know that our voices were raised enough that much of that conversation would have been audible. What would they think?

And the need to maintain a good front for our colleagues was one of the other problems. I inhaled to say that and then let the breath out before I did. He'd asked for time.

"It's okay." Nathaniel's voice was calmer. "And you're right. I should have told you."

"Thank you. And yes, you should have." I sighed. "This is not one of those forgiveness rather than permission situations."

Which just made me think of Leonard and the way he had suggested that maybe we shouldn't talk to Mission Control about the hopper. And Wilburt and the patch. Maybe it wasn't a conspiracy of the past but something about me now that made people think that I wasn't safe to talk to.

Nathaniel stopped and took my good hand. "But listen, Elma. This wasn't my first choice. I did look for other options."

"I believe you but—" Pressing my lips together, I sighed and studied the scuffmarks on the floor. And spotted what looked like the remnants of a bloodstain trapped in the scratched plastic. It had mostly been cleaned, but I'd had enough periods in my life for that particular shade to be unmistakable. What the hell had happened here last time? I dragged my attention back to Nathaniel because I could only solve one problem at a time.

"The thing is . . . part of why I'm angry is that I am supposed to be in charge. 'Deputy administrator,' right? It's hard as hell to get anyone to remember that, and when you are also cutting me out of decisions, it stings."

His mouth hung a little open. "I . . . I'll admit that I hadn't considered that aspect."

"I know." My gut twisted. He loved me so much and knew what I could do and still . . . still, he couldn't see me as someone in charge. "Listen, the timeline you proposed won't work. It'll take—at best—six spacewalks to salvage those parts and that's if nothing goes wrong. It's space, something always goes wrong."

He snorted and I could see him trying to lighten his mood. "Engineering 101. I always double the time I think everything would take."

"Sweetheart . . ." I closed my eyes picturing a spacewalk to the aft of the ship. It was a haul from the closest airlock and there were so many keep-out zones where something could puncture a spacesuit. "Sweetheart, you always delegated planning spacewalks. Mission Control is going to have to run this in the NBL multiple times to give us the right procedures."

"We can—"

"I'm going to stop you before you say that we can do a spacewalk without that step. When we're out there, we're running with elevated levels of CO_2. We get stupid. We can't come back in for tools. We can barely feel anything." I held up my bandaged finger. "That's why I delaminate nails, because the only tactile sensation I've got is all the way out at the tip of the glove and I have to shove my finger against it. So we need someone to go through the whole procedure start to finish and come up with the cleanest, most elegant way to do it. And then . . . then, that frees up our brains to deal with all the small things that go wrong because, as previously stated, something always goes wrong. Your timeline will get someone killed."

He rocked back on his heels as if I'd struck him. "That's a little hyperbolic, don't you think?"

"No." I reached out and took his hands, running my thumbs over the back. "When I said before that you weren't in charge anymore, that was true and also . . . you designed this mission.

People will trust you. They'll think you've thought everything through."

"You didn't."

"I'm your wife." I gave his hands another squeeze, smiling to soften my words. "It's my prerogative to question you."

He looked away, staring at the curve of the wall next to us. His mouth worked as if he were trying out different sentences before he finally said. "Will you sit down with me and go through the timeline to adjust it for a more realistic schedule?"

"Of course."

The thing we'd have to talk through was that when you added in the time that it would take Mission Control to develop the spacewalks and adjust to the things that go wrong, that meant we would wind up doing at least two of the spacewalks when the Earth was on the far side of the sun from us.

If anything went wrong while we were in the blackout zone, we wouldn't be able to consult Mission Control. We would be well and truly on our own.

THIRTEEN

Dear Florence,

I'm going to start with the bad news first. I'm afraid that Buster died this week. It was a good passing, I think, for a dog. Your daddy found him in the liriope out front, where he always liked to lay in the sun. He thought the old boy was just asleep, but when he called him for dinner he didn't move. We've got him buried in the backyard near the old holly tree where Superdog is buried. I'm so sorry. I know how much you loved that dog. He was such a good boy.

Now on to the happier news. I started volunteering with the Three Thirds to help with Meteor refugee children and they have already asked me to take on a management role. Retirement wasn't sitting well with me so it's nice to have a little bit to do. I'm having fun and feeling like I'm making a small difference. Everyone else is doing well and there's no real news to report.

Miss you and proud of you by turns.

Love,
Mama

Marm 39, Year 5, Monsol-Landing + 45 sols

Leonard and I were meeting in comms because it saved us from having to walk down there every time a reply from Mission Control came in, but the background chatter over the radio of the people doing construction work outside made it hard to concentrate.

Or maybe it was my lack of sleep.

The muscles in the right side of my neck had contracted into

THE MARTIAN CONTINGENCY * 117

a painful crick from napping at my desk. I kept tilting my head to the left to try to stretch it out. The room seemed impossibly warm and sweat beaded on my upper lip. I'm sure none of that was irritation.

Leonard flipped a page of the plans. "So if we use the greenhouse's HVAC for the second dome, that'll allow us to stay on schedule more or less for getting people down here. Am I reading that timeline correctly?"

"Yes. Things slow down after that while we're building the heat sink." Nathaniel hunched forward in his chair, elbows on knees. "I could really use your expertise on where to drill for that."

Leonard lit up a little, and I don't think it was the praise, I think it was just the thought of getting to do some geology. He hadn't been out of the dome since we got here. Leonard flipped to the revised timeline. "All right . . . but that new HVAC only affects the greenhouse. If it fails, then our worst-case scenario is that Earth sends a replacement with the Third Expedition."

"No." At her station, Florence wiped her eyes, which were red from lack of sleep. "Our worst-case scenario is a cascading failure. We can't get the HVAC built, something happens on Earth to prevent the launch of the Third Expedition, and then we don't have a way back to Earth. Right now, y'all can't even get Mission Control to answer you about adding a piece of equipment to a supply launch."

Leonard stared at her and I could see him remembering what it had been like while we'd been out of touch with the Earth on our last mission to Mars because of Earth First's acts of terrorism. Launch windows were not infinite. If Earth First struck and kept the Third Expedition from launching, what would that mean for us?

"That's true. But also, the scenario I'm proposing to build a new HVAC uses a redundant engine." Nathaniel's hand tightened on his knee. "We could lose two and still get home."

I sighed. "If nothing else goes wrong, that's correct."

Leonard met my gaze, then looked down at the table and

drew a circle on the vinyl with a forefinger. "We lost two people on the First Expedition and have been damn lucky this time." He sighed, stopping with his finger pressed against the table until the nail turned white. "This changes the potential contingencies but not the fact that all of us signed up knowing we might die on Mars and—"

The screen lit up. Florence straightened and turned to make sure we saw it. "Incoming. Oh. Well . . . sorry, folks."

On the screen, it just said "Received."

"That's it?" I tossed my pen down on the table. We were in a thirty-seven-minute time lag, but it had been over two hours since we'd sent our list of queries to Mission Control. "At least two of the questions were things they could have looked up in a bind—"

A massive thud reverberated through the ceiling. All of us were on our feet, turning toward the door. My brain flipped to a mental checklist from hours of contingency training. The emergency oxygen masks were stored in a cabinet at the foot of the stairs. They had five minutes of oxygen. The question was mask now or mask later?

"Stay here." Leonard moved toward the door, Nathaniel right behind him. "And talk to Mission Control. Get them to answer the questions."

"How am I—" But they were already gone.

Other people dashed past and I could hear shouting from upstairs. I looked at Florence, fighting the urge to follow Leonard and Nathaniel.

She tilted her head to the side, listening. "No alarms. Not a depress."

If the dome were punctured and depressurizing, there would be a lot more noise right now.

The chatter on the radio from the outside team remained steady without any breaks in rhythm. They just continued to work on excavating for the second dome as if nothing at all were amiss. I tilted my head and nodded at the radio. "They sound all right."

"So it's definitely something inside."

I started running through the list of things that had gone wrong in various sims. Equipment failures. Compressor malfunction. Plain old dropping things.

And what if it was something we hadn't planned for, like whatever had gone wrong on the previous mission?

"You think someone ran the rover into the wall again?"

"What?"

"Wilburt said someone punctured the garage wall with the rover. There's a patch there."

"Oh." She studied the gauges on her bank of instruments. "I'd forgotten all about that. It was only barely a rover accident. We were doing a repair on the antennas and, when moving the vehicle, bumped one of the struts, which impacted the wall. The hole was so small it was hard to notice."

Parts of that sounded exactly like what Wilburt had told me. As in, it sounded like the same words. "Maybe the outside team . . ." I trailed off because I could hear their voices on the big loop and everyone sounded boring and calm.

Florence shook her head. "Anyway, we wouldn't hear anything that happened in the garage in here. Too much dirt."

"Right." There were ten meters of regolith mounded around the main dome and a long corridor between us and the garage.

Florence tapped the screen. "Leonard said he wanted you to reply to Mission Control. What do you want to say?"

"What I want to say is 'Why are y'all being such assholes?'"

She barked a laugh. "I would pay good money to see that."

"Someday . . ." Really, though, I just wanted to ask people straight questions and get straight answers. Between Mission Control and my crewmates it was getting real frustrating.

Three chimes sounded as the public-address system activated. "All stations. All stations. All stations." Leonard's voice was unhurried and also had an edge to it. "We are doing an immediate work stop and a mandatory twelve-hour rest period. Find a good stopping point in whatever you're working on, then get food and go to bed. Do not make me come find you. Repeat, we are stopping for a twelve-hour rest period. This is mandatory."

The microphone went silent.

In the distance, Nathaniel's voice rose. It was so faint that I couldn't make out any words, only that I knew my husband's voice and I knew his tones and he was angry.

Biting my lips, I itched to go upstairs right then. Instead, I turned back to Florence. "Send a message to Earth and tell them that we're taking a twelve-hour rest period." I held up my finger to tell her to wait a minute. "Actually, belay that . . ."

I grabbed my white pad and wrote a longer note so she wouldn't have to take dictation. "Send them this."

We are taking a twelve-hour rest period, which should give you time to gather the material we requested. This station will be unstaffed during our rest period. This is the last transmission until we are given the material we require.

Florence's eyebrows climbed faster than a Sirius rocket. "Last transmission . . . I can't send this."

"Sign my name to it." I pointed at the comms interface as if I could point at Clemons. "Address it directly to 'Dear Director Clemons.' He won't fire me—I mean, if he wants to come here and talk to me in person . . ."

"Someday . . . someday your cockiness is going to get you in trouble." Florence sat down in front of the console. "But tosol, I am happy to help you pursue your goals."

"Great. Do that and then go to your rest period." I twisted my neck, trying to work that knot out of it. "I am going to find out what happened."

Comms was directly opposite the stairs to the main level. I bounded up and had enough speed at the top that I arced a little bit over the floor. It gave me a good view of what had happened.

The trellis for one of the greenwalls had fallen, twisted at an angle. Jaidev was pulling it to the side and had a bright green streak down the chest of his white kurta and a vivid red splotch on one shoulder. For a heart-stopping moment, I thought he'd been cut when the greenwall fell.

Then I remembered that tosol was Holi—the festival of colors. When we'd been planning the mission, we'd talked about how close it was to Purim this year and how to fling colors without getting dust in the air purification systems. Sponges were the answer. Jaidev just had celebratory color on his clothes. He was fine.

Beyond him, Catalina sat on the floor, one leg stretched out in front of her, while Kam knelt next to her manipulating her knee. Bolí stood behind her, with his hands on her shoulders.

Even from here, I could see that she was insisting that she was all right.

I could also hear the rumble of Nathaniel and Leonard talking. The bathroom module stood between me and them, so all I could catch were occasional flashes of Leonard's hand as he gestured. It looked like Catalina was getting the support she needed, so I went to the two men to see how I could be useful.

Their voices got clearer as I got closer.

". . . don't have time for a rest period now." As I rounded the corner, Nathaniel was facing me. His hair was sticking out at odd angles as if he'd run his hands through it recently. "We barely have time to do the things that were already on the list."

"We are past the point of diminishing returns. Well past it." Leonard gestured toward the sleep cubicles. "Do I need to have you escorted to bed?"

"I can do that, if it needs doing." I tried to make my voice flirtatious, hoping to reduce the tension crackling between the two of them.

Nathaniel turned to me, hand outstretched the way he did when he needed my help. "Elma. You've seen the numbers. You can explain it to him."

I shook my head. "I can also see the increase in accidents. Leonard is right."

With his head tucked back, Nathaniel looked as if I had betrayed him. "But we have work to do."

"Yes. And right now, our job is to take a break." I glanced toward Jaidev, who had done as much celebrating as he could. His wife was out on the surface working through one of their major holidays. "Listen, Nathaniel, tosol is Holi for the Hindu and Jain members of our crew. It's a kindness to take the rest of the sol off."

My husband rested his hands on his hips. "Fine. But it's not my holiday. I don't need a break."

"I can barely get you to celebrate *our* holidays, so that's not a valid argument. We all need a break." I gestured toward the kitchen module. "I'll allow a detour for dinner, but our *mission commander* is correct."

I may have stressed "mission commander" a little too much. Nathaniel's cheeks flushed. The muscle at the corner of his jaw flexed. He inhaled sharply, words nearly visible on the tip of his tongue.

Then he let the breath out and turned to face me fully. "I know we're tired, but if I can't get Mission Control to give me the information I need, then that's going to double our workload to stay on timeline. We have to work through this."

"On that point . . ." I moved my attention to Leonard. "I sent a message to Mission Control telling them that we were taking a rest period and that this would be our last message until they responded with the information that Nathaniel has been asking for."

"That sounds like an ultimatum," Leonard said slowly.

I nodded. "If you need to change that, I signed my name so you can always say I went rogue."

He snorted, looking a little pained. "No, thank you. Had enough rogue crew members to last me a lifetime." He rubbed his forehead. "Besides it's worth a shot and we aren't doing anything else until they answer us. Everyone takes a break before someone else gets hurt. Regardless of what department they are in. I trust you can control your husband?"

I flashed back to when Nathaniel had been asked to control me during my quest to get women into the astronaut corps. He had backed me then. "I'll talk to him, but control isn't the way our marriage works."

Leonard held up his hands and took a step back. "All I can ask. Now, I'm going to check back in on Catalina."

As he turned to walk away, Nathaniel took a step as if he were going to follow and keep arguing. I got in front of him and put my hands on his shoulders. "Hey . . ." He'd always been driven but this was beyond anything I'd seen since the early days after the Meteor struck. "Hey, what's going on?"

Brows raised and creased he looked at me as if I were an Earth Firster asking why we should go into space. "If I can't present a viable solution to Mission Control, they're going to pull us. The politicians are—I never should have come."

"Nathaniel." My heart went cold and I squeezed his shoulders to keep him from pulling away. I knew he'd come for me and that it had been hard but that was different from hearing him voice it. "I'm sorry this is hard for you."

"It's not that it's hard, it's—" He grimaced, looking at the group surrounding Catalina. "You haven't been—none of you have been in those meetings. I have spent the past eighteen years fighting politicians who want to ignore the problem until it's too late or who see everything in military terms or who understand and don't care about anything except lining their own pocketbooks."

"I'm sorry . . . but what do you think Leonard and I were doing from the moment we got home?" We'd taken the "Elma and Leonard Show" to every influential person we could. "You think that we're here because of your efforts alone?"

"No. No, I'm sorry. I shouldn't have said . . . Yes, I know how hard you and Leonard worked to make this mission happen." He pinched the bridge of his nose. "It's just that on all of your other missions, you had someone in Mission Control backing you. Me, Nicole, Halim . . . I thought things were stable. I thought I could leave. I thought we could leave."

"Clemons—"

"Has been authorizing orders that are consistent with an

abort, not with solving the problem. How long did it take you to convince him to let women into the program? Years." He scrubbed his face. "Years. He will play it safe, just like everyone else down there, and by the time they realize the problem it will be too late. Just like right now."

I inhaled, sliding my hands into his. "Do you want me to talk to Nicole?"

"No . . ." He sighed, squeezing my hands. "No. Thank you. Nicole understands. We talked a lot while you were gone. She's why I thought things were stable. It's just . . . I'm just frustrated."

"Listen, I'll make a deal with you. Have a meal with me. Then lie down for a nap. If you wake up without needing an alarm, then I'll support you when you go back to work."

He growled under his breath and put his hands on his hips, staring into the distance with an old familiar look. He was still working the problem in his head.

I closed the distance between us and slid my hands through the gaps made by his akimbo arms. His body was tight with frustration and anger, but he softened after a moment and hugged me. I leaned into him, pressing my face into the hollow of his neck.

Away from us, Catalina was being helped to her feet. I should be there, helping Leonard with damage control. Instead, I was "controlling" my husband. Kissing his neck, I worked my fingers into the base of his spine, keeping my bandaged one lifted.

He groaned, sagging a little against me. "You're not playing fair."

"I am." I kissed his neck higher, heading toward the corner of his jaw. Did I feel guilty for using intimacy as a distraction? A little, yes. But it was working and he needed to rest. I needed to rest. All of us needed that. I dug into his knotted muscles. "If you weren't sore, this wouldn't work."

Nathaniel pulled away a little, twisting to try to look behind him. "Your hand. You shouldn't be—"

"I should be resting? Is that what you were thinking?" I stepped clear and grabbed his hand with my undamaged one.

Tugging him away, I turned toward the kitchen. "Come on. We're going to eat and then go to bed."

I was pretty sure that if I could get him to relax enough to fall asleep in the first place, he'd sleep through the night. I knew I would.

I was significantly less certain about what tomorrow would bring when we were looking at our situation with clear eyes. The thing that kept tickling the back of my head is that maybe Mission Control was being slow to respond because aborting *was* the right call and they just didn't want to make it any more than we did.

FOURTEEN

ASTRONAUTS' REBELLION
SHAKES MARS MISSION

Demands for Recovery Materials
Ignite Controversy

SUNFLOWER, Kansas, March 24, 1970—The crew of the Second Mars Expedition has gone on strike, refusing to communicate with Mission Control in an unprecedented protest. Sources high within the International Aerospace Coalition say that Dr. Elma York, the famous Lady Astronaut, has vowed silence until their requirements are met. As the standoff unfolds, it raises profound questions about the governance and decision-making processes within interplanetary missions.

Marm 40, Year 5, Tuesol-Landing + 46 sols

When I woke up, Nathaniel was still asleep. We lay curled on the bottom bunk, sheet wrapped around our naked bodies. He faced the wall, with me snuggled up against his warm back.

Our little bunk was still dark, but beyond it I could see that early morning sunlight was letting a ghostly glow through our small skylight. God, Leonard had been so right about the rest period. I had no idea what time it was and that was okay by me.

I felt comfortably drowsy and warm. Even in a cramped bunk, I slept better when I was with my husband. Maybe not better—because I woke up a little more to reposition, but I slept more soundly. His even breathing and the warmth of his body pressed against mine was a comfort.

When we'd lain down, his breathing had been fast and erratic, so I hadn't even tried for an ignition sequence with him. He was too wound up in all the wrong ways. I had felt him twitching as he continued to think through problems. I'd rubbed his temples and snuggled up against him, trying to make the bed as appealing as possible.

Now I had one arm draped over his midriff and let my fingers play with the fine hairs on his chest. His breathing didn't change and I was grateful that I had won our bet. I curled more tightly against him, and made a mental note to check my calendar after he woke up to see if we could have a try at obtaining orbital velocity . . . Wait.

When was my last period?

I ought to be about due. That's the trouble with trying to keep track of so many calendars. Martian months were fifty-five or fifty-six sols long, but our biological clocks had been wound on Earth. I've always been like clockwork, which is why Nathaniel and I felt comfortable with the rhythm method.

We'd been married for twenty years and never had an accident.

And part of that was because I checked my calendar when I wasn't sure. Slipping my arm away from him, I sat up. The air was chilly against my bare skin as I got out of bed.

As I stood, Nathaniel rolled onto his back.

I froze. In the shadows, his face was still slack with sleep. There wasn't room for me to be able to get back into bed with him now, but I wasn't sure I'd be able to fall back asleep anyway. As long as he stayed sleeping, I would count my blessings.

As quietly as I could, I opened the top compartment in my half of our lockers. There was enough light for me to see what I was doing, thank God. I kept the calendar stuck to the side with a thumbtack in the plastic. When I pulled it down, I lost the thumbtack and it bounced across the floor.

Long practice at not swearing while on a hot mic kept my mouth sealed around the string of curses. I tilted the calendar toward the skylight. Marked with a red circle was the date that my period should have started. March twentieth or Marm thirty-sixth.

Either way you counted it, I was five sols late.

I'd never been late before. I mean, a day or two, sure. My heart started to beat a staccato rhythm against my ribs. I wasn't pregnant. It was just stress. And hard work.

It had to be that. I knew an astronaut who had stopped menstruating because she was a marathon runner. We'd been in a really hard push for the past four sols. See. That was just stress. I swallowed. I just needed to give it a couple of sols and then it would start.

My mind grabbed hold of all of the what-ifs and might-bes and ran straight down the path of worst-case scenario. My period might not start. If it didn't, I would need to talk to Kam about running a pregnancy test. It would get reported to Earth, regardless of the result.

And then . . . Nathaniel and I had made a conscious decision to not have children. My career as an astronaut had been so important to me that we had chosen it over having a family. It wouldn't have been fair to anyone because I was gone for months and sometimes years at a time.

But now we were on Mars. We were on Mars with the intention of creating a sustainable habitat for people to live in. Children were supposed to happen. Later. The next expedition was supposed to bring teens.

And also, we were still going to be launching into space. I was still an astronaut. It's just that my home planet was changing.

I took a breath, trying to stop the runaway greenhouse of my anxiety. *3.1415 . . .*

Wait a few sols to see if it started. Then deal with the parameters presented.

I turned back to the locker to put the calendar away. Damn

it. I had to find the thumbtack. Kneeling, I felt along the floor, which was getting almost no light from above.

"Well, that's a nice view." Nathaniel's voice was rough with sleep.

I popped up onto my knees. "You're awake." Brilliant.

He stretched and yawned so wide that his jaw popped. Wincing, he pushed himself up in bed. "What time is it?"

"Um . . ." I turned and reached for my watch. "Just after nine."

"Am I allowed to go back to work now?" He leaned forward and planted a kiss on my cheek. "I'm kidding. I mean, I'm not, but I am also ready to acknowledge that I was more tired than I thought I was."

"Should we put out a press release?"

He snorted. "It's not like I'm a pilot."

"Then you've picked up bad habits from me." Except that pilots respected the problems caused by exhaustion. Twenty percent of air fatalities were caused by pilot error due to fatigue. I reached up higher to turn the small light on so I could see the floor. "Watch your eyes."

He squinted as the light clicked on. "What are you looking for?"

"Dropped a thumbtack when I . . ." *When I was checking my calendar to see if maybe I'm pregnant.* I grabbed a clean pair of underwear. Don't ask me why it felt better to have this conversation clothed because Nathaniel definitely had seen me naked.

He took a breath and I could see him start to ask me what was wrong, but he held it while I pulled on my underthings. As I dragged the tank top over my head, I stopped stalling.

"I was getting my calendar out." I kept my gaze down so I didn't have to see his unguarded expression. "And then I just realized that my period is late."

"Oh." He slid to the edge of the bed, the sheet still wrapped across his lap. "Are you okay?"

"It's only off by five sols." I shrugged, as if this was no big deal, and looked up to meet his gaze. His brow was furrowed with concern, but I couldn't tell how he actually felt. I should have watched him as I told him.

"Do you . . . do you want to have Kam do a test?"

"It takes two hours to get a result." Turning from him, I grabbed the flight suit I had worn yestersol. "I don't want to waste the resources right now. I'll give it a few sols."

He got out of bed and wrapped his arms around my middle. Pulling me back against his chest, he kissed the side of my neck. "I love you."

"I love you, too."

Someone knocked on the door. "Elma?" Leonard's voice was suspiciously calm. "Can you and Nathaniel come downstairs? To comms?"

You learned to not have a lot of modesty when you were an astronaut but still, I was mostly in my undies, so I didn't open the door. "We'll be right there."

I also didn't ask him what was wrong, because if he'd felt comfortable with more details being public, he would have told me through the door. Behind me, Nathaniel was already standing up and grabbing a flight suit, which he pulled on without underwear.

I pulled mine on and slipped on my sneakers, not bothering with socks. My head was filled with rattling thoughts—Mission Control had responded with the information we needed. Clemons had said "no" to the engine scenario. Someone was dead. I tried to veer my thoughts away from that as fast as I could because I could feel the list of people that I loved on Earth and the Moon looming in a wave of anxiety.

With a forced smile, I checked in with Nathaniel and pulled the door open. Outside our cubicle, other folks were up, starting their sol. Graeham Stewman was doing push-ups in front of his cubicle. Helen and Reynard were having coffee next to the kitchen. Zainabu and Mosi were running along the exercise track we'd laid out.

Everyone seemed brighter than they had yestersol. There were no hints about any problems. Or rather, any new problems.

Catalina limped over to the kitchen in that way you do when something really hurts and you're trying to walk like it doesn't. This is a stride I've done a lot in my time with the IAC. She eased herself down next to Helen and Reynard.

I followed Nathaniel down the stairs and concentrated on just getting to comms as fast as I could.

When I walked into the comms center, Leonard was standing with his arms crossed over his chest and Florence sat with her chair tipped back. Dawn was sitting by her, doodling on her white pad.

They all turned and looked at us when we walked in. "What's going on?"

Nathaniel walked over to the console, where a stack of paper had spooled out of the teletype machine. "Are those the answers?"

Leonard looked as if he had eaten a rotten lemon. "Those are instructions on departing Mars."

It felt as if Earth's gravity were pulling down on us instead of Mars's. The anxious pit that had been forming in my stomach condensed, drawing all the blame and guilt down toward it. Florence had been right that she couldn't send my ultimatum. And now here we were. What could Clemons do, I'd thought. Well, now we had the answer.

I swallowed the hot acid at the back of my throat. "I'm sorry. I should have cleared that message with you before sending it."

Leonard thumbed through the procedures. "We knew it was coming. They were already planning to pull us out."

"What are we going to do?" Dawn capped her marker.

Sighing, Leonard looked to the side and scratched under his jaw with his thumb. He squinted in thought for a moment before turning to Nathaniel. "How confident are you that we can safely work around the HVAC and stay?"

"A high degree of confidence." Nathaniel had stopped his pacing next to the far wall. "I would feel better with the figures from Mission Control which would allow me to run scenarios to account for possible failure points if we lose another redundancy. Goddamn it. Why won't they answer?"

Florence stared at the teletype. "I bet the question about the engine tipped them over the edge."

I groaned, tilting my head back to stare at the ceiling. The hum of fans filled the silence as we thought. Outside the comms center someone walked down the corridor humming under their breath. Besides the five of us in this room, no one else knew that we'd just been told to come home.

"If we leave, there's no way for them to launch the Third Expedition." I lowered my head. "It's got teenagers scheduled to be on it. They can't land them if this is the only dome. It's one thing to ask us to rough it, but not kids."

"What if . . ." Nathaniel's voice slowed and his eyes were narrow, looking into a mission plan that no one else could see yet. "What if some of us stay and send the rest home."

Leonard's head snapped around so fast I thought he'd give himself whiplash. "That guts our safety net. We can't go back up to the *Goddard* if things fail."

Nathaniel nodded slowly. "I know. We'd need to use the *Esther* and the *Matsu* to bring down supplies to supplement the cargo drops. We'd have to crowd the main dome with extra people, because I'm assuming that some people will want to stay and also . . . we can't do this with twenty of us."

Florence scowled. "I'm not going back to Earth just to die when the oceans boil because some politician thinks they can get reelected on the basis of killing the space program."

"Same." Dawn nodded. "Not after what we went through just to be here this time."

I kept up with the climate news through my brother's work in meteorology. Even if I didn't get deep into the math the way I once had, the story remained the same. "The numbers are better than they were eighteen years ago, but we only avert the climate problem if everyone on the planet works together, and even then . . ."

"We can't put all our eggs in one basket," Nathaniel said.

"It's what the UN Secretary General said when we presented Elma's calculations for the first time."

Leonard looked at the clock, comparing the time here with that on Earth at Mission Control. He drummed his fingers on the procedure they'd sent up. "Elma . . . let's pull everyone in for a meeting. I'm not ready to pack it in and I want to get their take."

"Copy that."

Florence looked at the clock as she reached for her console. "I'll let the *Goddard* know to be ready. Set the meeting for eleven hundred?"

"Belay that." Leonard held his hand out to her. "Unless you have a way to talk to the *Goddard* without Earth listening in."

"If we wait until tonight, when we're both on the far side from Earth." She hesitated, glancing at me. "I've got a short code I can send up to the comms team to let them know to prep for that."

Why had she glanced at me before saying that? "I'm curious why you would have prepared that."

"What? You're asking about people setting up codes?" She made a derisive noise and turned her attention back to Leonard. "What do I tell Earth?"

"I believe we said there would be no further communication until they sent us the information the Doctors York requested." A wicked grin bent his nose farther to the side. "Don't say anything."

It was a foolish thing to be pleased about, but warmth swept through me as if I'd been picked to be on someone's kickball team. I'd made a risky call and Leonard had backed me.

At various points in our lives, Leonard, Nathaniel, Dawn, Florence, and I had all needed to handle classified material, which meant that we knew how to keep a secret. And that meant that somehow we got through the entire sol without telling the people we worked with that Earth had told us to pack it in.

Not until the Earth set and the *Goddard* started its pass.

Leonard gathered us all in the main dome in front of the mural. He had me set up the whiteboard with columns for "Pro" and "Con" and "Questions." As soon as Jaidev had heard there was an evening meeting, he'd set up a table next to the kitchen and preemptively rehydrated some bags of coffee, making the safe bet that they'd be consumed.

You could feel the electricity crackling off everyone as they waited, chatting among themselves. My gaze kept slipping toward Florence, who sat with the portable comms unit on a kitchen table, waiting for the *Goddard* to start its pass.

My brain kept flipping between two secrets. Earth wanted us to come home. And my period was late. *3.14159265358—*

"I've got them." Florence pulled one earpiece back and flipped a switch to put them on the speaker. "Go ahead, *Goddard.*"

Halim's warm voice filled the dome. "Hello, Bradbury. We've got you broadcasting shipwide, per your request."

Leonard met my gaze and I nodded to tell him that I had his back. He took a deep breath and turned to face our crew members on the ground and projected his voice toward the ones overhead. "This morning, Mission Control sent us the procedures for an abort."

People shifted in their chairs. They exchanged glances but there wasn't an explosion. What I saw was a controlled combustion. I saw Lance's face go bright red and him bite down hard on something. I saw Jaidev grab Aahana's hand. Nuan Su's fists clenched on her knees. Helen inhaled sharply and then her chin tilted down in that way she did right before she decimated someone in chess.

They were pissed. They were professional.

Leonard saw it, too. He nodded at them. "I want to start by saying that I am proud to be here with you. If nothing else, what we have done together and what we were prepared to do is remarkable. Regardless of the outcome, you should take satisfaction and pride in your work." He smiled at the group as

if we were students facing a final exam or about to graduate.
"Now—"

"Sorry." Howard raised his hand. "Can I ask why . . . I mean,
waiting till a night pass to tell us?"

"Fair question." Leonard nodded. "I have an idea and I want
to share it with you first before we talk to Mission Control
about it. Get your input. Kick the tires. See if it'll roll."

"Wait a minute . . ." Howard looked more than a little discom-
fited. "Wait. We're talking about keeping things from Mission
Control?"

The other First Expeditioners nodded as if this were a totally
normal course of action. As if they had a lot of practice choos-
ing forgiveness over permission. And yes, we had hit a point
on the way out when Parker had told Mission Control how we
were going to do things and did not accept their suggestions but
he *had* told them.

My gaze went to the mural behind the whiteboard. I clenched
my jaw and brought my attention back to the immediate problem, not a five-year-old mystery. We'd been told to go home.
We needed a solution to that.

"Yes, I want to keep this to just us. Only for a little while."
Leonard took a step toward the group. "Here's the thing. All
of you have dedicated years of your lives to getting here and to
helping humanity have a home beyond Earth. We came to Mars
with the intention of staying here permanently. Why did we
start that mission?"

Aahana raised her hand as if this really were a class. When
Leonard pointed to her, she said, "Because of the Meteor?"

"Exactly. Because the Meteor was a disaster that was everyone's problem. That problem remains unchanged. The Earth is
still warming and humanity needs to spread out. There's a saying in Latin." Leonard turned to the board and wrote out, *"Aut
viam inveniam aut faciam."*

Something about it was familiar, but I had no Greek or Latin.
But I had seen it, or part of it before.

"'I shall either find a way or make one.'" Leonard folded

his hands together in his full professorial mode. "This is what Hannibal, a Carthaginian general who fought the Roman empire, said when he was told that there was no path through the Alps. 'I shall either find a way or make one.' Now, I don't want to ignore Mission Control. What I want is for us to all get back on the same team. I want us to find a way or make one. So . . . the question that I have for the group is, 'How do we convince Earth to support our mission?'"

That question hung in the middle of the dome like a thunderstorm about to squall. For a moment, I missed rain so badly I could almost smell the petrichor and I wanted to go home. But I also wanted to be here and watch dust devils swirling in the sun and the unbroken Milky Way spreading across the sky.

"Can we stay?" Bolí rested his hand on his wife's banged-up leg. "I mean. Aren't they pulling us back because it isn't safe to stay?"

"I believe that we can stay safely." Nathaniel straightened on his bench. "For instance, we could build an HVAC from scavenged parts and use the *Goddard* for a lifeboat if that doesn't work. But if we go home . . ."

I twisted my pen between my fingers. "If we go home, no one else will come here."

"But even if we stay, they might not send anyone else," Lance said.

"Exactly. Exactly the problem. Good job identifying it." Leonard tapped his fingers against each other. "Let's rephrase our question, then: How do we remind them what our shared goal is?"

Graeham shook his head. "That's a PR question, isn't it, though?"

Him saying that somehow reshaped the problem in my head. As much as I hated being in the spotlight and public relations had been the bane of my existence, it was a thing I'd had to learn how to do to get here.

"Air show." The words slipped out of my mouth and I found Helen in the group.

It was as if we were formation flying again and she could read my plane's position from the turbulence across her wings. Her eyes widened and she nodded. "The birds."

Nathaniel had been there and he knew the incident we were talking about but he hadn't heard any of the conversations backstage that led up to that moment. He leaned forward and I could see him trying to follow us.

Drawing in a breath, I turned to Leonard. "Early on, when we were trying to convince people that women should be in the astronaut corps—"

"Because we bloody well should be," Dawn muttered.

"Anyway, we did an air show to demonstrate our competence, but . . . but during the show, my plane hit some birds. Lost engines. It made the papers."

"You aren't giving yourself credit." Aahana shook her head. "I heard about it in India. That was the moment when people started talking about women being in the space program and a lot of it was because you were completely unflustered after nearly dying."

I laughed. If by "unflustered" she meant that I had locked myself in the bathroom and threw up afterward, then sure, that was a way we could talk about it. Granted, that had been because of the press, not the accident itself, but still. "They made such a big deal about it. I knew that I survived because of my training, but to the public, they saw a near disaster and a miraculous recovery. They like disasters that get happy endings."

The speaker crackled as Halim said, "When Benkoski and I couldn't close the hatch door, everyone paid attention. The space program had become dull and the world tuned in to see if we would survive."

Helen nodded enthusiastically. "They want us to come home. If we *won't* come home, the politicians will do everything in their power to shut us down. But if we *can't* come home . . ."

"If we can't come home, everyone will be rooting for us to succeed." I looked at Nathaniel. "And you're sure we can stay here safely."

He hesitated. "A high degree of certainty, but . . . but there's no surety. If they'd send me the damn information, I could lock down the last questions."

"Hang on, hang on." Howard Tang held up his hands in a time-out. "Are you suggesting that we fake an emergency?"

"Yes." Wilburt nodded, and then laughed. "There was one time a man who swallowed invisible ink and had to wait in the emergency department for someone to see him."

"Not the time." I shook my head at him.

"No, it is exactly the time. We have already an emergency, yes. But they are not seeing the emergency. They are not seeing us."

Florence nodded slowly. "We could film the 'Elma and Leonard Show' with an explanation that the plan to abort is bullshit. Send it to Earth as if it were for the PR department to approve and then 'Oops! Did we forget to encrypt that?'"

My stomach clenched at the thought, but years of therapy meant that I just let the wave of unease ride through me. I turned to the board so my back was to the group. "I'll start writing down ideas as we have them."

Behind me, Aahana said, "I like this idea. The Lady Astronaut clubs would pick up on it and amplify that."

"So would the 99s."

"And the Negro flying clubs."

"Yes. All of that is true. And there are two probl—" *Brainstorming phase, Elma. So that means you don't get to shut down the ideas you don't want to do.* "Two things we need to plan to work around. One, it puts us on the opposite team from Mission Control. Long-term, we need them. And y'all know the folks back there. You know that they've been working toward having us here as hard as we have. So throwing them to the wolves—which is what this would do—that isn't going to solve the problem. That's going to make it worse. Different, but worse. Problem two . . . Public relations campaigns take time. It took years to change people's minds about women in space."

Helen nodded. "But it is another eleven months before the

next mission launches. What if the 'won't' is 'we won't quit'? The public likes Elma, and if she says that she won't quit, they will trust her."

Why did it always have to be me out front? Leonard was the mission commander. I knew that I had been in the public eye longer than he had, but goddamn it, I just wanted to be an astronaut and see space and fly. And I also wanted to save the planet. Again, I wished I had a way to talk to Nicole. She would know how to—actually, she would back us on staying. This would work. If I was out front again. Damn it. But this would work.

I swallowed hot acid and nodded to Helen. "So you're suggesting that Leonard and I frame the crashed cargo drop as this mission's bird impact. That we communicate our willingness to stay, despite the risks, and that we also talk about our faith in the IAC."

"Exactly."

Nathaniel slid off his bench and stood. He was looking at my midriff. Why was—oh. Right. "I just had a thought . . ." He shifted his weight and probably wanted to start pacing, which was how he always thought best. "You've been sending photos back of the crash site. What if the reason that they want to pull us back is because they found evidence of sabotage?"

I didn't know about anyone else, but I went cold all over. The engineering team all looked at each other as if they thought someone might have schematics they could study right then. Reynard took a breath, then rubbed the back of his neck, scowling in thought.

Opal leaned back in her chair, staring at the dome overhead as if she could take the measure of the *Goddard*'s reaction. Lance looked like he was counting on his fingers.

Halim spoke first. "But that doesn't change anything, does it?"

Tilting his head, Leonard said, "How so?"

"If there is sabotage, then it can hit us on the way home as well as here. We don't know where the problems are. But where you are . . ." He sighed into the microphone. "Bradbury Base. We know exactly who built it. It has run under its own power for four years. It is tested. We know who will build the second dome. That is us."

We knew who had built the dome, but I also knew that these people had a secret. "True, but—" I wasn't going bring that up in the group. It would derail everything and they would deflect the question. But now everyone was looking at me. I floundered and came up with, "Well, I mean, there was a saboteur on the Moon."

"Believe me, I'm aware." Halim's voice was dry.

"He thought he had a way home." Helen's spine straightened; her chin came down. "Halim is right. Sabotage from Earth does not change the strategy here. If anything, it makes the game-play clearer. We should stay."

Nathaniel took a slow breath and let it out. He nodded. "You're right."

Lance stopped counting. Opal lowered her head with a clear and focused gaze. She smiled at her husband. "I do love a challenge."

"Yes." Reynard took Helen's hand. "Yes, we have spent the last week looking at many contingencies. Better the problems we know."

God, I loved these people so much. After years of fighting to get people to listen it was such a joy to face a problem with a dedicated, competent team. All I had to do was record an episode of the "Elma and Leonard Show." They were the ones who were going to have to solve anything that broke and we would be there to support them.

I looked at Nathaniel and smiled. Did we know what the future held? No. But that was true every single sol. Here, we had a purpose.

Leonard surveyed us, pausing on me with his brows raised in a question. Did I want to record the "Elma and Leonard Show"? Did I support him? I gave a single nod to answer both unspoken questions.

He faced the group again. "I want to repeat back what I'm hearing, to confirm that we are all on the same page. The engineering team believes that they have the resources necessary to compensate for the crashed cargo drop. The comms team is ready to record one of the 'Elma and Leonard Shows' in the model the Public Affairs Office has established, in which we explain our commitment to the mission and then send it unencrypted so that the entire world can see it. So to confirm, as a team, do you want to stay?"

From the speakers, "Hell yes, from me. But it'll take a bit to get a vote from everyone."

There were eighty of us on the *Goddard*. And only twenty down here. Every hand on Mars went up. I raised both of mine. *We would find a way or make one.*

And then I realized where I had seen the Latin phrase. It, or part of it anyway, was written above the hashmarks in the south airlock behind a stack of boxes put there by our mission commander.

FIFTEEN

SCIENTISTS CITE
A METEORIC WEAKNESS

March 25, 1970—In this time of television, nuclear energy, journeys to Mars, and suborbital planes, the varied accomplishments of science and technology astonish the imagination and almost defy description. Yet in the midst of these technical triumphs, Dr. Durward L. Allen, an ecologist of Purdue University, directed attention toward "a critical weakness."

Scientists suggest that the weakness is not in physical science or the development and use of complicated hardware. The astronauts in the Second Mars Expedition are again demonstrating man's brilliant mastery in those activities. The weakness is rather in the biology and ecology of mankind. In addition to the changes wrought to our climate by the Meteor, human beings are multiplying on this planet at a dangerous rate. This is coupled with radical alterations to their physical environment and pollution of air, water and land which will make the greenhouse effect harder to mitigate if left unchecked.

Marm 41, Year 5, Wednesol-Landing + 47 sols

It honestly felt like I spent half my time in comms now. As soon as the Earth set, Leonard and I had settled in so that we could be there when the *Goddard* started its first night pass. Dawn was on duty this time and watching the clock for when the ship would likely be in range.

I pulled my hand away from my middle again. I wasn't bloated. I was just slouching.

"*Goddard*, Bradbury. Do you copy?"

As much fun as all the raised hands had been, we'd decided that an anonymous vote would make it easier for people who had misgivings about staying to voice that. It's one thing to sign up for a mission where you have the full support of Earth. It's quite another when you realize that the hundred people you came out here with might be the only people you can rely on. The twenty of us on Mars had voted to stay, but we were already down here. Now we needed to hear what the folks on the *Goddard* had decided.

"*Goddard*, Bradbury. Do you copy?"

My stomach was tied in knots. I was six sols late. But putting the test off until after the vote made sense because I didn't want the results to sway anyone's decisions.

"*Goddard*, Bradbury. Do you copy?"

"Bradbury, *Goddard*." Emily Garber's voice rang through the speakers. "Loud and clear. I'm handing the mic to Halim."

A moment later, his resonant tone rolled into the room. "Thank you, Emily." He sighed and waited a moment. "Okay. She's left comms. I need you to bring Helen in and—sorry, Dawn, I need you to go out."

She pursed her lips, brows rising, but nodded without protest. "All right. I'll find Helen and send her down."

Goddamn it. Someone didn't want to stay. Why else would he need privacy? Now we'd have to decide if it was possible to split the mission—except, wait. He'd asked for Helen and not Nathaniel. Frowning, I looked at Leonard, who had the same quizzical expression on his face.

Dawn left the room, shutting the door behind her.

Leonard reached for the mic. "Dawn is out. How many voted no?"

"Oh—no, it's not that." Halim cleared his throat. "Sorry. Yes, let's handle that part first. Everyone voted to stay—I mean, everyone who voted. Some people abstained, saying that they would abide by the will of the group."

"That's great news." I fiddled with the cord of the mic. If I were going to have the pregnancy test run tonight, I needed to do it before Kam turned in. I shoved that aside. Waiting until next sol would not change anything and right now my attention needed to be here. "So . . . why the secrecy?"

The mic cut back in on the tail end of a sigh. "You aren't going to like this. After the events on the Moon, Helen and I were both sent with codebooks in case anything went down that we needed to keep secret. Like sabotage."

Leonard's mouth dropped open. "So . . . that's good information to have."

"Sorry. I'm genuinely sorry that you were kept in the dark. I thought it was a bad idea, but . . . the easiest way to keep a secret is to limit the number of people who know. So. So it's just me and Helen. I think." I could almost see him shrugging. "For all I know, Clemons sent multiple codebooks with multiple people."

I was unreasonably annoyed that they had gotten sanctioned codebooks after I'd gotten in so much trouble for using codes to write to my husband. "He didn't send anything with me."

"Nor me." Leonard settled in his chair. "I take it you got a coded message?"

"I didn't. That's the problem."

A knock on the door made me jump, which gives some idea of exactly how tense I was.

Leonard half turned in his seat. "Come in."

Helen poked her head into the room. "Dawn said you needed me?"

"We're talking to Halim, and . . ." Leonard beckoned her in. "Shut the door behind you."

She came in, holding a notepad and slide rule in one hand. In the other, she had a paperback book that we must have interrupted her while reading. Her gaze lit on me, as if to wonder why they needed a computer when I was here.

I switched the mic to VOX so we didn't have to push the button each time we spoke. "Halim, we have Helen. You want to catch her up?"

"Helen . . . Rhode Island protocol."

Her slide rule hit the ground. "Sorry." She bent and picked it up, shaking her head. "Sorry. I knew that it might happen, but . . . here?"

"I think at the IAC."

What the heck were they talking about? Leonard looked as confused as I felt. Halim couldn't see it, but Helen could. "The Rhode Island protocol doesn't exist. When everything went down on the Moon, we used it to let Clemons know that we thought communications were compromised."

"And . . . and you think that they're compromised now?" Leonard hunched into the mic. "But you said that you didn't get a code."

"Right. Or, I don't think I did." Halim's voice changed a little as he shifted away from the mic. "Helen, I'm sending down the message I got back. Can you look to see if I missed anything?"

"Of course." She pulled a chair over to the console while I shifted back to give her space. Sitting down, she set the slide rule to the side and put her notepad and the paperback in front of her.

"Leonard and Elma, to explain while we wait for that to come down . . . I used the codebook to ask Clemons if we were being sent home because of saboteurs. There's a check phrase and it didn't come through." As he spoke, the message flickered onto the console in front of us.

Halim, good notes about the transfer time for the crew from Mars. We believe that bringing them up to the Goddard *closer to launch time will create more space aboard to allow for the reconfig. The MMT met briefly today to review the ship's systems and mission progress. The* Goddard *performed flawlessly during launch and continues to do so. A testament to all the hard work and dedication by the teams that have readied her for flight. Your team on orbit has done a tremendous job completing all the activities scheduled in the very packed FD1 and FD2 timelines. The planning teams send their thanks. The Lunetta crew and teams are ready and looking forward to your arrival.*

Helen put her hand on the paperback and frowned. "There's nothing here."

"Damn it. I was hoping I was wrong." His exhalation was a brush of static. "So Clemons didn't read it."

"Maybe he missed it?" I asked.

"If it had been an immediate reply, sure. But this had a five-hour delay in getting a response during their day. I . . . I don't think Clemons is there."

I shifted in my seat, uncomfortable with the possibilities that were starting to open up. At the same time, it somehow made more sense to me that the decision to bring us home hadn't come from him. We didn't always agree, but he was dedicated to the space program.

"Is this Earth First again?" The group had been responsible for major damage on Earth and at Artemis Base during our first mission.

Leonard shook his head. "The IAC has more than one facility. Even if Earth Firsters somehow took over Mission Control in Kansas, I don't see them being able to hijack Brazil or Algiers or France. Someone would have let us know."

"They took out the Deep Space Network before. That was a lot of—"

"They destroyed it." He pointed at the console as if it represented Mission Control. "This would mean taking and holding a facility and maintaining a fiction for multiple days. Not just with us, but with the rest of the IAC. I don't think that's within the Earth Firsters' abilities."

When was the last time a communication from Mission Control had seemed normal? Before the order to come home, they had felt focused on the wrong things. We had all cross-trained on equipment, so I went to the comms console and pulled up the queue for personal messages and news. The log showed electronic package bursts at their regular intervals so spotting the pattern break was easy. "We haven't gotten personal mail since sol before yestersol. Traffic stops around noon our time."

In the silence, I could hear the faint crackle of Halim's open channel. "So, my question then is . . . who is in control of the IAC right now?"

"Goddamn it." Nathaniel's muffled curse startled me awake into disorienting dimness.

I was lying on my side on the lower bunk at some unknown hour. He was a shadowy silhouette leaning against one wall. I rolled onto my back. "What's wrong?"

"Sorry." He limped over to the bed and sat. "Stepped on something . . . Ah. A thumbtack."

I sat up, resting a hand on his back. "I'm so sorry."

"It's okay. It doesn't hurt—just startled me." Nathaniel leaned over to push the thumbtack into the thin plastic wall of our cubicle.

The provocative unzipping sound of my husband removing his flight suit had a surprisingly Pavlovian response for me. I scooched over to make room for him. "Will you be able to slow down now? Since we're staying."

"That depends on if Mission Control starts cooperating or if we continue to have to compensate for them."

And Mission Control would not start cooperating with Nathaniel's team. I so wanted to talk to him about it, but—even if we hadn't agreed to keep the "Rhode Island protocol" conversation secret—now was not the time. The walls were very thin and I didn't want the word haphazardly getting out to the rest of the crew because I was careless with my husband.

Nathaniel rested his hand on my upper arm, rubbing it gently. "What's wrong?"

"Mm . . ." I reached out and found his bare thigh. "Classified things."

He rubbed my arm while he waited for me to finish thinking, then ran his hand down to my stomach, drawing a circle. "What about . . . ? Have you started yet?"

"No." I caught his hand because I had been thinking about this since we talked to Halim and everything changed. Again.

"If I don't start, I'm going to wait to ask for the test until I get up to the *Goddard* and talk to Ana Teresa. Although honestly, as a doctor she's scarier than Kam."

"Why wait?"

"Because if I am . . . they'll ground me. If they do that while the *Esther* is down here, that'll complicate getting the ship back up to the *Goddard*." I pulled him down to the bed.

"There's a reason people get grounded when they're—"

"Yes, because men are afraid of things they don't understand." I kissed his neck. "I wouldn't be the first woman to avoid mentioning it before a launch."

He stilled in my arms. "Really?"

"Really." Granted, my sample size was exactly one astronaut. "I'm not telling you who."

Chuckling, Nathaniel rolled so that he faced me. He ran a hand up my side, circling the ball of my shoulder and then tracing a line up my neck to let his fingers play in my hair. My right hand found his back while my left was pinned awkwardly between us. I twisted my wrist to find one of his nipples and used my thumb to trace a circle around the fine hairs there.

He grunted, stretching a little under my hands.

Smiling, I drew a knee up over his legs. "And how was your sol?"

"Frustrating, honestly." His hand came up to draw small circles at my temples. "We keep finding things that aren't the way they appear on the plans. I can't tell if those are changes to the base that the last crew didn't document or if I'm looking at outdated plans, and none of them remember."

Wilburt's face when he told me about the "rover accident" played across my mind. "Do you think they really don't remember?"

He sighed, breath warming my neck. "I don't know. Sometimes Wilburt seems genuinely baffled and dives in to help. Other times he or Graeham are just . . ."

"Weird."

"Yeah." Nathaniel rolled on his side to face me. "I'd feel better if

I had the full specs on the engine coolant systems instead of relying on my memory, so I'd know if we could actually use them to build the heat sink. I mean, I know I *could* use the turbopump to build a compressor but it's really not the right piece of equipment because . . . you don't want to hear any of that."

"Oh, you know I love it when you talk about your equipment." I sounded flirty but I was wondering if the undocumented changes were sloppiness or part of the larger problem. "Are you finding a lot of things that are out of place?"

"Not really. I'm just being cranky that there are any. But there are always differences between plans and execution." He shifted me to be on top of him. Trying to help navigate in the narrow bunk, I bumped my wounded finger against a metal support strut. I hissed. Just a little, but it was enough to make Nathaniel freeze.

"Are you okay? Did I hurt—" His hand went to my midsection.

"Just my stupid finger. I bumped it." I settled my weight on him, straddling his thighs, and was determined to not have that conversation now. It was one thing too many. "Fortunately, my other hand is still useful for priming thrusters."

It was a distraction, for both of us.

SIXTEEN

INDIAN HOME LIFE CAUSES CONCERN

Disruptions in Families on Reservations Deplored

By Edward C. Burks

KANSAS CITY, Kansas, Thursday, March 26, 1970—A group of experts on American Indian affairs, meeting here yesterday, called on Congress to alleviate the "catastrophic" disruption of Indian home life. Under so-called remedial and welfare programs, it was said, one Indian child in four is presently taken from his reservation home and sent off to boarding schools or to some form of foster care.

Marm 42, Year 5, Thursol—Landing + 48 sols

Helen stopped at Station 3 by the south airlock. "All right, do it again."

"Hm?" I pulled my hand away from my stomach, which I kept finding myself touching as if something noticeable had shifted. Was I bloated? Because I was a week late or because I was pregnant? Pasting on a smile, I pulled the Portable Fire Extinguisher off the wall to check the PFE's gauge and gave her the next line from the "Elma and Leonard" script I was practicing. "That's right, Leonard. You and I have been working and training together as a team for five years—except it's not actually five."

"Five is what your script says." She pulled the second PFE

off its bracket and set it on the ground. "Serial number and reading?"

"Why do you have the script memorized better than I do?" I turned the canister to find the label. "0993227—pressurized full."

"Because I have heard you say it ten times now." She jotted the number down on the logbook.

"I have not said it ten times." I crouched to read the number from the other one. "0993463—pressurized full."

"Got it." She entered the number and date and looked at the PFE I was holding. "Give. You are injured."

"One finger." I rolled my eyes. "On my nondominant hand."

"Give."

I didn't have a reason to be stubborn, really, except that it was annoying that such a minor injury was getting any attention at all. But Helen was not someone you could wear down just by being stubborn. I handed her my PFE. "Here you go."

"Thank you." She took it.

I stood in front of the south airlock. This was the one we stored the gear in. This was the one with the hashmarks and maybe a sentence in Latin. Putting my hand on the ratchet handle, I checked the pressure gauge.

Behind me, Helen said, "Are you avoiding doing the lines again?"

"There's just something I want to check." I pumped the ratchet handle and said the blasted lines as I did. "That's right, Leonard. You and I have been working and training together as a team for five years now. Serving on the First Mars Expedition was such an honor and now we're so fortunate to be back here on Mars."

Helen fished in her pocket and pulled out the crumpled script. Lowering her voice, she did her impression of Leonard, which made me giggle every time. "There are few people that I trust more than the men and women who have come with us for the Second Mars Expedition . . . then he talks for a while about how nice we all are and then says ... That's why we're so committed. We have a team that we can trust."

I hauled the inner airlock hatch open as I tried to keep the lines going. I figured if I could do that, I could sound natural and smooth when we did the recording. "Then I laugh and say, 'Why, on the first mission to the Moon there were only three of us, and when I went around the backside of the Moon, I was more alone than a skunk on a dance floor'—that is not a real Southern saying. And also, I liked being alone."

"Talk to Dawn and Florence." She opened the case containing the portable breathing apparatuses and pulled one out. "Or change it."

"I know I can ..." Inside the airlock, my voice was muffled by the stacks of bins we'd brought back. I studied the wall of bins trying to remember roughly where I'd seen the writing. "It's just that they worked so hard on the script."

"They worked hard on it, but you are the one saying it. You've never asked for a change to a script before?"

"No ... not really. I corrected some numbers in one, but that's just because it was wrong and would have been confusing." The script supervisor at *Watch Mr. Wizard* had started letting me look them over before they were final after that, which I very much appreciated.

"Well, I think that if it is not something you would say then that is also a mistake."

As I pulled bins down and set them aside, I turned her words over in my head. That line of logic sat uncomfortably with me. There were two modes in which I had been deployed by publicity. The ones in which I was carefully coached, like *Mr. Wizard,* and the ones in which I said whatever came to mind, like late-night talk shows. My therapist back on Earth said that my anxiety about being in front of people had given me the gift of an ability to read folks. "What will people think?" The refrain from my mother, which I could never quite erase, gave me a path through conversations, in which I plotted the likely trajectories of any given quip.

When the anxiety was bad, that paralyzed me. The rest of the time, if I could keep from panicking, I'd learned to see it as a useful tool. Mind you, that had taken years of work.

But it also meant that right now, Helen's offhand comment that I could change the script made me start thinking that maybe . . . maybe I was resisting practicing because I knew the script was wrong.

I bit my lower lip and focused on clearing the bins so that I could get back to the work that I was supposed to do. I fully expected Leonard to suddenly appear and ask me what I was doing. Helen hadn't been on the First Expedition and didn't seem to care what I was doing and—

Aut viam inveniam aut faciam.

The letters had been scratched into the wall of the airlock with some sort of rough, improvised tool. Someone had made an effort to buff them out but they were still clear. I couldn't tell if it was Leonard's handwriting.

I shall either find a way or make one.

Below them were ranks of hashmarks. I could see twenty-five without moving anything else. If I knew the exact number, what would it tell me?

"I don't hear any script happening." Helen leaned into the airlock and saw the stacks of boxes in disarray. "What are you doing?"

"Oh—I . . ." I wasn't going to lie to her. I pointed at the letters. "I saw this earlier and remembered it when Leonard said the same thing in the meeting the other sol. I wanted to . . ."

I wanted to investigate this because it was easier than thinking about the fact that I might be pregnant. I wanted to talk to Helen about that so badly and also wanted the secret to not exist.

Helen walked closer, head tilting as she considered the writing. "What did Leonard say it was?"

"They were counting the remaining sols."

She looked around the unused airlock. The door on the other side of it led to a wall of regolith and wouldn't open. "Here? Curious. How many hashmarks are there?"

"I don't know."

"Let's count them, then." Helen grabbed a box. "But you still have to say your lines. You were more alone than a skunk on a dance floor."

"I was more alone than a skunk on a dance floor." I shifted another box. "It's ever so nice to have company this time. With twenty of us living and working on Mars, every sol is filled with purpose because we're getting ready for our friends to come down from the *Goddard,* which is in orbit around Mars right now."

"And then Leonard says . . ." Helen stopped to drag the script out of her pocket. "Won't that be swell, Elma, when we have a hundred people on Mars?"

"Ninety-seven."

"I thought it would actually be eighty-two, with the skeleton crew that—"

"No, I mean there are ninety-seven hashmarks."

"Oh." She lowered the script and looked at them. "What does that tell you?"

"I don't know." I shook my head and started to restack the boxes. "The First Expedition was on the surface for three hundred and eighty sols. That was about fifty-four Martian weeks. Ninety-seven doesn't fit any patterns for that to be tracking total mission time."

"But that's what Leonard said it was?" She helped me start to put the bins back.

"Yeah. Have you noticed anything . . . odd?"

She hesitated and my fear made me stop moving bins to look directly at her. Her face was still and quiet except for a tiny, pinched frown. "No. Or only that I had been very close to all of them before . . . before you replaced me. Now there is a distance."

"Was that—"

A klaxon went off.

Not just any klaxon, but the one for a solar event. Earth monitored for solar flares because the Moon and the space stations were vulnerable without Earth's magnetosphere to protect them from the radiation. So were we.

We had one hour to get to shelter. My heart ran fast, but I moved out of the airlock, looking at my watch. 1043. "Our window closes at 1143."

"Confirmed 1143." Helen was looking at her watch, too.

A similar alarm would be going off on the *Goddard* and everyone up there would be crowding into the "cellar" behind the water tanks right now.

I turned toward the wall next to the airlock hatch, where the emergency procedures were pasted. Helen was right beside me. Around us, I could hear other people moving, calmly and professionally, the way we had trained.

We'd learned procedures by station, since there was no way to know where we'd be during any given emergency. The checklist was written on the wall so we didn't have to think at all. Confirm the airlock was closed and had a good seal, then go to the "cellar" on the equipment floor with everyone else.

It was buried under the surface plus we had an additional ten meters of regolith mounded on top of the dome, all of which was an excellent shield against radiation. We would be a heckuva lot safer than the folks on the *Goddard.*

Except for the people out on the surface. Leonard had told the survey teams to continue working on the excavation plans for the second dome. Which team was out right now?

I bit my lips and kept my mind fixed on the procedure in front of me. We needed to seal this hatch, since I'd opened it, before we could move on to next steps. I grabbed the door and pushed it closed.

The klaxon cut off.

That was weird. I kept moving, although I was grateful for the silence. I tested the latches and all were dogged tight. Helen bent to peer at the pressure gauge. "We have a good seal."

"Copy. We have a—"

Three tones sounded. "All staff, all staff, all staff. This was a sim. You may return to your duties. Repeat. This was a sim and we are not completing it." Leonard paused. "Elma. Come to comms."

A sim? I straightened and found Helen, who was turning from looking at the intercom. Her brows were drawn together in confusion. "Why would they do a sim now—oh. Bastards."

She was a step ahead of me, but the moment she said it, I understood what was happening. We hadn't answered Mission Control. They were trying to force the issue.

"Leonard is going to be furious." Which was not far off from my own internal barometer. Sighing, I reached for the intercom mounted beside the airlock to let Leonard know I would be en route once I helped Helen restow the gear I'd pulled down.

I pushed the button to talk to comms and it slid in without engaging. I pressed it again, waiting for the click and buzz of activation.

Behind me, Graeham said, "Is that broken again?"

I jumped with an undignified squeak. I may have been carrying some residual tension.

"When did it break?" As I asked, I realized that I hadn't seen it in any maintenance reports.

"I . . ." He looked back toward the stairs and then across the dome to where Wilburt was talking to Lance next to the mural. "I'm not sure. I just remembered that I tried it earlier and it didn't work."

So, was he looking at Wilburt, Lance, or the mural? Or just away from me? I pushed the button one more time in misguided hope before turning my back on it. "Did you log it?"

"I . . . Leonard called a work stop and I lost track." He put his hands in his flight suit pockets and gave an affable, very British shrug. "I'll go let engineering know. Ta."

He turned and skip-bounded back toward the stairs. I called after him. "Let Leonard know I'm on my way?"

"Wilco!" He half turned before continuing on to the stairs, where there was a little bit of a traffic jam from people who were coming back up from the cellar.

I grabbed the hatch's ratchet handle, shaking my head at the shenanigans that Earth was pulling. Running an unscheduled sim was one thing. Using the alarm as a means to get our attention? That was quite another. That would lead to people ignoring the alarms.

Helen shook her head. "This alarm business is a very bad strategy."

"You can say that again." I pulled the door open.

As I released the handle, I had time to register some resistance, but not that I'd caught the edge of my bandage on something. It pulled the bandage off.

"Damn it!" I glanced down at my index finger. The black stitches where Kam had tacked my nail in place to hold the nailbed open while the new one grew in were even more disconcerting than the throbbing.

"Oh dear." Helen paused.

With my right hand, I yanked the gauze free, tucking it into my pocket. "Well, that's annoying."

"I'll finish up and you go see what Leonard needs and then show that to Kam."

"I don't want to leave you with this mess." I curled my left hand inward to mask the index finger a little. "And I don't need to talk to Kam."

"I look forward to seeing you say that to Kam." She paused on the airlock threshold. "I think he will skewer your soul with a spinal probe."

"Who?"

"Kam." Helen tilted her head.

"Oh—oh, sorry, you said 'he' and I got confused."

She snorted. "English pronouns are stupid."

"Anyway, you're right. And I promise to do it after I talk to Leonard." I fled before she could make any other snarky comments.

When I got down the stairs to the first subfloor, I could hear them talking before I got into comms. Nathaniel's voice was tight and controlled. ". . . say that we should transmit the plans to them without—" A brief flash lit his face as he saw me walk in and then worry buried that moment of light. "Elma."

"Sorry." I took a step farther into the room. "And the intercom by the south airlock is broken."

"Oh, that's not—" Florence raised a finger toward the ceiling and then cocked it at me. "Got it. I'll make a note."

"That's not what?"

"Surprising, given the sol."

I didn't push, but damn it, I was tired of people keeping secrets. "So, did they send a message with the alarm?"

Florence tapped her screen. "You can read it, if you want. The gist is that they express concern that the leadership may be suffering from the strain of managing a floundering mission."

Anger surged through me. "Floundering? Did they use that actual word?"

"They did." Leonard's mouth was tight. "You know I kept having the thought that it's a good thing I'm not the first Black commander or they would use any mistake to make sure I was the last."

"They'll try anyway." Florence scowled at the screen. "They always do."

He snorted. "They were always going to take this mission away from me at the first chance they got . . . Someday, maybe they'll learn that you can't put people in a position where they have nothing to lose."

The look that he and Florence shared had a lot of layers to it that I couldn't begin to unpack. Or maybe it was more accurate to say that I could begin to unpack it from watching the way our Black friends and colleagues had been treated over the years, but my understanding wouldn't get beyond the outer wrapping.

Leonard shook his head and faced me. "They want Halim to take over the mission."

I looked back at the screen. "It . . . it doesn't say that."

"During our 'solar event,' they sent the *Goddard* a different message." Florence grimaced. "Halim had comms send it down to us."

"That doesn't make any sense . . ." It wasn't that I had an issue with Halim. He'd taken over as chief astronaut after Parker. And yes, he'd apparently been a bit of a hero on the Moon, but he'd never been to Mars. Leonard had. I found myself wanting to talk to Nicole even more. "Who's CAPCOM this shift?"

"Ed Olhava," she said.

My brief flurry of an idea about trying to come up with a secret message that the CAPCOM would pass to Nicole vanished. "He's a PAO."

"Yeah." Her mouth had a sour twist.

Public Affairs Officers were a necessary part of the IAC, but the CAPCOM seat had always been an astronaut. CAPCOMs went through the sims with us and knew how to parse the information coming in from the backrooms down to only the things that we needed to hear. PAOs were in Mission Control to explain things to the public, not to us.

"What is going on down there?" I rubbed the back of my neck.

Leonard grimaced. "I don't like it either, but it doesn't fundamentally change anything. They still can't make us do anything unless they come out here."

"They could." Nathaniel rested his hands on the table. "The same link that lets them sound an alarm from Earth. They could set off alarms at random intervals to disrupt work. Or . . . they can regulate life support from Mission Control."

Which I knew, in the sense that we'd talked about emergency overrides but not in the sense of using environmental controls to force us to do things we didn't want to do. I couldn't imagine anyone in the astronaut corps agreeing to . . . Oh. "Are we talking to a PAO because none of the astronauts would participate in whatever baloney this is?"

My question sat leaden in the room. Nathaniel paced in a small circle. Leonard bent his head, one arm crossed over his chest, the other hanging loose by his side. Florence shifted in her chair and looked back at the monitor.

Lifting his head, Leonard turned to Nathaniel. "The link between Earth and our systems . . . can you just disable it?"

"There is no 'just.'" Nathaniel shook his head. "It's not like there's a single switch that we can flip. We can prioritize removing the remote control capabilities or we can prioritize setting things up to stay here longer."

Leonard hissed through his teeth in a grimace. "Well, that's not a great—"

"We can." Florence turned back from her console. "There is a switch we could flip. They have to be able to send a signal. If we take our radio arrays out of alignment with Earth . . . they couldn't do anything."

She and Leonard and I had been through that. Being out of contact with Earth on the First Mars Expedition had been . . . difficult. The idea of doing it on purpose . . . I bit the inside of my cheek.

Leonard's nose narrowed as he inhaled. He shook his head. "We'll keep that as a last resort. The goal is still to try to make Mars a home for people from Earth, which means we need to stay and we need the Third Expedition to come. So, right now . . . Right now, let's try to get the Earth back on our team. Elma . . . you and I have a show to record."

"Copy that." *3.141592 . . .* "But there are some rewrites I'd like to make first."

SEVENTEEN

ASTRONAUTS' PLEA FOR MARS MISSION CONTINUATION STIRS EMOTIONS WORLDWIDE

KANSAS CITY, March 27, 1970—The television appearance by Dr. Leonard Flannery and Dr. Elma York has sparked a groundswell of support for the Second Mars Expedition, with public opinion tilting decisively in favor of continuing the mission. Dr. York argued, "Our research is vital to the future of humanity and the potential risks are a necessary part of scientific exploration. Being here, to make a home for you, is what we signed up for."

The astronauts' unwavering commitment and expertise have garnered widespread admiration, with an increasing number of individuals rallying behind their cause. Johnny Carson stated, on *The Tonight Show,* "I've got faith in that little lady's capability to navigate the hurdles created by the supply drop crash." Meanwhile, others have criticized them for disregarding the potential dangers of their continued stay on Mars.

Marm 43, Year 5, Frisol-Landing + 49 sols

It had been a while since I was as nervous about a routine meeting as I was the sol after Earth set off the false alarm. My flight suit was stuck to my body with sweat as I waited next to Leonard at the whiteboard in the front of the room.

Leonard stood with his hands clasped behind him in his

professor stance. I really wanted to get a white lab coat for him. "Good morning, everyone."

"Good morning, Dr. Flannery," we all responded in a sing-song the way we had started doing every morning.

His familiar crooked smile seemed like it had an extra dash of pride as he looked at us. He had this way of making you feel like you'd won a math tournament. "All right, class . . . Before we get to this." He tapped the board on which I'd written up the duty roster as if we weren't about to introduce A Problem for everyone. "We're going to start with departmental reports so that we're all working with a Big Picture view of our plan. Engineering, you're up."

After Nathaniel and engineering would be Kam with the medical report. It would be fine. We had a game plan. It would be inconvenient but not dangerous.

Nathaniel nodded. "We're in good shape with the groundwork laid for the changes that we'll need to make to connect the second dome with this one. I'm going to switch part of the team back over to assembling the solar collection system under Reynard and just keep Bolí and Lance to work with me on fabricating the connections to use the greenhouse HVAC in Dome Two."

"You have to tell them what we named it." Lance leaned forward. "The Compensator 5000."

"The Compensator 5000 is going to be the first machine designed and built on Mars—"

"Excuse me, no." Wilburt shook his head and I could see his mechanic's heart being deeply wounded. "When we were before here, I designed and built—"

"A lot of things." Leonard cut him off. "Which we don't have time to list if we're going to get through this meeting. Engineering, anything else?"

"Yes, actually. Could we send the *Esther* up to the *Goddard* this week? I realize it's earlier than we had originally planned, but it would allow us to bring down some supplies and additional personnel that I could use as we make changes."

The *Esther*. By which he meant, could *I* go up to the *Goddard* early.

This was so I could talk to the doctor sooner. Because he couldn't leave well enough alone, he had to try to orchestrate things in my best interests. I suppose I should consider myself lucky that this wasn't a decade ago when he would have just made an appointment for me.

To be fair, there was a time in my life when I had needed that, but we were no longer in that time. Nathaniel's gaze was carefully for Leonard only. I knew that my expression was calm and unruffled, but he would have been able to see the irritation that was burning through me as if the entire dome's environmental controls had been set to broil.

Leonard looked back at the duty roster. "I was going to send Elma, Wilburt, Graeham, and Howard out to the crash site, per Mission Control's request. We'd wanted to give them some of the mission objectives they requested since we aren't doing any of the departure tasks. But . . . but we could probably bump that to next week."

I shook my head. "We've upended the entire schedule that Mission Control sent us. I think, if we're trying to play the role of dedicated scientists, that we should make as few changes as possible."

"I really could use those extra hands." Nathaniel met my gaze now and I saw the tiniest compression of his lips in a barely suppressed flinch.

"I'm sure you could, but we'll need time to rig sleeping berths for them." I opened my notepad all nice and helpful. "Also, I suspect other departments might have wish lists from the *Goddard*. My suggestion would be that we try to avoid deviating from the original schedule as much as possible."

"We will have to deviate." He tugged at the collar of his flight suit. "I mean, the HVAC situation alone."

"I am aware . . ." I smiled at my husband, who, bless his heart, meant well. "I think we could compromise and find an earlier launch time if warranted, but for the moment, I don't think there's a compelling reason to change the current duty roster, do you? Besides which, I'm fairly certain that your team has not had time to fully service the *Esther* and we don't want to rush that."

He could not argue with that, because the only reason to rush, now that we'd decided to stay, was that my period was late. Damn it. I would deal with that when I got to the *Goddard* next week, but not now.

Right now, we had to deal with the fact that we were staying on Mars and we had no idea how Mission Control or the planet Earth would react to that.

"All right." Leonard nodded. "After the meeting, Elma and I will look at the upcoming schedule and see if working in an earlier launch is in the cards."

Nathaniel had that slightly bewildered look he gets, where he can tell that I'm mad but he can't tell why. His eyebrows turn up in the middle and he gets a little scrunch in his forehead. "I can shift people to servicing the *Esther*?"

"Wonderful." I smiled brightly at him and was aggressively polite. "It is so nice to see what we can accomplish when we work together. Moving on . . . is it medical next, Leonard?"

As if I didn't know. When Kam had come to us with the list of supplies that had been on the lost cargo drop, we'd all agreed that the best approach was to treat it as a nonissue.

"Yes, medical is up." Leonard said. "Kam?"

Our doctor offered us a cleared throat. "We'd had trouble finding the drip lines, so we did an inventory of the material brought in from the drop sites. The drip lines had wound up in the south airlock and they were supposed to have come to the med station." Kam straightened the edges of a notepad, easing into the heart of the matter. "In doing so, we identified other items that are missing—not mislaid or stolen. They were also on the cargo drop as filler."

I watched the room, keeping the gentle smile on my face that I'd learned from years of publicity. Who was going to react badly?

"While we have redundancies for everything, this is now going to create shortages—specifically in birth control. The majority of our birth control options were on that cargo drop, so we're going to have to do immediate rationing."

Lance laughed and then cut off. "Wait. You're serious?"

"What do you mean, rationing?" Bolí looked at Catalina. "Are you saying that my wife and I can't—"

The outburst that didn't happen when the cargo drop crashed happened now. You would think we'd told the men that we were going to remove a precious body part. All of them had questions.

Kam waited, tapping one finger on the notepad. "Let me try to answer your questions . . ." A pursed mouth did nothing to mask our doctor's amusement. "In addition to anything you brought in your personal stores, each married couple will be issued forty condoms. The pill will be reserved for a subset of women for whom it provides additional therapeutic effects. The rest of you will need to find workarounds."

"Forty condoms per month?" Bolí relaxed. "You had me scared for a moment."

"Forty condoms until the Third Expedition arrives."

"Wait—what?" Jaidev sounded aghast. "But don't we have more on the *Goddard*?"

"Yes, those are in the tally. We have two thousand in stock on the *Goddard,* some of which need to be reserved for equipment use—"

"My equipment has needs, too . . ." someone in the group muttered.

Kam's mouth curved in a wicked grin. "Look, on the First Expedition, we went three years without sex. You can survive."

Florence shook her head, laughing, and I was so grateful for the way she was working to calm the fellows down. "Some of us can thrive. But all you poor little boys . . ."

"This is a serious problem for health, physical and mental." Boli seemed like he was going to have a conniption.

Wilbert said, "Do you know what the difference is between a tire and three hundred and sixty-five used condoms?"

"No, Wilburt." I fell into the rhythm of his voice, glad for the help. "What *is* the difference between a tire and three hundred and sixty-five used condoms?"

"One's a Goodyear. The other's a great year."

As people laughed and some of the tension diffused, I made a mental note that Leonard and I would need to be on the lookout for condoms being used as currency the way they had been on military bases during the war. This was a mission with a *lot* of married folks. There were a handful of special cases—single folks, who had either been on the First Expedition or who had a specialty that was so niche and necessary that an exception had been made.

"Come on." I waved for them to settle down. "I know this is hard, but y'all have to suck it up."

The entire room—the entire base—the entire planet burst out laughing at me. I froze, face heating bright red, and was right back in college again. A fourteen-year-old girl being the punch line for jokes. It took me a long moment before I realized what I'd said. That it was, legitimately funny. I'd frozen too long and gone too red in the face to pretend that was intentional.

Kam glared around the group. "Listen—I need to be clear about this. Don't take any chances. We are planning to have children on Mars but are a good decade of research away from human conception here. Do any of you want your wives to be the subject of science papers on fetal development under Martian gravity? No? I didn't think so."

The bellyaching and laughter stopped. But they wouldn't be the last complaints we heard.

And then, of course, there was the fact that I might be the first of those subjects. Could I have talked to Kam about it when we were briefed on the missing supplies? Yes. Why didn't I?

I would. Once I was off the planet. We'd talked about contingency plans as part of the prep as habitat administrators. Abortion. Consent to monitoring for science and then abortion. Spin up the *Goddard*'s centrifugal ring to Earth gravity and carry to term.

If I was pregnant, I was going to have to make a hard choice, and God help me, I didn't know what I would choose.

Marm 46, Year 5, Monsol—Landing + 52 sols

Three sols later, I was strapped into my pilot's chair on the *Esther*. Nathaniel had decided to prioritize sending me up to the *Goddard*, and the case he laid out for why was pretty compelling if you didn't know the underlying reason.

My period still hadn't started.

All those years of convincing politicians had given him the tools to explain why something was mission critical. It was very annoying, and after Kam's speech at the meeting, I let him.

Over the comms, Dawn's voice was calm and soothing. "I am happy to report that we are approaching T-minus five minutes. Initiate abort/recycle procedures."

I leaned toward the console for the Backup Flight System controls. "Roger that, Bradbury. Initiating BFS safing." My gloved fingers were clumsy as I entered the command so that we didn't accidentally trigger the BFS during flight. "Definitely don't want a premature injection . . ."

I'm not sure whose snort I heard over the comms. Beside me, Howard Tang continued with the copilot tasks because he understood the glory of checklists. "MOX safing in progress."

It felt a little weird to have him there instead of Leonard, but the base administrator couldn't take off and go to the *Goddard*. Howard and I had done sims together back on Earth and he had this warm, calm tone that managed to make everything seem like he was inviting you to an afternoon of polo.

Behind us, Helen sat in her NavComp seat following along on her own checklist.

Over comms, Dawn said, "Copy that. Initiate APU shutdown on my mark."

The seconds ticked by on the watch strapped to the outside of my suit.

My latest hope was that I'd skipped a period because of

perimenopause. I knew the word because Mama had been a doctor. I knew it was possible because I was almost forty-eight. But
I had no idea when my mother had started going through the
change, because I'd gone away to college when I was fourteen.

"Mark."

I flipped the switch. "APU shutdown in progress."

Once that was underway, I closed the fuel tank valves and
watched for the hydrazine pressure to drop below 200. It's a
little funny how many things we have to turn off to be able
to launch. It's all about conserving power and making sure
that nothing that could be damaged during the high-g loads of
launch is put in an unnecessarily compromised position.

Compromised position. Like launching while potentially
pregnant. My LCVG had been tight when I put it on. Not a lot
and the damn things are spandex, but still.

It could be bloating and salt retention. Or maybe the fluid
shift on Mars settled things in different places than it had on the
Moon or in microgravity.

I bit down on the inside of my lip to get my mind back on
the flight.

Howard, Helen, and I were getting to launch from an entirely
new planet. We were going to fly tosol and that was amazing
and should take all of my attention. Except that my breasts had
become incredibly tender.

Howard watched a gauge on the console. "Heater reconfiguration complete."

From inside the base, Dawn said, "Understood. Proceed
with MPS heater reconfiguration."

In five minutes, we would lift off and then spend six hours
chasing the *Goddard* while we orbited around Mars with the
best views. In my LCVG, every cooling tube that ran across my
bosom felt as if it were iron digging into my flesh.

Everything was fine. I was definitely not pregnant. "MPS
heater reconfigure—"

"*Esther*, stand by." Dawn cut into the rhythm. "We are stopping the clock."

My gaze immediately went to the bank of gauges. Everything was still nominal as far as I could see. "Roger, wilco. What's going on?"

"Stand by." The only reason that I knew something was wrong was that she didn't elaborate. Her tone of voice was mildly pleasant.

I exchanged glances with Howard, but we couldn't talk about it privately with the current comms configuration. He had a furrow in his brow and shook his head, which was the closest you could get to a shrug in a spacesuit. I wanted to turn to check in with Helen, but that was physically impossible in a suit.

She was probably doing the same thing I was—running through a list of reasons we might have stopped. Fuel leak. Weather. Sticky valve. There were so many, really. It could be something on the *Goddard* for that matter.

Or Nathaniel had told them that he thought you might be pregnant.

The comm crackled and Leonard's voice came into the cabin. "Shut down and come inside." I could hear his inhalation. "We just got word from Earth that Clemons had a massive heart attack. He's dead."

I felt like I'd been kicked in the stomach and also felt nothing at all. It did not seem real or possible that Norman Clemons was dead. "When?"

"The heart attack was a week ago." Leonard's voice was grim. "They didn't want to worry us while his fate was uncertain and . . . we'll talk about it when you get inside. But the short of it is that we're hearing about it now because there's a new interim director. It's Parker."

The earpiece buzzed as someone sucked in their breath. A moment later I realized that it was me and that I was still holding that breath as if stopping breathing would stop the world from moving forward.

I should be thinking about Norman Clemons and grieving him. But all I could hear was *Parker*.

The years and years in which I had been the target for his

unpredictable anger meant that hearing his name made me break out into a sick sweat. The man who had tried to keep me out of the space program entirely was suddenly in charge of my life.

I let the breath out slowly, blowing down to avoid activating my mic again.

Parker wasn't my enemy anymore. After Terrazas had died and I'd stepped into the copilot role on the First Expedition, things had started to change. He'd still dig at me sometimes, but I'd begun to understand that it wasn't about me. The year that we had spent on orbit above Mars had made us, if not friends, then colleagues.

When we got back to Earth, he had been my wingman on more than one occasion when the reporters had pushed too hard. I'd been his when grief had caught him by surprise.

The fact that he was in charge would be good. We were past the point when he would sabotage me for fun.

Having Parker in charge would be good. He believed in the space program. He was an astronaut. He'd been to Mars. Of all the people on Earth, he was uniquely suited to understand what we faced here.

This would be good. So my heart could slow down and I could stop sweating. Everything would be fine now.

EIGHTEEN

DIRECTOR OF INTERNATIONAL
AEROSPACE COALITION DIES

SUNFLOWER, Kansas, March 30, 1970—The aerospace community is in shock following the sudden death of Director Norman Clemons, who suffered a heart attack while overseeing operations for the Second Mars Expedition. Clemons, a British national, was widely respected for his commitment to the advancement of space exploration. He was sixty-seven.

As the mission continues, Clemons's absence is deeply felt by his devoted wife, Mildred Clemons, their two children, John and Alice, and the entire aerospace community. Clemons, known for his exceptional leadership and unwavering dedication, also possessed a deep love for reading science fiction. His passion for the genre, which fueled his imagination and sparked innovative ideas, was a testament to his boundless curiosity. His legacy as a visionary director will endure, leaving an indelible mark on future missions.

Marm 46, Year 5, Monsol-Landing + 52 sols

When we got back into the base, Leonard had pulled us all into the main dome. Someone had set chairs up in a circle. Nathaniel had the same look of baffled sadness that a lot of us wore. Clemons, dead?

It shouldn't have been shocking, because he smoked cigars

constantly and I knew that he had a bad heart, which was why he'd never gone into space, but still . . . dead?

In the center of the circle, Dawn finished threading the portable Nagra reel-to-reel and looked up to Leonard. "Ready when you are."

He nodded, shoulders slumped. "Parker sent this message. Dawn recorded it for us and it seemed like a thing that we could all do with hearing."

Dawn pressed play and that familiar, cocky, charming voice rolled into the dome as if he lived here. But like me, Parker had never come down to the surface of Mars on that first mission. "Hello, this is Stetson Parker. Even though there are 340 million kilometers between us, I believe that we are united in mourning our friend and colleague Norman Clemons. I believe that the space program exists because of him. You are on Mars, or in its orbit, because he constantly championed the role that space plays in the future of humanity."

Parker was right. Clemons had run the space program since the IAC was founded. He'd been stubborn and opinionated and also willing to admit when he was wrong. I was never going to see his cloud of cigar smoke again.

"I am grateful that he got to see your arrival on Mars and the great successes you have achieved there so far. From the moment he received word about the crashed cargo drop, he was here in the offices overseeing the IAC's response. At some point, the news will get to you that he was on the floor of Mission Control when he had the heart attack that ultimately took his life, and that is true, but I do not want you to link any guilt or blame to the work you are doing. He was here because he loved space and he cared deeply about you."

Nathaniel slipped his hand into mine and squeezed it. I leaned into him, my heart tightening in my chest as Parker spoke.

"His great regret was that he never got to go into space because of his heart. I want you to know . . ." His voice wavered a little. "I want you to know that we're sending him up to the Moon to be buried there."

Tears burned the rims of my eyes. That wasn't enough. It wasn't the same. Clemons was still never going to get to see the stars outside of an atmosphere or from the surface of another planet.

"I also wanted to speak to you as your interim director. First, you have my deepest apologies for the silence and conflicting objectives that you have been sent over the last week. When the UN asked me to take this role, one of my conditions was that you deserve to have answers and complete truths." I could hear the wry smile in his voice. "Those of you who have worked with me before know my feelings about keeping things from astronauts on a mission."

Across the circle, Florence snorted. I met her gaze and gave a little nod because oh, yes, did I ever know that. Sure, he'd kept his own share of secrets, but he'd always believed that you should not withhold news from astronauts in some sort of bid to preserve morale. He had been furious with Mission Control—with Clemons, when he'd directed them to censor the news we were being sent during the First Expedition.

Like the fact that my husband was hospitalized. Parker had gotten that news and immediately sent Kam to brief me. And when they'd lied to him about his wife . . . well. That had been a bridge too far.

"You had asked for information about a number of things. We are sending that up now."

Nathaniel let out a huge sigh of relief and straightened in his chair. I held his hand, just in case he was about to stand up and head straight to the comms room.

"I cannot speak to nor will I second-guess the choices that caused a delay in sending it to you, other than to say that the past week here has been . . . difficult. But I'm here now and you will have my full support with your efforts. To that end, there are—"

Leonard reached past Dawn and paused the tape. "I want us to have time to mourn Clemons before we listen to the rest of this." He ran his hand over his hair, pausing with it at the back of his neck. "Anyone who wants to write a message of condolence can give it to Dawn or Florence and they'll batch them to send down. Elma, can you and I—"

To my surprise, Dawn cut him off. "Play the rest of it."

"It can wait."

Florence stood up, glaring at him, and crossed her arms. "Dawn and I have already heard it. You're about to share it with Elma. After all Parker's grand words about not keeping things from us . . . seriously? Play the damned tape."

Sighing, he shook his head. "Okay."

"—things I disagreed with Clemons about and places where we agreed. As interim director, your safety and well-being are now my charge. I've read through the department reports to catch up. Thank you for your many good notes." He paused and cleared his throat. "I know that there was a suggestion to bring you all back to Earth after the loss of Cargo Drop Four. I don't believe that's necessary, but I do think that Clemons was correct to be concerned about your safety."

By "suggestion" he meant "an order," which we'd ignored.

"But given the increased hazards, I believe that the best course of action is to change the staffing plans to keep the women in the safety of the *Goddard* while our brave men prepare the way for them." It was as if he were staring directly at me and smirking, because he'd always, always thought it was a mistake to have women in the program at all. "This is not a permanent change, of course. It's only until we can resupply you with 'certain provisions' on the cargo drops ahead of the Third Expedition, but our best-case scenario is another eighteen months—Earth months. Given that, separating our crews by sex seems prudent until we can resupply you."

Dawn stopped the tape. "That is the bullshit everyone needed to hear."

"He can't be serious." Catalina looked deeply appalled.

"Oh, he is." I shook my head, wanting to get on a ship only so I could fly back and strangle the man. "He has fought the presence of women in the program from the beginning."

"That's the damn truth." Florence sucked air through her teeth. "On the First Expedition, every time you thought that we'd proven ourselves, he'd do another little undercut about 'the ladies.' We were all on kitchen duty and laundry duty on the way out to 'play to our strengths.'"

I remembered that change but hadn't known Parker had been involved. "I thought that came from Mission Control. After the dryer incident."

Graeham looked uncomfortable. "I did not know that there was a lint trap."

"See!" Wilburt sat up in triumph. "I am not the only one who skips pages in procedure manuals."

"I had done laundry before. I simply . . . I simply did not know that—"

"It doesn't matter." I waved my hand to get their attention. "Folks, it doesn't matter. Point is—"

"Point is that he made it sound like those duty assignments were coming from MC." Florence scowled and shook her head. "But he sent the suggestion back to Earth, which I know because he dictated it to me. Like I wasn't sitting right there with opinions."

Understand, Parker and I had come a long way. He, Heidi, and I were the only ones who didn't land on the First Expedition. That sacrifice had surprised me when Parker had originally made it. Later, as we got to actually know each other during those long months on orbit, I understood that it was because he had a long and intimate history of depression. The loss of his wife had broken him. There had been entire sols when he hadn't left his sleeping module. Whenever Heidi came over from the *Pinta,* or someone came up from Mars, he pulled himself together and presented a convincing mask.

No one knew about the depression. Except me.

We were at a point now where he liked me enough that he felt it was his duty to protect me. Just like he thought he was being gallant and doing the right thing by trying to limit women's roles. No matter what we did, he would always think we were the weaker sex. He would shove us into a box because he cared.

Bolí said, "But his idea. It's not bad, this idea of separation—ow!" He rubbed his arm where Catalina had just thumped him. "What? It means that we don't have to worry about not having enough condoms."

Leonard clapped his hands together. "People. This is why I wanted to delay the rest of the tape." He looked at us all and the disappointment at the focus of our conversation rolled off of him in waves. "A good man died this week. Let's take some time to give him the respect and mourning that he deserves."

After the meeting, when Nathaniel stood, his shoulders were stooped, as if everything weighed more. I alternated between a leaden blanket of sadness for Clemons and burning rage at Parker. But Leonard was right. We could give Clemons our thoughts tosol because Parker was still going to be there next sol.

"Hey." I took Nathaniel's hand and pulled him toward our cubby so that we could have some time to unpack the grief and set it aside. "I'm unscheduled right now."

"I need to work." But he tightened his hand in mine, looking at the floor.

I knew this look. After his father had died he'd built a deck at our house. When we lost all of our colleagues and friends and family who were in Washington when the Meteor hit, he'd buried himself in work.

"Then let's help with the chairs. Hm?" I didn't let go of his hand until he nodded.

We weren't the only people who needed to do something tangible. Zainabu and Wilburt were folding chairs and carrying them back around to the kitchen.

I folded a chair and Nathaniel grabbed another. As we worked, I asked, "You remember when you and Clemons testified in front of Congress?"

The corner of his mouth curved. "Yeah, he was a rock during all of that." We carried the chairs to the kitchen. As we set them down, Nathaniel cleared his throat. "That's why I was feeling so . . . betrayed when I thought he was telling us to abort."

"It was hard to reconcile, which is why I thought something worse was happening."

That's why Clemons hadn't answered Halim. God. At least Parker would be frank with us. Even if he was going to use the position to shape the program to match his own ideals.

It did not take long to reset the area to its nonmeeting configuration, with space for people to do their mandatory exercise and areas set aside for assembly of new dome components. Nathaniel caught my hand after I set down the last chair and pulled me into a hug.

We stood quietly, his head bowed and resting on my shoulder. I squeezed him tighter and whispered, "Baruch dayan ha-emet."

Clemons. A good man. Infuriating. Cigar-smoking. Dismissive. But ultimately a good man who loved space as much as any of us and would never get to go.

When I lifted my head, I saw Wilburt watching us. He turned away, but not before I saw that his eyes were red.

Nathaniel squeezed my hands. "I really need to work."

"I know you do." I leaned in to kiss him on the cheek. "I'll come get you for dinner."

We all have our own ways to cope with grief. Nathaniel's was to bury himself in work. Mine? I suppose it was not that far different and on another sol I would have tried to carry on. But that morning I was supposed to have flown up to the *Goddard*, and that meant I had nothing on my schedule now. I couldn't even bake something because the kitchen we had here was still only geared for rehydrating freeze-dried food and warming things.

I stood in the middle of the floor, looking for someone who needed help.

By the kitchen, Helen had set up a game of chess with Reynard. Over at the whiteboard, Florence and Dawn were breaking down the sound gear and they already had Howard helping them.

Kam was walking down the "street" toward the tiny medical module. It was one of the storage containers that had been set up to make our streets and was catty-corner to the kitchen and opposite the bathrooms so that all the plumbing was in a single area.

I had nothing to do. And I had something to do.

Swallowing as Kam came even with me, I fell into step with our doctor. "Busy?"

"You are saving me from paperwork." Kam's easy smile flashed at me, but above that, the doctor's eyes were measuring me. "What's up?"

I was convinced that one look at me would allow a diagnosis, and I wasn't sure if it would land on pregnant, menopausal, or paranoid.

Or something worse, because the part of my brain that never stopped being anxious had started remembering stories about cancer and thinking about the amount of radiation we got during the early days before they figured out lightweight shielding.

I swallowed but did not beat around the bush, although my hands were slick with sweat. "Can you do a pregnancy test? My period is late."

Medical training must be amazing, because there wasn't even a hitch in stride. "What was the date of your last period?"

"Sol or day?"

"Whichever way you're calculating it."

I don't know why I asked, since the date was now burned into my brain. "February twentieth, Marm ninth."

"And you're pretty regular?"

"Yes."

"Okay." We stopped outside the small medical container and Kam pulled the door open for me. "After you and let's see what's what."

"What . . . what do I do?" I resisted the urge to look back and see if anyone had noticed me go in.

Opening a cabinet, Kam pulled out a small cup. "To start, I need you to pee in this."

That was fine. I had peed in many cups during my time as an astronaut. There was a small curtained-off toilet in the corner by the sink and I slipped behind that illusion of propriety. Kam and multiple doctors at the IAC had seen me naked and jabbed me with needles and inserted various astonishingly cold metal devices into my nether region.

But this made me sweat. At the end of this, I would know one way or the other.

"Did you have much interaction with Clemons?" I undid my flight suit, letting it puddle around my ankles, pulled down my briefs, and attempted to untense enough to pee. There's always the little dance you have to do as you make guesses about what direction the urine's going to come out.

"He was around a lot when we were setting mission parameters for the First Expedition." Kam paused and I could hear cloth rustling. "That was before you came on board. I always got so mad that he could break the smoking rules."

"Yeah. The only time I saw him without a cigar was when he used to come by pre–launch quarantine during the early Moon missions." The cup warmed in my hand. I profoundly did not want to be pregnant, because it would complicate everything.

"He'd stopped visiting quarantine by the time I started working there. Too many of us, I guess. And half the time we were launching from Brazil." Glass clinked. "I was surprised when he showed up before our Mars launch on the First Expedition. He was . . . he was very kind, actually."

"His soft side was always a surprise." In the back of my head was a small voice that had grown up assuming I would have children. That loved my niece and nephew. That still felt so alone after the loss of so much of my family. That wanted to have a legacy that wasn't just a moniker that sounded like a comic book character. "Did he ever recommend a book to you?"

"Did he?" Kam laughed. "You missed the library meetings. Clemons had *very* strong opinions about what we should have access to. That's why we have such a deep science fiction collection. 'The people looking toward our future are who we should be reading.'"

Laughing, I set the cup on the edge of the sink and washed my hands. "I didn't know that. I was always vaguely terrified of him."

"Oh sure. That way he'd blow a cloud of smoke right before he pronounced your fate?"

"Yeah, he and I had a lot of those conversations when we were trying to get women into the space program." Sweat made my underwear stick to my thighs as I pulled my clothes back into place. "Years later, he actually apologized."

"He was good about that." Kam sighed. "Now we've got Parker."

"Yeah." When I pulled the curtain aside, I briefly thought a young man had come into the room and jumped. I sloshed a little of the urine up the side of the cup and barely avoided spilling it. "Crap. Sorry."

Kam had a crew cut, but I was used to that. The lab coat, though, had appeared while I was behind the curtain, and it smoothed out all of the doctor's curves. Also, my nerves were definitely keyed up.

"You okay?" Pausing with a jar in one hand, Kam studied me.

"I—yes." I handed over the small cup. "Just everything going on."

"Okay . . ." Kam had set up a rack with a couple of test tubes standing over a mirror. Using a dropper, the doctor added three drops of my urine to each tube. "There's a reagent already in here. If you're pregnant, in about two hours we'll get little red rings at the bottom of the tubes."

"Thanks." I looked around the little room, wishing for some

activity to keep me occupied, knowing I would have to find that elsewhere.

Kam paused, watching me, and put a hand on one of the cabinets. "Do you need a Valium?"

I balled my fists and shoved them into my pocket. "I'm fine."

"You understand that because you're a pilot, I need to ask again."

"I do and I really am fine." I nodded toward the test tubes. "I can survive two more hours."

I had survived weeks of testing and a month of waiting to find out if I'd gotten into the space program. Two hours should be nothing. We waited longer than that for a launch. This was only two hours.

Just two. I wiped my palms on the thighs of my flight suit.

T-minus two hours and counting.

NINETEEN

UNSEASONABLE STORM BATTERS TAIWAN

TAIPEI, Taiwan, March 27, 1970—(AP)—Torrential rains battered Taiwan today as an early typhoon swept across the southern part of this island. The police have reported 126 casualties thus far and that cliffside highways along the east coast have collapsed in multiple places. Ferry services along the southern coast had been suspended because of lashing winds and heavy downpours.

Marm 46, Year 5, Monsol-Landing + 52 sols

Two hours. Two hours before I would know what happened next.

I wound up helping Catalina and Nuan Su with the greenwall. It was satisfying work but did not consume enough of my brain to keep me from looking at my watch every ten minutes. It also did not take long enough.

One hour and twenty minutes.

From there, I went to our cubby and remade the beds.

One hour and ten minutes.

I went to see if Nathaniel had any math that needed to be done.

He glanced up as I came into engineering and then back down at a box of something that he was wiring. "I just need another minute."

"Oh." Of course, it was nearly time for dinner. I'd told him I would come for him. "I can wait."

One hour and seven minutes.

I looked away from my watch. "Do you have any math that you need doing?"

"Mm . . ." His lower lip was tucked in between his teeth. "Done."

"Great." I traced my finger across the end of his workbench. The other people in the room were concentrating and the mood was subdued. I wanted to tell Nathaniel I'd taken the test and couldn't do that with everyone in here. "Let's go up and grab something to eat."

Across the table, Reynard set his calipers down. He straightened, cracking his back audibly. "I will come with you."

"Okay. Wonderful." I smiled brightly at him.

One hour and five minutes.

We went up together. Helen joined us. So did Aahana and Jaidev. I know that we talked but not what the conversation was about.

Forty-seven minutes.

I know that I even laughed.

Thirty-two minutes.

But it felt like I was sitting behind my body and watching them. Our conversation had been veering between stories about Clemons and about Parker.

Reynard was gesturing with his spoon. "So then, Clemons told me to go turn the lights out in the engineering department because someone would not stop working."

Laughing, Nathaniel spread his hands. "I will grant that I had lost track of time."

"I honestly don't know how you function when I'm not—" I stopped as Catalina arrived at our table.

Twenty-nine minutes.

"Sorry to interrupt." She leaned on the table. "Ladies, could you join us? We need to talk about sex."

"Um . . ." My heart sent a wave of heat through me. She couldn't know. I blinked and glanced at Nathaniel.

"Ladies only." She shrugged with a trace of a smile. "Sorry, gentlemen."

"Yes." Helen wiped her mouth and pushed her empty vacuum pack toward Reynard. "Do the recycling for me?"

"But of course."

Shrugging, I pushed mine toward Nathaniel. "Be a dear?"

He did a terrible French accent, mimicking Reynard, "But of course!"

Aahana followed suit. "Jaidev, would you mind?"

His French accent was even more outrageous. "Budov coooorrrrse!"

Laughing, I stood, and the three of us followed Catalina to the far side of the dome by the greenwall we'd assembled earlier. Opal and Florence were already there. As we walked up, Dawn was talking with Zainabu and Nuan Su.

Twenty-four minutes.

Catalina nodded. "Okay, it looks like we have everyone."

Nuan Su looked around the group, "Where's Kam?"

"Working on something." I swallowed. "Mentioned some paperwork earlier. I can go get—"

"It's all right. As flight surgeon, it might put Kam in a tricky position anyway." Dawn looked around the group. "On comms traffic, I've heard more than one fellow mention that they're worried they won't have orgasms."

Aahana frowned and raised her hand a little. "But aren't they separating us? Won't they be able to . . . help themselves while we are gone?"

"It'll take a while for us to be ready to go. So we need to remind the gentlemen that there are nonpenetrative forms of sex."

Catalina nodded. "Blow jobs, hand jobs, fingering, fisting—"

"Arguably that is penetrative," Opal said.

I kept my face neutral and nodded as if I had any idea what she was talking about. The room got very warm.

Twenty-two minutes.

As the other women talked, adding ideas to Dawn's suggestions, my face flushed and my skin felt as if I were standing in a sauna. Nathaniel and I have a healthy relationship, but I suddenly had a clear and vivid understanding that I *was* a prude. I wasn't the only one who felt uncomfortable, though.

Florence was quieter than I was used to her being. While Dawn and Catalina seemed to have been waiting for the entire mission to break out this particular topic.

Twelve minutes.

"I have it!" Zainabu clapped her hands. "Earth loves procedures. We write up extremely detailed procedures for nonreproductive sex."

Opal bounced on her toes. "Oh, it needs an acronym. DPNRS."

"Pronounced 'Deepners.'" Nuan Su grinned. "We can give them a pocket checklist."

I laughed, imagining the men in our crew if we handed them a checklist. "Wilburt will skip half the steps."

"I didn't know you were that close," Dawn said.

"That's not what I meant." The room was impossibly hot as they laughed at my discomfiture.

Nine minutes.

Catalina said, "Can we really give them a checklist, because that will definitely help my own orgasm situation. Men have not gotten female equipment figured out."

"You didn't take Nicole's advice and pack a vibrator?" Opal laughed.

I drifted back to stand with Florence. I mean, I thought it was hilarious, but my one attempt to chime in had also made me feel very old.

"I wish I could add to this," Florence said under her breath. "But all I can say is 'maybe just don't have sex.'"

I was listening to the other women and learning all sorts of new words. I was fairly certain that their idea of "playing canasta" was very different from mine. "Honestly, I don't understand the fuss . . . Why aren't people just switching to the rhythm method? The only times we use condoms are during my fertile periods."

Which I had apparently badly mistimed. Or not.

Five minutes.

Aahana leaned forward, brows raised. "Does that work?"

"Condoms and birth control pills are supposed to be more reliable." I shook my head, listening to the other women and feeling like I was learning more than I had during my entire marriage. Who knew that kneeling beside the man while he's seated helped you provide a "deeper throat"?

"But you and Nathaniel will have your twenty-first anniversary this year, will you not?"

"Um . . . yes. Yes, that's right. Which reminds me that I need to figure out what sol it's happening on." I smiled to cover my unease that Aahana was tracking when our anniversary was.

Dawn looked past me, smiling. "Kam, hey. It's okay if you don't want to join us."

The doctor's hands were shoved deep into pockets that showed the outline of fists through the fabric. Kam stood awkwardly at the edge of the circle. "I thought I'd check to see if a medical perspective would be helpful."

Mark—two hours.

I did not want to know here. I could feel Aahana deflate a little as I moved around the circle to get closer to Kam.

With a salty grin, Dawn winked at the group. "And, of course, we also need to take care of ourselves." She briefly glanced my way as if checking to see if I would shut the conversation down. "Fingering is something we can do for ourselves or each other."

Florence cleared her throat. "Okay, this is all well and good, but not a problem that all of us have."

Pursing her lips, Dawn sobered. "No, you're right." She glanced at Florence, then across the circle to Kam. "I'm sorry. You're right. We need to have each other's backs if there are any problems. We need to watch out for everyone."

Looking down, the doctor checked the time. "Actually, that reminds me, Elma . . . I promised you some paperwork, didn't I?"

"Yes, sorry to pull you away." I shrugged as if this were about Clemons and Parker and not a rack of test tubes.

As we walked away from the group, each step seemed to lower the doctor's shoulders. We didn't talk on the way to the medical module. I kept queuing up sentences but they were all in the category of "What if . . ." and none of them were useful.

0, 1, 1, 2, 3, 5 . . .

Kam held the door for me as we went into the little space. It took only two steps to get to the rack of test tubes.

. . . 8, 13, 21, 34 . . .

The doctor leaned over the table. "No rings. You aren't pregnant."

I slumped against the table, bracing myself with my elbows locked. "Oh, thank God." I started to cry.

Kam came around the table and pulled me into a hug. I didn't get asked any awkward questions. Breaking away briefly, Kam grabbed a tissue and handed it to me. "You okay?"

"Yes." I blew my nose. "I didn't want to be so I'm not sure why I'm crying."

"The body reacts to the release of tension in different ways." Kam shrugged. "You hold a lot in. It's like you're a pilot or something."

I snorted. "Thank you."

"Now the question is, why aren't you having your period?" Kam turned to the cabinets. "I'm going to do a blood draw just to rule out some things but my guess is that it's perimenopause. Have you been having any other symptoms?"

"Um . . . my breasts are tender. And I feel bloated."

Nodding, Kam pulled out a syringe. "Hot flashes? Trouble sleeping? Mood swings? Although honestly, those last two would be impossible to differentiate from background stress at this point."

I rolled up my sleeve, remembering my mother complaining about her "own personal summer." And also how often I'd felt like the dome was too hot recently. "Maybe hot flashes."

"Okay, you may also notice increased frequency of urination, vaginal dryness, and a lack of interest in sex." Kam swabbed my arm and paused as if weighing something. "And to be clear, women going through perimenopause can still get pregnant. Don't take any chances."

"Copy that."

From there, it was a straightforward medical visit. I walked out feeling like a band around my chest had been snipped. Nathaniel would probably be with Reynard still, so I would need to pull him away and—

As I stepped out, Leonard was waiting for me.

He had a worried pinch around his eyes. "Everything okay?"

"Paperwork . . ." I waved generally as if it should be apparent that I was dealing with important and boring things. "I feel like I should ask you the same question."

He nodded and gestured me toward the stairs. "Parker wants to talk to you."

"Talk?" I fell in alongside him. "It's a nineteen-minute lag right now."

The time delay made conversations impossible even during close approach. At best, we could hope for a ten-minute delay, which essentially made it a set of linked monologues.

"Yep."

Frowning, I looked across the dome to the kitchen, but Nathaniel was already gone. I turned my attention back to Leonard. "You'll sit in, of course."

He gave a single nod in response. "I was hoping you would ask me to do that."

"Of course." I hurried down the stairs and briefly thought about ducking into engineering because I wanted to tell Nathaniel, but that conversation would not be short . . . so I went into comms, where Florence was waiting. I raised my eyebrows to see her. "I thought you were upstairs with the Deepners."

She snorted. "Not my cup of tea."

"Deepners?" Leonard frowned in question.

I flushed, remembering the entire sex conversation. "In-joke."

"Okay . . ."

"According to Mission Control, Parker's standing by." Florence stood up from the chair and handed her headset to me.

Another lay prepped on the table all ready for Leonard, but without a mic. "It's encrypted, so you'll have about thirty seconds more delay than usual, but at this distance, that doesn't make any noticeable difference."

"Good note, thank you." I sat down at the mic, adjusting the headset. The fact that it was an encrypted call tightened the knot in my stomach.

Florence headed for the door. "Tell Parker I said he's still an asshole."

"Probably will." I waited until she was gone and pressed the talk button on the mic. "Sunflower Mission Control, Bradbury Base. This is Elma York standing by for Stetson Parker."

I leaned back in my chair, listening to the quiet hiss of interplanetary space. Making certain that the mic was in the off position, I slid the right earphone back and looked at Leonard. "What do you think he wants?"

He shook his head. "I was going to ask you. You know him better than I do."

"He's going to want to make his mark, so it'll be an order of some sort."

"That was my guess as well." Leonard settled his headset, leaving one ear clear for in-room conversation. "So . . . you want to tell me why you were really talking to Kam?"

"You want to tell me what DeBeer did on the last mission?"

"His main focus was the same as yours, piloting and navigating during surveys and—"

"I thought I might be pregnant. I'm not." I was so tired of all the secrets and lies. We were supposed to be a team. I couldn't even get my goddamn mission commander to talk to me. All of the frustration and fear boiled up and over and out in a froth. "Goddamn it, Leonard. I'm supposed to be your second-in-command. Stop it with the damn lies."

Leonard blinked at me. People get this idea of me that I'm demure and gentle and they forget that I'm a pilot until I start cursing. I leaned into his surprise, because it was the only break I'd found in his armor.

"For fuck's sake. There was blood inside DeBeer's boot. There are spatters of blood in the hall of this level. A patch in the garage. Hashmarks in the goddamn south airlock, which has a broken intercom. Dawn painted over racist language. Here's what I think . . . I think that DeBeer was shitty and racist and that things got out of hand and eventually y'all locked him in the south airlock."

I have heard that Leonard is very good on poker nights. His surprise at my language was gone. He just stared at me and slowly nodded. "I can see how you could infer that from the items you've mentioned."

I rolled my eyes at the deflection. "So, that's a 'yes.'"

"That's an 'I can see how you could infer that.'"

I snorted. "What I don't understand is why you didn't tell me before we got here and why you are so determined to keep it a secret now."

"Do you remember how you used to send coded messages to Nathaniel?"

"The ones where I was accused of being a spy when I was just trying to talk to my husband?"

"And do you remember how Florence and I asked you not to help? On more than one occasion?"

I gaped at him. "I did stop."

"No. You just changed tactics." Leonard swiveled in his chair to face me. "You are fundamentally incapable of seeing a problem and not trying to fix it. The things that happened on the last mission were not fixable."

"We could have talked to Mission Control or—"

"You see how you're trying to fix it now, it's—"

"Bradbury Base, Sunflower Mission Control." Parker's voice popped into my left ear, making me jump. "Hey, York . . . listen, I know that you're mad at me about the directive to move the women back up to the *Goddard*. I need you to back me on it, though."

My heart was still thundering in my chest from the argument with Leonard. There was nothing wrong with trying to fix things. And now it was literally my job and he wasn't giving me the tools—

Meanwhile, Parker was continuing to talk. "We've got a real situation down here. Wargin had to pull all sorts of favors to get me into the interim director position. You remember Gilbert Mason?"

I did. He had been a senator from North Carolina and had spent his career promising to end the space program. I'd testified in front of him at congressional hearings and he had been officious and either willfully oblivious or an idiot.

"She had to give him the UN ambassador position—the reasons why don't matter, but he is angling in the UN to become the head of the agency with promises to bring costs down and improve safety. The usual racket. He doesn't understand anything about the space program but he's talking a good talk about 'keeping our people safe.' He'd been putting pressure on the IAC already and Clemons had the track record to resist. I don't. I need to make a mark and I need to make a compromise. I promise it's temporary." As he talked, Leonard and I were staring at each other. "Look—you know me. I will not bullshit you. I *promise* that this is temporary, but if Grey and Schnöhaus release one of your films again, then Mason will use it to say that I can't control the agency. Please. Please, this is me, *begging* you, to not fight me this one time. Please get all the ladies back up to the *Goddard* until I'm confirmed. Then we can say it's safe later when it's time to bring everybody back down to the colony. Do you understand? Over."

"That's nice." I'd been working on training the word "colony" out of my vocabulary and somehow fixated on it when he just dropped it in there. I was still thundering with rage, but years of training kept me from out right cursing on a hot mic. "Bless your heart, Parker . . . I'm surprised given your love of language that you've never objected to the word 'colony.' Now here's the thing. You know there are women with expertises that are needed down here now. Most of the greenhouse team, for instance. We'd lose most of our suit techs. I don't know that we can move all the women to the *Goddard*. I'm going to have to talk to Leonard about it, though, because ultimately, it's not my decision. Over."

I sat back in my chair and made sure the mic was off. My hands were shaking, I was so mad. "What do you think?"

Leonard stared at the ceiling and shook his head. "He's right that you have the weight to fight him on it. The question is, should you, and . . . I don't want to ask you to, but my concern is that following his plan will make things less safe, not more safe."

I nodded. "The crew did cross-training but not that much. We'd lose key personnel."

He pressed his palms together, tapping the forefingers. His eyes were tight and his gaze darted back and forth as he thought. "We could just straight-up lie, but that'll make reports harder. Which in turn will make asking for help harder when we need it."

"Yeah . . ." I chewed the inside of my lip. There had to be a flight path through—what did I know about Parker that could help here?

I spent part of the wait thinking through the years I had known him. He was less volatile than he had been when we'd met—although in hindsight, that had been in the middle of a war—but he'd always been dismissive of women. Mind you, he thought he was gallant. But at his core, all along, he was a pilot. That was true now, too, no matter how much he was trying to remake himself in politics. He was always a pilot and would default to the structure he'd learned in the Air Force.

I turned toward Leonard, teasing an idea out of the thinnest of possibilities. "York. Wargin. Grey. Schnöhaus. What does Parker call you?"

"What?" Leonard rocked his gaze back down. "Flannery. Why?"

"Surnames. What if we do duty rosters that are surnames only? Let the IAC assume that we're following instructions and it's all men."

"Huh." He rubbed his forehead. "Except most of the couples aren't in the same department."

"True . . . and we'd still have to switch who was on comms down here, because that's voice sometimes."

"We've got enough warning on those that we could pull someone from engineering in to cover a voice call." He nodded toward the door. "They're just across the hall."

"Good luck getting any of them to respond in a timely mann—"

Parker's voice was in my ear, chuckling. "Wow. I did piss you off. Cursing on a hot mic like that? Over 'colony'? Come on, York, it's a standard term. On the front about moving the lady *colonists* up to the *Goddard*, I love that you think it isn't your decision. Leonard and I had this whole long talk about how you get when the bit is in your mouth. You are on Mars because you fought for it. I thought that I could keep you out of space altogether and was very wrong. And yes, I just admitted that I was wrong about something, go ahead, I can hear you being smug from here. But . . ."

He sighed and the sound took me back to flying with him in a T-38. Even when we had hated each other, he had been a generous and patient teacher. It had always given me a glimpse of this other person that I had finally gotten to know after a decade of working together. I mean, he still picked people to hate, but if you weren't on that list, you only got charming Parker.

"I knew this wouldn't work, so . . . I'm passing the mic to Wargin and leaving the room."

I bet that Leonard and I looked really funny from the outside because we did a double take straight out of the cartoons. Nicole was in the room with Parker and he was only just now mentioning that?

"Hello, Elma." Nicole's patrician voice strolled onto Mars like she owned it. "I'm assuming that Leonard is there and listening in, so hello to you as well. Knowing you, I'm also assuming that you will have already figured out a workaround to the directive. Parker is still getting up to speed, so I need you to get the women to the *Goddard* and the men to Mars before he does. Nathaniel's plan has you scavenging an engine from the *Goddard*. That's going to mean a lot of spacewalks. And if we do Parker's plan, then that means that all of the most hazardous work will be done by an all-woman crew. Let's send a very clear message about what we're capable of, hmm? Over."

"That's audacious. Aren't you worried about what will happen if one of us gets injured or makes a mistake? But—I trust you and your assessment of the situation on the ground. We'll make it work. But I have conditions. One, change the official language to replace the words 'colony' and 'colonist.' Suggestions are 'habitat' and . . .'" I still hadn't gotten a good suggestion to replace the word "colonist." "And something that's not English at least. Two, we need clear communications from the ground. We're not getting the reports that we need. Like what happened with that cargo drop? Why didn't we know it was smashed? Also, hello and how are you? Over."

I sat back and glared at Leonard. "So you had a long talk about me? 'Bit in my mouth'?"

Leonard spread his hands. "Parker told me that you have this image of yourself that you're deferential but when you get an idea that a thing needs to be a certain way, that's the way it's going to be. Like, for instance . . . 'colony.'"

"Habitat. And that's why you won't tell me what happened?"

"It was four years ago, Elma. Let it drop." Leonard sounded genuinely annoyed. "It doesn't have anything to do with any of the very real problems we have in front of us."

He wanted me to ignore the fact that multiple people who had been on the First Expedition were lying to me. If I pushed, he'd just say that it was me with the "bit in my mouth." I ground my teeth together and turned my head so that I wasn't glaring at him, just at the microphone. "Fine. Then let's work the problem. Medical. Both of our doctors are women."

"Well, shit." Leonard ran his hands over his face. "Do you think Parker remembers that?"

"He will." So I had been a problem worth having a meeting over. And what were they even talking about? I took back seat all the time. The only time I was out in front was when publicity was forcing me to be a shield. And they were mad at me because I tried to fix things? Fine. They could damn well let things break then. I grabbed my anger and strangled it so I could focus on the mission. "What do you think we should do about the medical staff?"

"Kam and Ana Teresa have backups. Sheldon Spender could cover."

I shook my head and then tried to soften it. "Sheldon Spender is a great guy. As our inventory specialist, will his emergency medical training be enough if there's a serious injury?"

The only time I got stubborn about something was when I was right. Men could do that, but heaven forfend a woman have an opinion. Except that Nicole could get away with it.

Leonard pursed his lips. "He was approved as a backup. You and I both vetted the final lists. Are you saying he *can't* do the job?"

"Of course. You're absolutely right. I'm sure Sheldon will do a great job."

He sighed and threw his pencil on the desk. "Okay. So, what? We leave Kam down here?"

I kept trying not to fume and to prove that I was a team player. Again. "I'm sorry. I'm frustrated. We're pulling someone who's the best suited due to political pressures. I hate this. I hate it so much."

"What happens if we do keep Kam down?" Leonard sat forward. "What if we use your surname idea?"

"Kam's not married." But I wanted it to work. I gnawed on my lower lip trying to find a path through. "It's not like there's another Dr. Shamoun on the mission."

"But 'Kam' sounds like a man's name. Circling back to your point of frustration . . . the issue isn't that Mission Control or Parker thinks Kam is a problem. It's that Ambassador Mason wants the women off Mars. So, to rephrase my question from earlier. Will *he* remember who Dr. Kam Shamoun is? If all of our reports talk about the men on Mars, then Kam could just blend in as one of the guys."

"We'll have to get Parker to buy into that."

"So let's ask him. And if he doesn't buy it, then we find out what plan he's proposing." Leonard looked at the clock. "Seven more minutes. Let's run through the other departments."

We spent the remaining time working through the staffing and by the end it almost felt like we were on the same page again.

But I was honestly grateful when Nicole finally responded. "That's good news. Thank you. Parker? You can come back in—" In the distance, I could hear the timbre of his voice, but couldn't make out the words. "Mm-hm. She'll do it, and this is a reminder that I'm on a hot mic. While he's getting the headset back on, I'm largely fine and am enjoying the freedom of being in my second term. Ah—Parker, Elma wants you to change the official language from 'colony' to 'habitat' and to drop 'colonist' in favor of a non-English title. Given your store of languages I suspect this will be a fun game. While we're at it, I'd like you to stop calling them 'manned' missions, but I'll make my case for that with you later. She would also like assurances that the people at the habitat will get the information they request in a timely manner. I trust that you can provide that. She also wants to know about the cargo drop and, frankly, so would I."

"Seriously? She's holding me hostage over 'colo'—ow—yes. Fine. 'Habitat.' I'm guessing the German *kolonist* won't fly. Maybe the Arabic *sakin* or, oooooh, the French *habitant* would play well with habitat. Or would it be confusing over comms? Damn it."

I could hear his polyglot love of languages kick in, and while it had not been a tactic, I was glad that my flailing about for a "colonist" replacement had given him some excitement. It made him forget to be mad at me for challenging him. For the moment at any rate.

"I'll work on it. On the other points. Yes, absolutely on the information flow. Confirmed. The cargo drop . . . that's still under investigation. The satellite photos of the area are tagged as 'clear' but all of them are obscured by cloud cover. The two theories that were on Clemons's desk were that the mislabeling was either active sabotage by someone who deliberately didn't run the scan of the area again or that it was just human error."

In the silence, I thought I heard the soft thwap of a ball hitting the palm of his hand, but that was probably my imagination, remembering the way he used to toss one in the air when he was in the CAPCOM seat. He wouldn't be there, he would be in Clemons's office.

"As soon as we know, I'll share that with you. Meanwhile, thank you for not fighting me—even if I had to bring in the president of the United States—hey! Seriously, though, thank you for agreeing to be in charge of the *Goddard*. It'll give me time to fix things. Parker, over and out."

And then they were gone.

"We didn't talk about Kam. Do you want me to reinitiate the call?" I started to reach for the console.

"No. No, I think I'll check with Kam, first. Get the good doctor's take on it and then we can do a follow-up." He hesitated. "You know Kam is . . ."

I nodded, remembering the way our doctor had transformed over the course of the First Expedition, starting with a haircut and then a change of names. Parker had set the tone by not even blinking, which had surprised me. He was such a pilot and such a sexist asshole and then sometimes surprisingly compassionate. I think being away from Earth gave us all more space to be ourselves.

But it was also something we didn't talk about. I straightened the cords of my headset. "Will it be safe? If Kam stays down?"

"I'll make it safe." Leonard scrubbed his face and stared at the ceiling. "But I'll let it be Kam's call. And if I'm feeling generous, I'll ask Helen to use her codebook to give Parker a warning."

"Don't let it be a surprise. Please." Because Parker's thanks reminded me of how things had changed on the First Expedition as he'd started to trust me. He'd started to see me as a friend. It had been a disorienting change, because if you were on his good list, he would give you unflinching loyalty. He just expected it back.

That was the problem—*one* of the problems with Parker . . . When he trusted you, it was possible to betray him and that was not something he forgave.

This change in staffing—the thing that was only just starting to percolate into my brain was that I wasn't going to be back seat. I was going to be the captain of the *Goddard*.

Parker was trusting me. And when you're in charge there are a lot more opportunities to mess everything up.

PART II

TWENTY

GODDARD BECOMES REFUGE
FOR WOMEN ASTRONAUTS

KANSAS CITY, April 13, 1970—In a strategic reorganization of the Second Mars Expedition, the women astronauts who were part of the initial landing party are being relocated to the *Goddard* spacecraft. The *Goddard*, which delivered the expedition to Mars, will now serve as a sanctuary for these trailblazing astronettes. Simultaneously, plans are underway to shuttle down the forty men remaining in orbit in two separate trips. Stetson Parker, acting director for the International Aerospace Coalition, said, "Our top priority is the optimal functioning of the mission for both the astronauts on the *Goddard* and the ones in our Martian habitat, and this reorganization allows us to uphold that objective." As the brave men prepare for their descent to the Martian surface, the women will keep the home fires burning aboard the *Goddard* until it is safe for them to return.

Aprim 4, Year 5, Sunsol-Landing + 65 sols

Through the thin walls, I could hear other couples having one last morning of conjugal bliss before we split the teams. Nathaniel and I lay curled on the bottom bunk. His chest was a solid presence and I stretched, pressing back into him. His right arm was draped over my ribs and he pulled me in tighter.

I felt his attention and rolled in his arms. "Dr. York . . . my

202 * MARY ROBINETTE KOWAL

procedure manual indicates that a condom would be in order now."

"Is that so, Dr. York? Well, we can't skip a step on the checklist." He reached for the box shoved under his pillow, but there was something flattened in his smile.

I put my hand on his side as he stretched. "Nathaniel?"

He paused with his hand under the pillow and then rolled onto his back, holding the foil wrapper. "I just . . . I was just thinking about, you know, your change."

"Perimenopause." My period still hadn't started, so we had no idea if I was fertile or not. When I'd told him that I wasn't pregnant, he had seemed relieved. He did not look relieved now. "What were you thinking about it?"

"That we're having to be more careful than we've ever been. It's not that I mind wearing one, it's just . . . I don't know, maybe because they are so rationed and here we're using two in one sol. It makes me . . . it really drives home the fact that I won't see you for months." He kissed my neck and laid his cheek against me. "I'm going to miss you."

"This will be shorter than my missions to the Moon."

"On the Moon, you weren't disassembling a rocket engine in space."

Missing me and worrying about me were two different things. I rested my hand on his cheek. "And on Earth, you weren't building a heat pump in a Mars suit."

He drew a circle around my navel. "That's mostly the geology and construction teams. All of the wiring I'm doing will be inside."

"Mm-hm . . ."

He grimaced and took the circle wider. "Okay, a little is outside, but only one trip."

"And how many spacewalks have you done?"

"It's a Marswalk." He shifted so that he was holding himself up on one elbow. "And it depends on how you count it. I was going back and forth a lot during unloading."

"I count it as suiting up. So, two." I ran my hand down his

chest and slipped over the smooth scar on his stomach from his ulcer repair. "Promise me that you'll eat while I'm gone."

Nathaniel's hand stopped. "I don't—it's not intentional. I just . . . I just get busy."

"That sounds like a preemptive excuse." I squeezed his side. "I need you to promise. You can come up with engineering solutions for almost everything. Come up with one for this."

He sighed and looked toward the end of the bed, lips curling in like he was biting them. He sighed again and the scar shifted under my hand. "Nicole had suggested that I get a lunch buddy at work. I will ask Reynard."

"Thank you." I pulled him down to rest across me and then had to shift because my breasts were still tender. It was deeply annoying. "And what about the other meals?"

"I don't know." He ran his hand up to my hairline. His gaze traced my face as if he were trying to memorize it. "But I promise I'll come up with a system."

"Make a checklist."

"You." He grinned and leaned in to kiss my nose. "Are such an astronaut."

"I am." I drew my knee up along his side. "And I think it's time to resume the countdown for one more liftoff."

Four hours later, Opal and I were strapped into our seats, ready for launch. Florence sat in the NavComp seat and kept looking at her checklist and then fiddling with her slide rule. She'd trained as backup NavComp but had clearly not expected to actually need to deploy those skills. With all the men staying behind, that put Opal in the copilot seat instead of Leonard.

But in my helmet, Dawn's voice still sounded over comms. "The countdown is now approaching T-minus five minutes. Initiate abort/recycle procedures."

Helen, Dawn, and Zainabu were staying behind to bring our second lander, the *Matsu,* back up after the first group of men came down. The plan to get everyone where they needed to be was like that riddle about the fox, chicken, and bag of grain, with the gravity well being the river. If you need to keep one lander on Mars and one on orbit, and you can only fit twenty people including pilots in a lander, how many trips does it take to get everyone where they need to be?

"Roger that, Bradbury. Initiating BFS safing." I reached for the Backup Flight System controls and entered the command "O6 GPC MODE 5—HALT."

Beside me, Opal went to her next checklist item. "MOX safing in progress."

"Copy that. Initiate APU shutdown on my mark." Dawn's voice was a comforting familiarity. "Mark."

I flipped the switch. "APU shutdown in progress."

"Heater reconfiguration complete." As Opal watched the gauge, my spine tightened a little.

This is where we had stopped the countdown before. Because of Clemons. Damn it. All of my early memories of launches involved him standing at the back of the room in a haze of cigar smoke.

"Very good. Proceed with MPS heater reconfiguration."

As I waited for the heater to process, my gaze lifted briefly from the banks of switches to the window. Beyond it, a wisp of a cloud drifted across a pale pink sky. The light on the console drew my gaze back. "MPS heater reconfiguration complete."

And then Dawn said the magic words. "NavComp, launch trajectory is a Go."

Florence let out a sigh that triggered her VOX. "Copy that, launching trajectory and checking system summary."

I put my hands on the controllers. "Checking main engine gimbal profile. Stand by for motion."

Rocking the controls through their quadrants of motion made slight vibrations run through the seat and up my spine. A smile spread across my face as I felt my ship come to life.

Returning the gimbals to neutral, I lifted my hands and looked over at Opal. "Close tabs and visors. Turn on LES oxygen."

As if it were choreographed, and after all the sims, I guess it was, we both reached up and closed our visors, locking the helmets in place and switched to ship oxygen. A tinny metal hiss replaced the ship air as O_2 wooshed up and over the vent in my helmet.

A chorus of women's voices repeated the call back to me. "Tabs and visor closed, LES oxygen on."

I don't think I'd ever heard that before without male voices mixed in.

Ten. I exhaled, conscious of directing my breath away from my mic so that I didn't accidentally trigger the VOX. *Nine.* I put my hands on the controllers. *Eight.* Florence rested her hand over the clock. *Seven.* I rested my head against the back of my helmet. *Six.* Inhale. *Five.* My stomach muscles tightened in anticipation of launch forces. *Four.* Throttle and the *Esther* lurched as the main engine ignited. *Three.* A roar built beneath us. *Two.* Exhale. *One.*

Liftoff.

Florence started the mission clock as we began our rise. Mars reached into my seat and pulled me down. It was gentler than the Earth. The squeeze against my chest built in a slow crush as I watched the instruments and the sky beyond them.

There is no sim on any world that can truly prepare you for riding a column of fire into the sky. The *Esther* vibrated in ways that were familiar and also new. The ride was softer than I had expected.

"Roll's complete and the pitch is programmed."

"Everything is looking good."

"One Bravo." Florence watched the gauges for the information I needed.

From the ground, Dawn said, *"Esther,* Bradbury. You're good at one minute."

"Roger."

As we rose, any thoughts I had about the gentleness vanished as the months of living at 1/3 *g* made the *g* load of liftoff feel

206 ★ MARY ROBINETTE KOWAL

like three times that. I kept my diaphragm tight and breathed through my mouth in a pattern that honestly sounded like I was constipated.

The sound abruptly faded and took the vibrations with it. Instruments—the instruments were all green. A laugh surprised its way out of me. "We already hit max q. I guess that's an advantage of a thin atmosphere."

"Elma, Opal. Look at the sky." Florence had taken this ride before.

"Wha—oh." Opal's voice broke.

Outside, the sky was brightening from rose to a deep blue that made my heart hurt. Over the comms, I heard someone make a soft "Oh" of wonder and I think it was me.

"Bradbury Base, *Esther*, everything okay?"

"The sky is blue, on the way up . . . Earth-sky blue." I swallowed. "It's getting dark now. Heading into night."

The main engine cutoff, when it came, was an anticlimax because it was so familiar. The silence and that brief moment where you feel the pressure from the harness as your body keeps flying upward. And then we were on orbit.

Six hours later, I had done a docking that I'd done so many times over the years that I'd lost count. Some had been with the *Goddard* during training or to do hull checks during the trip out. Some had been with *Lunetta* or the Orbital Telescope. Some of the dockings had been with the *Pinta* or *Niña* on the First Mars Expedition.

Not that the *Esther* was a BusyBee, but all of them used the same basic flight path to the same docking configuration. All of them had been slow and careful, because space is not a place where you want a collision of any sort.

Where things changed was with the hatch opening.

Each ship was different. Floating into the large work hangar of *Lunetta* felt expansive, while the long spindle of the *Niña* had felt almost cozy. The *Goddard* had the same basic configuration as the *Niña*, with a long spindle running through three additional centrifugal rings to accommodate the larger crew.

During the six-hour trip to the *Goddard*, we had stripped out of our suits, and weightlessness felt like coming home. But home was Mars, now. Still, it would be good to see our friends up here. I opened the hatch, and the interior of the *Esther* flooded with music.

A band waited in the spindle, with their feet hooked under rails, playing "Chattanooga Choo Choo." It was a joyous and raucous sound that stopped me mid-transit, so I forgot to grab a rail and floated up. I had to correct with a hand against the ceiling like a rookie. Florence had the opposite reaction and came to a sudden, startled halt on one handrail. Behind me, I heard a chorus of surprised laughter.

The music was so joyful that my face hurt with smiling. I saw Ida Peaks and Darlene Ritika on flute, Ray Rotor with his guitar, Chan Tzu Pheng on the erhu, Peter Alsdorf on the dizi, and Anita Lindgren on clarinet. Near her, Modesto Westenberg and Linda Grossman played trumpets and Josh Lawrence had his euphonium, while Halim floated at the front playing an oboe. Beyond them, it looked like the rest of the crew had filled the spindle and as the song came to an end, they burst into a cheer.

Halim raised his oboe, and as a group, they chorused, "Welcome to the *Goddard*!"

"Oh my word." I grinned at Halim and pushed off to hug him. "What prompted this?"

"It's not every sol we get visitors." Holding his oboe to the side, he gave me a one-armed hug. "And also, twenty of us are heading down this week. This is a welcome and a send-off."

Then he turned to welcome Nuan Su and the others as I got pulled into the crowd and passed from friend to friend.

Ida's hug was fierce and her flute pressed against my spine like extra armor. "After your dinner, we've got a 99s reunion planned. If you are up for it."

"I am literally up for it." I squeezed her arm as I let her go. Ida and I had been members of the same 99s club of women pilots on Earth. At the time, the idea that we would all be on orbit around Mars was inconceivable. "Where do we meet you?"

"We've got the observatory reserved."

The group vanished into various spokes leading from the spindle and down to the centrifugal rings, so the crowd seemed to drain away.

Halim grinned and hooked a thumb toward the spoke on our left. "Ladies! We've got dinner waiting for you."

"That sounds swell." I pushed off with my toes and grabbed the handrail to change my state vector and followed him into the spoke. It was a long narrow tube with a ladder running along one side of it. At the top of the ladder, I had to pull myself down, and then gravity began to make itself known.

Grinning, I put my feet on the outside of the ladder rails and slid down the last couple of meters the way I used to. Funny, the things you miss. I kicked a little free of the ladder so that I could clear it for Florence.

And I failed to compensate for the Coriolis effect. The ship turned around me and I staggered, as "down" wasn't quite where I expected it to be.

Halim caught me under the elbow. "I see you have your ground legs."

"I got cocky." I laughed as I got my feet under me and straightened carefully. Florence stood at the bottom of the ladder and she was bright enough to hold on to the rail as she turned.

Savory aromas of tomato sauce and melted cheese wafted on the circulated air. Aahana lifted her nose and sniffed. "Is that . . . is that lasagna?"

"We have salad, too." Halim grinned and beckoned us all into the cafeteria, which was the entirety of a module, and long enough to see the curvature of the floor. Behind the aluminum counters, the kitchen team worked with induction burners and ovens to make a wider range of food than we had the capability to do on Mars. Someday. Someday, Mars would have salad.

"Fresh greens?" Catalina looked like she was going to swoon. "You are my absolute hero."

Someone had made a welcome banner out of old procedure pages and taped it along the top of one wall. People I knew and had worked with for years saw us, waving and grinning. I wanted to stop and give everyone hugs, but . . .

But there was an old familiar stickiness originating in my nethers. Seriously? Now? I tightened everything I could, as if that ever helps.

It marked the first time that I was absolutely delighted to be wearing a diaper.

Aprim 5, Year 5, Monsol-Landing + 66 sols

When I got to Halim's office the morning after we arrived, he was unpinning a paper banner from the wall over his desk. The deep blue paper had dense Arabic calligraphy swirling across it. At the start of the voyage, he'd told me that the letters were a line from the Quran that translated as, "O assembly of Jinn and men! If you can pass beyond the zones of the heavens and the earth, then pass!"

Halim looked over his shoulder as he removed the last pin. "Ah, Elma. Good morning. Is it time already?"

"You have fifteen."

"Swell. I'm going to leave the fabric wall hanging, if that is all right."

Opposite his desk, a geometric cloth in blues and golds against a neutral background stretched from floor to ceiling and made the tiny office feel like we weren't on a spaceship. "It's more than all right." I shoved my hands in my pockets and leaned against the door. "Do you need help packing up the rug?"

"Hm? Oh, no." He rolled the banner into a tight tube. "No, that's for whoever the commander is. Which in half an hour will be you. Unless you don't want it?"

"The captain's seat?" I had such mixed feelings. Even though the *Goddard* would never leave Mars orbit again, it was still one of the big rockets. We would need to maneuver occasionally to adjust orbit. I would take my flying where I could. And also, I would gladly give up being the commander, but he didn't want to hear doubt or fear. "I mean, it looks like you just do paperwork."

"Funny." Halim slid the banner into a cardboard tube. He'd gotten to actually fly the *Goddard* on the trip from Earth to Mars. "The rug. If you don't want it, I could—"

"I do." The rug was one of the most beautiful things on the *Goddard*. Halim had used some of his weight allowance to bring up a small, vibrant red rug, which had a deeper burgundy border with organic flowing shapes, framing a diamond medallion in the middle. "But it's . . . it's not a prayer rug?"

He laughed at me. "Sorry—sorry, no. I wouldn't keep that on the floor for anyone to walk on. No, this is just something I liked. Being commander of the ship is mostly paperwork and meetings, so having a small luxury? It seemed like a good thing to do for the team."

"I aspire to be half as good at leadership as you are." My stomach had been tying itself in knots all morning. Some of that was my period and the rest was regular old anxiety. On paper it made perfect sense for me to take over as commander of the *Goddard*, since Halim was heading down to the surface. I'd been Leonard's second, and I was the most senior of the astronauts after Halim. I swallowed the sour burn at the back of my throat. "Are you looking forward to seeing Mars?"

"You'll be fine, Elma." He winked at me, then bent to tuck the tube into his carryall. "And yes, I am. I have been intensely jealous of you all."

I glanced at my watch. "We should translate over there."

"I really don't need a fancy ceremony."

"I know, but the crew does." He had been the commander of the *Goddard* for more than a year. Even if I hadn't thought it was right to do a real send-off for him the way we did for commander changeovers on *Lunetta*, I had been approached by no fewer than three crew people who wanted to know when the command change ceremony would be.

He sighed. "I know. Do something twice in space, and it's a tradition. Do it three times, and it's a long-held tradition."

"Just be happy Parker hates publicity as much as we do, or he'd make us broadcast it."

"Thank you, no." Halim shuddered and picked up his bag. "I'm dreading when he forgets what being an astronaut is like."

"You think he will?"

"It was hard for me to remember as chief astronaut." Halim stopped at the door of his office and looked back in, sighing, before he flipped off the light. "That's part of why I assigned myself to this mission before I stepped down."

One of the perks of being chief astronaut was that, in exchange for putting up with meetings, paperwork, and personnel squabbles, you got to assign yourself to a plum position when you stepped down. It suddenly occurred to me that Halim would have to have known about whatever happened on the First Expedition.

"Say . . . apropos of nothing. Do you know what happened with DeBeer?"

He rolled his eyes. "The man is a monster. I wanted to pull him from the first mission before you were even assigned, but Clemons insisted that we needed the South African funding."

We arrived at the foot of the ladder up to the spindle. "There's a place where he painted the n-word."

"I know." He winced, slinging the strap of his bag over his head. "When they were on the surface, we were getting nearly constant reports, but . . . I have to give the shrinks some credit. After we had them talk to him and a couple of other crew members things seemed to straighten out."

"That's surprising." I started up the ladder, feeling the gravity load come off with each rung.

Below me, Halim said, "I didn't think it would work, but the flight surgeons and their damn protocols insisted. What brought it to mind?"

"Just thinking about the things waiting for you on the surface. Dawn put a mural over it that's beautiful but you can still sorta see the original letters." We hit the tipping point and I pulled on the ladder, propelling myself up into the weightless joy of the spindle. At the top, I grabbed the handrail and changed my vector to curve into the long hollow tube that ran the length of the *Goddard*.

Halim popped out, bag floating against his back. He tucked and curled neatly to align himself with my "up." With the natural grace of a space dweller, he hooked a foot under one rail while he realigned his bag with one hand. "Well, he's not coming back on the next mission or any of the rest. There are plenty of South African astronauts who are not assholes about their racism."

I stared at him. "You . . . you let them come, even if they are racist?"

Halim looked down the long stretch of the spindle and his mouth twisted as if he'd eaten something he regretted. "Elma . . . and I mean no offense by this, but coming to work at the IAC, which, though an international organization, is based in the United States, I have learned that everyone I work with is racist. Some of you try not to be."

My pulse buzzed in time with the fans in the spindle. I didn't know where to look or what to say.

"DeBeer embraced it and believed that his prejudice made him a better person. His government agrees with him, but . . . but Clemons discussed the problem with them and convinced them that other South Africans with less 'firm' beliefs would have 'an easier time in our international work environment.'" He wiped his hands together and glanced at his watch. "Shall we? The masses await."

"Absolutely." I kicked off, supermanning down the spindle to the next ladder entrance. We had been at the administrative and science ring, which housed offices and laboratory modules.

I slowed at the D-ladder on Ring 2, which housed the kitchens, gardens, and recreation modules. Catching the rail with one hand, I twisted into the tube, rotating to face the ladder. For the first several rungs, I had to pull myself downward, and then the gravity well caught me and sucked me down the ladder. I put my feet on the outside of the rails and pressed my hands against them, metal hissing against my skin as I dropped. Tightening my thighs slowed my descent to a constant and manageable state.

When I emerged from the ceiling of the module, I kicked free to land with a small bounce at the bottom. I stumbled a little, which was embarrassing, but not as bad as the sol before. I'd just gotten the direction of the centrifugal spin wrong.

Fortunately, I recovered before Halim landed.

Even carrying a bag, he hit the ground and controlled his rebound as if he'd been born moving from zero-g to one-third gravity with a Coriolis effect. He even naturally compensated for the spin. I'd get there. I'd been there on the trip out, but the reacclimation period was still annoying.

Together, we walked into the Large Meeting Assembly room. The LMA was where we ate, had meetings, and did maintenance work that required more room, like prepping cables. Or having a command handoff. The wall of sound that hit me when we entered the LMA made me stop for a moment. After months being one of only twenty people on Mars, the full complement on the *Goddard* was overwhelming.

Tomorrow, our number would drop from eighty-six to sixty-six as twenty men descended to Mars. Right now, the LMA was a swarm of activity. Some people were sitting. A clump was trying to keep a balloon aloft as it twisted in the air with the spin of the ship. I spotted a group of Jewish folks along one wall and could tell by Osher Pereira's body language that he was having a theological discussion that was probably related to what time it was in Jerusalem or maybe complaining again about the rabbis who said that on Mars, given our small numbers, women could complete a minyan or how Kabbalah would need to be adapted. Rachel G. was actively laughing at him and Rachel B. had her head in her hands. But Daniel Shapiro was leaning into whatever argument it was.

"Oh boy . . ." Halim swung his bag off and dropped it next to the door. "You sure you want this crew?"

"I'd rather be on Mars."

"Me, too." He scanned the room and spotted the *Goddard*'s inventory specialist, Sheldon Spender. Beckoning, he pointed across the room to the small "stage" that was built against one wall. It was really an arrangement of packing crates coffin-locked together so that they couldn't shift.

Sheldon met us there and handed Halim a logbook. "I want you to appreciate that I stopped Gagarin and Haise from having a literal pissing match."

"Well done, and of course it was those two."

"They're going with you to the surface, right?" I made very firm eye contact with Halim. "Right?"

"First ship down." He slapped the logbook against one palm and bounded on stage. Putting his fingers in his mouth, he made an ear-splitting whistle. "Friends, crewmates, and Martians, lend me your ears."

Sheldon snorted under his breath even as the room quieted.

The lights caught in the silver hairs at Halim's temples as he turned his head to regard the crew. "I have been proud of you for years but never prouder than I am now. Many of you I hired. But I have trained with all of you for the past three years as we prepared for this mission. You have been steadfast, goofy, and a joy to work with. I look forward to spending time with you on Mars and seeing what you get up to now that I'm no longer in charge."

"A lot more shit!" someone shouted from the back.

Halim laughed and then waggled his finger. "You say that, but given who your next commander is, you know that is not true. If you get out of line, your next commander can quiet you to death."

The room went hot all over as everyone turned to look at me and the old desire to run made the muscles in my calves tense. Practice let me laugh at Halim and mostly mean it. I put my hands on my hips to mask their shaking. "Y'all don't want me to be disappointed in you, do you?"

Halim made an exaggerated shudder and beckoned me onto the stage. "Come on, let's get this over with."

I climbed onto the crates to stand beside him. "Halim, I've known you since you joined the astronaut corps. I think I speak for all of us when I say that serving with you is always an honor." Straightening my shoulders, I moved to the part of the ritual that I had seen multiple times but had never taken part in. "Commander Malouf, I stand ready to relieve you."

"I am ready to be relieved." He held out the logbook. "Your ship is in good repair and the personnel are as solid a group as one could ask for."

"Thank you." I took the logbook in both hands and it seemed to carry its own localized gravity field.

"Also, for the real emergencies." He fished in one of his flight suit's pockets and pulled out a small bar of chocolate.

My eyes widened because a bar of chocolate was irreplaceable out here. "I will guard it and deploy only when necessary."

"Then I have no further duties."

The air in my lungs was cold. "I relieve you, commander."

Halim grinned and stuck out his hand to shake mine. "I stand relieved."

And with those words, the command of the *Goddard* became mine.

TWENTY-ONE

CHINA HINTS AT A MANNED SPACE PROGAM

By John Noble Wilford

April 19, 1970—China published yesterday the first clear hint that it might have plans for a manned space program.

An article in the *Peking Daily Kwangming Jih Pao* said that a recent unmanned space flight, which apparently demonstrated the capability not only to orbit a spacecraft but also to bring the capsule back to Earth, constituted an "important aspect in the development of the technology of manned artificial satellites."

American space observers said that the newspaper article was the first public acknowledgment by the Chinese of what some International Aerospace Coalition experts had grown to suspect in recent weeks.

Aprim 10, Year 5, Satursol-Landing + 71 sols

Even though it was less than a week since we had seen Helen, Dawn, and Zainabu, it seemed right that they should get the same welcome we did.

Which is why we were crowded in the spindle, waiting for the airlock hatch to open. I didn't play an instrument, so I floated to the side and let Sue McBerry and her orchestra fill the space in front of the hatch. It was a different configuration than last time, since she'd lost some of her musicians.

And tomorrow morning, we would send the *Esther* back down with the second set of twenty men on it. After that there would only be forty-nine people on a station built for a hundred. All women.

The ripple-bang sounded through the corridor and Sue swung the orchestra into a rendition of "The One I Yearn For" by Yi-Feng Hong. With accordion, tambor drum, a smaller horn section, and our string players, the spindle became a resonant hall of joyful sound.

Helen's face, shocked with mouth dropped open and eyes wide with delight, was everything I could wish for. As she drifted into the spindle, Dawn and Zainabu floated out, both with grins brightening their faces.

Zainabu abandoned the foot rails and began dancing to the music in zero-g exuberance. She swung in front of me, and I found myself dancing with her. Heidi launched herself over the band to Dawn and swung her into a fierce hug that transformed into a dance. The movement seemed to ripple down the spindle, and moments later, everyone who didn't have an instrument had followed our lead and found a partner or danced in a group.

Do something twice in space, and it's a tradition. Do it three times, and it's a long-held tradition. I would not mind this much joy becoming a long-held tradition.

When the shrinks had asked me what "enrichment activities" I wanted, I'd asked for baking, and they'd doubled my requests in that beautiful IAC redundancy. The *Goddard* had a full kitchen, which was a joy and a comfort.

But the thing that was best?

The *Goddard* had butter. Real butter, frozen in glorious blocks of creamy wonder. I worked the butter into the flour and felt the tension in my shoulders evaporate. The kitchen was quiet after the welcome dinner, and having time to myself felt like the most precious of gifts.

Helen walked into the kitchen. "Oh good, I had hoped I would find you alone."

"That sounds suspicious." The week since the handoff had

been largely devoted to paperwork and meetings. Helen had just come up so wouldn't start in the duty roster until tomorrow. "What's up?"

She walked to the intercom and turned it all the way off. "The hashmarks in the south airlock. I asked Graeham about them."

My hands stilled as I stared at her. "What did he say?"

She leaned against one of the broad counters. "He said that they had been storing things there and that he'd forgotten to bring a pad in to do inventory so scratched on the wall."

"That is wildly out of character for him." The British astronaut had always been very thorough. "And also, Leonard said they were counting sols before they left."

She nodded. "I did not note the discrepancy to him, but yes, it occurred to me as well."

"Did he have a reason for the Latin?"

"He changed the subject when I inq—"

Ida walked into the kitchen. "You are the most predictable person."

"We all have our ways of coping." I ran my fingers through the flour, checking the consistency, to give myself time to reorient again. "The goal is to get two pies made before the *Esther* leaves so I can send them down with the boys."

"Well, you're going to have a hard choice, because I could only get one of these." She reached forward and set a chicken egg on the counter.

I stared at the pale brown shell.

My hands were covered in flour and I found myself not wanting to get fingerprints on the egg's pristine surface. Swallowing against a sudden lump in my throat, I didn't dare look up.

Tomorrow was Passover and we needed a Beitzah for the table. I had canned pickled eggs in my personal allotment, but roasting a pickled egg was really and truly not the same. A fresh egg? It was a beautiful gift.

"I did not know that the chickens were laying enough to spare any," Helen said, and I was grateful for the time to gather myself.

"The first generation, no. But the second generation seems perfectly happy to produce. There's one condition, though—well, not a condition, but a request." Ida rested her finger on the egg. "Can you blow the egg—I mean. Why does everything sound like an innuendo now?"

"Wait until I start talking about rolling pins. May I ask why?"

"So we can keep the eggshell."

But I wouldn't be able to roast it if I blew the egg—everything really did sound like innuendo. "I meant why do you need the eggshell intact?"

"I have this idea for Easter and—"

Helen blinked at her. "Easter was March 29th."

"Yes, but we had to work through it because of . . . " Ida waved a hand as if she were trying to encompass Clemons's death, Parker's orders, and the crew change on the *Goddard*. "Anyway, Oksana is Ukranian Orthodox and their Easter is on April 26. So we thought that—"

I held up my hand to stop her. "Wait. Y'all have two Easters?"

"Orthodox and Protestant," Ida said.

Helen held up a hand. "Catholic."

"Three Easters?"

"No, I just meant that I'm Catholic and the Protestants got their date from us."

I shook my head. "And here I was thinking the Jewish calendar was hard to map onto Mars time."

"And some dioceses move the holy days." Helen wrinkled her nose in a smile and then looked at Ida. "So . . . you and Oksana are proposing that we celebrate Orthodox Easter."

"Yes, and then we can still do the egg hunt we'd planned." Ida turned back to me. "That's why I need the eggshell intact."

I almost said yes and if it had just been me, I might have. I cleared my throat. "For Passover, we need a roasted egg. Would it be okay if I used it for that?"

"Oh! Sure." She nodded and it was that easy. "There are others that we can—"

Florence walked into the kitchen. She stopped by the wall

and flipped the switch on the intercom with an irritated click. "This is supposed to be on."

"Then why does it have an off switch?" Helen asked.

Florence just rolled her eyes and faced me. "Sorry to bother you, but we have a message from Mission Control. Change of plans."

"Of course there is . . ." I sighed and wiped my hands on a towel. "I'll come with you."

"This will be fast." She shook her head, waving me back to the pie crust. "Also, I'm not letting their choices deprive me of one of your pies."

"These are going down to the planet with the boys . . ." I set the egg aside, glancing at Ida. She had faded back to stand with Helen, but pointedly neither of them left the room.

"In that case . . ." Florence's mouth twisted and she shook her head. "Just got a message that they want ten of the men to stay. All spacewalkers."

So Parker had finally had a chance to look at Nathaniel's plan in detail and realized that an all-woman crew on the *Goddard* meant that we would be the ones to salvage the engine. I scowled at the bowl and kept forming the crust. "Well, that was only a matter of time."

"Listen, we haven't acknowledged receipt yet." She stood across the counter from me, arms crossed. "What do you want us to do?"

"Me?" I lifted my head in surprise.

"Yes, you." Florence has this thing where she'll look at you like you don't have the sense that God gave a fence post. Right now, she looked like I didn't even rate as a stump. "You're the commander of the ship, so spacewalks are your area."

"Oh. Right."

"Oh right . . ." She shook her head, lip curling as she snorted. "So, *commander*, what's your call?"

We'd only done the handoff last week. It did not feel real. I added four tablespoons of water to the crust, which is more than I used on Earth, but I knew from experience that the air was drier on ships and in habitats. Okay, so Parker wanted ten men to stay behind. Ten spacewalkers. Damn it all. They were going to keep us trapped on this ship, which was not what I signed up for.

I bent my head and formed the dough into a shaggy ball as I thought. With Clemons, I could have pretended to misinterpret the order. He would have known, but he would have granted me the plausible deniability.

Parker wouldn't. Parker would see it as a betrayal. Parker would double down and we'd find ourselves with no spacewalks at all. Sighing, I transferred the dough to a sheet of waxed cloth.

"All right, I'll head on up to comms to make the case for letting us do the spacewalks."

Florence *tsk*ed. "You could wait until the pie is done. He won't expect you to get the message until our morning."

"It's better if it chills anyway." I turned to the nearest sink to wash my hands. "Besides, Parker will be in the office now."

"I'll come with."

I shook my head. "It's your rest period. Take it. With a forty-minute lag this conversation is going to take a while."

And maybe I could come down to the kitchen in between messages to have some quiet time to myself.

The comms module was in the zero-g part of the *Goddard* so that the spin of the centrifugal rings didn't interfere with its orientation. In the middle of our "night" the module was dark, lit only by the glow of the monitor telltales. Without one of the comms team there, a part of me wanted to back away as if I weren't allowed to be in the module without supervision. For part of the First Expedition, that had been true.

Now, as the ship commander, it wasn't. I flipped the lights on. I had the right to be there and the training to use the equipment. My heart beat a little faster anyway, which was annoying.

Sighing, I pushed across the module and hooked a foot under the rail next to the system that was dedicated to Earth.

Resting my fingers on the keyboard brought back old memories of sending messages with Nathaniel.

Message for: Stetson Parker, interim director of the IAC
Message from: Dr. Elma York, commander of the Goddard

I paused because the title felt more like a Purim costume than something that belonged to me. I didn't want to include it, but Parker was a man who believed in the sanctity of hierarchies. He was in charge here, yes, and also he needed to be reminded that as of last week, I wasn't just an astronaut. I wasn't just "York."

I had briefly considered asking for Helen's codebook so I could talk to Parker in private, but if I couldn't make the case for it in public then he would see it as an attempt to manipulate him. It was also why I didn't send a message to Nicole. She would see the orders through other channels and would take any action she thought was necessary.

I needed to keep this simple and I also had to give him something he could use to justify changing his mind.

We received the staffing instructions about keeping ten men aboard the Goddard. *I am concerned about the morale among the crew with this ratio. When I was in the computer department, Mrs. Rogers had a policy to not hire men because she found that their presence was disruptive in a largely female department. When the numbers are more even the problem balances itself. Given your previously stated concerns about the "optimal functioning of the mission," I would like to continue with your original plan for crew separation.*

For the upcoming spacewalks, Druzylla Pacanowska was one of the engineers who worked on building the Goddard. *I recommend her for EV1. She has more spacewalking time than anyone on the crew and the majority of it was spent in constructing this ship. For EV2, I would recommend Mavis Davis, who has been running the*

Goddard's engineering department since our arrival. She was also instrumental in the events on the Moon so should have a good eye here.

That last sentence was a euphemism for "The woman defused a bomb, so if you're worried about sabotage, send her."

I drew in a deep breath, reread the message, and hit send.

Then I went back to the kitchen. The dough should be chilled enough, and if I didn't do something with my hands while I was waiting my brain would eat itself.

The empty kitchen hummed around me with circulation fans and the buzz of the refrigeration compressors. I put the pies into the oven and stood back as the heat triggered a hot flash.

Scowling, I turned to the sink and ran a rag under the water. As I pressed the cool cloth against my neck, I glanced at the time. 0134. I should go up to comms to see if Parker had responded.

Or I could clean up my mess. Flour coated the counter where I'd rolled the crusts out.

I sighed. Smarter to go to comms and check for a message. I could reply and then come back down to clean. I wiped my hands off, then left a quick note so that if someone wandered in they wouldn't think I'd abandoned the mess entirely.

Heading up the ladder to the spindle felt as if gravity had reversed itself. Parker was going to be so mad about that message. He would see it as an absolute challenge to his authority. There was no way I could pretend it was anything but that.

At the top of the ladder, I twisted to head forward to the comms module. Damn it. I should have left well enough alone. Nicole was the one who wanted the all-woman spacewalk. I should have let her deal with him.

The hot flash hadn't abated, and by the time I got to the comms module, sweat slicked the back of my neck. Grabbing the rail by the door, I stopped my forward momentum. The dark hatch waited.

Grimacing, I turned the light on and pulled myself into the module. Across the small space, a blinking light signaled that a message from Earth was waiting. How could a small light be so terrifying?

I hooked my foot under the rail and clicked on the screen.

Message for: Dr. Elma York, commander of the Goddard
Message from: Col. Stetson Parker, interim director of the IAC
Good note re: staffing of Goddard. Consulted with adviser who concurs. All men to report to surface of Mars. Note received re: spacewalk staffing.

I stared at the page. He'd agreed? I read it again. He'd agreed. The adviser had to be Nicole, and I wanted to kiss the screen in lieu of her.

Parker had not, however, liked my suggestions for the spacewalk. Knowing Parker, he would need to punish me for challenging him about the staffing. Not that he thought he was punishing anyone, but the man had a strong need to be right, and if he was wrong in one area then he would double down in another.

For now, however, I had a reprieve.

And a kitchen to clean.

On the First Mars Expedition, I'd been the only Jew—except Wilburt, I guess, but I hadn't known that. With a hundred people on the Second Expedition, I'd thought there would be one or two others. But during the first weeks of training, people kept coming up and quietly letting Nathaniel and I know that they had joined the space program because of us. It still baffled me, but I was delighted not to be alone this time.

Around the LMA, six other Jewish women bustled around doing last-minute things before our guests arrived. I was having a wonderful time and I was filled with anxiety. I have found, in general, that there are few things on any world that can simultaneously delight and dismay in the same manner as a formal dinner party.

Not that this would have passed muster as a formal Seder on my mother's watch. We had cloth napkins, yes, but they had never seen an iron. Our plates were aluminum. The cups were plastic and scratched from a year of use.

Francesca flurried into the room with a stack of matzo boxes six high clutched to her chest. "Is this going to be enough? I don't think it will be enough. I should get more out of storage. Is this enough? You made place cards?"

"I said I was going to." I set one of the folded punch cards in front of Aahana's spot at a table far from mine. "Mama always said that place cards were a kindness because they saved everyone from that horrible 'where should I sit' moment. And yes, that's enough matzo."

"Are you sure? About the matzo, I mean."

Across the room, Dolores chimed in, "It's enough matzo." She set a tin can on the table with a single orange zinnia in it.

In fact, in the middle of each of the six tables we'd set up in the LMA there was a zinnia, which Dolores had grown as a personal project. Each table had a runner cut from a parachute that Wilburt and I had scavenged from one of the cargo drops. It was unhemmed and unadorned, but the apple-green sheen of the nylon still made the room look surprisingly festive.

"Are you sure? I didn't think they would all RSVP yes." Francesca stopped at the nearest table and set her stack of boxes down. Opening one, she pulled out three pieces and set them on the aluminum plate in the middle that was serving as our matzo tray.

"It surprised me, too." I set another card down. When we'd been planning the mission, we'd talked as a group about the holy days. We coordinated our personal allotments to have supplies for the fourteen Jews on the mission, plus a couple of guests. Having all forty-nine women RSVP yes to dinner had been a delightful problem to have.

"Really?" Druzylla, from engineering, raised an eyebrow.

"The invitation came from the captain. Of course they were all going to say yes."

I stared at her, place card frozen above the table. Intellectually, I understood that I was the captain of the *Goddard*. I ran the meetings. I did the scheduling. I flew her when she needed to be repositioned. But I had not thought about the ripple effects of that.

"Hot plate, coming through!" Cipiora came in carrying a steaming pan.

"Is that rice and beans?" Francesca moved to the next table with her boxes.

"She's Sephardic." Had I pressured the crew into coming? I set Dawn's place card down next. "That's why we're doing a buffet, so you can skip the things you can't eat."

"Right. Right. It's just surprising."

"Eating only matzo and jam is surprising." Eva from comms glanced down at the place cards as she dodged around me with the stack of Haggadot she'd printed on quarter sheets of paper. "Put Dawn and Heidi next to each other."

"We eat more than matzo and jam." I covered my racing thoughts by laughing and stuck my tongue out at her. "And I'm trying to split the First Expedition folks up so we aren't cliquey."

"Yes, but . . ." She paused, biting her lips and then tried again. "But they got to be close on the First Expedition and I know that Heidi has missed having Dawn up here."

"Good note. Thank you." I swapped Dawn and Catalina, since I was also trying to split up those of us who had been on the surface.

More dishes started to come out of the kitchen. Our friends were helping, and the room filled with women and the astonishing aromas of home cooking. Chicken and almond matzo ball soup, potato kugel, carrot tzimmes, and dishes that were less familiar to me but smelled amazing, like a rice and ground beef dish steeped in cinnamon and allspice, a lemony-mint soup, and hand pies made with matzo and stuffed with ground beef and tamarind paste. And multiple versions of the charoset! Chopped apples and walnuts with cinnamon sat next to a ginger, fig, apricot, and date version.

My mouth watered as I put the last card in place and checked my watch. Twenty more minutes for my pie, which meant I'd have to jump up during the meal and also that it would be hot when it was served. I'd made my mother's recipe for an apple crumble with matzo meal and pecans as the topping— granted, with rehydrated apples, but other than that it was the same.

"Place cards!" Someone clapped their hands together in delight. "Now I have to find mine."

Another woman said, "I'm feeling justified in bringing my pearls."

In moments, people began shifting around, finding their places, and all the while the room was filled with laughter and chatter. I drifted toward my seat, smiling and nodding and saying pleasantries along the way.

Across the room, one of the comms team caught Rachel G. and handed her a note, nodding to me. I glanced at my watch: 1800 here, and that would be nearly 0900 at Mission Control. Parker had probably just gotten to the office.

Rachel hurried up to me and handed over the printout. "Sorry."

"It's fine." I wrinkled my nose, unfolding the page.

Spacewalk staffing: Elma York, EV1. Druzylla Pacanowska, EV2. Mavis Davis, CAPCOM. Standing by for reply.

I loved spacewalks and also I was under no illusions that this was a reward. This was a classic Parker "if you screw up it will be your fault" maneuver. I bit my lips against the desire to dictate an immediate response and nodded. "Thank you." I folded the paper to shove it into my pocket.

"He said he was standing by for reply."

"And Parker also knows that I'm Jewish and that this is

Passover. I'll reply next sol." I smiled with the bubbly warmth I'd perfected from years of hiding anxiety. "Because this night is different from all other nights."

We took our places, and as I looked across the long narrow module, the slight curve in the floor made the people at the far end appear to be uphill from me. The women. My throat tightened as the reality of an all-woman Seder kicked in. Before the Meteor, my father led the Seder and recited the Kiddush. After the Meteor, when Nathaniel and I celebrated with Jewish friends, whichever man was oldest took the lead. Tonight . . . tonight, there were no men and I was the oldest Jew on the ship.

And I was their captain.

I swallowed, standing so they could all see me, and smiled. "Fellow lady astronauts. Welcome to our Passover Seder. Seder is the Hebrew word for 'order,' and we use it tonight because Passover Seders all go in the same order, and we are happy to share it with you. At your places, you'll find the Haggadah, which will explain the order for tonight."

As paper rustled and I saw women studying it with the same earnestness with which they would prepare for a spacewalk, a warmth spread through me. "To translate this slightly into our common vocabulary . . . the Haggadah is our procedure checklist, so just think about the Hebrew you see in there as being a list of acronyms and you should get along just fine. And with that . . . Seder is Go for launch."

TWENTY-TWO

VIOLENT STORM IN SWEDEN

STOCKHOLM, April 26, 1970—(Reuters)—Roofs were ripped from houses, store windows were shattered and thousands of window panes broken tonight as a violent storm hit Sweden. Cars were blown off the streets and parked vehicles overturned by the storm. A policeman at Södertälje, south of Stockholm, was killed by an uprooted tree.

Aprim 17, Year 5, Satursol-Landing + 78 sols

Floating in the aft nadir airlock, the cooling system in my spacesuit seemed to suddenly fail. Sweat broke out over my entire body in prickles of heat. I held up my wrist mirror to check the controls, since I must have bumped them somehow while we were waiting for the airlock to finish depressing.

The control was set to the 22 degrees Celsius that I liked, but I was roasting.

The words "I think—" had gotten out of my mouth before I realized that the controls were not broken. This was, in the words of my mother, "my own personal summer."

"Something?" Druzylla pushed off from the outer airlock hatch where she was watching the gauge and turned to check on me. "Are you okay?"

"Mmm." I nodded, frantically searching for a topic as cover. I did not want to discuss menopause with CAPCOM, or Druzylla, for that matter. I adjusted the temperature to compensate and the cool air was a relief. "I was about to say that I think we should have taken an Easter egg out with us to hide but stopped myself because, of course, no one could go find it."

"Also, we are not Christian." The Polish engineer's sense of humor was . . . dry. "And also pressure has equalized."

"Copy that, y'all have a Go to open the cover and egress." Mavis drawled through the speakers in my Snoopy cap. She would be sitting in comms as our intravehicular CAPCOM with her sip pack of coffee and the full procedure book laid out in front of her. "And you'll tether to the aft starboard stanchion of the airlock rail."

"We're opening the hatch now." In the near vacuum of the airlock, the latch was silent as Druzylla worked to release the fifteen catches inside the mechanism.

A moment later, she pulled it back and up and the quality of light in the airlock shifted to be warmer and starker. Druzylla paused at the threshold of the airlock, hanging there for a moment before she reached out and tethered to the outside of the ship, and then released her interior tether.

"EV2's anchor tether hook is on aft starboard stanchion. Slider locked, black on black."

"Bag is still RETed to the airlock." I unclipped the Retractable Equipment Tether and passed the white tool bag out to Druzylla. "You have the bag."

"I have the bag." She took it and clipped the RET to her suit, then twisted to clear the hatch for me to egress.

As soon as she did, I saw why she'd paused on her way out. Mars.

I knew that Mars would be there, of course I did, but my mind was still prepared for the views of all the other spacewalks— the inky black of space or the blue-and-white glow of Earth or maybe, maybe the grays of the Moon.

Mars.

I was captured by the beautiful sand and salmon and rust surface that passed below us as if the view had its own gravitational pull. Pale wisps of clouds flirted with mountain ranges. In the distance ahead of us, Valles Lucilas was just coming out of the terminator into the daylight. Leonard had named it after his mother, Lucille, when we'd gotten close enough to really see it. He'd said that it was as deep and wide as her love. The canyon was so large that if you were standing in it, you wouldn't be able to see the other wall, and from here, it was a vast wrinkle on the surface of the red planet.

Mars.

There would be time to look at it later. Shaking my head to break the spell, I reached out and tethered to the outside handrail beside Druzylla. I made sure the carabiner was fully engaged with an unbroken black line on the safety. "EV1's anchor hook also tethered to aft starboard stanchion. Slider locked, black on black."

Our CAPCOM couldn't see us, so we had to narrate everything we were doing to allow Mavis to follow along. We had some cameras on the outside of the ship, but the image quality wasn't great and couldn't really catch the details of what we were working on. As per Parker's instructions, Druzylla was EV2 on this spacewalk. But she knew the ship better than I did—heck, she'd built large parts of it—so even though I was technically in charge, she was taking the lead.

So I looked to Druzylla to make certain she was set before I radioed to Mavis. "Are you ready for us to translate?"

"Sure enough. Druzylla, you're always going to work a little nadir of Elma on this route, so make sure to keep your tethers parallel and not crossed. For optimal translation, both of y'all go nadir under the lab along handrail 1175. Past the grapple fixture, down the gap spanner, to handle 0362."

"So over the river and through the woods, eh?" I followed Druzylla as we pulled our way aft along the spindle of the *Goddard*. We always say "spacewalk," but it's really just a hand-over-hand crawl along meters of handrails, dragging a tether. "Gotta wonder if that'll have any meaning for future generations of Martians. Maybe the song'll be 'over the dry creek bed and through the boulders.'"

"Y'all. They ain't going to completely forget the Earth. I

mean, we still talk about record 'albums' and the album was originally a book of sheet music." Mavis cleared her throat on comm as if suddenly remembering her job. "Anyway, y'all let me know when you're there and we'll go over the next procedure."

My back was to Mars and everything in my field of view was the austere pockmarked skin of our spacecraft. Cables snaked along it with no concerns about aerodynamics because the *Goddard* would never enter an atmosphere.

When I first started doing spacewalks, my hands ached from almost the minute I came out of the hatch, because I gripped the handrails so hard in order to be able to tell I was touching them. And, honestly, to feel safe. Now I'd learned to use a lighter grip. Oh, my hands still ached, just not immediately.

Druzylla's VOX caught bits of her humming under her breath, but I couldn't quite make out the tune.

"Whatcha singing there?"

"This song is now stuck in my head. I am trying to come up with something that scans but keep only coming up with Polish words."

"Why not use Polish?" All of the conversations that we'd been having down on the surface bubbled up in my mind. "It's an international group, so why not rewrite the songs that way, too?"

Druzylla gave one of her small "hms," which meant that her brows were coming together as she gave your idea serious consideration. "'Over the *wąwóz—*' No. When I say it out loud I do not like it."

Mavis said, "It sounded good to me."

"It matches the meter of 'river,' I will grant that, but we do not use articles in Polish and it sounds strange." Slightly zenith of us, one of the small, round windows looked into the spindle. Druzylla made another small "hm," then lifted a hand and waved. "Yes. Hello. Yes. Very nice."

As I got to the window, Helen was looking out, smiling and waving. She held up a beautifully decorated egg with thin white lines creating a geometric pattern in beet fuchsia and onion yellow. "It's beautiful!" I said, even though she couldn't hear me.

"What is?" Mavis asked.

"Helen was showing us an Easter egg she'd found."

"We are at handle 0362." Druzylla hung by the handle, even though it was obvious she knew where to go next.

"Great. Follow the gap spanner nadir aft below the Lesser Cupola and do a tether swap before proceeding."

"Roger, wilco." Druzylla grabbed the stiff nylon strap that spanned the gap from one handrail to the next. "I will not try to draw the full map in my head to this change in topic—it is very over the river—but I am thinking now of our Passover Seder. Why do they get so many eggs and we had to make do with a single one?"

"They're using just the shells." I took the nylon in hand and followed her to the next handrail. We were heading so far back on the ship that we would run out of length on our primary tether. "They blew the eggs—which sounds dirty every time I say it—"

"Because it is," Mavis interjected.

"It is a perfectly normal baking technique involving two holes. All you have to do is cover one with your mouth . . ." I could hear myself and I was not proving my point. I cleared my throat. "Anyway, you can do that and still preserve an egg for dyeing. We needed whole ones."

"Mm." Druzylla checked her tether arrangement on the new handrail. "Slider locked, black on black. But they also thought ahead to needing them and have been saving eggshells for . . . how long?"

"Don't ask me," Mavis said. "I was raised Jehovah's Witness before I got out. All my cultural references are very skewed."

"Besides, we thought ahead, too. That's why we had the pickled eggs for the seder plates on all the other tables. There was no way to be certain the chickens would lay." I secured my tether to the handrail. "Slider locked, black on black."

"I'm passing six o'clock on the side of the spindle here."

Druzylla paused and lifted a hand to wave at the window she was passing. "Genevieve has found a really nice one."

The Lesser Cupola was just big enough for a person's head and shoulders in case we needed a visual line-of-sight spotter at the rear of the ship. And sure enough, when I got to it, Genevieve was showing off a lovely pale blue egg with broad gold bands.

I gave her a thumbs-up, which made her grin and showed the gap between her front teeth. She could whistle through it and it was hilarious watching the men jump when she did a wolf whistle behind them. Unbelievably loud.

Mavis said, "Now stay totally nadir till y'all get back to the engine."

"So, it is then occurring to me that we should think of Rosh Hashanah now." Druzylla carried on as if we hadn't stopped talking and it took me a moment to catch up with her.

"Well, we did work through what we needed to pack for—"

"Yes, but when will we celebrate it? And for how long?"

"Um . . ." I was suddenly cold as the hot flash ended and the temperature I'd set my environmental controls at became a huge overcompensation. You don't understand cold until you're in a shadow in space. "It's supposed to start on September thirtieth, which is . . . early Julm here."

"Exactly." She paused in front of me and transferred her tether to the next handrail. "Slider locked, black on black."

I reached across the span and snapped my tether to the new rail. "Slider locked, black on black."

We had reached the part of the ship without people inside. No windows broke the surface of the fuel tanks, but the snaking cables and pipes became denser as we approached the engines. When we got back there, all this chatter would come to a halt as we concentrated on the task at hand.

Mavis piped in. "Okay, I got to know. 'Exactly' what?"

"Just remember that you asked . . ." I muttered as Druzylla drew breath to explain.

"So, here you have to understand that because calendar Jewish is calendar lunar and not Gregorian, Rosh Hashanah's day of the week changes itself with year on year. But there are three days in week when first day of Rosh Hashanah, it should not fall. These are Sunday, Wednesday, and Friday—so it cannot start Saturday night, Tuesday night, or Thursday night. But now we are also on Mars. So much like this Easter is normally on a Sunday on Earth, but for us, it is a Satursol. So, then, are we to keep the holidays aligned with Earth or are we to shift for Mars?"

"Interesting question." I paused on the rail to adjust the temperature of my suit back to 22 degrees Celsius. "I guess it depends on the priority. Maintaining a connection with our heritage on Earth or making Mars truly home."

"For Shabbats we have already shifted. Why not also for High Holy Days?" She stopped ahead of me, swinging to the side so that her feet were out of my direction of travel. "We are here."

There were five engines mounted at the aft of the ship. I'd seen them from BusyBee flights when I'd gone out for visual inspection, but hanging at the back of the *Goddard,* within touching distance, the scale of them really hit home. Each cone of the engine was about as big as the capsules we used to fly in during the early days. The extreme heat they had generated on the way out had left the metal with a patina of soot and the rainbow swirl of oxidized steel.

"EV2, you'll proceed along handrail 1438, which is going to be sandwiched between two WIFs. I need you to maintain a keep-out zone as you pass the bolts on the hoist point. Tether to the starboard end."

Druzylla said, "Translating on handrail 1438 to starboard end. Will maintain a keep-out zone."

"Good readback." Mavis said, "EV1, tether to the same rail, but stay at the port end. Insert your APFR into WIF Papa 557. From there, you'll be oriented nadir to reach the bolts holding the coolant lines in place."

I nodded inside my suit, as if anyone could see me right then.

"Tethering to 1438." I had to reach over and around the arm mounted on my Mini Work Station. The MWS was handy, but there were times when having a horizontal bar of tools strapped to your chest was a little awkward. "Slider locked, black on black."

Releasing my Articulated Portable Foot Restraint from the MWS, I plugged it into the Worksite Interface Fixture's socket and gave a quick pull test to make sure it was actually seated. Getting myself into the APFR was always slightly unnerving because I had to let go of the handrail, but with two tethers there's no real danger—or, I mean, no more than just being in the vacuum of space to begin with.

Feet secure, I straightened up and faced nadir, looking straight at Mars. It is so much smaller than Earth and more of it fit into my field of view. Reds and golds and tans swirled beneath us, more beautiful than any egg could be.

And I could also see the terminator coming up, which meant that I should get started before we orbited around into night and it got harder to see. "EV1, in the APFR at Papa 557, facing nadir. Ready for the next step."

"Copy that, Elma. And I have a caution for you. The grapple shafts and curvet coupling are no touch."

"Copy that." And I couldn't quite resist during my readback. "No touch shafts or coupling."

Mavis snorted in the mic. "Good readback. Wait for motion to dampen out before imparting loads. Elma, get out your PGT. Clockwise two, torque one. Expect six turns to back out the bolt. Start on the block bolt. Stow the loose bolts in your trash bag."

"Copy." I pulled out the Pistol Grip Tool, which is just a big ole space drill, and set to working the bolts out.

Meanwhile, she coached Druzylla through peeling back the insulation blankets to be able to get to the electrical systems. We settled into a rhythm of call-and-response as Mars spun below us.

And then, two hours into the spacewalk, I couldn't get a bolt to budge. "Mavis, I've got a stuck bolt here. Any trouble if I increase the torque?"

"Should be fine to go up to torque three."

I adjusted the setting on the PGT. Even through the gloves, I could feel the drill jerk and then the clutch disengaged the motor. I did not curse on the hot mic. If I couldn't get the bolt out, Parker would say it was because I was a woman and not that the bolt was stuck because it had been subjected to a bazillion degrees of heat and then the vacuum of space.

"No luck here. Torque four?"

"Mm . . ." Mavis sounded like she was consulting a manual, which she probably was. "Stow the PGT and switch to a manual hex driver. I want you to give it a tap and see if that jogs it loose."

"Copy." I attached the PGT to my MWS and then fished around in the crewlock bag for the manual hex driver, which was a hex socket with a big T-handle attached to it. I snapped its thin tether to the handrail. "You got a preference on what I use to tap it with?"

"Use your crowbar tool to start."

My fingers were clumsy in the gloves and I had to press them against the silicone tips to feel the socket. My nails gave a warning ouch and I closed my eyes, trying to feel that subtle moment when the hex driver was seated.

"Hex driver is in position." I opened my eyes and pulled the crowbar tool on its tether out of the crewlock bag. I braced in the APFR and gave the hex driver a solid rap. It jarred loose, spinning away from the spacecraft.

My heart seized in my chest and I went hot all over. Lurching forward, I brushed the bare edge of the driver. It tumbled away and jerked into an arc as it reached the end of its tether. This was why we used tethers, and yet I could not help but imagine it drifting farther away until it deorbited and burned up in Mars's thin atmosphere.

This tool was literally irreplaceable. Every tool we used was. And something was spinning away from me. Just a small thing, tumbling and winking in the sunlight as it drifted away from the spacecraft. I did not curse on the hot mic.

I inventoried everything on my MWS. Then I checked the crewlock bag. Nothing was missing. "Mavis, be advised that I lost something—it was small—the size of a quarter, maybe? I saw it tumbling away from me when I was breaking the torque. It's heading aft and nadir of us."

"What'd you lose?" She was calm, but I could hear the dread in her voice.

"I don't know." Whatever it was had drifted too far away to be visible. "Looks like I have everything, but I definitely saw something floating away."

"Druzylla, you lose anything?"

"Negative."

"All right, I'll log it." Mavis had to do that because if it stayed at our level, we might smack into it on a future orbit.

"Thanks." I turned back to reseat the manual hex driver and stopped. "Oh. Well, the good news is that I know what the object was."

"And the bad news?"

"The head of the bolt sheared off." I stared at the jagged piece of metal sticking out from the spacecraft. A memory of watching Nathaniel and Lance work on the backup O_2 generator bubbled up from Mars and made me laugh in surprise. I knew how to handle this. "There's enough of a stub that I can do the hacksaw trick and back it out by hand."

"I did not expect you to know that." Druzylla's voice had a rare smile in it. "You sound like an engineer."

And that was possibly the best compliment she could give me.

There is a particular tiredness that comes after a spacewalk. Your hands ache. Your shoulders and arms ache. And you feel so damn proud of yourself. It doesn't matter how long I have been living and working in space, going outside a ship in your own personal spacecraft of a suit and hanging over a planet is a privilege.

We worked removing the parts we needed in turns and shifts. I'd just come in from my second spacewalk and floated in comms talking to Nathaniel. Because my turn for a personal call came right after the shift, and I had no one to blame for that bit of scheduling but myself.

I kept my foot anchored under the rail closest to the mic. "Tell Lance I said thanks, because his hacksaw trick worked like a dream. Well . . . I mean, it was a pain in the ass in microgravity but I did get the bolt backed out."

"He'll be thrilled." Nathaniel's chuckle was a warm burr in my headset. "You're thinking like an engineer now."

"You mean staying up too late and living on coffee?"

"Ha! It's going to be like this for another Mars month at best—there's nowhere to work without bumping into someone's dirty underwear."

"Please tell me that people are doing laundry."

"Yes. But some people seem intent on wearing the same thing until it wears out."

I laughed, shaking my head. That used to be the way we did things because the capsules were too small for a change of clothes. "Now I'm trying to remember who would have been going up in the early *Lunetta* days before we had laundry facilities. It's not Halim."

"No. I swear he starches his shirts." Nathaniel groaned. "I'm just so frustrated."

"Me, too." I tried to sound sexy without making anyone in comms look at me too closely. When they'd built the *Goddard,* they'd made some assumptions about comms that did not match the reality of where we found ourselves. Artemis Base and *Lunetta* had private comms areas, so that people could call home as part of their overall wellness.

With the lag to Earth being what it was, no one would be calling back for anything except official business. And calls to

Mars? They weren't supposed to split husbands and wives up. It made being astronaughty a challenge. "What's frustrating you most?"

He didn't take the bait. "Well, the scrubbers are wearing out faster than they should because there are too many people living in the dome."

"But you knew that would happen."

"Yes, but it's faster than I expected so now I'm worried that there's a leak someplace. Oh! And then. And *then*, I had the team look for a leak, just in case, and Lance actually found a patch on one of the hoses leading to the south airlock hatch."

"You had a leak?"

"No, no, nothing like that. You would have heard the alarms if we had." I could imagine him picking at the edge of the microphone stand. "No, it's just that it wasn't logged, and that always makes me nervous."

"Wait." I pulled closer to the mic, frowning at it as if I could see through space to make eye contact with Nathaniel. "Which airlock did you say?"

"The south one. Where you found those hashmarks." He made another noise of annoyance. "We emptied it because we're going to use that airlock for access to the new dome. I asked Wilburt about the Latin and he said that it was part of a beautification contest."

I snorted. "They did not plan a consistent story for that. But back up a second to the patch. Why . . . why would someone have needed to do a patch there?"

"I have no idea. Probably something was overpressurized, or maybe there was a small manufacturing flaw. Maybe someone just needed a temporary bypass on life support while they were doing a repair. I really have no idea."

"You just had three ideas." I laughed at him, but my spine was tight with unease. I know Leonard said that it was a four-year-old problem but I didn't like the fact that they kept lying about it.

"Three ideas is not the same as three answers. None of the

First Expeditioners remember patching it. I'm hoping that Rafael did the repair. Which reminds me that I need to message Mission Control and see if he remembers. Because right now, I don't know what is out there waiting to break."

Orbiting Mars, it was easy to forget that something had happened down there on the last mission. "That's the problem, isn't it? What's going to break next?"

TWENTY-THREE

MARS EXPEDITION EXPANDS
LIVING QUARTERS

June 16, 1970—The astronauts of the Second Mars
Expedition have reached a pivotal milestone with the
completion of Bradbury Base's second dome, marking a
significant expansion of living quarters on the Martian
surface. Its completion stands as a testament to the in-
domitable spirit and collective efforts of the brave men
who are pushing the boundaries of human achievement.

Maym 11, Year 5, Sunsol–Landing + 128 sols

Laughter and applause bounced off the walls of the LMA module as Liz Hara finished her tiny puppet show. Clipboard in
hand, I stepped to the mic to fulfill my role as MC and buy
time for the next act to get in place. Over the past month, we'd
fallen into comfortable routines punctuated by spacewalks and
celebrating at any excuse. As we were doing tonight, with our
radio talent show.

My smiles were for the women in front of me, but my words
were for the men below us. Mostly, I imagined Nathaniel. "I
know you boys are wondering why we did a puppet show for
radio, but if it can work for Charlie McCarthy, I sure hope it
worked for you. If not, you can ask Liz to reprise this when we
rejoin you."

As I spoke, the comms team reset the microphones for a duo.

"And I have to say that we are all a little surprised that you
finished your work setting up the second dome ahead of sched-

ule. Not complaining, mind you, just surprised. Next thing you know, y'all will be picking up your socks without being asked." The ladies laughed and I have no idea what the fellows did. Nathaniel would likely still be at his work desk, with the radio playing so he could hear us. He would probably laugh and then look slightly guilty about his socks. Comms gave me the nod that they were ready, so I looked at the clipboard and read the next part of the script that had been given to me. "Next, we have Carol Mack, from the biochemist team, singing her rendition of 'Moon River' accompanied by Kendra Zzyzwyck on the violin."

That was all I had to do.

Oh, I would have preferred to be in the audience, but also recognized that for morale, I needed to be involved in this little talent show. We wanted a way to celebrate the men completing the second dome, and since we couldn't actually be with them . . . radio. I volunteered to be the MC, which might look like I had to be on all the time, but it wasn't my talent being scrutinized. I was just there as filler in between the real talents.

Like the fact that one of our biochemists turned out to be an opera singer.

This was why I wasn't doing a talent. Smiling and reading a script? That was well within my wheelhouse. Now. It definitely had not always been. And I was clearly, completely, obviously not riddled with nerves. I'd learned to hold a clipboard so no one could see my hands shake and to just accept that the back of my mouth would taste slightly sour. But it wouldn't get any worse than that.

On the other hand . . . Aahana, who was a little bit farther down the roster looked positively green. I bit the inside of my lip and stepped next to her. Keeping my voice low, I said, "Anything you need?"

Compressing her lips, she shook her head. "You were very funny. The line about the socks. I suppose it turns out that when you cram fifty men into a place built for twenty people, they find their motivation."

"Or maybe it was because they were all horny and wanted us to come down. I mean, not come—you know what, never mind." On our improvised soundstage, Carol and Kendra's song was drawing to a close. I smiled an apology to Aahana and fled from her compliments. "Excuse me."

Back at the microphone, I let the applause fill the room for a moment. "That was simply wonderful. Thank you so much, Carol and Kendra. I wonder if someone is going to write 'Mars River.' Or maybe . . ." What was that Polish word? "Maybe 'Mars Dry Creek Bed.' How about it, boys? Are any of you secretly composers? And now, we've got Helen Carmouche with 'You Can't Raise a Goldfish in a Wineglass,' which she assures me is the actual title of the song. She's accompanied by Yung-Chiu Wang on the keyboard."

Helen stuck her tongue out at me as she stepped to the mic, but Yung-Chiu mouthed, "I know. So silly."

I faded back from the stage area and smiled at Aahana. "You're next. All set?"

"I am—" She stopped and pressed her hand to her mouth.

A lifetime of anxiety, combined with years spent watching people experiencing zero-g for the first time, made me especially attuned to the face of someone trying not to vomit. I scanned the area for the nearest trash bin, which was by the door and thankfully not wire frame.

"You know, I always used to get so nervous before an appearance." I kept my gaze forward, watching Helen sing a song in Hokkien. "Still do, truth be told."

"I find that hard to believe." Aahana lowered her hand.

"Yep. In the early days, I had a terrible time before almost every appearance on live television."

She turned to face me. "But you always seemed so calm and polished."

"Lies." I smiled out the side of my mouth. "Two secrets. First, just think about one person that you're talking to. I think about Nathaniel most of the time. Sometimes my niece, depending on the show. Who would you think about?"

"Jaidev." She turned back to face the stage. "Maybe my cousin."

"Good choices." I glanced at her and she still looked nervous, with a little sweat on her upper lip. "The second secret is that I also learned to breathe better. Which helps."

"What do you mean, 'breathe better'?"

I rested my free hand on my stomach by way of demonstration. "Push all the air out through your mouth and then hold your breath . . ." I counted to four with my fingers. "Now inhale."

As I demonstrated, I realized that over the course of the afternoon, I had let my shoulders tighten and my stomach clench. So often, I don't become aware of the tension in my body until I manage to release it. I smiled as Aahana took in a deep breath.

"Now, the secret I've learned is that I can't make the fear go away, but I can know that it's coming." The secret my therapist had taught me, but I wasn't quite ready to open up that much to the younger astronaut. "I can know how my body reacts to it. My hands shake. I want to vomit and—"

In hindsight, I should not have said that word. Aahana just barely made it to the garbage bin. The *Goddard*'s doctor, Ana Teresa, materialized out of nowhere.

It wasn't happening to me, but I felt the old shame of making a scene rush over me in a wave of empathy. God, how I hated putting people out and being the center of a fuss. When I had been in Aahana's place, I had always felt mortified. I'd gotten so good at hiding it.

Standing outside the moment, watching it happen to someone else—no. This wasn't the same thing as what used to happen to me. Everyone who moved around her and guided her out of the room did so with gentleness and compassion.

In college, when I had been the only girl and so, so much younger than everyone else in my class, my nerves had been met with open mockery. That was why I had gotten so good at hiding.

Helen's song was coming to a close. I put the regulation smile on my face and in my voice and stepped to the mic.

After the show, I floated in the Greater Cupola with Helen and Ida. The large hexagonal windows overlooked darkness. We were on a night pass, and without the artificial lights of humanity, the planet was a paler darkness blocking the deep void of space.

Ida pushed a net bag of fresh snow peas toward me. "I swear to God, I'm going to spend my entire personal allotment on chocolate when they send the Third Expedition out."

"At least that travels. I keep dreaming about these cannoli that we used to get when we would go to New York before the Meteor." I caught the snow peas. "Even if I could match the crust, there's no way to do the filling with freeze-dried dairy."

Helen stretched, body suspended in the air. "When do the goats come out?"

"Fourth Expedition." I pulled a snow pea out of the bag. "Assuming they send it. So . . . six years? And I've never worked with goat's milk before."

"You think they won't? Send the Fourth Expedition, I mean." Helen relaxed from her stretch, curling inward a little.

"Dunno." I took a bite of a beautiful, crisp, and succulent snow pea. "I guess I could try with sweetened condensed milk . . . but then there's the ricotta."

Ida shook her head. "Now you're making me miss fresh cheese."

"The sun is coming up." Helen had rotated to stare out the window where the thin silver atmosphere of Mars was glowing in an arc.

I reoriented so that I fully faced the glass. Yes. I had spent a lot of time doing spacewalks and the view was better without frames supporting the windows, which were made of four panes of glass that were each three centimeters thick. But there wasn't a lot of time to stop and appreciate the view. Even when there was, you had to hold yourself in place.

Here, I could just float.

When you see that fragile sliver of atmosphere begin to glow, it is so like Earth that my heart tightens in my chest. Then dawn breaks, sending shadows chasing across the red surface as mountains and valles spin into view. Where there had been darkness, we had swirls of ochre amid vivid reds.

Helen sighed. "I will never get tired of—"

The intercom crackled. "Elma York to comms. Elma York to comms."

I spun in place and kicked off the glass, aiming for the intercom. Grabbing the handrail next to it, I slapped the call button. "York here. I'm on my way."

Tucking, I pulled on the handrail to swing through the door of the Greater Cupola and into the spindle. It was after the workday, so this wouldn't be a problem on Mars. Probably. What time was it on Earth? But if something had happened to Nathaniel, Mars would call me just like this. Or maybe it was innocuous, like Parker made a change to the schedule again and just wanted to exert power by calling me to the phone.

Comms was only a little way down the spindle from the Greater Cupola, so I was able to superman straight there without touching a wall to reorient until I got to the hatch. Grabbing a handrail, I changed my vector to enter comms.

Loretta Olivas looked up from the mic as I swung in. Her eyes were wide like the proverbial deer in the headlights. "Yes, sir. She's just coming in right now."

Ana Teresa clung to a footrail and glared at me with jaw clenched. Glaring was her natural expression, but this was a whole different level of angry for the doctor. The sort of glare that made me realize I'd only ever seen her be annoyed before.

"What—?"

"Headset." Ana Teresa pointed at the one that Loretta pushed toward me. "We have a medical problem."

Ana Teresa abruptly switched to Spanish and addressed Loretta. It was too rapid for me to follow, but it made Loretta raise her brows and push to the door. Loretta switched back to English, for me, no doubt. "I'll be in the observation dome. Let me know when I can come back."

My breath shallowed as questions buried me. Sending Loretta out meant this was confidential. Had something happened to Nathaniel? But why would that make Ana Teresa angry? I reached for the headset Loretta had left floating in the air and pulled it on. "Bradbury, *Goddard*. This is Elma. What's going on?"

In the headset, I caught the tail end of Leonard's sigh. "Ana Teresa tells me that Aahana is pregnant."

I'm ashamed that my first thought wasn't for Aahana. It was that Ana Teresa had told Leonard. Not me. She should have come to me, as captain of the *Goddard*, but instead she had made her report to Leonard. I pushed that selfish hurt away and concentrated on Aahana.

How must she be feeling? If those test tubes had shown a ring when Kam had run the test for me, I would have been sick to my stomach, but would some part of me have been, maybe, happy? Aside from the thousands of complications of a pregnancy away from Earth that made the prospect terrifying. "How's she taking it?"

"She is very upset. Understandably." Ana Teresa shook her head and faced me. "I am about to give off sparks. Why the hell did you tell her to use the rhythm method?"

"I—what . . . ?" I didn't know which of my questions to start with, in part because I had no idea what Ana Teresa was talking about. "I'm sorry. I'm confused . . . I don't remember telling Aahana anything like that."

"You told her that the rhythm method had worked for you and Nathaniel for decades."

"Oh . . ." The memory wormed its way out of the haze of anxiety I'd been navigating through. "Okay. Yes. I remember saying that's what we did, but . . . I didn't tell her that she and Jaidev should—"

"Elma." Leonard cut me off, voice firm. "You are in a command role. She looks up to you. She absolutely took that as advice."

I blinked, chest tightening. Some fear. Some anger. This was why Ana Teresa had gone to Leonard. She wanted him to discipline me, so she'd gone right over my head, and now they were both acting as if this were somehow my fault. "They must have miscounted."

"I am up to my nose! The rhythm method, it does not work."

"It does. Nathaniel and I have—"

"Used it for decades. I know. Aahana told me." Her nostrils flared with anger. "It. Does. Not. Work."

"But . . ." I gestured toward the door as if the room where I had taken the pregnancy test were just on the other side instead of 400 kilometers below us on Mars. "But I've never even had a scare until . . . until recently."

"Well, that is likely because Nathaniel is sterile."

The room went cold. The breath sucked out of my open mouth as if a vacuum had opened in the module. I floated, staring at the doctor, not even able to shake my head or ask a question. Nathaniel was sterile?

I curled my toes under a rail to keep from floating away in shock. "I don't understand. How do you even know that? About Nathaniel, I mean."

"Since the goal is to *eventually* have babies on Mars, we checked the fertility of everyone coming up."

"Does Nathaniel know?"

"No."

"Does *Kam*?"

"Yes."

"Then why make me jump through a hoop to get a pregnancy test?" My skin heated. "Oh my God. Y'all thought I was having an affair?"

She muttered something in Portuguese. "No. You always assume a gun is loaded, even if you're sure it isn't. But the fact is that an exception was made for the two of you because of who you are. A shitload of exceptions, actually. He should not be on this mission at all."

I shook my head, swallowing the sour taste that was gathering at the back of my throat. "He's the lead engineer—they needed someone who could adapt to conditions on the ground here."

"There are other engineers who could have done that." Leonard sounded tired. "They didn't need his skills specifically. Clemons thought that if you knew about his chronic conditions, you would decline the mission. They needed *you*."

My skin felt like it was two sizes too small. I was so angry I couldn't even find words to spit at Leonard or Ana Teresa. "Chronic. Conditions. So not just sterility."

Ana Teresa groaned, head tilting back to stare at the ceiling. When she straightened, some of her fury seemed to have dissipated. "I will tell you and then we will move on because Aahana is the primary concern now. Your husband has neuropathy, primarily affecting his fingertips and the soles of his feet."

The memory of him fumbling to undo the gloves on his suit bubbled up out of my brain. I'd thought it was because he was less experienced. The thumbtack that hadn't hurt. I'd thought he was being polite. The fork that he'd dropped. I'd thought it was just regular clumsiness.

I ordered numbers to calm my racing mind. *3.1415926535 . . .* There was worry about Nathaniel and fury about not being told and the beginning of sorrow and I did not have the luxury of sitting with any of that in the moment.

There was a problem that we needed to work. I remembered the contingency plans, and we had hard choices ahead of us. "All right. All right. So. Aahana. Has she . . . has she decided what she's going to do?"

What I got in response was a snort. "She wants to abort, and I quote, 'I came here to do science, not to be a science experiment.' Not that it much matters what she wants. She's from India. Abortion is illegal there. And I am from Brazil, where abortion is also illegal."

I almost said that we were on Mars but stopped to count so that I could think things through. *0, 1, 1, 2, 3, 5, 8* . . . Right. For regular operations, we were each governed by the IAC. But for crime, each of us was governed by the laws of our home country. My mind blipped over to the slur painted on the dome on Mars. Was that why they hadn't reported DeBeer? Knowing that in his home country he hadn't committed a crime?

In the headset, Leonard said, "Whoa, whoa. We have set contingency plans. Why are you bringing up legalities back on Earth?"

"Because politicians are stupid. I will tell you that this was a subject of a lot of debate with the flight surgeons—or rather, we were all very clear that at this time abortion was the only ethical choice. But . . . but not every member nation's UN representative agreed with that." Ana Teresa grimaced and grabbed the table to reorient. "I am not looking forward to writing up this report for Earth."

"Do you have to?" I wanted to make eye contact with Leonard to see what he thought. "I mean . . . there are a lot of things that never get reported. Does this have to be?"

Ana Teresa's mouth twisted in a sour line. "Yes, of course. Then I'd just have to perform an abortion in one-third gravity or provide prenatal support and then deliver a baby in one-third gravity who may or may not be viable or deal with a miscarriage. None of which I feel like doing by just winging it."

"I'm sorry." I held up my hands trying to placate her. "I just thought that since we have flight rules for everything else that—"

"OF COURSE WE DO." Ana Teresa's fists clenched. She cut off and let out a slow breath. "Elma, I know that you're used to being the smartest person in the room, but stop talking about my area of expertise."

"I'm sorry."

"I know you are. I know that you *meant* no harm, but as a physician, I've sworn to *do* no harm."

I almost apologized again by reflex, and the only thing that kept me from doing it was that my throat was clamped nearly shut. I couldn't take in a breath and my gut was churning. I needed to get out of here. I needed to get to the head before I vomited, I—I was panicking.

I was having a panic attack.

It had been a long, long time since I'd had one. What was the checklist for getting out of this spiral? *This is upsetting but not dangerous*—not to me. Nathaniel was ill. I had just endangered the life of a crewmate and—*0, 1, 1, 2, 3, 5, 8, 13* . . . I swallowed. I took a slow breath and held it as the numbers mounted in my head. I let it out. Anxiety was fear without an outlet. It was a problem that couldn't be worked. Except that there was a problem that we could work. I shoved all of my fear for my husband to the side to look at later. Right now, we needed to focus on Aahana. "What can I do that will be helpful?"

Ana Teresa took a matching breath, as if she were also trying to calm down, and nodded. "Yes. Correct. We do have flight rules for this, and the first is that we need to spin the *Goddard* up to Earth gravity."

I didn't ask questions. I didn't raise the problems that it would cause. This was in the contingency plans and smart people had already worked through the complications we would face. I nodded, grateful to have a direction. "I can do that."

TWENTY-FOUR

June 25, 1970

Dear Helen,

Each time I sit down to write, something has gotten in the way. Now, I feel I must because your name came up today (I'm working on my memoir with a ghostwriter, because honestly, who has the time?) and I told her about our long-distance chess games. The fact that I lose every single one and how it keeps me humble. You should know, though, that really it's because I miss you and this gives me a reason to think about you every day.

Speaking of which . . . R-QN1.

On other subjects, how is Reynard? By skimming the public briefing reports, I see that he's been assigned to "Regenerative Environmental Control and Life Support System Recycle Tank Drain." Probably because the CO_2 scrubbers are taking a beating with all the extra bodies in the main dome.

Do give Reynard my regards. Elma and Nathaniel. Leonard. So many friends up there. Unless I miss my guess, I know fully half the crew. Just tell everyone I said hello. Needless to say, I'm wishing everyone the very best. Mars sounds very, very appealing after a day of cabinet meetings.

I don't get to fly as often as I would like. Finding time in my schedule is tricky. Very, very tricky. Unfortunately, my trick for taking politicians up to schmooze them has been complicated by increasingly rough skies. A lot of the time, we have to do lunch instead. My God. You have no idea how these men like to hear themselves talk.

Be well, my friend.

Love,
Nicole

Maym 20, Year 5, Tuesol–Landing + 137 sols

I crouched in front of the oven and checked the chocolate chess pie that I was baking instead of calling Nathaniel in the middle of the night. The crust was perfectly browned and golden. It was tangible and in front of me and not the phantom conversations that I was having with my husband about why the hell he had not told me about the neuropathy.

I knew why.

You could literally poison the man and Nathaniel would just tell you that he had chosen to leave the office early. I could not change his nature.

But I could bake a pie for Aahana.

I wasn't under the illusion that it would fix anything for her. Her pregnancy was all over the news on Earth. I don't know who was leaking things to the papers, but I hoped all of their teeth fell out, except for one, which was rotten.

I was also hoping that something chocolate would be a comfort to her. Or at least allow me to go back to sleep. Anxiety and night sweats do not make sleep easy. In the morning, I'd get someone else to take it to her, because to say that she was uncomfortable around me was an understatement.

Pulling the pie out, I grimaced as my arms protested. Standing under Earth gravity took so much effort after over a year of living with Martian gravity. The pie weighed three times what it should. I'd spun the *Goddard* up slowly, but even increasing the gravity over the course of three sols did nothing to prevent it from feeling like I was living under three-g thrust at all times.

I turned very carefully to set the pie on the counter. Out of long habit, I kicked the oven door shut with my foot.

The Coriolis effect spun the ship around me, throwing off my balance, and I stumbled—

I was on the floor. The pie plate was upside down. Molten filling coated my left hand.

I shook my hand, trying to fling it off, but it clung to my skin, so hot that it felt cold. Just enough presence of mind kept me from swiping at it with my right hand. I turned to grab one of the potholders I'd dropped and moved too fast again. Landing on my elbow, I snatched the potholder with my free hand and wiped the chocolate away.

The skin underneath was bright red. Around me, the pie was smeared in sticky fragments across the floor.

"Goddamn it." What a waste of resources. "Damn it all to hell."

"Elma?" Helen seemed to appear from nowhere. Rounding the counter, she took an awkward sidestep and almost went down, too. But she caught herself on the end of the counter, dropping a paperback book. "What happened?"

"Coriolis effect." It was worse since we'd spun the ship up faster. Every time I turned, I could feel the ship rotating around us. The diameter of the rings had been designed for Martian gravity and a slower spin. I rolled onto my knees, and my hand was starting to throb. "Dropped the damn pie."

I was aware that I was cursing a lot, but there are times when I am more a pilot than my mother's daughter, and the sheer tomfoolery of my mistake was infuriating.

"Are you hurt?" Helen went to the drawer and pulled out a towel.

"I'll be fine. I'm just mad about the pie." I grabbed the counter to brace myself as I stood up fighting the gravity and the spin. "Damn it."

"One of your chess pies?" Helen sighed and carefully lowered herself to the floor to start cleaning up my mess.

"Yes." My hand felt tight and tender. I turned the faucet on and stuck it under the cold water. "You don't have to do that. I'll get it in a sec—damn it all."

I turned the faucet off. What was I doing? Wasting drinking water by running it over my hand? Sure, it would get recycled, but filters only lasted so long. Everything, from pie to filtration, came from Earth. I couldn't waste anything.

Without the cold, the throb started building again.

"Here." Helen handed me a damp towel, which was a better plan to try to cool the area.

"Thanks." I draped the cloth over the burn. The cool soothed it. A little. To distract myself, I nodded to her book. "What are you reading?"

"Oh." A line appeared between Helen's brows. She picked up the book and riffled the pages, then looked around the kitchen almost as if she were checking to see if anyone else was in here at this time of night. "I got a message from Nicole."

"How is she?" I rotated the cloth, trying to find a part that was still cool.

"Fine, but . . ." Helen opened the book and pulled out a sheet of teletype paper with pencil marks scribbled above the lines. "No. I don't think she's okay. Or . . . she's asked me to do something. I could use your thoughts."

I didn't have to take the paper to recognize a cipher. "Rhode Island?"

She shook her head. "Aahana."

With my free hand, I took the page and tried not to read the letter, which seemed innocuous. In the margins, a completely different message was scribbled in pencil.

DO NOT LET ABORTION HAPPEN

I frowned at the page. "Okay, I have two questions. No, three. One, how many people do you exchange coded messages with?"

Helen smirked. "What are your other two questions?"

"Are you sure this is from Nicole? It seems out of keeping for her to ask for that." I handed the page back. "And how is that encrypted or coded? I don't see anything in there."

Looking down at the page, Helen rubbed a corner with her thumb. "It's definitely her. And it's not out of keeping, but my problem is that I don't know if this is a political request or a personal one."

"And you'd treat them differently?"

Nodding, Helen folded the page and tucked it back into the book. "I trust her to see the big picture on a political request. For instance, a space baby might attract public interest and encourage continued funding for the program."

"Or the pregnancy might go very badly and make people think that Mars isn't safe at all." I shifted the cloth on my hand. The skin was already getting puffy. It throbbed with every beat of my heart. "We aren't ready for babies, and anyway, Aahana doesn't want it."

"Exactly. To me, it seems like there are too many variables for this to be a purely strategic request. Politics are annoying, but I can understand that tactics sometimes mean sacrificing a piece."

My head came up. "Aahana is not a pawn."

"Elma . . . all of us are." She grimaced and shook her head. "I don't mean that it's right, but that is what we are to the countries in the UN and specifically to the IAC signatories. You and Parker are higher-value pieces, but even those will get sacrificed to win the game."

The air in the room seemed to thin. She wasn't wrong. That had been true for my entire career. Inhaling deeply to fight the closing of my throat, I leaned against the counter. "And the personal reason?"

She sighed and opened her mouth. Closing it with a grimace, Helen looked away. Then she eventually nodded. "I think this is a matter of public record, though not widely known." Looking back to me, she said, "Nicole had multiple miscarriages and stillbirths, resulting finally in an emergency hysterectomy. I don't know what that will do to her decision-making on this matter."

I had known Nicole for longer than anyone in the program and I hadn't known that. I guess I could add her to the list of people who didn't trust me, and—that wasn't a useful train of thought. Obviously, Helen trusted me since she had just come to me with this. "So . . . you need to decide if you should get involved?"

"Exactly."

Tilting my head to the side, I tried to work through the scenarios, but my hand kept pulling my attention. The skin was lit up and throbbing and rotating the cloth was doing nothing and I was also cold and—"I'll think about it, but right now . . . I think I need to go to the med center."

Helen went to full alert immediately. "That bad?"

I pulled the cloth away and let her see. The skin on the back of my hand, wrapping around my thumb, was swollen in a tight blister.

Helen sucked in her breath. "Yes. Yes, you should go."

I looked at the smears of chocolate on the floor, and then at the clock. "Actually, wait. They won't be there yet." I waved the cloth at the mess. "I'll get this cleaned up and—"

Helen snatched the cloth out of my hand. "I will clean up. You will wake up a doctor because that is a very bad burn."

"Yes. But there actually isn't anything they can do, so—"

"Go." Helen pointed to the door, which would lead me around the ring to the MedMod on the far side. "Do not make me call Nathaniel."

I snorted. It would serve him right to be kept in the dark about this. "I'll go." Not that I was going to wake anyone up. "But I want to register a complaint."

"Confirmed. Go."

Helen is very intimidating for someone a head shorter than I am. I went. The walk took me through the LMA to a connection tube to the human habitation module, which held the gym and the MedMod.

In the gym, a handful of people were still up doing their mandatory workouts. It seemed ridiculous now that we were operating under Earth gravity, since the entire purpose of the workouts was to maintain bone density.

I made a mental note to check to see if that schedule could be lightened.

At the far end of the gym, there was a short hallway with the medical center on one side and a couple of offices on the other. The door to the medical center was ajar and I could hear voices.

So, they were up. There went that excuse. I flexed my hand and the movement stretched the burn, making hot and cold wrap around me in sickening waves. I'd really done a number on it.

I knocked.

The voices cut off and Ana Teresa swung the door open. She glared up at me, which was her natural expression, so I didn't take it personally.

"What?"

"I, um . . ." I held out my hand. "I burned my—"

She grabbed my free shoulder and guided me through the door. "How did you do that? When?"

"I was baking a pie and dropped—oh." Aahana was in the room, sitting on the examining table. "You're busy. I'll come back."

"We are finished and were just talking." Ana Teresa usually had the bedside manner of an angry terrier, but right now she rested her arm on Aahana's back as if she were afraid to break her. "Yes? Are you okay to go now?"

Aahana nodded, looking at the floor rather than either of us. "Thank you. I didn't mean to wake you up."

"Nonsense. It is my job." The terrier turned back to me, baring her teeth. "Tell me you didn't put butter on your hand."

"No. Just a damp cloth. No ice, either."

"Good." She beckoned me farther into the room as Aahana hopped off the bench.

She wasn't starting to show yet, but her shoulders were hunched and her face drawn down. She shoved a small bottle of pills into her pocket. Heading to the door, she moved as if her gravity were even higher than ours.

At the door, she stopped. "Elma? Elma, can you tell Mission Control to let me abort?"

"I—" Nicole's letter flashed to the front of my memory. "I'm sorry."

Because the one person I knew who might have been able to influence matters was set on Aahana seeing the pregnancy through.

The command module hummed around me with quiet tension as we waited for the *Esther* to arrive on her supply run. Floating behind the pilot's chair, was there actually anything I could do if they misjudged the approach and rammed us during docking? No.

No, because the burn on my hand was bad enough that I'd been "grounded." Ana Teresa had "deroofed" the blister, which was not a term I'd previously known, and I'd been content with that. My hand was wrapped flat on a plastic board and she was making grumbling sounds about a skin graft.

Even if I'd been in the pilot's seat, instead of Helen, there would have been nothing I could do to save the *Esther* or anyone in a depress zone, but I could course correct if an impact knocked us out of orbit or get us free of a debris field. The same way Helen could. I just wanted to be useful.

"*Goddard,* we don't see a flyout." Halim's announcement eased the tension a little. He had the *Esther* perfectly lined up with the docking port and didn't need to do any additional alignment. "We're initiating final approach."

Helen depressed the mic. "*Esther, Goddard,* copy."

A collision hadn't happened, but it could, so I sat watching their glacial approach. Three centimeters per second, just the way it should be.

From the *Esther,* Halim's voice crackled over the comm, "*Goddard, Esther.* Contact light."

Even trusting him as a pilot, I still relaxed as the board on our side lit up. Helen toggled her mic. "Capture confirmed. Welcome to the *Goddard.* We'll see you aboard shortly."

"Is there pie?"

"There are plenty of other desserts, but no pie. *Goddard* out." Unbuckling her seat restraints, Helen twisted in the air to face me. "You need to teach me how to bake those."

"It's all about the pie crust." I flexed my fingers as much as I could, feeling the sting of the skin stretching under the bandage. "Ready to go meet the boys?"

We floated in the spindle, facing the hatch of the airlock that the *Esther* was docked to. I'd heard the choir and band rehearsing but until the *Esther*'s hatch opened, I had not experienced their full-throated glory. Susan McBerry had orchestrated "Fly Me to the Moon" for voice, flute, trombone, accordion, violin, oboe, and erhu.

She took the ripple-bang of the hatch opening as her cue and counted them in. The woodwinds flourished, and by the time the hatch swung inward, a choir of twenty women filled the spindle with their voices.

Halim floated in the open hatch with Wilburt and Howard behind him. He pulled himself out, grinning wider, and grabbed a rail to reorient so he was facing the same "up" that we were as he listened to the chorus.

I couldn't help it; I looked past them for Nathaniel even though I knew he wasn't scheduled to come up. He'd surprised me before by adding himself to maintenance crews for mission inspections when we had been in Earth orbit.

The hatch remained empty.

They needed the space. Halim and his small flight crew were here to pick up the salvaged parts from the *Goddard*'s engine. Of course my husband wouldn't hitch a ride.

I packed that small sadness away and kept a smile on my face as the boys enjoyed their welcome. The song ended and I joined in the cheering because I sure as heck wasn't going to join in the applause. Nuan Su Tang kicked forward to wrap her husband in an embrace. Wilburt and Dawn waved at each other. And Halim . . . Halim looked at the couple smooching and for a moment sadness washed over his face.

His wife and children were still back on Earth. They were scheduled to come on the Third Expedition.

Halim turned his grin back on full and spread his arms wide, as if he could embrace all of us. "I love this tradition. Thank you for the welcome!"

"Happy to have y'all back." I floated over to him and gestured down the spindle. "We've got a chicken dinner waiting for you."

He did a double take. "Actual chicken?"

"Yep." Because the chickens that had been raised in Martian gravity had been struggling to breathe under Earth gravity loads. But right now, let the boys think that it was for them. "Gotta welcome y'all back proper."

"Happiness abounds." He eyed my hand and nodded at it. "How bad is it?"

"Annoying but fine." Unless I poked it, in which case it let me know that it was definitely burned. I'd rather that he didn't know about it at all, but given the reports we all had to fill out, everyone knew. I was still so put out with myself. "Want to head for the kitchen?"

He followed me down the length of the spindle, which was still filled with women as people filtered back to work. "As soon as it's clear, I'm going to superman down the entire thing."

"I see someone misses being in space." We translated toward the ladder that led down to the kitchen. Flying down the spindle never got old. We weren't going far but it was so freeing and what I think I had been reaching for since I had started learning to fly planes. I grabbed the handrail next to the ladder to stop my momentum and tucked in next to it instead of dropping straight down.

Halim was slightly less graceful, but only because he'd been in gravity for the last seventy-five sols. I eyed him. "Hey . . . be careful going down the ladder. It's Earth gravity at the bottom."

"I know." He rolled his eyes. "Kam has had us doing weighted squats for sols in prep."

"Trust me, it's not the same." Besides the more recent experience, I also remembered returning to Earth after the Mars mission. "You're also going to have the Coriolis effect to deal with."

He gave a small salute. "Thank you for the good note."

Nodding, I went first into the tube. In Martian gravity, I used to put my feet on the outside of the ladder rails and slide down the last third. With Earth gravity? That last third was . . . very fast, so I tended to get a little closer before sliding.

Especially since I burned myself.

I used my right hand to do most of the work and slid the last couple of meters to the gently curved floor outside the kitchen module. The air was filled with garlic, and crushed tomatoes mingled with the bright green freshness of oregano and basil grown here on orbit.

Stepping clear, I made way for Halim to come down. Before his feet cleared, I heard a small sound of surprise and then his body dropped through the ladder tube. He hit the floor with a thud I could feel through my feet and staggered backward.

With another small yelp of surprise, Halim lost his balance completely and landed flat on his ass. I really did try not to laugh. Fortunately, Halim beat me to it, laughing as he flopped the rest of the way back down. "This is terrible."

"I warned you." I offered him a hand up.

He waved it away. "You're injured."

"That's why you're only getting one hand." I beckoned. "Come on. Let me help you up."

He pushed himself up, still chuckling, but there was a strain in his voice. "I can't believe we used to live like this."

"For generations." I offered my good hand again. "Maybe gravity is too hard for you delicate fellows. We can just keep y'all sequestered in the spindle."

"Or we just start taking turns about who lives here." Ignoring my offered hand, he rolled to his knees and reached for the ladder to pull himself up.

And he fainted. Gravity. It does a number on you.

I stood at the whiteboard in the LMA. I kept trying to tuck my clipboard under my arm and bumping the burn with the edge.

264 * MARY ROBINETTE KOWAL

Holding it in one hand, I faced my crew. Forty-nine women and three men. Halim, Wilburt, and Howard looked miserable. Poor Howard had fainted and then vomited when he got down to the ring for the first time. It was like returning to Earth plus a constant spinning.

"Morning, folks." I smiled at my crew.

"Good morning, Dr. York." The singsong response that we'd greeted Leonard with had somehow translated up from Mars and gotten applied to me.

"We're going to go over this week's duty roster, with our priority being to finish loading the *Esther* so the boys can head back down to Mars."

"Yes, please." Halim tried to sit up straight but kept sagging back into gravity's grip.

"I told y'all to stay in the spindle."

Wilburt shook his head and then closed his eyes, swallowing. I'm sure he'd been about to say that he was fine and make a joke but none of them had acclimated yet. It had taken us a week to feel even vaguely normal. What would the future hold for the generations born on Mars?

My gaze went to Aahana, who sat near the back. She had her game face on, but her cheeks were hollow.

Turning back to the board, I started at the top. "Engineering, y'all are going to do a breakout session after this with Mavis. She's got a detailed roster for you. Mavis, you want to give the high-level view?"

She nodded and stood where she was. "Short form is that we need to get caught up on maintenance on the ship. We're doing fine, but a bunch of stuff got put off while we've been concentrating on salvaging the engine. I figure we can turn it into a contest."

"What's the prize?"

"I got a box of chocolate for the team that gets through their tasks—with the caveat that I get say-so on if the task is actually done."

Ida said, "A box of chocolate? Can I switch to engineering?"

Everyone laughed and I looked at Wilburt, waiting for his joke. He was bracing himself with his elbows on his knees.

"Request denied, but nice try. Moving on to biology." I winked at her and started to turn back to the board but a raised hand stopped me. "Beth Anne?"

The petite blonde wore her hair in pigtails, which always made me think about Ruby Donaldson. "I just noticed that the schedule has us working over the Fourth. Can we have the sol off?"

I stared at her for a long minute. It was Maym 26th. The schedule I had on the board didn't go into the next month—no. Wait. She was talking about an Earth date. "The Fourth of July." I gave a little laugh of disbelief. "Goodness, I'd switched over to Mars dates so thoroughly I was trying to figure out why you were talking about Jum fourth."

Beth Anne wrinkled her nose. "Sorry, I should have said Independence Day to remove the ambiguity."

"It was only Independence Day for some people," Florence muttered.

"I know everyone isn't American." Beth Anne twisted the end of a braid. "But I thought that maybe we could take turns. Like Americans get the Fourth off and the French folks get Bastille Day. You know. Keep the connection to Earth."

"That's not what I meant." Florence lifted her head. "I meant that some of our ancestors were still enslaved. Why should you get the Fourth off, when we rolled right over Juneteenth?"

"What?"

Ida said, "June nineteenth. When Black folks celebrate the end of slavery. In the US."

"I guess that should be a sol off, too? Maybe we could make a calendar of which holidays we want to celebrate and coordinate that with the duty rosters." Beth Anne looked so young and so earnest.

"There wouldn't be a single workday left then. Celebrating every little thing."

I didn't see who said that.

Florence turned in her seat, looking for the voice. "Every little thing? You think the end of slavery was a little thing?"

Oh no. I knew that voice from her and had been on the receiving end more than once. To pull the focus back to me, I stepped forward. "As we adapt to living on Mars, the way we celebrate holidays will change. Maybe we'll have a purely Martian holiday to commemorate Landing Day. Maybe it'll have fireworks, but the chemical formulation will have to be completely different to ignite at all."

Mavis said, "If we weren't salvaging and recycling everything, we could jettison garbage and stage meteor showers for Bradbury."

"That would be appropriate for the Fourth." Ida snorted. "Burning gar—"

An alarm went off.

It was the triple-pulse pattern that signaled a problem in Bradbury Base. In moments like this, my anxiety vanishes and is replaced by a clear map of what needs to be done, as if all my background fretting had been in preparation for this.

"Florence, Kciko—comms. Halim and crew, prep the *Esther* in case we need to send help down. Ana Teresa, prep a med kit to go with them. Helen, Ida, and Anita, prep the *Matsu* in case we need to do an evac for Bradbury." We had two landers, but they would only hold forty people total. Six of those people would be crew. There were forty-eight people on Mars. Fourteen would get left behind. "Mavis and Heidi with me to the command module. Everyone else, secure your stations and listen for orders."

Everyone moved. Quiet, and calm, and professional. I headed for the ladder, tossing my clipboard on the table as I went. But even as I climbed out of Earth's gravity well, I knew that there wasn't a damn thing we would be able to do from here.

Best-case scenario would put the shuttle crews on Mars in six hours. Bradbury was on their own.

TWENTY-FIVE

PREGNANCY ON MARS

UNITED NATIONS, Kansas, July 1, 1970—The issue of abortion has been thrust into the spotlight, following the news that Aahana Kamal, a colonist on the Second Mars Expedition, has become pregnant during the mission. The news has sparked a heated debate among the members of the United Nations, with both sides arguing passionately for their respective positions.

Sources within the International Aerospace Coalition have reported that Kamal has expressed a desire to have an abortion, citing the extreme conditions of space travel and the potential dangers to both herself and the fetus. Stetson Parker, the interim director of the International Aerospace Coalition, stated, "We will be following the directives of the United Nations in consultation with our flight surgeons. Clearly, this matter will require careful consideration and discussion to balance the concerns of the international community and the safety of our *habitante*."

Maym 26, Year 5, Monsol—Landing + 143 sols

Nicole once told me that she thought not knowing was the worst. I am inclined to agree with her. We were waiting in the command module, looking at the board that contained telemetry from Bradbury Base. I kept picking at the bandage holding my hand flat on the plastic board. I wasn't going to need to fly the *Goddard*. I didn't have to take it off.

It was so hard to be smart and leave it alone.

We knew that there was a CO_2 alarm on Bradbury. We could tell that the levels in the main dome were dangerously high. We had confirmed—albeit with a forty-three-minute delay—that Mission's Control telemetry was the same as ours and that they had recorded a sudden, massive spike in levels. They reported that they also could not get a response from Bradbury.

We could not tell anything beyond that.

I reached for the mic to call comms and then pulled my hand back. Asking them to try to raise Bradbury again would be obnoxious because it would show a lack of trust. Of course, Florence would contact me when they had reconnected with the base. We had satellite coverage, but sometimes the handover periods created a Loss of Signal.

This was longer than any LOS should be.

3.1415926535 . . .

"CO_2 levels are dropping." Mavis tapped the gauge and frowned. "Not fast."

"That's good though, right?" My neck was tight and stiff. I rolled it to the side to try to crack it. "It means someone is working the problem."

"Maybe. Or maybe the scrubbers are catching up after the initial leak." She winced. "Sorry. I just . . ."

"I understand." All of us had friends or husbands down there. I picked at the bandage. I wanted that level drop to be Nathaniel working the problem. I wanted them all to be in emergency oxygen masks and evacuated to the other dome. I wanted to know.

The radio crackled and my heart tightened with hope. But it was Halim. "*Goddard, Esther.* We're ready to disengage on your orders."

"Thank you, *Esther,* stand by." My brain could spin out all sorts of scenarios. Everyone dead. Some dead. Some brain damaged. Everyone fine, but with nasty headaches. Everyone was fine, but comms was flooded with CO_2 because it was downstairs—like Nathaniel's office—and CO_2 was heavier than oxygen.

. . . 8979323846 . . .

One of the reasons we place so much emphasis on contingency plans and sims was so that in moments like this, we didn't make decisions due to panic. I took another breath to keep my airways open. We had run a comparable scenario in a sim, except the crews hadn't been split like this. "*Matsu*, what's your status?"

"We're on step forty-seven A of the preflight checklist." Behind Helen's voice, I could just barely hear the rhythm of Ida and Anita doing a call-and-response as they worked their own lists. "We should be ready to disengage in another hour."

"Thank you, *Matsu*." They were having to play catch-up because none of the preflight work had been done, whereas the *Esther* was already prepped for a departure. The part of me that used to be a NavComp could see the trajectories traced across the inside of my skull. Departing an hour later would give them wildly different arrival times. And we still didn't know what they would find when they landed, which elevated the likelihood of sending them prepped for the wrong emergency. Repairs were a far cry from an evacuation. I wet my lips and toggled back to the *Esther*. "Halim, the *Matsu* crew is an hour away from departure. We're going to hold you until they are prepped."

"Copy that." The line was silent for a moment. "Should we use the time to unload some of the cargo to make more room for passengers."

"Negative. You can off-load on the surface if needed." We could only make so many trips. If we sent them down and it was unnecessary, then that slowed down building the new HVAC and wasted resources.

I looked out the window and saw the terminator approaching. We were going to the night side of Mars while Bradbury Base still lay close to morning. Forty-six minutes to cross the far side of the planet.

Below us, the last light of sol rolled past, leaving the planet dark. Before, that lack of man-made lights had seemed like potential. Now it was a terrifying reminder that Mars might have become uninhabited. Floating against my harness, I rubbed the space between my brows, then turned to Heidi, in the NavComp seat. I could do this math, and honestly wanted to, because it would give me *something* to do, but it was Heidi's job. For the moment, my own awareness of what the flight paths meant was enough to make a decision. "Will you calculate a trajectory for the *Matsu*, with a departure seventy-five minutes from now?"

"On it."

That would give them time to complete their preflight check and put us back in range for a good trajectory to Bradbury.

I opened a channel to both ships. "*Esther, Matsu, Goddard.* If Bradbury remains nonresponsive, I'm going to have *Matsu* drop to do recon, because they aren't loaded with cargo. Halim, you'll disembark an hour later and move to a lower orbit, which will allow you to join them quickly if evac is necessary or return to the *Goddard* with minimal fuel expenditure if not."

And now all I could do was wait.

. . . 2643383279 . . .

I lost count working pi and had to start over three times before we came out of the shadow of Mars at 1216 Bradbury time. Below us, the thin slice of atmosphere rimmed the void where the planet slept. Then the sun burst over the edge, chasing shadows back, and unfurled the reds and umbers of Mars.

Without preamble, the comm circuit lit up and Florence piped a male voice into the command module. ". . . update from Bradbury Base." That was Parker's voice.

But why the hell was Parker giving us an update? Chills chased themselves over my arms and legs. Who was dead?

"The information he sent is that at 0914 local time at Bradbury, there was a rupture in the cooling system, leading to its compressed CO_2 flooding Dome One. Sensors worked as planned, but the rise in CO_2 was so sudden that they were forced to evacuate to Dome Two."

He? Who was he? And 0914? That would have been during their morning meeting, at the same time we were having ours. I tugged at the bandage, starting to unwind it and stopped myself. *Do not act rashly. Do not make the situation worse.*

"All crew members are now present and accounted for. They are receiving appropriate medical treatment."

Mavis curled toward fetal which is what happens when the tension sags out of you in zero-g. "Thank Darwin."

My breath was still shallow because Parker was now the head of the IAC. If this were only an update, we would be hearing from the CAPCOM on shift. "Appropriate medical attention" could mean so many things.

"By this time, your console should be showing you telemetry from Bradbury. You'll note that the CO_2 levels are still elevated. In order to reach comms and reestablish contact, Rob Kimbro had to wear a Mars suit." I could hear Parker's inhalation. I could see the way his jaw tightened before he had to deliver bad news. "Three members of the crew were on the lower level in the engineering department when the breach occurred."

Nathaniel.

"Reynard Carmouche and Nathaniel York had been completing some work. Lance Woolen was sent downstairs to retrieve them from engineering at the start of their morning staff meeting. Carmouche is conscious and was able to give us a report that York succumbed to the CO_2 before the alarms went off. Carmouche had a mask at his desk and was able to retrieve a mask for York. He found Woolen while attempting to get York up the stairs to the main floor. Carmouche was unable to get both men up on his own."

The masks held five minutes of oxygen. They were only intended to buy you time to get to safety. I boxed up all my feelings about the phrases "Carmouche is conscious" and "attempting to get York up the stairs" while I listened to the rest of Parker's report from the end of a long tunnel.

"He requested help from the other dome, but the intercom at

that airlock was malfunctioning and did not transmit." Again, the inhalation from Parker, as if he were giving us time to process this. "Because Carmouche went immediately back downstairs to swap masks on York and Woolen, he did not realize that Dome Two had not heard him. Fortunately, Flannery had done a head count in Dome Two and had realized that the men were missing. They are all currently in Dome Two and Shamoun is treating them for CO_2 exposure now."

A part of me noted that I had made the right call to hold the ships until we knew more. Sending them down would have meant sending the wrong aid and six hours too late.

The rest of me stared straight out the window of the *Goddard* as Mars blurred in my vision. I wasn't crying, but my face was so rigidly calm that I had forgotten to blink. I had forgotten to breathe.

"Bradbury Base will be in contact with you at 1300 hours about the specific needs they have. I want to assure you that we here at Mission Control stand ready to support you in any way we can. Message repeats. *Goddard*, Mission Control. This is Acting Director Stetson Parker of the IAC. Rob Kimbro reestablished comms with us at 1112 during one of your LOS's and I'm relaying his update from Bradbury Base. The information he sent is—"

Florence cut it off and spoke into the mic. "We're recording it so you can listen back later. Do you want to send a response?"

I blinked. I inhaled and from the tunnel, I watched my hand flip the comms switch to respond. "Yes, thank you. Voice, please. Let me know when you are ready to proceed?"

The speakers hissed in the pause, then she said, "I've got you patched in. Go ahead."

"Mission Control, *Goddard*. This is Elma York, captain, speaking. Thank you for the report. We will stand by to assist Bradbury Base in any way they need. From your report, the lead engineer and two of his staff are down for the count. My suggestion is that we send a small team of engineers to assist in their repairs. The *Esther* is nearly loaded with material for the HVAC installation and standing by for departure. Can you ask the engineering backrooms at Mission Control if there are any additional supplies we should include in that shipment? York out."

My hand turned off the mic. I stared out the window. I blinked. There were things that needed doing. I looked at the clock. "We have half an hour before we're scheduled to talk with Bradbury." I stared out the window and my brain made lists of things, stacking tasks into a neat order almost like pushing numbers into alignment. "You two can stand down while we wait."

Heidi unbuckled and pushed closer. "Elma . . . are you okay?"

I think the answer to that was no, but a blanket of numb distance filled the space between my heart and my body. "I'm nominal." I needed to let Helen and Opal know about their husbands but those would be in-person conversations.

Actually, I needed to give everyone a status update. My hand reached for the mic, toggling it for shipwide broadcast. "Attention all crew. Attention all crew. We've reestablished contact with Bradbury through Mission Control. They had a CO_2 leak but everyone is present and accounted for. You may stand down from your readiness stations and return to normal duties. I'll have a full update after I've had a chance to talk with Bradbury directly and we'll adjust duty rosters as necessary at that time. Good work tosol. I'm proud of y'all."

My hand turned the mic back off. *3.1415 . . . 3.141 . . . 3.14. Three.* Three members of the crew were on the lower level in the engineering department when the breach occurred.

Shaking my head, I flipped the toggle to address the *Esther*. "*Esther, Goddard.* Halim, y'all can stand down. It sounds like Bradbury needs to do some assessments so we're going to stand by before sending you to the surface."

"Roger, wilco. That announcement was good to hear. Glad they're all okay."

3.14 . . . Three. Three. Three.

"Yes. I'll keep you updated." I turned the toggle to *Matsu.* "*Matsu, Goddard.* Y'all can stand down. It sounds like the Bradbury needs to do some assessments but there's no urgent need for you to go to the surface." I dug my fingers into the burn so that I could feel something. "Ida and Anita, will you handle shutdown? I need to borrow Helen for a bit."

There was silence for a moment. When Helen replied, I could hear the panic in her calm, calm voice. "I'm handing control to Ida. I'll meet you in the spindle in five."

"Copy that." The mic was turned off. That task was finished. I unbuckled my harness and twisted free of the gear. Heidi reached out a hand but I waved her off. "I have to tell Helen and Opal about their husbands."

"But Nathaniel—"

"I trust Kam's skills and there is nothing I can do for him. But I can help Helen and Opal." My body knew how to orient itself to go to the door. I followed it, aware that Heidi and Mavis were still staring at me. I supermanned into the spindle and hooked left to go to the shuttle airlocks.

The zero-g toilet was next to the command module. I stopped and then pulled myself inside. I had five minutes.

I wanted to react. I wanted to weep. Or vomit. Or shake or something. But all I felt was cold.

Squeezing my burned hand, I waited for the bright pain to mean something, to bring tears to my eyes or to melt the ice that surrounded me.

Nathaniel had been exposed to high levels of CO_2. He had been unconscious, even after being moved to an oxygen environment. He was not okay. And here's the thing they teach us about CO_2 exposure. You think it's dangerous because it's not oxygen, but that's not the real problem. The real problem is that it binds to hemoglobin in the red blood cells. Even after you've been given oxygen, that CO_2 is still hanging out, reducing the amount of oxygen in your bloodstream.

Nathaniel was still unconscious.

He already had nerve damage and there was no telling what other health problems he was hiding. *He shouldn't be here at all.* I started to shake. The cracks let the real fear push out. Go long enough without adequate oxygen to the brain and you got brain damage.

Nathaniel was still unconscious.

My throat closed and I pressed my hands across my mouth, squeezing my eyes shut. I would prefer a BusyBee to the bathroom, but I had a lot of practice at crying silently.

And I had three minutes until I needed to be there for Helen. Three.

Helen and Opal both took the news about their husbands as calmly as I appeared to. All of us were lying or in shock or both. Now I clutched a clipboard, floating in comms with Helen, Mavis, and Florence. I had invited Opal, but she declined because she felt like she would be a distraction. The clock ticked over to 1300, and right on the mark, the circuit from Bradbury came alive.

"*Goddard,* Bradbury." Rob Kimbro's voice joined us in space. "I have Leonard, Kam, and Bolí here."

"Bradbury, *Goddard.* We read you loud and clear. I have Elma, Mavis, and Helen here." Florence nodded to me that I had the go-ahead to talk.

"Hey y'all. Sounds like you had quite the morning." I tightened my fist around my next question. *How is my husband.* "How can we help?"

"Hi, Elma . . ." Leonard cleared his throat. "Before we dive in, I want Kam to give you and Helen an update on your husbands."

Helen's gaze cut sharply to me. When I told her about Reynard, I hadn't told her about Nathaniel because I had wanted to make sure she could focus on her husband. My back was sweating and the room was too warm.

"I appreciate that, Leonard." I tucked my good hand in my

pocket and felt the comforting smooth surface of a folded emesis bag.

Kam's voice was calm and soothing. "Helen, Reynard is doing well. He's got a headache and some nausea, but is otherwise unaffected. He says that you told him to keep a mask at his desk and we're lucky that he did."

Nodding, Helen's face was impassive. "I am glad that my paranoia was of use."

"Paranoia?" Kam asked.

"Ah . . . yes." She looked down as if embarrassed by this. "Well, during the events on the Moon, I was caught in the equipment room without a mask. Since then, I . . . I find it easier to go downstairs if I have one with me. I asked Reynard to do so as well for my peace of mind."

When I'd come back from the First Mars Expedition, I'd heard stories about what had happened while we were gone but always in that joking way which masks past trauma as comedy. Helen's version of realizing that she was breathing CO_2 was funny and full of overplayed confusion.

It hid the fact that the real event must have been terrifying.

"We're all glad that you did or things would have been much worse." Kam's voice softened. "Elma, Nathaniel is awake now. He's confused, but that should pass."

I wanted to know if his "chronic condition" would affect the outcome. I should have talked to him about the neuropathy instead of deciding to wait until I saw him face to face. Then I would have more information with which to make decisions.

"Thank you for that good report." If I let myself ask any questions about Nathaniel, the meeting would become nothing but my concern for my husband. "And Lance?"

"Concerning. He has not regained consciousness. From our reconstruction of the timeline, I think it likely that he was exposed for seven minutes before Reynard found him and got the mask on him."

I swallowed. Brain damage started happening at the two-minute mark. "Prognosis?"

"Won't know until he wakes up." Kam left the "if" unspoken. "But . . . and I say this for information, even knowing that it will make you both worry more, but . . . brain damage from CO_2 poisoning can show up a couple of weeks after it happens. We'll keep a very close eye on them and, honestly, on everyone else. We were all exposed."

"That's terrifying as hell," Mavis said. "And y'all are down three engineers."

I nodded, even though the people on the ground couldn't see me. My brain felt sluggish, skipping and returning to Nathaniel in every silence. I uncapped my pen and wrote *Actions* at the top of the clipboard, trying to externalize my thoughts so that they could be useful. "We can send a team down to help with repairs."

"Good, thank you." Leonard's voice was ragged. I would bet anything that he had run his emergency oxygen out evacuating folks from Dome One. "Mission Control is putting together a list of suggested supplies for you to bring down."

That should have been Nathaniel. My throat closed and I pressed the cap of the pen into the burn until I saw spots of white at the edges of my vision. I swallowed. "Mavis, why don't you take lead on coordinating the repairs."

She nodded, scribbling notes of her own. "I'm going to need everything y'all know about what happened."

"Copy that. I had Bolí and Sheldon compile a report. It's still incomplete but we can give you the preliminary overview now."

They started talking through the problem and I floated there, trying to stay focused. My attention skittered from the piece of tape holding a checklist on the teletype, then to Nathaniel, and then back to Bolí saying ". . . overpressurization event likely caused . . ." to the hum of the fans. I took copious notes, writing down what people were saying without fully hearing them.

My breath was shallow and the room was too hot.

"Excuse me. I need to visit the facilities. Back in a bit!" My voice was chipper. I smiled even as I kicked out of the room, twisting through the hatch.

I needed to come apart. Just for a little bit and then I could go back in and be useful. I supermanned down the spindle, passing Anita and Meredith, and waved and smiled and made it past them to the hatch of the *Esther*.

She wasn't a BusyBee, but she was soundproof and empty except for supplies. I pulled myself in and shut the hatch behind me with a ripple-bang of safety. Hanging in the middle of the ship named after my aunt, I drifted, curling into a ball.

The Too Much of everything pushed up into my throat. *Neuropathy. Brain damage from CO_2 poisoning can show up a couple of weeks after it happens. Chronic condition. Confused.*

He had to be all right. If Nathaniel couldn't work, it would kill him. I couldn't do anything. None of this was something I could math my way through or—or . . . I buried my face in my hands, throat burning with salt. Even here, even alone, I was quiet when I cried.

But I was so scared.

The ripple-bang of the hatch made me flinch. I spun away from the door to put my back to it.

"Elma?" Helen said.

I cleared my throat and wiped a globe of tears away from my eyes. "Yes. Do they need me?"

"No. Mavis has it under control right now." She floated just behind me. "Nathaniel . . . what do *you* need?"

"I—"

Whatever thin hull of control I'd been able to pull around me shattered against the wind of her kindness and I disintegrated into racking sobs. She wrapped her arms around me, as if she were trying to keep the pieces of me from spinning off into space. I hung in my friend's arms. One hand latched on to her sleeve and dug in as if that would keep me from dropping down the gravity well of overwhelming fear.

We rotated in that cluttered space as my fear spun out around us and she reminded me that we were safe. That whatever came next, we would face together. I wasn't alone.

And neither was Nathaniel.

We had a crew. We had friends. It would be okay.

He would be okay.

TWENTY-SIX

MARTIAN COLONY STILL
REELING FROM TOXIC GAS

BRADBURY BASE, Mars, Sunday, July 5, 1970—
With the lives of three astronauts hanging in the balance,
the remaining crew members of the compromised Bradbury Base worked around the clock to repair a breach in
their environmental systems. The International Aerospace Coalition plans to send an emergency repair team
down from the *Goddard* in a drastic change of plans
caused by Wednesday night's massive surge in CO_2 levels
in the Martian habitat.

Interim Director Stetson Parker of the IAC called it
"the most critical situation" in the history of the international space program. Though the source of the breach
is as yet unknown, he said, "the chances of our *résidents*
making a full repair to the habitat are excellent." Compli-
cating the repairs, tomorrow Mars will pass behind the
sun, cutting off communications to Earth for twenty-two
days.

Maym 29, Year 5, Thursol–Landing + 146 sols

Three sols after the accident, I secured my pen on one of the
Velcro patches on the comms desk and stared at the clipboard
where I'd been tracking the conversation. Mavis had it well in
hand, but she and Wilburt did not always see eye to eye, so my
job was to make sure they were having the same conversation.

I tried to paraphrase back the details that Leonard and Bolí had just shared with us. "Okay . . . so the fact that the CO_2 levels still aren't coming down is either due to a problem with the scrubbers or the original breach is still leaking." I wanted Nathaniel. Beyond my personal yearning for him, he had talked about a problem with the scrubbers. We needed his input on this before we lost contact with Earth. "How do you determine where the problem is?"

"Well, that's just tracing the CO_2 lines." Mavis drummed her pen on the edge of her board.

"It would be more efficient to look at saturation levels." Wilburt shook his head. "Many parts of the system are only accessible if we excavate."

"But you can test line pressure without that."

Florence hung near her station, working on an embroidery project with radiant green thread. I watched her needle rise and fall through the fabric.

From Mars, Bolí said, "Mavis has a point and it does seem as if—oh. Nathaniel. Hey."

"Does Kam know you're up? Whoa—" Leonard's mic thumped and his voice got distant. "Sit down."

My heart stopped and flung itself toward Mars.

Muffled and tiny, the shape of my husband's voice sounded wrong. The microphones both went silent.

The comms module fans hummed. Mavis stared at me, wide-eyed. Florence's needle paused, glistening in the light. Between them, Wilburt gnawed on his lower lip.

I unclenched my fists and then toggled my mic. "Can I talk to him?"

My clipboard was floating across the room. I had let go of it at some point.

The speaker crackled. "Yeah. Um." Bolí cleared his throat and there was a conversation behind him that I couldn't make out. "Yeah. Just give us a minute to switch over to speakers, Elma."

"Sure. Of course." I pulled my hand back from the mic and stared at the black and chrome base of it. I wet my lips and turned to Mavis. "I think we should add Opal to the list of people going down. Engineering department. Been to the surface. And seeing Lance will probably help both of them."

She stared at me and opened her mouth. Then shut it, shaking her head. "Suuuure . . . yeah. Yeah, I'd been thinking the same thing. Yep. Have you fly us down and—"

"Negative." I wanted to go down to see Nathaniel. God, how much I wanted that, but I had this ship to run and there were people in Bradbury that I trusted to look after him. It was still hard to breathe past the longing to go. I held up my hand as if my burn were the entirety of the reason. "We'll send Helen as pilot."

"Okay . . ." She exchanged a look with Florence. "But we would be okay if you wanted—"

The mic from the surface crackled and she shut up.

"Elma, hi." Nathaniel's voice was low and slower than it should be, as if he had the flu.

I closed my eyes so I didn't have to see Wilburt or Mavis or Florence watching me. "Nathaniel." My throat tightened with yearning for him. I swallowed so that I could speak. "How are you feeling?"

"A little dizzy, but otherwise fine." His voice did not sound fine. I couldn't even define exactly what was wrong with it. A sluggishness. Or a hint of slurring but not really. Just . . . just not right. "Glad I caught you. I was just coming to talk to Leonard about the accident."

I could hear Leonard's voice behind him and made a bet that he was telling Nathaniel to go back to bed. The same way I was. "Sweetheart, you're supposed to be resting."

"I'm fine." He cleared his throat. "Listen. Listen, I want to look at the—"

"No, Nathaniel, you're not." I bent my head, eyes still closed and tried to imagine him sitting in front of me. His hair would be mussed, but he'd be hunched forward drawing pictures in the air with his hands. "I need you to go back to bed now."

"I've been doing nothing but sleeping. We can't afford to be down any engineers and—"

THE MARTIAN CONTINGENCY * 283

Bolí cut in. "Your hands are shaking like a leaf. You'd short anything you tried to wire."

"What?" Nathaniel sighed. "I . . . I just had coffee. And I'm talking about going over plans, not wiring."

I knew this pattern. He was going to dig in and keep pestering people until they gave him schematics to quiet him the way you'd give a pacifier to a baby. But he wasn't a baby. "Nathaniel Ezra York, you are going to stop talking to me and go straight back to bed where you will stay until Kam tells me that you are allowed up."

"Wow. All three names?"

"Your refusal to address your health is affecting the mission. I love you, but right now I am not speaking as your wife. Go. To. Bed."

"But there's a problem. We need to—Leonard, I'm fine. Just listen to me for a minute."

"Bed." I hated making him feel useless but he wasn't helping. "There are other people who can do this work, Nathaniel. We're sending engineers down from the *Goddard* who are completely capable of tracing saturation levels."

"No. That's just it. Using the plans to track the problem isn't going to work. There are undocumented changes and the breach has to be in one of—let go of me." Fabric rustled. "No. I'm not imagining things."

"Wait—" I opened my eyes and reached out as if I could touch him. "Wait, what do you mean undocumented changes?"

Florence had looked away and was staring at the microphone closest to her.

"Before the breach. Remember, I'd found a patch and no one could tell me what it was for? So, I was trying to reverse engineer it to figure out why it was there and where I should look for related changes." As he picked up speed, Nathaniel's voice started to sound a little more like him. Still dragged out and rough, but more activated. "I've been lying in bed thinking about why this happened. I think it was an overpressurization event because there's a loop of life support that isn't attached to the main system."

A murmur in the background.

Wilburt laughed uneasily. "Nathaniel, you aren't making any sense. Why would part of the life support not be attached?"

I knew the answer. All the pieces had been there and I kept being told that it wasn't important. That it had happened four years ago. That I was imagining things. "Because the First Expedition diverted life support to make a prison."

Florence stowed her needle, weaving it into the fabric. She stared at the microphone.

A sharp crack sounded as if another mic were being plugged into a hot channel, which is probably what happened. Leonard said, "Elma, Nathaniel's not looking great, so we're going to take him back to medical."

All of the emotion that had been at a distance flared up and I wanted to scream at him and I wanted to cry. I don't know what my face was doing, but my hands were knotted into fists.

"Do not use my husband as a tool to avoid this conversation, because if he is right then your silence has led directly to harming our crewmates." My voice was pilot calm. "I need you to explain to Nathaniel, Bolí, and Mavis what happened on the First Expedition."

Florence flicked the switch on her mic. "Leonard."

"I know." He sighed. "I know."

Wilburt sagged in on himself. "Thank God."

Mavis spun on Wilburt, slapping a hand against the ceiling to keep from over-rotating, and her voice was *not* pilot calm. "What the fuck. We've been trying to work this problem and you knew that there was an isolated subsystem?"

He flinched. "Yes. I mean, no. I didn't build it. I knew there had been changes but I thought we had all of them reversed."

"Next time maybe tell me I should be looking for 'changes.'" She looked mad enough to spit literal nails. "This was irresponsible, unprofessional, and reckless. Do y'all not have a—"

"Mavis." I flattened my hand. Sweat filmed my palm. But my voice was so steady. "This is a blame-free mission. What happened on the First Expedition happened for reasons I don't understand, but right now we are all on the same team here. We have not been. I think what we've learned is that when we withhold information everyone suffers. So, let's all get back on the same team and work this problem. Okay?"

"Yes, ma'am. Noted." She drew in a deep breath as if she were sucking all that outrage back down into a vacuum-sealed box for later disposal. When she looked at Wilburt again, her cheeks were still red with anger, but her voice was calm and professional. "I would appreciate a full briefing on the changes made during the First Expedition."

Wilburt looked cowed and relieved at the same time. "I will provide as much information as I have."

"Let me take the initial briefing." Leonard's voice was rougher than I'd ever heard it. He cleared his throat. "Elma, you got some of it right. When we got down here, DeBeer was a real problem. Parker had been the only one who could really keep him in line. After the sign incident on the *Pinta,* Parker told him that he'd do everything in his power to keep him grounded when we got back. And then when the shit down here started up, Benkoski reported the problem to Mission Control. They said that we should 'work on our interpersonal communications.'"

Mavis rolled her eyes. "Of course they did."

Leonard snorted into the mic. "I was given time with one of the shrinks to 'talk about my feelings.' But I knew how that was going to go."

Halim had told me that. He'd told me that the shrinks had thought they'd solved the problem but these men had just clammed up and not talked about it. What would have happened if they had felt free to talk? In a world where either of them would have been honest about their feelings, it might never have gotten this far. But maybe that was me trying to fix things after the fact. "And DeBeer?"

"Nothing happened to DeBeer so . . . knowing he was getting booted out of the program when we got back, he had nothing to lose and no consequences here. Benkoski had been reporting the problems to Earth and at a certain point I think he just gave up."

I winced, remembering how often DeBeer had been offensive in training and on the way out. On the way back . . . I realized that I hadn't seen him until we docked with *Lunetta*.

"Benkoski confined him to quarters after each infraction. And then he'd come back out because we needed him. Then he stopped obeying the order to stay confined. It's not like the dorms lock, right?"

"Is that when you built the jail?"

Wilburt shook his head. "It wasn't—DeBeer built it."

The room seemed to unfocus and refocus.

Aut viam inveniam aut faciam. "I shall either find a way or make one." I blinked as pieces that hadn't made sense began to rearrange themselves. "Leonard. You were in there for ninety-seven sols?"

"All of us were." Florence's eyes were closed and sweat beaded her upper lip. "Everyone from the 'separate but equal ship.'"

Fans hummed in the module. Wilburt had hunched in on himself, hands clenched together. He looked green. I remembered him telling me that if he'd been the right age, he thought he would have been a Nazi. Was *this* why he thought that? Had he helped DeBeer?

Over comms, Bolí made a long whistle that crackled over the speakers. "How the hell did this one asshole keep you all—"

"A gun." Florence yanked her headset off and pushed away from the comms console. "Excuse me."

The headset drifted in her wake, cord kinking on itself as it twisted in the air. Mavis grabbed it, looking at the hatch Florence had gone through. "Should—"

Wilburt slashed the air with his hand. "Leave her alone."

Over the speaker, Leonard's voice was as calm as if he were discussing a sim. "DeBeer made an improvised projectile weapon with compressed gas. He shot Florence."

It felt as if those words silenced even the fans.

On Earth, we had too many examples of a single person using their hatred to dominate and terrorize. Mars was supposed to be different. My palms were sweating. I wanted to say something to fix that awful silence.

Some things can't be fixed.

I took a slow breath and counted to ten. My heart wouldn't support anything more complicated than that. The harm that their silence had allowed was unchanged, but the reasons and decisions around it reshaped themselves into a different pattern. I let the breath out again, counting down as if I were approaching a launch.

"Thank you for that good report." I flexed my toes under the rail and reoriented to face Wilburt, who was the only member of the First Expedition I could see in this moment. He looked as if he wanted to vomit. "What would be most useful now?"

"Speaking only for myself, I would like to work through the plans and notate the deviations I know of." Wilburt wiped the back of his neck with one hand. "I am now afraid that there are others. DeBeer saw what Earth First had done on the Moon and made a remote detonator that he kept on his person. You asked how one man could do this? Because we—those of us who were white—we helped him."

Mavis made a full body shudder that pushed her away from the wall. "You helped him do what, exactly?"

"Wilburt kept us alive." Leonard's voice remained calm and detached. "He pretended to be DeBeer's friend so that we got food and life support."

"You're telling me that—"

"Stop." Every connection in my body had tightened to the point that I was trembling. I wanted to know what had happened. I wanted to know exactly whose fault it was. And I'd seen the way gentiles leaned in to stories of Holocaust survivors as if their curiosity were the most important thing. "We are not making these people relive their trauma. We only need to know what was changed."

Wilburt closed his eyes, clenching his hands so that the

knuckles were white. Mavis's jaw was set as if she were about to fight me.

Over the speakers, Leonard murmured, "Thank you."

"Okay." I grabbed my clipboard out of the air and turned back to the microphone, as if I were the mission commander instead of him. "Nathaniel, Bolí is going to escort you back to bed. We'll update you when we hit a stumbling block. Until then, your mandate is rest."

"Elma, you know that I'm not going to be able to rest after learning about . . . all this."

The problem was that I did know that. Work was going to kill him and not working was going to kill him. If he went to bed now, he would lie awake working the problem. That drive made him Nathaniel. It gave him life as much as overwork hurt him. For years, I had known where that line was for him and could pull him away.

Now . . . now his health was in a different place. "I do know that, Nathaniel. But you're going to have to learn to rest." My eyes were dry and burned. With the information that the First Expedition team had just shared, they actually did need Nathaniel looking at the plans with them. "Mavis is lead on the repairs and will be coming down to the surface soon. You may stay for this briefing so that you are up to date. After an hour, you will take a mandatory rest period. Is that clear?"

Static hissed on my headset. I closed my eyes and could see him, mouth opening to protest.

"Yes, ma'am." He didn't sound bitter, only resigned. "Confirmed, briefing then rest period."

"Good." I opened my eyes and found Mavis but focusing was hard. My body went through the motions of giving a nod and a reassuring smile. "Mavis, you have the meeting."

I left the comms center and the temptation was to find Florence. But she did not need me trying to fix things. She had needed space and I understood that.

My own heart was unstitching itself as I slid down the ladder closest to medical. Earth's gravity matched my inside. I felt heavy and a little queasy, shaping and reshaping sentences in my mind. I walked through the gym, smiling at people. I waved hello at Anita and Yung-Chiu.

At the door to medical, I let the mask drop. Knocking, I waited, all emptied out inside. Ana Teresa opened the door and looked at me. I halfway expected to see Aahana because that was how the sol was going. Instead, she was alone, and her small desk was strewn with forms. "Come in. What's going on with your hand?"

"Oh—it's fine." I held up my hand to stop her protest before it could get rolling. "I'm not just saying that. I'd honestly forgotten it was burned. No, I'm here because I'm . . . I'm not okay."

Her face softened. The pilots joked that she was the Terrier of Space, because most of the time she was mad at us for lying to her. Which . . . fair. But terriers could be soft and loving, too. The concern that welled up in her eyes made my chest constrict. She pulled another chair up to her desk and gestured to it. I sat down, hands pressed flat on my thighs.

Ana Teresa waited.

"I don't." My eyes burned again and my pulse pounded in my ears. It was hard to speak. "I don't want to be the next thing that breaks."

"Elma." I fully expected her to make a joke about me being a pilot and admitting that something was wrong, but she sighed and locked the door to the MedMod. "What are the things that make you feel as if you might break?"

My mind coughed out a list that was so full it crowded out words. Where to even start? Nathaniel? The First Expedition? Aahana? Being in command? The CO_2 problems? Parker?

Ana Teresa waited. She filled a sip pack with water and set it in front of me.

"I am . . . I am frightened about Nathaniel. Then there's running the ship. And the CO_2 leak. And Aahana. And Lance. And relations with Earth. And . . ."

"And we are 390 million kilometers from home."

I shook my head. "That's fine. It's just the 400 kilometers from Nathaniel. I . . ." I didn't know how he was or what I could do for him. "May I see his medical files?"

"I'm not in the habit of discussing my patients with others. Even his wife."

"Of course, I—" I held up my hand. "Wait. I think I'm not asking as his wife. I'm asking as the captain of the *Goddard*. I have too many unknown variables and this is one thing that can become known. He is our lead engineer and his health is affecting the mission. I need to have an understanding of how the neuropathy is likely to interface with the CO_2 poisoning."

Ana Teresa sighed heavily and some of the angry terrier came back into her expression. She cocked her head to the side, staring into the middle distance as if she could shake the fabric of space. "I thought you knew. I'm sorry. I told them that this was going to be a problem."

"This." His health. His chronic condition. Neuropathy. Nerve death.

Ana Teresa pulled a filing cabinet open and riffled through until she found a file and extracted it. "This does not leave my office. You are going to look at it and then we are going to talk about it. And by 'it' in this context, I mean your feelings."

My instinct was to object. I swallowed it. "Copy that."

She pushed papers aside to make space for the file. One tumbled to the floor. Grateful to have something useful to do, I picked it up. And stopped. It was a printout from the comms center of a citizenship application to Iceland with Ana Teresa's information half filled out. "What's this?"

"Oh." She took it from me. "I'm trying to get this submitted before we go into the blackout period."

"Okay, sure, but . . . I mean. Iceland?"

"Well. I am tired of being told that I can't treat Aahana, so I thought I would apply to be a citizen of a country where performing the abortion would be legal. It's an international program, so really what difference does it make?"

"Maybe you should just declare yourself a citizen of Mars." It shouldn't make a difference which country she was from. It shouldn't matter for any of us. I opened the folder she had given me and my breath caught.

A photo of Nathaniel was clipped to the inside. It was just a standard IAC mug shot but seeing him healthy drove home how very wrong he had sounded.

"If that would help Aahana, I would." Ana Teresa settled in the chair across from me. "You should talk to her. I think it would benefit you both."

I had a moment of not knowing what she was talking about, trying to link "it" in some way to Nathaniel or to DeBeer. But Ana Teresa was still talking about Aahana's pregnancy. "I don't think Aahana wants to talk to me."

"You have little monkeys inside your head. Of course she does. She is frightened and you are her idol. Of course she wants to turn to you."

I looked up from the folder, which was full of phrases like "residual neurological disability" and "chronic polyneuropathy." I blinked to clear my vision. "I thought she blamed me for her pregnancy."

Now Ana Teresa looked like she wanted to bite me again, which weirdly made me more comfortable. "Aahana looks up to you and you have been avoiding her. She thinks that it is that you are disappointed in her because she made a mistake by getting pregnant."

It felt as if someone had dropped a wet sleeping bag over my shoulders. I knew the younger woman had looked up to me. I just didn't think that she still did. It had been a relief, in a way, because it meant I didn't have to feel guilty about avoiding her.

Or, I thought I didn't.

"Elma. You are deflecting." She sat forward, face softening again. "As concerned as we both are about Aahana, I do not think that she is what brought you here."

"No." My gaze dropped back down to the file. "What does demyelination mean?"

"It is the loss of fatty myelin sheath which insulates of the nerve axons—" She shook her head. "Too much science. It means that his fingers and feet have a loss of sensation and dexterity."

Nothing she said seemed real. My skull echoed with the words but I couldn't connect them to anything. "That's from the thallium poisoning?"

She sighed and beckoned for the folder. "He worked on the Manhattan Project for a time?"

"This predates the poisoning?" How had I been married to him for twenty years and not known? I couldn't find anger or distress. Just shocked silence where my heart should be.

"Possible. I have my own theories . . ." Her brow furrowed as she glowered at the folder. "Here is what I think. I think that he experienced some damage then, but perhaps not noticeable. Then, that the thallium poisoning caused more neuropathic damage than it would have were the myelin sheaths not already weakened."

"And now?"

"And now. CO_2 poisoning can also result in damage to the basal ganglia and also demyelination . . ." Ana Teresa sighed. "Kam tells me that his hands are shaking and that he has weakness in the legs. It is possible that this will improve. It is possible that this will get worse. I am sorry."

I had information and different variables. How did I plot a course through that? "If it gets worse . . ." I had always joked that his work would kill him. "How much worse are we talking?"

"I don't know."

He shouldn't be here. "Does he need to go back to Earth?"

"Even if we were on Earth, if the neuropathy turns out to be progressive, there would be nothing that could be done." She rested her hand on mine, eyes full and soft with concern. "Do not fret about maybes. Work with what we have now. Tell me . . . what are the things that we know."

"He can't work—"

"No. No, that is not correct. His hands shake. Yes. That is correct."

"Okay . . . Okay, so he can't do wiring. But he could do plans or . . . or program or something." I could feel the emotion just outside but starting to crowd in. My eyes began to burn. It didn't matter what happened to his body. Or if his thoughts were slower. What did I *know*? "He's still Nathaniel."

My job would be to help him remember that.

Part of my job. I still had a ship to run and we had a base to repair. *I shall either find a way or make one.* "What should I say to Aahana?"

Ana Teresa settled back in her chair and folded her hands in her lap. "What would you want to hear, if you were in her position?"

I knew the answer to that. Not the specific words yet, but I knew. It was the same thing that I had wanted for my entire career.

I wanted to know that I wasn't alone.

TWENTY-SEVEN

Second Mars Expedition Mission Log, *Goddard*, Captain Elma York: Maym 48, Year 5 1147—All operations complete unless otherwise noted:

- Standard Measures Post/Pre-Sleep Questionnaire
- *Matsu* Cargo Operations
- EDV Deiodinated Water Fill
- Bio-Monitor Operations
- 2nd EDV Deiodinated Water Fill
- FBCO2 Scrubber Bed clean filters
- Vacuum Bag R&R
- LSG Primary Crew Restraint Unfold/Fold
- WHC Manual Fill
- Inspect Emergency OBT Simulator Functionality

Maym 48, Year 5, Tuesol—Landing + 165 sols

I floated in the comms module, aware of Dawn pretending to ignore me, and waited for Nathaniel to pick up for our scheduled call.

"*Goddard*, Bradbury. Nathaniel York here."

I closed my eyes so I could paint him against the darkness. "Hello, Dr. York. Happy anniversary."

In my imagination, his lips curved in a smile framed by lines from thousands of happy moments. "Dr. York. A very happy anniversary to you as well." Paper rustled near the microphone. "Thank you for sending down a present with Halim. I've got yours here. I'm sorry I couldn't send it up."

"It'll be something to look forward to when I come down."

"Any idea when that will be?"

"That is completely up to Ana Teresa. I can't put a suit on yet." Even if that weren't the case, the truth was that I would have stayed put because it didn't feel responsible for me to leave while Aahana was pregnant, especially not while we were in a communications blackout period with Earth. "There are some things I need to take care of before I'll feel good about handing command over."

"Mm." I could hear the unasked questions in his voice.

"You sound a little better. How are you feeling?"

"Fine."

"Nathaniel." I waited for him to tell me about the neuropathy.

He sighed, breath brushing across the microphone in a popping hiss. "Thinking feels like I have the flu. I'm used to being able to hold a design in my head and rotate it, but pieces keep disappearing . . . I don't like it. How about you?"

"The burn is healing well. Honestly, where she took the skin graft hurts more." I flexed my hand in the brace, aware that I couldn't dissemble if I wanted him to be open with me. Dawn had known me a long time. I could trust her with this. "I'm exhausted and worried, but the anxiety is just sort of a low-level background radiation, which will hopefully dissipate when we can talk to Earth again. I had a good talk with Ana Teresa and that helped."

"The Terrier of Space?" He chuckled in the way that made his eyes squint nearly shut. "I've been glad that I've had Kam as my doctor. He's been great."

"He?"

"Oh—" He laughed again. "Right. Early on Leonard said he'd talked to Kam and that they'd agreed it would be easier to treat him—her?—as one of the guys."

Relief and guilt flooded me. Guilt that we'd talked about how staying might not be safe for Kam. Relief that Leonard had gotten out in front like that. "And that's . . . that's been okay?"

Nathaniel hesitated and I could hear that it hadn't been

entirely okay. "There was a little friction with a couple of the military guys, but Leonard shut that down real fast. The rest of us have been watching Kam's back. Well, I *was* until he confined me to bed rest."

"Keep going with your kvetching and I'll ask him to take your slide rule away."

"Cruel." Nathaniel chuckled and I could picture his dimple forming. "I'm sorry I'm not there."

"Me, too." I stretched a little, setting myself drifting. He wasn't going to tell me. I didn't want to push, not now. Not on our anniversary. My shoulder bumped against something, and I had to open my eyes to reorient myself. Pushing away from the desk, I saw that Dawn had put on headphones and faced the wall to give me some privacy. I had the best crew. "You should open your present."

"I thought maybe I would save it until you came down."

"It's perishable—well, part of it is."

"Dr. York, did you bake me a pie?"

"Open it." I listened to the paper rustle and was grateful to him for leaving the mic hot while he unwrapped it, so I heard the soft exhalation he made when he saw the gift. I knew the pie had made it down intact because Opal had carried it on her lap.

"Elma . . ."

"It's not the original." He was holding a nine-inch yellow-ware pie plate. "But it has the heart feet on it and I think it's from the same mold as your mom's."

"Where did you find it?"

"A thrift store with Pearl before we left." His mother had made pie in a yellow-ware pie plate just like that. When she'd passed, it had been one of the few things of hers that we'd kept and I used it as my pie plate. Until the Meteor wiped away it and every other possession we owned. This wasn't her plate, but I'd thought of her the moment I saw it.

"You know, Mom did the Charleston once, balancing this on her head." He laughed again. "I hadn't thought about that in years."

I'll be honest. In that moment, I felt like I'd won at anniversary presents. "I remember the year she did the hula wearing a newspaper skirt."

"God. I wish we still had those home movies." He sniffled. "And is this . . . is this rhubarb?"

"It is." Freeze-dried and reconstituted, but I'd tested this on Earth before committing some of my weight allowance to it. "But I didn't make the crust, so you'll have to thank Helen for that."

"I was wondering, with your hand."

"I'll be out of the brace and doing physical therapy next week. By the time the *Esther* makes her next round trip, I'll bake you a pie crust."

"I would rather have you."

"Me, too." I wanted to lean into him and feel the warmth of his neck against my forehead. I wanted to smell the light, indescribable musk of him and rest my hand on his thigh and—"I miss you so much."

A part of me wanted to tell him that I would be down the instant my hand allowed me to wear a spacesuit. But we would both know that for a lie, because I had responsibilities here and passing them off in a crisis would be an awful thing to do. The moment Parker had split the mission into women in space and men on Mars, I'd become the mission commander on the *Goddard* in the same way that Halim had been for the crew in space. But now that we were out of touch with Earth, my responsibilities had multiplied because there was no one above me to consult.

I opened my eyes, comms module resolving itself around me in white plastic and aluminum. I was a mission commander. Earth was behind the sun. On Mars, I had been the deputy administrator and had never felt like I had power, only responsibilities. When I'd come up to the *Goddard*, I had been so focused on the responsibilities of the position that I had forgotten that being a mission commander came with powers which I had not used.

Things had shifted after the First Expedition team started talking to me. There was still a distance between us, in part because I was so angry about how their silence had endangered the whole mission, but they weren't shutting me out any more. Leonard had deferred to my judgment on more than one occasion.

I was the captain of the *Goddard* and I was a mission commander. I was his equal right now. And the communications blackout with Earth meant that for four more sols, I wasn't required to get a superior's permission. I needed to review some handbooks to see if my memories of procedures matched the realities.

"Nathaniel, I'm sorry, but . . ."

"You need to get back to work." I could see him nodding, a lock of his straw-blond hair falling into his eyes. "Thank you for making the time to talk. And for this. I'm really . . . This is a wonderful gift."

"Of course. I love you."

I found Aahana in the gym, running on the treadmill. She stared across the module as if looking ahead on a long road. Her dark ponytail swung behind her with each step. In her sweat-soaked tank, the slight thickening of her middle was more apparent than it had been.

Or maybe that was just because she was farther along.

I slowed as I approached her station, and checked my watch. Her exercise slot was scheduled to be done soon and I'd timed my arrival just a little wrong. Maybe I should try this later.

Aahana saw me standing there. "Do you need me?"

I shook my head. "It can wait."

"I'm nearly done anyway." She turned the treadmill off, slowing to a walk and then dismounted holding the handrail for balance against the spin of the ship. Her voice was bright but she swallowed twice, hard. "I'm happy for an excuse to stop."

Maybe I was projecting, but I saw myself in that cheerful mask.

"Sorry, I meant to catch you after you'd had time to shower." I had thought this would be the kinder approach, instead of announcing at the end of a meeting that I wanted to talk to her the way Clemons used to do to me. Leaving everyone else to wonder why I'd been kept after school. But now, I'd created a situation where she would need to wonder herself. "Do you want to do that and then come to my office? But I also don't mind you being sweaty if you'd rather shower after."

She glanced at herself, wiping a hand down the perspiration slicking her forearm. "May I . . . may I ask what this is about?"

Around us, other women were working out as part of their assigned times. None of them were watching us but all of them were aware. Or at least, I felt like their attention prickled against my skin. My therapist has told me that I'm probably wrong about that. I lowered my voice. "Your situation."

Aahana did not. "The pregnancy." She lifted her head, but looked across the room at God knows what. "I'll shower first."

My office belongs to the captain of the *Goddard*. I could have used Leonard's office, but I was a pilot more than I was an administrator. Plus the touches that Halim had made to it softened the room and made meetings less intimidating. I hoped.

Aahana knocked on the door, even though I'd left it open. Her hair was wet and slicked back from her face in a tight bun.

"Come in." I half rose and gestured to the fold-down seat bolted to one wall. "Pull the door shut?"

She inhaled deeply as she nodded and turned to shut the door, resting one hand against the wall for balance. When she sat across from me, her face was calm with a little bit of a smile, but her eyes were tight.

I wet my lips and forced myself to meet her gaze. "I want to apologize to you."

Her eyes went wide. "Oh. No. You don't have to—" She rested her hand on her belly where the rounding was more obvious when she was seated. "This was—Jaidev and I could have made different choices."

I wanted to tidy something to avoid the earnestness in her expression but all my notebooks were already at neat angles and secured by straps as if we were in zero-g. "You were acting on information that I gave you that was false." I held up my hand to stop a further protest. "You can argue with me about that, but Ana Teresa has already been real clear. I don't think you want to argue with her."

She gave a little laugh at that.

"Also, I've been avoiding you because . . ." I looked down now, because I had written this out as a script for myself. "Because I have been embarrassed, not just of misleading you, but because I had forgotten that I was speaking from a place of authority. This is a problem with my own understanding of my position on this mission. I should have spoken with more care to begin with and should have approached you as soon as your situation became clear. I let you down on multiple levels." I lifted my gaze out of the gravity well to face her. "I am very sorry."

Her mouth was rounded into a soft O. She blinked, shaking her head. "You are very busy. I understand that you don't have time for me."

I had the time, but I was scared to be around her because every time she treated me like a role model or a hero or whatever I was to her, it meant that I felt like I had to live up to her expectations and I was sure that I would fail. I said none of that, because she didn't need the burden of my own insecurities more than I'd already shared.

"You are a member of my crew. Of course I have time for you." I drew in a breath to dampen the prickling unease in my gut. I wouldn't vomit, the way I used to, but the desire to flee from attention would probably never go away. "Even if we were only talking chain of command, you would be my responsibility. But you are also a person I care about."

THE MARTIAN CONTINGENCY * 301

"Thank you."

"So . . . let's work this problem." Slipping a notepad from under its strap, I flipped past the lists I'd made last night to the one about Aahana's situation—assets, responsibilities, barriers, consequences—and turned to a plan behind it, which was a list of contingencies.

She leaned forward and I saw Aahana put herself back into a box of being unimportant. "You have so many other things to worry about, though."

Had I been part of building that box around her?

"Again, I have time for you. But to reassure you about allocation of resources. I can't do anything about the repairs on Mars beyond what I am already doing, which is enabling people to do their jobs and staying out of their way." And I couldn't do anything about Nathaniel, because we were in a wait-and-see pattern. But I could do something about Aahana and the longer we waited, the worse the consequences. "I'm going to authorize the abortion."

"Oh—" Her eyes widened, tears welling at the rims. She pressed her hands over her mouth, and then shook her head. "Thank you. But I don't want to get you in trouble."

"I've been trouble for my whole career." I felt Parker's shark smile twist my lips. "I'm the Lady Astronaut of Mars."

"That doesn't give you the authority to . . . The IAC and the UN and my home government have all said no."

"I know. I had to redefine the problem—problems, actually—to see the solution." I looked down at the table, running a finger along one of the elastic straps. I hadn't realized where the problem was until I had to put Nicole into the barriers column. "The immediate problem isn't that you are pregnant, it's that no one has been willing to risk their political career to support the choice you want to make. I've read through every procedure manual and contingency plan I can find relating to crew health. In every single instance, the mission commander has authority to override Mission Control."

"That's Leonard, though."

"On Mars, yes. But Halim was the mission commander for the *Goddard* until the moment Parker split us into two missions, men on Mars and women in space. The moment he did that, he made me mission commander of the *Goddard*. And we're in a communications blackout, which also grants me the power to use my best judgment for the good of my crew. So there are two avenues through which I can authorize this." I leaned forward across the table so that she could see my resolve. "I'm sorry I didn't recognize earlier that I had the power to issue this order. As soon as you're ready, we'll talk to Ana Teresa."

Across the table, Aahana's face froze, mouth partially open. She stopped breathing. Blinking, she closed her mouth and drew in a shuddering breath. She opened her mouth again as if she were going to speak but folded forward, resting her head on the desk, face hidden behind her hands. A single sob coughed out of her and then her shoulders tightened as if she were holding her breath.

The Coriolis effect kept me from bounding up to comfort her and that gave me enough time to think about the effects of my actions. To her, I was Clemons. I was Parker. I was her captain. If I were her, would I want to come the rest of the way apart or be given space to put myself back together?

Both. I put my hand on her arm the way I had seen Parker bolster a flagging crew member. "I'm going to step into the hall to get some water for us. I'll be gone for about five minutes."

She nodded, another sound escaping the shelter of her arms.

I hesitated then pulled my desk drawer open. Inside, was the emergency chocolate bar that Halim had left for me. I took it out and set it on the desk in front of Aahana before I left.

In the hall, I leaned against the wall for a moment, feeling the ship spin around me. How did I get here? I could see the path and still be surprised because I had not been paying attention.

I was the NavComp, watching the numbers and never looking out the window at the destination.

Right. I told her I was going to get water for us. Wiping my hand down my face, I pushed away from the wall and set a timer. Five minutes, on my mark.

I sat across the table from Aahana. The chocolate bar lay between us, two pieces gone because we were both savoring it.

Aahana's eyes were red, but her shoulders were square and her voice was steady.

"You are why I went into the space program." A strand of hair escaped as she shook her head. "I have been thinking about your offer and how you said 'problems.' What are the other problems?"

I turned the sip pack of water in my hands. "You won't be the only woman who gets pregnant accidentally. So how Mission Control handles you sets a precedent. If you were on Mars, I don't know what Leonard would do."

Maybe he would have just ordered it and not made the report. Maybe Kam would have been willing to do the abortion in one-third gravity. Maybe they would have all toed the line. I had no way of knowing.

She tucked the stray hair behind her ear. "Just so. I have been thinking about the uneven application of the rules. If this had happened to Sigur, she would have been allowed to have an abortion by the Icelandic government, but the doctors would not have been allowed to administer it."

Which was why Ana Teresa was in the process of trying to change her citizenship. "Maybe we should all just be citizens of Mars."

"That will be true someday. I mean, that's the goal, right?" She broke off a tiny piece of chocolate and stared at the dark sliver as if it held all of her attention. "I always said I wanted to be you when I grew up, so . . . what would you do, if you were me?"

My stomach tightened. If I were her . . . I *had* been her. Even if it turned out that the choice we made hadn't been an actual choice, I'd thought it was. "Nathaniel and I made the choice to not have children."

"Oh." She rolled the chocolate between her fingers. "I hadn't realized."

"Well, as it turns out, the reason we thought the rhythm method worked was because we *can't* have children." No need to go into which of us was the problem. "But when we thought we could, we—*I* decided that I wasn't willing to give up my career for that."

"Yes. It's not that I don't want children, but I don't want a child now and I don't want either of us to be a science experiment." Then she shook her head and set the chocolate back down, looking up at me fully. "But I actually meant . . . you have always been the Lady Astronaut, even before you were able to go into space. You made people pay attention to the problem and the inequities. How . . . how do I do that?"

"I haven't always been. The Lady Astronaut, I mean." I looked at the geometric hanging on the wall, tracing the lines as if it would give me some answers. I had intended to be the support behind a woman pilot who was flashy like Nicole, or Princess Shakhovaskaya, or Sabiha Gökçen, the same way I had been the support behind Nathaniel. But an accident—a literal accident—had pushed me into the spotlight. "I guess . . . you're already in the news. If you want to, I can coach you on how to use that. How to be . . . how to . . ."

"How to be a Lady Astronaut of Mars?"

"Basically. Yes." I had initially tried assigning numerical values to assets and barriers to math my way to a solution which had been profoundly unsuccessful. I sat forward as the path unfolded in front of me and for the first time I could see the equation and the destination. "When we were trying to get women into the space program, I was the public face of the problem but I was representing a group of women who were all working together. That's the key here. That's what we do. It doesn't have to be me out in front by myself. Or just you."

What do we call ourselves if not colonists?

"It's all of us—we are Martians."

TWENTY-EIGHT

IAC CHIEF, AT U.N., PUTS STRESS ON JOINT PROGRAMS

Special to The National Times

UNITED NATIONS, Kansas, July 28, 1970—Col. Stetson Parker, interim director for the International Aerospace Coalition, spoke before the assembly today about the role of the joint programs in improving the overall trajectory of Meteor recovery. He pointed to the increased life of batteries and the introduction of electric cars as being a direct result of technologies developed for the space program.

Maym 52, Year 5, Satursol–Landing + 169 sols

I floated in comms by myself. Unlike when I'd talked to Nathaniel, I sent the crew out for this after they set up an encrypted call with Parker. They knew who I was calling and they knew why, but they did not need to hear Parker's raw response to me.

"*Goddard,* Mission Control. Parker here. What the hell is going wrong now, York?"

Sweat coated my entire body and my throat tightened the way it used to every time he walked into a room. I took a breath, knowing that the extra seconds wouldn't make a difference with the forty-four-minute lag between us. He wasn't mad at me. Yet.

Parker was just worried because we'd been on the other side of the sun for twenty-two sols after a major disaster. I'd asked for a voice call, which we only did for sensitive matters. He was afraid someone was dead. And he was going to be fretting for forty-four minutes until my voice got to him.

That's when he would get mad.

"Good morning, Parker. All systems are nominal and everyone is in good health. I'm sorry to have worried you." I rotated the paper I'd written my script on so I wouldn't lose my train of thought as I talked to him. "This is a courtesy call to let you know that during the comms blackout, I authorized the abortion for Aahana. In my judgment, as mission commander, it was necessary for her health. We have not included this in our reports through official channels to Mission Control, and will wait until you have a plan in place to spin this the way you want. I've come up with a list of possible contingency plans for what comes next and I'd like to go over them with you. You asked me to back you when it came to getting the women to the *Goddard*. I did. I may not have always run this ship the way you wanted me to, but we've had a good track record and the only injury thus far has been me with that damn pie plate. I'm doing what I can to support you. I need your support here. Over."

And then I settled back to wait. Helen had loaned me a book but when I opened it, all I could do was stare at the pages. The words wouldn't come together to make sense.

I must have read the same paragraph a dozen times during that forty-four-minute wait before I gave up and started doing my physical therapy exercises. The entire time, my brain kept serving up the different ways Parker would tear into me for my decision.

I had entire imaginary conversations in which I responded with fiery rhetoric about how he had delegated responsibilities to me during the First Mars Expedition but none of the authority and how I hadn't complained. Imaginary Parker scoffed in real time and I unloaded everything about DeBeer and how that situation wouldn't have gotten so out of hand if he'd been doing his job. None of these were things that I would actually say to him, because you didn't manage Parker by confronting him. That just made him dig his heels in.

But the man loved hierarchy. My challenge this time was that I needed to remind him that as captain of the *Goddard,* I had responsibility *and* power.

Forty-four minutes later, the real Parker responded, "I can't do that, York. The ruling from the UN to the IAC is that the country of origin is still the deciding factor for anything that doesn't affect the overall safety of the mission. Personally, I think the outcome of the pregnancy is something that Mission Control ought to decide, given the needs of the crew on Mars, and were it up to me alone, I would give the okay to do the abortion. But I'm still not confirmed. Between you and me, given all the international politics involved, I don't see that ruling changing. So you should make plans for her carrying that baby to term. I'm sorry. I really wish I could do something different here." There was silence on the line for a minute and I almost started talking again, but the mic crackled. "How's your hand? I was tracking the reports before the blackout period and it sounded like it was doing okay. It's not going to . . . You'll still be able to fly after this, right? Over."

His concern always startled me, but the fact that he focused on my flight readiness did not. Mind you, I don't think he was worried about that from mission parameters—or not as his primary concern—but he was a pilot and so was I. He knew how much I loved flying.

"My hand is healing well, thank you. I'm out of the brace and doing light therapy. I'm not cleared to do anything that might put it at risk of shearing the skin graft off for at least another month so you'll be happy to know that I can't do any spacewalks now. But yes, I'll be able to fly and could now, if they'd let me. You've met Ana Teresa, and . . ." I cleared my throat. "None of that's why I'm here. Parker, I'm sorry. I wasn't clear. The abortion has already happened. It's like when they sent Terrazas out. It all looks fine on paper, but everything about it is wrong. Trust me to know my people. This was going to kill Aahana by degrees. You can use the comms blackout to use me as a scapegoat if you need to. When I asked for your support, what I should have said was that I want your backing to make sure that Aahana and Ana Teresa's careers aren't affected by this. It was my call, as mission commander for the *Goddard*. I'm willing to accept any consequences that you need to assign to me. I thought this through and I have some ideas but I'd like it if we worked the problem together."

I leaned forward and pushed a button on the keyboard, sending him a coded message I'd already written.

"I borrowed Helen's codebook—and I'm seriously hoping that you have Clemons's copy. This was the only way I could think of for sending you plans without tipping off whoever has been leaking stuff to the press about Aahana. The message contains the three different plans I'm proposing. In brief, they are: One. The order appears to come from you. Two. We report this as a miscarriage. Three. The order comes from me with two variants—Three-A. You approve and Three-B. I'm a scapegoat. In all of those, we also release a recording of Aahana talking about her experiences and offer her for interviews. The shape of the recording and the interviews depends on your opinion of the best way to handle this. Over."

I stared at the microphone as if there was something else I could do. Forty-four minutes. I grabbed the book again and tried to distract myself. How hard did I have to concentrate to get through a single short story? According to the cover, these stories were the World's Best Science Fiction of 1967. They ought to be able to hold my attention and yet I stared at the book continuing to not read it for I don't know how long.

Words had never been my comfort.

I flipped to a random page. 147. The square root of that was 12.124355653 . . . Page 216. Square root. 14.6969384567 . . . Page 93. Square root. 9.64365076099 . . .

The headset crackled and I flinched, propelling myself backward.

"Acknowledged."

And that was the sound of a pilot who had learned not to swear on a hot mic. I let go of the numbers I'd been holding and tucked the book under an elastic strap, waiting for Parker to get his reaction under control.

"I'm going to take time to read through your proposals and consult with an adviser. I will talk with you in two hours—wait, your hours are longer. What time is it . . . You're about three and half hours behind us. Right." I could hear the cursing contained within his sigh. He'd always hated the time differences. "For clarity, I will talk to you at twelve hundred GMT. Parker out."

Twenty-two minutes to the hour, I had Florence connect me to Mission Control. "Mission Control, *Goddard*. Elma York standing by. I have Aahana and Florence in the room with me."

That was nearly true. I'd told Aahana to arrive twenty minutes past the hour, because there was no point in her waiting around. Florence floated in the comms module with one foot casually hooked under a rail, needle rising and falling with a calm that I envied. She had made progress on her embroidery and the meadow was now framed by trees. Would she start doing pieces inspired by Mars someday or continue looking back toward Earth?

I stretched in place, trying to work some of the tension out of my shoulders and back, then repositioned myself next to one of the fans and opened the small craft box I'd brought up with me. Inside were punch cards bundled with a rubber band and the start of a new paper sculpture. A dragon, this time. In theory. I was having trouble getting the snout quite right.

Florence paused and looked across the module at me. "Don't leave little bits floating in my space."

"That's why I'm next to an intake vent." I pulled out a small set of scissors. This might, in fact, be a disaster, but attempting to pass the time by reading had been a useless endeavor. "And yes, I'll clean the vent out afterward."

"Thank you." She lowered the embroidery. "Hey . . . thank you for inviting me to participate in this. I'm not sure I agree with your plan, but I appreciate being included. Especially after . . . I'm sorry we didn't tell you."

I didn't want the apology because then I would have to stop being angry. I didn't want explanations that came from guilt over what happened to Nathaniel because of their silence; I wanted her to trust me. That was something I would have to earn somehow. I concentrated on snipping a small dart where I wanted to bend the card. "I'm sorry I made you talk about it."

Our apologies met in the silent space between us and all they did was keep a door open, but neither of us was really ready to step through. I took a breath and lowered my punch card to look square at her. "But right now, I want you here because you don't agree with me. You always see things that I don't. Besides, you and Dawn literally wrote the script that got public support behind us for staying in the first place. I figure it'll be easier if you're here for the conversations."

"Did you forget that you rewrote that script?" She eyed me over the rim of her embroidery hoop.

"Only in a couple of places to make it sound like me."

She laughed and the door between us cracked a little wider. "You keep telling yourself that."

Aahana swung into the module, followed by Ana Teresa, who looked like she was herding the geologist. Ana Teresa looked from Florence's embroidery to my papercraft. "If you had told me this was a crafting circle, I would have brought my quilting."

"Forty-four-minute lag. I needed something to do with my hands." I slid the scissors back into their little sheath and tucked them into the box. I pulled out a blank card to make notes on. "This time, I'm betting that we'll be occupied with conversation about—"

"*Goddard,* Mission Control. This is Stetson Parker standing by for—Jesus Christ!" Parker's voice came through the speakers so we could all hear. In the background, I caught the sound of my voice from forty-four minutes ago. Which meant that he had us on speakers, too, and that meant he wasn't alone. "Okay.

Got it. So you got there early, which I appreciate. So, um . . . I guess we'll just start. I have President Wargin with me as well as Betty Ralls from our PR department. Betty, go ahead."

I raised my brows, exchanging a look with Florence and wishing that Helen were there. Betty, Nicole, and I had been among the original six women astronauts. She'd eventually left the corps to focus on PR, so it wasn't completely surprising that she was there but a shock nonetheless. Looking back down at my punch card, I started jotting notes as Betty spoke.

"Hi, Elma, I hope Mars is treating you well. We appreciate the heads-up so that we can get out in front of the news cycle and break this ourselves. I'll be sending a script to you later today for the recording that you mentioned. My recommendation is that you be the one to record this, as the public is familiar with you while Aahana is an unknown—no offense, Aahana, but you know how things are with the public. I'm passing the mic to President Wargin now."

I made sure my mic was off and looked at Aahana who was hurriedly making a note on her pad. "We'll look at what they send and deci—"

"Hello, Elma, Florence, and Aahana." Nicole always had so much command in her voice. Even when we'd been at parties back on Earth, she'd seemed able to just will everyone to have a good time. "When Stetson asked me for advice, I offered to come speak to you directly. I'm not sure where communication broke down before, but I sent explicit instructions not to allow the abortion to occur—we are past that point now, I understand, but in order to minimize the consequences to you all we've got a very narrow and very specific path we need to walk. We can get through this, but I need assurances from you that you will follow our instructions to the letter from this point forward. Separately, and on a personal note . . . Elma, how is Nathaniel doing? I've read the reports, but . . . how is he? How are you? I'm passing the microphone to Stetson now."

My mind split into three responses. How was Nathaniel? How was I? I didn't know the answer to either question. Another part of me noted that Nicole was calling Parker by his first name. What was going on there? They weren't . . . I shook my head to clear it. None of my concern and the rest of me was just mad. It had hit so suddenly that I couldn't even put my finger on why and I didn't have time to think about it because Parker started talking.

"Of the options you presented, we're going to go with the version in which I issue the order." Parker leaned closer to the mic and his voice dropped. "York . . . York, I promised you that when I was confirmed I would send the women back down to Mars. Now, we've already needed to send some of you down to deal with the repairs and they've been doing good work. You're damn right that I haven't appreciated some of the ways you've run the *Goddard*, but I also can't argue with the fact that your safety and performance records are exemplary. In fact, they'd be spotless if not for your injury, but the important thing is that the public loves you. They loved that damn stunt you and Nicole pulled with the all-woman spacewalks. So if I question your judgment, they are going to question mine. Thanks for that. Now, Nicole recommends—and I agree—that I can issue the order on ethical grounds. Betty is going to spin it to show that I'm not beholden to pressures from any particular government."

Nicole cut in. "I've been very public in my belief that the pregnancy should continue."

"Yes." Parker sounded annoyed. "Yes, you have. York, we'll give you time to respond. Over."

"Thank you, Parker. Betty and Nicole, it's good to hear your voices. Give me one moment to check with my crew." I muted the mic. "Well?"

Ana Teresa huffed. "She has some nerve, sending 'instructions' to me. First, Nicole is incapable of following instructions herself. Second, I am Brazi—Icelandic and not subject to the authority of the United States."

"Good note." As I jotted a reminder to myself, the anger surged again and spotlit what had annoyed me when Nicole had been talking. She had always been my friend, from before the astronaut corps even existed when we were Women Airforce Service Pilots in World War II, and now she was assuming that she could issue orders. I looked up from my note card to Florence and Aahana. "What about the recording?"

"I want to do it." Aahana's cheeks were a little hollowed, but her shoulders weren't tight anymore. She pushed a piece of paper across the module to me. "If you join me that would be welcome, but I do not think that India will listen to you the way they will to me. I've made a list of the points I want to hit in the recording."

"Copy that." I glanced at them and started to tuck them behind my notes. "Do you want to present these yourself?"

She hesitated, tucking her lower lip between her teeth, as she looked at me. I could almost see her weighing what answer to give. My question probably sounded like it might be an order.

I winked at her, and tucked the list under a strap where either of us could reach it. "Not a veiled command, but an offer. You can think on it and let me know when we get there. Florence, your thoughts?"

Florence spread her hands, thread drifting in a tail after her. "I'm changing what I was going to say. I was going to agree with Betty that you ought to be in front to take the heat, but if Aahana wants to get her hands dirty and has the energy, then I can respect that."

"I do." Aahana took a breath and nodded. "I do."

"Good for you." Florence twisted so she was facing Aahana fully. "But listen, you have to understand that the press will treat you differently than they will Elma."

"Believe me," Aahana's smile was thin and dry as she reached for her list. "I am fully aware of that. But that is part of what we are trying to change, is it not?"

Florence pulled her embroidery toward her again and nodded to me. "I can work with Aahana and Dawn to modify whatever Betty sends up. No other notes."

"Thank you." I inhaled to gird myself and glanced over my

scribblings, numbering the order in which I would respond to Parker's points. Then I toggled the mic on. "Parker, York. Thank you for giving me the time to talk to the team. Just a note that Ana Teresa has also joined us. One thing I need to push back on is the note from Nicole about the instructions she sent. I was aware of them. However . . . Nicole. You're the president of the United States and you sent instructions to a Taiwanese woman about something that affected an Icelandic woman and an Indian woman, none of whom are in your purview. For that matter, as the mission commander on the *Goddard*, neither am I." What was the phrase she used to use? "We'll take your counsel under advisement."

Florence snorted, a smile rounding her cheeks.

"But on a personal note, Nathaniel is improving and I'm staying busy, which helps. I'll tell him you asked after him. Betty, thank you for the offer to do a draft of the script. We'll look over the information you send up and incorporate that into the one that our comms team is writing. As a note, plan for Aahana to be in the recording with me." I muted the mic, glancing at Aahana. "You want to take this?"

She nodded, kicking forward to position herself in front of a mic.

Toggling mine back on, I said, "I'm passing the microphone to Aahana."

"Hello, Director Parker, President Wargin, and Ms. Ralls. I would like to be included in this recording as the person it most directly affects. Currently, the rules are applied unevenly. Imagine what would have happened were I and Sigur, who is from Iceland, to have become pregnant at the same time under the current conditions. She would have been allowed to have an abortion, but no one would have been allowed to administer it. In addition, forcing a human to become a science experiment would violate the ethics of many countries—were I on Earth I find it difficult to imagine that any new drug, which might affect a fetus, would be administered without animal testing, and certainly none would be administered against the mother's

316 * MARY ROBINETTE KOWAL

will. Yet that is the situation in which I found myself. I believe that this appeal will be heard most clearly from me rather than from Dr. York."

Ana Teresa beckoned for the microphone.

Aahana glanced at me for confirmation before she said, "I am passing the microphone to Dr. Brandão."

Taking the mic, Ana Teresa scowled as if Parker were directly in front of her. "Listen, you're letting the water in. It will affect many more women before we have enough animal data to know it's safe. It may very well be that all the mothers and children have to stay in the centrifuge under Earth's gravity for some period of time. We simply don't know." She drew in a deep breath and if she could have bitten Parker, I think she would have. "I know this will get me into trouble, but I don't care. Aahana was not the only pregnancy. After we saw how this was done, I chose not to report the other because the mother miscarried naturally and very early. Another pregnancy will happen again before the arrival of the Third Expedition and we will still have no idea if it is safe. Do you have no understanding of how much we have to learn before it is ethical to try to birth a human here? The Third Expedition will bring with it postpubertal teens who are old enough to agree to participate in finding out how being on Mars affects their development. And you wanted to see what would happen to someone who didn't agree, for whom the consequences would be lifelong? It will be a decade before we are ready for the birth of a child on Mars. There is no foolproof form of birth control, so there will be many pregnancies between now and then. The way we handle this will set a precedent. And do not dare suggest that women stay home. I'm passing the mic to Elma."

I cleared my throat, blinking with shock at her tirade. Another pregnancy? Who? Should I know? I shouldn't know. If I knew then I would have to act like I didn't know. It was safer for whoever it was if I didn't know.

Wetting my lips, I glanced at my notes to orient myself and toggled the mic. "Parker, I really appreciate you backing us.

Again . . . listen, I know there's the formal statement that you'll make and what you'll say when you speak to people privately. I want to reiterate my willingness to be the scapegoat. It was my call and I know I put you in a bind. But thank you. Over."

I toggled my mic off and glanced at Florence who said, "All mics are muted. You are Go to talk and I want to start by saying . . . I'm surprised as hell that Parker is backing you."

I scrubbed my face. "If he didn't, then he'd have to admit that he couldn't control me anymore."

"Could he ever?"

"Oh, yeah." In the shadow of my hands, memories rolled over me of sitting in the back seat of the T-38 as I realized that Parker knew I was taking medication for anxiety. That same sick, twist of my gut as he blackmailed me pushed sweat out of all of my pores as if it were happening right now. Or maybe that was just perimenopause. I dropped my hands. "But the thing about Parker is that he's always, always been protective of his people."

"True, but he also hates having people buck the hierarchy." She glanced at Aahana and Ana Teresa to explain. "First Expedition, he was a holy terror if you got out of line. Softened on the way back though but still, I expected him to go full vengeance."

"I played dirty in the initial communication." I picked at the bandage on my left hand.

"Leave that alone." Ana Teresa snapped. "And do your exercises during the break."

"Aye-aye." I spread my fingers as wide as I could, feeling the skin prickle under the bandages as I did.

Across the module, Aahana raised her hand. "May I ask how you played 'dirty'?"

"Oh . . ." I answered her, but I looked at Florence. "I brought up Terrazas. Parker didn't agree with Mission Control's decision to send him out on the spacewalk instead of Leonard but he didn't buck the order. It weighed on him. So . . . I told Parker that he needed to trust my assessment of my crew."

Florence whistled. "That is dirty pool. Respect. Glad it worked."

I stretched my hand again and looked at the clock. "And now, intrepid adventurers, we've still got forty minutes, so this is a good time to grab a craft project or take a bathroom break if you need to." I pushed toward the door. "And I do."

Once upon a time, after a conversation like that with Parker, I would have needed to throw up. Now all I wanted was to wipe the sweat off before we started again.

This was going to be a long, long sol.

Forty-six minutes later, Parker said, "Copy that. We're discussing. Stand by."

I snorted. "I wonder if he was the only one cursing."

Aahana lowered her knitting. "What do you mean?"

"That was a forty-six minute response." There was a moment where she smiled and nodded as if she got it, but I could see the confusion she was masking. She'd come into the program as a colo—as an inhabitant, and she wouldn't have any reason to know. Parker, Betty, Nicole and I had all joined when you still had to have a pilot's license and have logged time in a jet. I nodded toward the speaker, as if it were actually Parker. "We're on a forty-four-minute delay but it took him forty-six to respond. He's a pilot. All of them are, actually. We're trained not to curse on a hot mic."

"Oh . . ." Her mouth rounded as she looked up in thought. "Does Mission Control track that?"

"Oh yes." Florence snipped a thread on her embroidery. "When we're working CAPCOM, it's one of the ways you can tell how pissed an astronaut is. On this side, it's one of my favorite things about working comms. I get to hear this string of profanity and then when their mic is hot again, they sound like they're having a warm bath."

I grinned at an old memory. "One time Lebourgeois didn't

realize he'd switched to VOX and cursed about a schedule revis—"

"*Goddard,* Parker here. Thanks for your patience." Parker sounded all business now. "I just wanted to say that we're all glad to hear that Nathaniel is improving. He's a good man."

Damn him and his unexpected compassion. My eyes burned and I swiped a thumb under them.

"We appreciate the note from Aahana about why she wants to be involved in the recording. Betty will take that into consideration while she's working on the script."

Nicole said, "Meanwhile, I'll talk to the prime minister of India privately. Indira is an old friend and the presidency is in a bit of a shambles right now. She'll have more sway and will appreciate the opportunity to be prepared. Elma, make sure you coach Aahana on the public pressures, because this is going to be a bumpy ride for her."

"Oh, York knows all about public pressure." I could hear the shark surfacing in Parker's voice. There's this sharp, nasal edge that he gets and I could imagine him leaning toward the mic with a smile that looked charming to everyone else. "And I don't want to cause you to feel overtaxed, what with everything going on with Nathaniel. It doesn't seem right to ask you to take the lead on this *and* to run the *Goddard.* I'm going to reassign you back to Bradbury Base so you can be closer to your husband. Over."

The thing about where my relationship with Parker was now was that I couldn't tell if he was trying to be cruel or if he was trying to be kind. I'd fought for a career in space and I had one. But a part of me wanted to thank him and just go be with Nathaniel.

Ana Teresa shoved her quilting hoop aside and snatched the microphone. "Listen, you monkey, Elma has a skin graft on her left hand. Did you not hear the part about not being able to put a spacesuit on? She is on the *Goddard* for another two months— two *Martian* months. Minimum. And that's only if she does her exercises and does not injure it or cause it to get infected. So, you can do many things, but sending her down to Nathaniel is not possible at this time. I'm passing the mic to Elma."

"I . . ." My mind emptied of everything except that number. Two. Two more months until I got to see Nathaniel. Goddamn it. I just wanted to go home. To him.

Florence opened her mic. "Parker, you've always been an asshole. Don't tell us that she's doing a good job and then punish her by taking command away. I know you. This isn't you being considerate and you damn well know it."

"Yes, and I can take lead on the public relations." Aahana spoke in a low, calm voice that was full of authority, but her hands were clenched around the neck of the microphone. "Dr. York will not be the only one coaching me. We have quite the team up here."

I cleared my throat, but the module had gone hazy beyond a swelling globe of tears. I brushed them away and they soaked into my bandage. Ignoring Ana Teresa's hiss, I opened my own microphone, because he would see all of this support as the challenge it was and he would escalate. "Parker, unlike Florence, I think you were being kind. I've also known you a long time and the one thing you would never do is use my husband as a weapon. So if you need me to step down as captain of the *Goddard,* I will. Or I'll keep serving until I'm cleared to land, because I want to see Nathaniel more than . . ." I squeezed my eyes closed to hold the tears back. My throat hurt with longing. "But I also want you to know that Aahana and Florence and the rest of the team up here have this. I asked you before to trust me to know my team. I do. And I know that I am not the only Lady Astronaut of Mars."

TWENTY-NINE

KASHMIR ASSEMBLY TO GET BILL LEGALIZING ABORTIONS

SRINAGAR, India, August 11, 1970—The government will introduce a bill in the Kashmir state legislative assembly next month to legalize abortion as part of its birth-control program.

The Muslim majority in Kashmir is probably the first in an Indian state to take this step despite opposition from orthodox teachers and some Muslim organizations that ask Muslims to boycott family planning programs.

Acknowledging that opposition existed, Health Minister A. G. Goni said at a news conference Tuesday that a recent interview with Dr. Aahana Kamal, an astronaut on the Second Mars Expedition, had shifted the tenor of conversations. Dr. Kamal's difficulties in getting approval for an abortion had highlighted the ways in which climate refugees in India faced many of the same dangers and challenges surrounding an unplanned pregnancy in space.

Jum 9, Year 5, Frisol-Landing + 182 sols

Over the next month, the *Goddard* changed—I'm not talking about the ongoing work to convert it to a space station—but the fact that more of my crew had gone to the surface to help out with Bradbury, so we were down to the staff of eighteen needed for maintenance and conversion. If it weren't for our communal meals, it would have been possible to go an entire sol without crossing paths with another woman.

And yet the amount of paperwork and reports that I had to deal with every sol did not seem in anyway diminished. I was going through a report on the health of a new batch of chickens now that we had spun back down to Martian gravity, when Florence knocked on my door.

I sat back in my chair with a groan. "I don't know what you need, but you are saving me from reading about sexing chickens."

"I don't know if I'm saving you." A furrow was between her brows as she handed me a folder. "Coded message came in from Kansas. Figured you'd want it right away."

"Thank you." I took it, feeling the panic rising along my back, and nodded to the chair in my tiny office. A coded message meant it was something from Parker that contained classified information. The list of items in which classified information was connected to something good consisted of exactly nothing. "Do you mind waiting while I check to see if it needs an immediate reply?"

"Made a guess that you might want that." She held up her other hand, which had her craft bag. "It's long."

She was right. There were three pages inside when the longest message that Parker had sent up prior to this had been half a page. My chest got tight pinpricks of nerves wondering what had gone wrong. I pulled the decryption key out of my desk and set it beside the folder, looking at the calendar for the date. Then I grabbed a portable whiteboard and started working through the decryption.

Florence pulled an embroidery hoop out of the bag. "Here I thought you did all your decryption in your head."

"One, it's a one-time pad, so it changes daily. Two, these are words, not numbers." But I was fast at it, and I knew that. Maybe I even took a little pride in that fact. But the opening lines of the letter wiped everything else away.

York, the investigation committee is about to release the public report regarding the crash of the cargo vessel. I didn't want you or anyone else from the First Expedition finding out via public channels and I'll trust you to explain the situation to them.

I inhaled slowly, trying to soothe the jitters back down. Across the desk, I could feel Florence pretending not to watch me as her needle rose and fell through the fabric.

Appended to this is a summary of the formal report. The crash of the ship itself has been ruled definitively as an accident. I'm including the technical specs so you can show Nathaniel because I know your husband and he'll ask.

There was no reason for that to be sent in an encrypted message if it was going to be released publicly. I bit the inside of my lip as I translated the next line.

You're going to see Vanderbilt DeBeer's name in there.

I must have made a sound, because Florence looked up, mouth opening as if she were about to ask a question. Then she shook her head and shifted the embroidery hoop in her hand.

He was overseeing the South African team that was processing the survey photos. Contrary to what I initially told you, the investigation team found that the photo of the site was actually clear and shows the damage to the cargo vessel. However, it was miscataloged and the committee has determined that it was an honest error. But people will see conspiracies where they want to and I'm certain that the press will take this and run a story about "revenge for being left at home." Nothing I know about DeBeer suggests he would do that, despite being one of the most racist pricks I've ever served with and I was Air Force in the South.

I stopped, staring at the tip of my marker as the letters around it went hazy. *Nothing I know about DeBeer . . .*

"Florence?"

She stowed her needle in the fabric and lowered the hoop. "I know that tone and I don't like it."

"No. I don't, either." I capped the marker and set it down on the desk. I considered five different ways to tell her and then just turned the pad around and handed it to her. "This is bad."

She snorted, reaching for it.

I saw the moment when she read DeBeer's name because her eyes stopped moving. Her shoulders hitched just a little, as if she were inhaling to yell. Florence's mouth pursed, she took a slow breath and then she read the entire thing again.

When she was done, she set it on my desk and leaned back in her chair. "Well." She opened her craft bag. "That is some bullshit."

"He doesn't know." I gestured vaguely at her. "No one told him what happened."

"Because he didn't care." She pulled the needle free. "He kept saying that Benkoski was in charge and that he'd back him. Or telling us to talk to you."

Because Parker had been sunk in a deep gravity well of depression, which was not my story to tell. But I remembered those bland reports from the surface.

I almost snapped that they'd never asked *me* for help. I wanted to shove back verbally but as I opened my mouth, I remembered what had happened to her. What DeBeer had done. What the IAC had allowed to happen because they had known he was a problem while we were all still on Earth. All of us had. None of us had said anything.

I let my breath out, with anger unspoken.

Instead, I opened the desk drawer and withdrew the partial bar of emergency chocolate that Halim had given me. I put it on the desk, within reach of her. "I'm sorry."

Her needle froze. Florence bit her lips, closing her eyes. I got to the eleventh digit of pi before she shook her head and opened her eyes again.

The rims were red. "Thank you."

I nudged the chocolate toward her, in case she hadn't seen it.

She set the embroidery hoop in her lap. "Where'd that come from?"

"Halim. In case of emergency." I took a piece to give her permission to do the same. "This is the second time I've broken it out."

Aahana and I had each had two pieces and then, unspoken, we'd both stopped to preserve it for a future need.

Florence leaned forward and snapped off a piece. She nibbled a small corner, eyes closing in reverie. I don't know for sure that she had the same experience I did, but you do not understand how glorious chocolate is until it becomes irreplaceable.

The sweet bitterness coated my tongue with silk. I let the piece dissolve in my mouth and, for a moment, replace all the tension with a curtain of dark comfort.

I sighed, looking at the square in my fingers, wondering how long I could make it last.

"Don't let Nathaniel know you make that sound."

"He already does." I set the little piece to the side and licked the remnants off my fingers. My mother would be appalled, but on Mars wiping my fingers would have seemed like a rude waste of something precious.

I rested my hands in my lap. We had to tell Parker. "Florence—"

"I know." She nibbled another little bit off the square. "Just let me enjoy my damn chocolate first."

She knew the same thing I did. If we continued to say nothing, DeBeer was going to get away with it. He'd try again. And someday, he'd convince someone that he was a good guy who deserved to come back to Mars.

THIRTY

**FOUR EARTH FIRSTERS
HELD FOR CONSPIRACY**

KANSAS CITY, September 21, 1970—Four men identified by the police as Earth Firsters were arrested here yesterday and charged with conspiracy to commit robbery and possession of dangerous weapons.

Jum 49, Year 5, Wednesol-Landing + 222 sols

After talking it through with Florence and Leonard, the message I sent back to Parker wound up being very short.

> *Be advised that the First Expedition members have reason to believe that the miscategorization of the survey photo was a purposeful act of sabotage by DeBeer. They want you to talk to Benkoski and Rafael before the report is made public. Tell them explicitly that Leonard gave them clearance to brief you.*

The reply I got back was shorter. *Acknowledged.*

I could only imagine how much cursing went around that single word. Benkoski had been the mission commander for the surface crew on the First Mars Expedition. He and Parker had been friends since before the Meteor. On the First Mars Expedition, Parker had been the overall mission commander. Parker should have been on the surface.

Parker should have been dealing with DeBeer. But he'd shut down and handed things off to me, who no one trusted.

He was an asshole who was also deeply loyal to his team.

This was going to be a gut punch to him. He would feel betrayed that no one had told him and he would feel like he had betrayed them because he hadn't been there when they needed him.

And he would assume that I had known and deliberately not told him.

I was watching every communication that came in, waiting for him to lash out. He didn't. He didn't mention it at all.

But I noticed that the crash investigation report hadn't come out yet.

Meanwhile, life on and around Mars continued. Tosol we were welcoming men back to the *Goddard*.

Helen had brought the *Matsu* up to pick up supplies and drop off a small mixed crew who would serve as relief for some stations on the *Goddard*. The timing of the flight was so it could serve as a medical transport for Lance. Eventually, Mars would have better medical facilities than the *Goddard*, but now that we were back to spinning at Martian gravity levels, they'd be able to give him better attention up here.

One more month before I got to see Nathaniel.

The entire crew of the *Goddard* floated in the spindle—all eighteen of us—facing the hatch of the airlock that the *Matsu* was docked to. The ripple-bang of the hatch opening served as the cue and our quintet started up without a conductor. I'd considered canceling the welcome music for this flight, but it seemed important to build traditions even when it was hard. They had settled on "Fifteen Minutes of Kissing" because Anita had remembered that it was one of Lance's favorites. It was not one of mine, but the music wasn't for me.

I was facing the hatch when it opened and Reynard floated through. Even though I knew better, I still looked past him for Nathaniel. There was no reason for my husband to be on that shuttle. The ailments he had couldn't be addressed by anything except time.

Other men and a few women followed Reynard out, reorienting in the spindle so that we were all facing the same "up."

But not Opal, or Helen, or Lance. Not yet. It felt suddenly crowded and I gripped the handrail harder than I needed to stay put.

As the song came to an end, everyone applauded. Ana Teresa tapped Anita and the two of them slipped overhead.

I forced the smile back to my face and drew everyone's attention to me. "Welcome aboard the *Goddard*! We're so glad to have you here. Our home is yours." I gestured down the spindle. "We've got lunch waiting for you, if you'll follow the band."

Spontaneously, the band skirled into a march and as a group arced backward to superman down the spindle in a move that was completely showing off. The new folks laughed and followed, streaming after like a legion of superheroes.

Reynard hung back as people vanished down the D-Ladder to the first ring.

I pushed over to him, anchoring next to the airlock. "Anything I should know before I go in?"

His face twisted into something between happiness and despair. "He laughed. When we got to orbit and MECO, Lance laughed."

"Oh God." My heart compressed into a tight ball. Lance had been in a persistent vegetative state since the accident. "How is Opal?"

He shook his head and shrugged, setting himself drifting. "She is an astronaut. Who can tell?"

I sighed. The culture we had inherited from the Air Force pilots who started the astronaut corps was such a dismal box sometimes. I hooked around the corner, through the airlock and into the ship.

Lance was still tethered in his couch. Opal floated next to him, holding his hand pressed to her forehead. Helen was behind Opal, arms wrapped around her torso, anchoring them both with a foot hooked under a rail.

Lance was smiling.

Ana Teresa and Kam were anchored near the airlock, in

whispered conversation with Anita, and Helen's copilot, Michael Collins.

Ana Teresa looked up when I came in and beckoned me over. The hiss of her voice almost vanished under the fans. "We are discussing whether to keep Lance in the zero-g section or take him to the MedMod as planned."

Hooking a thumb at Lance, Kam said, "He's been completely nonresponsive since the accident. He laughed when we got to orbit. Opal says she felt his hand twitch."

"She is probably imagining that." Ana Teresa rubbed the spot between her brows. "And the laughter could have been a breathing irregularity."

Michael shook his head. "It was the full Woolen laugh and it wasn't short."

I asked, "Is it because of the zero-g?"

"I don't know." Kam exchanged a look with Ana Teresa. "There's a fluid shift, but I wouldn't expect this. It might be the familiar environment."

"There is no data. At all. The space program is only fifteen years old. There are no studies of brain damage in space environments." Ana Teresa stared across the shuttle at Lance, and then back at Kam. "He is your patient. What do you want to do?"

Something about that made Kam look sad and then guilty. "He is."

Belatedly, I made the connection that Kam had been on the surface with the First Expedition and was among the people who knew about the jail. Kam had been one of the people that DeBeer imprisoned and did who knows what else to. I put my hand on Kam's shoulder. "Don't make the mistake of thinking this was your fault. Leonard runs a blame-free mission and so do I. We learn from the past and we move on, making different choices based on what we've learned." I nodded to Lance. "If you want my input—and I know I'm not a doctor—it'll be easier to move him down the ladder than back up it. If there's no harm in keeping him in zero-g, let him stay up here longer and we can always move him later."

"I think that's a good plan." Kam hesitated, and then caught my arm, pulling me a little closer. "Can I talk to you after we get him settled?"

"Sure." There was a tension in that grip that made me feel confident this wasn't about Lance. I smiled my best version of Mama's "don't worry the neighbors" smile. "Come by the LMA for the welcome lunch. We can talk after. Unless it's more urgent?"

The hesitation before Kam's nod made my heart squeeze into a lump of fear. I did not believe the smile that went with the nod. "After lunch sounds fine."

"Great—I'll check in with Opal. Ana Teresa, can you work with Druzylla to sort out a berth for him?"

When I got their confirmation, I pushed away from the group. Helen looked around as I translated down the aisle and that shift in her body position must have been enough to alert Opal. She lowered Lance's hand, swiping tears away from her eyes with her sleeve.

When her eyes were clear, Opal looked at me and tried for a smile. "Hi, Elma. We're ready whenever you are."

"Sounds good." I tucked my foot under a rail and rested my hand on Lance's shoulder, which had atrophied over the past month. "Hey, Lance. Good to see you."

"He laughed on the way up."

"They told me. It's a great ride, isn't it, Lance?" I checked in with Kam, who nodded. "The doctors have been talking. We'd like to see if keeping Lance in zero-g a while longer helps him some. Is that okay with you?"

Nodding, she bit her lower lip and her breath was rough. Rubbing his hand, she swallowed. "He—he liked the music."

"I'm glad of that. We'll ask the musicians to come by and play for you some more."

He didn't respond, but the smile was still there.

Even if he never woke up more than this, at least he was happy being in space. Lance was an astronaut and this was where he belonged.

The laughter of my suddenly expanded crew almost made me forget that Kam wanted to talk to me. I tracked the doctor out of the corner of my eye all during lunch. I was not reassured when Kam and Florence wound up sitting together a little apart from everyone else.

Across from me, Helen held a pair of chopsticks and stared reverently at the last bite of her salad. Thin ribbons of carrot made a bright orange splash against vivid green spinach. At her side, Reynard said something in French that made her laugh.

"What?" I pulled my attention away from the other table and focused on the friends that I had not seen in a Martian month.

"Nothing." Helen took a very prim bite of the salad.

Reynard winked at her. "Then I should not be worried about your interest in carrots?"

Helen's cheeks pinked and she replied to him in Hokkien. And I don't know what she said, but I do know that Reynard laughed and went red all the way to the tips of his ears. I envied them to my core.

He reached across the table and took her tray. "That is it. I am clearing the table before an indecency occurs."

Their shared laughter made the empty place where Nathaniel should be beside me feel colder. For a moment the room pulled away and dimmed.

Then Reynard stood up too fast and didn't compensate for the Coriolis effect. He tipped to the side as the ship spun around him. Helen reached for where she thought he would fall, but she was still reacting with Martian instincts. Laughing, I got there first, intersecting the arc of his fall as if I'd been born in space.

"Easy there." I held him steady while Reynard got his feet under him. Somehow, he'd held on to the trays. "You okay?"

"Only my pride, which had already been threatened by a vegetable." He straightened and turned carefully, walking away with the trays amid the good-natured teasing of our crewmates. We'd all been there. And he hadn't actually fallen on his ass.

Across the room, Florence and Kam were staring at us. I sighed or groaned, I don't really know which, and looked down at Helen. "Sorry to abandon you, but there's something I need to check in on."

She glanced over her shoulder and compressed her mouth into a line. Tipping her head back, she looked up at me. "Just in case it is relevant, Nicole wanted me to tell you 'thank you.'"

I sat down. "What? Why?"

Helen shook her head. "The entirety of the message was, 'Tell Elma I said, 'thank you.'"

I stared at her flummoxed. "And no context?"

She lowered her voice a little. "Just that it was in code. Do you know why?"

"I do not." The last coded message I'd had from Earth had been Parker's terse *Acknowledged.* I could, strangely, imagine him talking to Nicole about the DeBeer situation but did not understand the train that would have led to her sending me a thank you via this roundabout route. I didn't know why those words couldn't have been sent in the clear. "If I figure anything out I'll let you know."

"Only if you can tell me." Helen slid carefully out from the table. "And now I'm going to find my husband and then some zero-g."

"And a carrot?"

"Unnecessary."

I laughed as I stood and missed Nathaniel so much that I ached.

It took me a few minutes to work my way across the module. Once upon a time I would have been invisible, but now I was the captain and people had small things they wanted to touch base about.

The ones just up from Mars complimented me on the lunch as if I'd cooked it myself. I just smiled and told them that we'd have pie for dinner. The ones on the *Goddard* had questions ranging from if they could adjust a schedule to an update on chickens to a proposal for another talent show.

By the time I got to their side of the module, Florence and Kam had cleared their trays and were waiting for me. I smiled at them as I walked up. "Garden?"

"Sounds good." Florence gestured for me to lead.

The garden spans multiple modules on the *Goddard*, all on the same ring as the kitchens, so we were able to walk straight there without climbing back up to zero-g. Stepping through the hatch into that first one, the soft humidity feathered against my skin and smelled like the rich green of summer.

My shoulders relaxed the way they always did. I ran a finger over the leaves of a tomato plant, not able to help myself. I would wear that wonderful spicy fragrance as a perfume if I could. I led us to the benches in the middle of this module and turned to face Florence and Kam.

They were both tense through their shoulders with a matching uncomfortable tightness around their eyes. They exchanged glances. I waited for one of them to start, and when they didn't, I sighed and settled on a bench.

"Have a seat, y'all," I said as if this were my aunts' front porch back in Charleston. "Kam, you must be wrung out from getting Lance up here. How's he settling in?"

The medical question seemed to unlock Kam a little. "Fine—or, I mean, he's as comfortable as I can make him." But the guilt was back inside the tension.

Florence sat down opposite me. "Parker called Leonard."

"I see." That was the Southern version of *acknowledged.* There was a forty-three-minute lag time with Earth. They would have been exchanging a series of voice memos the way Parker and I had done.

A part of me had a sudden bitter jealousy that Parker had called Leonard, which, honestly, was a little funny given how thoroughly I'd tried to avoid Parker's notice for so many years.

The rest of me was aware that this meant he wanted the conversation to be off the books and I knew it meant he'd talked to Benkoski and Rafael.

After a moment, Kam sat next to Florence. "So . . . so I'll give you the big picture, and then you can ask any follow-up questions you want."

"Fair."

"Parker talked to Benkoski and Rafael. After being briefed, he told the committee to reopen their investigation into the crash. Parker told them that he believed DeBeer was capable of intentional sabotage but that he hadn't said anything previously because he had not wanted to sway their investigation and had expected them to at least look at the official records from the First Expedition on their own."

I could hear Nicole in that language as if she were reaching through the solar system to say "hello." It gave me a sudden, incongruous image of Parker saying that he was disappointed in them.

Kam took a deep breath. "It turns out that Benkoski *did* make a full report to Clemons when he got back. And that the official records had been heavily classified at the request of the South African government to protect the reputation of—"

I was standing in front of the tomato plants. I didn't remember moving. My hands were clenched around the racks holding up their grow lights. I don't know if I was supporting myself or about to tip them over.

Letting go, my hands ached and the new skin at the base of my thumb had a crease running through it. "Is there any action I need to take?"

"Are you okay?" Kam stood behind me, using the same voice of concern as when we'd found out that I wasn't pregnant. Which, it turns out, wasn't a test I'd needed.

"Is there any action I need to take?"

Florence answered me and I don't think I've ever heard her voice that gentle. "No, honey. We just wanted you to know. Before it's in the news."

"Thank you." That was the correct response and I delivered it with calm. Inside, the anger had started to boil again because them telling me about things now did not fix Nathaniel or Lance. I pushed it away and the room seemed to recede with it. The greens became gray and the air smelled empty. I stared at the perfect tiny red spheres of the cherry tomatoes rather than face either of them. In that moment, I didn't want to know if they were looking at me with pity or concern.

One of them shifted weight so that their shoe squeaked on the rubber floor. Kam said, "I'm sorry."

The anger sighed out of me into weariness. "I know." And I did. As mad as I wanted to be—as mad as I was, they were still below me in the chain of command and I had a responsibility to them. I turned to face them both then, with the regulation smile that you put on when you're wearing a spacesuit in Earth gravity and the photographer wants to take "just one more photo." I nodded to my crewmates and tried to mean it. "I appreciate the briefing. If there's nothing else, I promised folks pie with dinner."

I was suddenly glad that our crew had doubled in size because I had a lot of stress baking to do. And if the pies were seasoned with tears of anger and longing, well, a bit of salt always made the sweetness brighter.

THIRTY-ONE

CRASH REPORT STUNS SPACE COMMUNITY

JOHANNESBURG, South Africa, November 16, 1970—Following an investigation into the crashed Martian supply vessel, the UN subcommittee report concluded that Vanderbilt DeBeer deliberately hid the fact that the vessel had crashed. The report said that the former astronaut was angry about not being selected for the second mission and that his misconduct on the First Mars Expedition had been the subject of numerous reports.

President Nicole Wargin of the United States said, "I think it would be appropriate for South Africa to pay reparations for their part in this unfortunate event. They knew the problems with him and left him in a position of command."

Another source, high in the IAC, has speculated that the other problems the Second Mars Expedition has faced might have been due to sabotage left behind by DeBeer.

Julm 49, Year 5, Tuesol—Landing + 277 sols

A banner of paper moons and stars left over from Ramadan fluttered in the breeze from the LMA's fan. I smiled and waved at people as they came in, quietly cursing myself. When Halim had departed after those months of being the commander of the *Goddard*, it had felt right to do a real send-off for him the way we did for commander changeover on *Lunetta*.

Now my crew wanted to do the same for me, and if I said no then it would not happen for the next commander. Do something twice in space, and it's a tradition. Do it three times, and it's a long-held tradition.

I walked across the room to check in with Florence and Dawn. Listening to something on her headset, Florence nodded. "Okay. We're all set to broadcast to Mars, and Mission Control on Earth has confirmed that they are recording."

I couldn't delay this any longer. It wasn't handing over command that I wanted to delay; it was needing to give a speech. It was being broadcast on Earth, since they were less than an hour behind us right now. *This* was the punishment that Parker was meting out. He knew how much I hated publicity, especially something that focused on my "achievements." I hadn't done anything to merit attention—I mean, I'd done my job, but that was what any of my crewmates would have done. People had stopped coming in. It was five past the hour. I walked to the mic in the middle of our makeshift stage. I'd learned so many tricks to seem calm.

Now, I let out my breath, as unobtrusively as I could so that my lungs emptied and my diaphragm nearly folded in half. The inhalation that followed lifted my soft palette and opened my throat.

"My fellow astronauts and *gentlemen* astronauts." The little dig at all the times I'd been called a "lady" astronaut made the folks in the room chuckle. My voice was steady and strong enough that I shifted back a little from the mic. "I've been your commander for two hundred and eleven sols—not that I'm counting—and some of you have yet to venture to the surface of Mars. But you have been . . . well, I won't say 'tireless,' because I know y'all have been exhausted on more than one occasion, but you have been consistently excellent. I couldn't have asked for a better crew."

The lights were set so that I could see all of their faces and I knew every person in the audience. I knew every person on the world we orbited. My voice was being recorded to be shared on a planet full of strangers surrounding small clusters of folks that I knew.

"I also want to thank our trainers at the IAC and all of our friends on the Moon and in low Earth orbit for preparing us for this mission. And, of course, the folks staffing our flight control consoles and working with us—despite the significant time delays to solve problems none of us expected." I looked across the room to the camera that Dawn held, and I smiled, thinking about my brother watching this. "Especially our families. Thank you for supporting us. We all miss you. Come visit real soon now, you hear?"

Was that too folksy? I didn't know and I wasn't sure that I cared. Despite my genuine desire to see my brother and his family, my words weren't for them. This moment wasn't for them. It was for my crew here and on Mars. In the audience, I found Florence and Dawn, and Kam, and Heidi. These people were who I wanted to build a future with.

I imagined Leonard and Wilburt and Graeham on the surface. Parker would be listening at home. Would Rafael? Or Benkoski? Would DeBeer hear my words?

"There's a mural in the main dome on Mars that was not part of the plans for any expedition. The artist painted over things brought from Earth that are part of the canvas of society there but have no place here. What it shows me is that here, in the Martian sphere of influence, we can paint any futures we want. Imagine cities reaching out from the walls of Gale Crater. Not just a habitat. A home. That is the work that I am most proud of, during my time as your commander. That together, we are building a home."

I would walk from here to the shuttle and then drop down to the surface of a planet where my husband lived in the middle of Gale Crater. Nathaniel was my home.

"Now, to introduce the next commander of the *Goddard*, I'll just tell you what the director of the IAC said when he sent the assignment up." I fished the flimsy teletype paper out of my pocket. "Director Parker said, 'She's a damn fine astronaut and better suited to this job than you ever were. Don't fudge up the ship before you hand it over.' Except he clearly did not say 'fudge.'"

That got a laugh, because everyone knew Parker, even if just by reputation. They started to applaud in anticipation. The smile on my face matched their laughter and was not a regulation smile. It was pure joy as I beckoned my replacement to the stage.

Helen let out a quick breath and stepped forward with a small wave to the assembled crew. "Commander York, I stand ready to relieve you."

"I am ready to be relieved." I held out the logbook. "Your ship is in good repair and the personnel are a credit to the program."

"Thank you." She took the logbook in both hands.

"And this . . . is for when a real emergency happens." I held out a small note card. "It's my recipe for a chess pie. Including the crust."

Helen's eyes widened and I swear that they started to water. "That is very kind. I will deploy it when necessary."

"Then my work here is done."

Helen took a very deep breath. "I relieve you, commander."

Grinning like a rookie on their first launch, I shook her hand and it felt as if the gravity had dropped to lunar standard. "I stand relieved."

THIRTY-TWO

Julm 50, Year 5, Wednesol–Landing + 278 sols

The *Esther* shuddered around me as atmosphere brushed over the skin of our lander for my second landing on Mars. In the NavComp seat to my far right, Meredith called out our approach to Mars's surface. "On my mark, 3:30 until ignition."

"Confirmed 3:30." Every part of me felt alive in focused concentration. Behind me, ten people were silent. Three of them were returning to Mars. Seven were seeing that beautiful red surface spreading out to meet us for the first time.

I checked the horizon, then returned my gaze to the mission clock instead so I would be ready when Meredith called it.

"Mark. 3:30."

"Confirmed." The digital numbers flicked over in the countdown.

To my immediate right, in the copilot seat, Ida read out the checklist the way Leonard had on my first landing. "Thrust translation, four jets. Balance couple, On. TCA throttle, Minimum. Throttle, Auto CDR. Propellant button, Reset. Prop button."

In response, I flicked the appropriate switches, and there was a sense of déjà vu as memories of sims blended into the memory of landing before, which blended in with the *now* of it. Mars's atmosphere was too thin to be useful but I could still feel the eager kisses of it as we passed through.

"All right. Abort/Abort Stage, Reset. Att. Control, three of them to Mode Control. AGS is reading 400 plus 1."

The remaining numbers bled away from the countdown clock. "Ignition." I squeezed the control, firing four of our jets.

They kicked, roaring, into life. The gravity load increased, shoving me deep into my seat. I yawed the ship over so the engines pointed down to the planet and hid Mars from sight. Outside the viewport, red and orange tongues of plasma licked the glass as we began our descent in earnest.

I kept my gaze split between the window, watching for the horizon, and the altimeter. "Throttling down."

Ida nodded at my side. "1,500 meter altitude. 30 meters per second."

The horizon was in my viewport, level and steady, exactly where it should be.

"900 at 20."

Beside us, Meredith said, "Confirmed. You are Go for landing."

I eased off the throttle more, dropping us lower toward the surface. At one thousand feet, the glint of Bradbury Base's dome separated it from the rusty landscape. Beyond it, another mound of Martian regolith covered a second dome, and beyond that, the landscape was ripped open where excavations had begun for the greenhouse dome.

I kept the base centered on the grid of lines that were etched into the inside of the window. Horizon level. Dropping speed, but not too fast so I wouldn't land us off the mark.

"225 meters. Coming down at 5 meters per second."

My speed was better this time than on my first landing and I shoved that pleasure away to enjoy later. Right now, I still needed to land. We roared past the near wall of Gale Crater and the ground dropped away again. I throttled down farther as the transmission tower at the Bradbury beckoned me toward the beautiful clear square of the landing pad, as ruddy as the rest of the landscape.

"30 meters, 1 down, 3 forward."

Grin curving my lips, I edged us over the landing pad. At the bottom of the window, ochre dust swirled as if Mars was reaching up to say welcome home.

"10 meters, down 2.75." Ida's voice was as steady as if she were on a leisurely Sunday flight with the 99s. "There's the pad."

The feet of the *Esther* connected and a light flashed on the dashboard. "Contact light."

"Shutdown." I pulled my hands off the control stick and set it to neutral. I inhaled deeply for the first time since we started entry. I flicked four switches on the dashboard and confirmed that against my checklist. "Engine stop. Welcome to Mars, ladies."

That last bit wasn't on any checklist, nor were the cheers. I grinned. "Ida and Meredith, nicely done."

Meredith said, "I thought it would be a better view from up here, but . . ."

"You didn't look up?" Ida chuckled as she undid the straps on her seat. "Neither did I the first time I landed. Or this time. Much."

"I have to look out the window. Perks of the job." I reached for the mic. "Bradbury Base, *Esther*. We're home."

"Welcome home, *Esther*." Leonard's voice greeted us on the big loop, so every member of the crew on the shuttle could hear him. "There's a team coming out to help off-load and we've got lunch waiting for you."

"Copy that. Looking forward to it." I started to disconnect but the quality of the sound changed.

Private comms. Leonard said, "I'm dropping the big loop from this. Elma, after you're in, I need to talk to you."

My back was to the rest of the cabin so no one could see the worry on my face and my suit would mask everything else. With my helmet still on, no one could read my lips or hear me talk. "Understood. As soon as I'm out of my suit. I'll come find you."

My brain started to turn toward all the terrible things it could be. Nathaniel. Earth. Another failure point in the dome. I bit the inside of my lip and thanked the IAC that I had an entire shutdown checklist to distract me.

I would know what this was about soon enough.

By the time I jumped down on the surface of Mars, straightening slowly as if I still had a Coriolis effect to compensate for, the off-loading process was well underway. The rover was backed up with its trailer as people put some of the bulkier items onto it.

A line of people trundled between the cargo hatch and the base, carrying supplies to the airlock. I looked at all those bright green Mars suits, as if I could spot Nathaniel in the mix. We all looked alike in the suits except for height. Nathaniel wouldn't even be out here.

The urge to go help carry things was pretty strong, but right now I needed to do my walkaround and complete my checklist to make sure that the *Esther* was secured. Then I needed to go talk to Leonard. About . . . what? Turning away from the line, I flipped my comms to the common band and my headset filled with chatter.

"You have the trunk," Aahana said.

I tested the tension on the tie-down strap by the starboard landing leg.

"I have the trunk." After months of only women on the comms, the male voice that replied was almost shockingly low and then switched to Hindi: *"Aap Chorni Ho—"*

"Jaidev!" Aahana laughed. "I was only looking at the case—what did I steal?"

"Mera Dil."

I don't know what he said, but I could recognize flirtation when I heard it. Aahana's laugh was bright and infectious.

I didn't hear anything in the voices that indicated a new problem with the base. But maybe they didn't know yet. Did that mean it was Nathaniel? I didn't know what I would find when I saw him. Would there be a visible difference?

I looked down at the checklist strapped to my left forearm. More tie-down straps. As the conversations started up again, I walked around the outside of the ship, checking the straps tied at each compass point. I let the path carry me away from the group. The worry and the chatter made it hard to think.

After a minute, I switched away from the group channel and worked in silence. Just me, my checklist, and anxiety.

I followed a group into the outer airlock of Bradbury and pulled the hatch shut since I was the only one not actively carrying something. It was crowded with crates and six other astronauts. When the door was shut, I activated the suction fans to keep us from tracking Martian dust into the base.

As the automatic cycle ended, the airlock began to pressurize, faster than our littler hopper could. As the sound of a train roared on Mars, the checklist hanging on the wall fluttered. At the interior end of the airlock, the gauge light went green.

Suit fabric settled against my undergarments. Pulling off my gloves, I tucked them under my right arm and removed my helmet and the smell of Mars caught me by surprise.

On the *Goddard*, I'd had time to forget the sweetly chalky rotten-egg smell that crept in from the surface. Now my eyes

THE MARTIAN CONTINGENCY ✳ 345

prickled with tears at the smell of home. This smell meant that I would get to see Nathaniel soon.

The airlock swung open and folks were waiting to help clear it for the next load. I dropped my gloves into my helmet so I could free up a hand to carry a box.

Howard reached in and batted my hand away. "Let the inside team do the lifting."

"Stand back and let the women do the lifting." Mavis reached past him and hefted the crate I was aiming for. "Don't want to hurt the weaker sex."

"You've got an unfair advantage." Howard laughed, reaching for a different crate. "Two months at Earth gravity and—"

"Don't worry, little Martian boy, one sol you'll grow up to be big and strong like a real woman."

Sighing, Howard grinned at me and jerked his head over his shoulder. "Unless you need to head back out, they're ready in the donning station."

"I have a free hand."

"Don't worry, there will be plenty to do later." He turned and preceded me out of the airlock. I don't know why it made me uneasy to walk out without carrying something. I didn't have to prove anything. There were plenty of people to carry things.

I ducked out of the airlock and made my way over to the donning station that abutted the hallway. Most of the bays were filled with people stripping down after the end of a long sol. I faced the wall and walked into one of the empty slots.

The magnetic catches latched to my suit, taking some of the weight off, and I realized how tired I was. Sighing, I reached back to fumble for the catch so I could slip out.

At the edge of my vision, a suit tech seemed to appear from nowhere, in that way that happens sometimes in space when the ever-present fans can drown out footfalls. He rested his hand on my shoulder. "Hello, Dr. York."

At the sound of my husband's voice, my heart beat sideways

and upside down as it tried to slip out of my chest and snuggle up against him. A goofy smile plastered itself across my face. "Dr. York, what a pleasant surprise."

"May I help you?" He released the seals and a shiver went all through me that I don't think had much to do with the temperature differential.

"Why yes, thank you." As I pushed out the back of the suit, his hands were on my sides to stabilize me. The tubes girdling my LCVG left me with only the pressure of his touch and spots of warmth. I turned, still attached to my Mars suit by tubes and cables, and did not care that I hadn't finished the checklist or that I was covered in sweat or that we were standing in a room of our peers.

I kissed my husband.

God. I had missed him so much. The distinct, indescribable scent of him. The way he always missed shaving a spot right under his lower lip even with the electric razor. The way his face was alight as he looked at me. I pressed against him as much as I could, relishing his solid presence.

He had lost weight.

I wouldn't ask now. I didn't know if it was a side effect of the neuropathy or if he hadn't been eating. Asking here and now wouldn't help. I ran a hand up his back, squeezed my husband one more time, and released him. His smile when he looked down at me made one beam back from me in return.

Nathaniel handed me a towel and as he released it his fingers were shaking. "Let me know if you need help with decoupling your LCVG."

"I'd rather have help with coupling." I wiped the sweat from my face. "Unfortunately . . . I need to go talk to Leonard."

"Ah." Nathaniel turned to my suit so he could stow my helmet and gloves in their bags until the suit techs were ready for them. He took them one at a time, tongue held between his lips as he concentrated on sliding the bag over the helmet. "Do you know why?"

I slung the towel over my shoulder and decoupled the tubes of my LCVG. "Trying not to guess."

"Well, I can walk you over there and then afterward . . . ?"

"Afterward, I'll slip into something more comfortable."

I don't believe that I've ever shucked an LCVG as fast as I got out of that one and into one of the generic flight suits. Still zipping it up, I met Nathaniel in the hall. Taking my hand, he turned to walk toward the airlock to the main dome.

He slowed and looked down at our entwined hands. Lifting them, he ran the fingers of his other hand across the skin graft. "How is it?"

"Ana Teresa is very smug about her work." But as his fingers traced the edges, sensation went from vibrant to dull depending on which side of the scar he was on. "And you?"

"Frustrated." He held up his hand, showing the tremor. "This gets tiring but I'm finding workarounds."

"This does not surprise me." I leaned into him as we walked down the hall toward the airlock, which led into the main dome. "I've missed you."

"So have I." His voice was rough. "Very much."

Light shone through the open hatch in a testament to how much work had been done. Just like on the Moon, there was a new electromagnetic catch holding it in the open position, ready to release if the pressure dropped.

I whistled appreciatively. "Y'all were busy."

"We were very motivated." Nathaniel nodded at the hatch. "If Parker's rationale for keeping you all away was safety, then we had reason to make sure every new safety feature was installed ASAP."

Hand in hand, we ducked into the main dome, and I stopped.

The walls around the outside of the dome were a rich verdant green, and smelled of moist earth, and the young leaves of plants rustled in the fans. "Oh, wow." My eyes watered at the sight of all that life. "Y'all got the rest of the vertical gardens installed in here."

"Yeah. I mean, Catalina did." He ran a hand through his hair. "We're only just starting to get lettuces but it's nice to look at."

We took the long way around to the stairs, walking past the garden walls. I reached out my free hand and ran it along the leaf of a young tomato plant, releasing a sweet spice to mix with the sulfur scent of Mars. As we went, I nodded at astronauts I hadn't seen in months.

One part of me was amazed by the changes. The rest was concentrating on Nathaniel and trying not to look like I was worrying. I couldn't feel his tremors as we walked, but I could feel a difference in his gait. Ducking my head, I watched his feet. His right one was dragging a little. He slowed as we rounded the curve and arrived at the stairs to the lower floors. "You remember where the emergency oxygen masks are?"

"Bottom of the stairs." I squeezed his hand and leaned in to kiss the hollow of his cheek. "I'll be back ASAP."

He nodded and let me go downstairs alone. I knew that he'd gone down there since the accident, because he'd called me from comms, but I was unaccountably glad that he was staying upstairs.

Downstairs did not feel different. More people, yes, but the space itself was unchanged. I was changed, though. I walked around the curving hall feeling like the floor should be curving up, the way it appeared to on the *Goddard*, instead of around.

Leonard's door was open, but I knocked anyway.

He looked up from his desk. Dark bags weighed under his eyes and I would swear he had more gray hair at the temples. He stood, beckoning me in. "Elma. Welcome back."

"Thank you." I folded down the small chair opposite his desk and sat.

Leonard shut the door. Then he took his seat across from me. He stared at his desk, mouth compressing, and I braced myself for news from Earth.

Drumming his fingers on his desk, he cleared his throat and looked up. "Do you want some water?"

"I'm fine, thanks." I folded my hands on my lap and crossed

my ankles, sitting the way my grandmother had taught me to sit like a lady.

Leonard nodded, looking into the corner. He took a breath, opening his mouth as if to speak, and closed it again. The fans fluttered a quick reference booklet hanging on the wall. Leonard took his hands off his desk and rested them on his legs.

He met my gaze. "Elma, I owe you an apology."

Startled, I pulled my head back. "Sorry?"

"That should be my line." His smile was sad, and then vanished altogether. "I'm sorry that we kept things from you about what happened on the First Expedition. We shouldn't have done that and you were absolutely right when you said that my silence—my decisions as commander—led directly to . . . I'm so sorry about Nathaniel."

For some reason, this made me angry instead of helping. "Then you should apologize to him. And to Opal and Lance."

"I did. I mean . . . I apologized to Opal and Nathaniel. And Lance. I don't know if he heard or understood me, but I did try."

Even though I knew that the accident had been unintentional. Even though I knew that Leonard cared deeply about every person on the crew. Even though I could see how it was weighing on him, I was so angry at what his willful negligence had done. The entire First Expedition team had caused irreparable harm with their silence and they had done it because they had been following his lead. I understood that they were managing their own trauma and I also wanted to tear into him and make some horrible cutting remark that would hurt and leave a scar.

Slow is fast.

I took a breath. I let my heart hammer in my chest as if I were afraid, but the heat that filled my veins bore no resemblance to anxiety. I let the breath out. Leonard had once told me that an apology was because you cared about the relationship more than you cared about being right. I'd known him a long time. He hadn't meant for any of this to happen. He had been the victim of a system that had failed him.

"Thank you." I sat forward. The apology was appreciated but it wasn't what I wanted. "I am angry because you made the same choices Mission Control did. You chose not to listen or communicate. Why didn't you tell me? I'm your second-in-command."

He sighed, looking down. "Because you keep trying to fix things. I was . . . I was afraid that if you knew that you would go to Mission Control to try to do something about a thing that couldn't be fixed. And if they knew how completely we'd lost control of the First Expedition . . . There are so many factions that would have used that as proof that we aren't meant to live away from the Earth and they would have kept the Second Expedition from launching."

I stared at him. "Florence went back with a bullet wound. That would have turned up in the post-mission physicals."

"If you don't know it's a bullet wound, it's just a scar." He sat hunched at his desk. "By the time we got back it was nearly two years old."

I massaged the base of my thumb where the scar tissue was. "Those are reasons to not tell Mission Control. Not why you hid it after we got here."

"I know. I'm sorry. I was afraid and I made the wrong choice. That choice hurt you, it hurt someone you love, and it hurt the entire crew." He took a deep breath. "So, I want to relinquish command to you."

I laughed at him.

I didn't mean to. It just startled out of me and bounced in loud, brash, staccato bursts off the walls. Leonard looked appalled.

I shook my head. "No. Absolutely not. Parker would never—"

"He already approved it."

Mouth hanging open, I stared at him. "I don't want it." I didn't even have to think about it. "I want to fly and I want to spend time with Nathaniel. I don't want to manage. I don't want to be in charge. I just want to be with my husband for however long—"

My voice broke and I stared into the corner. I was a professional. I shook my head again. "Thank you for the honor, but I decline the assignment."

"Oh. Okay." He ran his hand over his hair again and I could almost see a script evaporating in his head where somehow giving me command would have absolved him of culpability for his silence. His shoulders bowed again.

I stood. "Thank you for the explanation and apology. Now, if you'll excuse me, I haven't seen my husband for several months."

"Of course." Leonard pushed back from his desk. He looked uncomfortable for a moment and then cleared his throat. "I built your schedule around the assumption that you would say yes to the handoff. So, you have some free periods now. I could use your help in identifying a successor."

My head cocked to the side almost on its own with surprise. "You're still stepping down?"

He half shrugged and half gestured at his tiny office. "I'm a geologist. I haven't been on the surface since we arrived. I . . . yeah. I had thought there would be time for me to take surveying shifts."

I hung by the door for a moment. The feel of standing on Mars was subtly different than the same gravity load on the *Goddard.* I wasn't subliminally aware of a ship spinning around me. Down was a constant now.

I shall either find a way or make one.

I wanted to see Nathaniel, but I was also still a member of the Second Mars Expedition. Leonard had apologized. The regret was etched into his being. An apology was because you cared about the relationship more than you cared about being right. So was accepting an apology.

"What about Sheldon Spender?"

"What?" Leonard looked up from his desk.

"He took over deputy admin duties while I was on the *Goddard.*" I stepped back from the door. "Let's pull up the crew member files and look at candidates to propose to Parker. I can go through them with you."

Leonard held up his hands. "No. No, I've kept you from Nathaniel long enough."

"We've been married for twenty-one years." I went to the filing cabinet and pulled open the first drawer. "Neither of us are going anywhere."

Did I want to be here? No. But if I left now, it would break the fragile trust rebuilding between Leonard and me permanently. So was this where I needed to be for the next two hours? Yes. As much as work was part of Nathaniel, I was an astronaut. The love of my crew was part of me.

We were Martians and we were here. We would either find a way, together, or make one.

THIRTY-THREE

**DISASTER TOLLS NEEDLESSLY HIGH,
CONFERENCE ON CLIMATE IS TOLD**

GENEVA, Switzerland, November 17, 1970—Every year 250,000 inhabitants of the earth, 95 percent of whom are in poorer nations, die in natural disasters that cause $25 billion in property damage, most of which is in developed countries. It is estimated that 85 percent of the deaths and half the damage could be prevented with existing know-how.

This assessment of vulnerability to abnormal weather conditions is derived from a prolonged international study conducted at forty sites in twenty countries. Some 5,000 people, from peasants to leading citizens, were interviewed by geographers and other scientists from the United States, Europe, India, and elsewhere.

Julm 50, Year 5, Wednesol–Landing + 278 sols

I expected to find Nathaniel in the engineering offices, even though he hadn't come downstairs with me. Instead, I found my husband in the recreation area with a set of weights. He had unzipped his flight suit and wore the upper half tied around his waist with only his tank top underneath. A fine film of sweat glossed the ball of his shoulder. I paused for a moment to appreciate the sight of his biceps as he raised a pair of dumbbells in a curl.

And then I realized that he was doing physical therapy.

Putting a smile back on, I walked up to him. "Well, hello, Dr. York."

"Dr. York!" He grinned at me and set the dumbbells down.

I sat on the weight bench next to him. "How much more do you have to do?"

Around us, other members of the expedition carried boxes, or unloaded gear, or lounged with a book, or crocheted on a rest period. Somewhere, someone was playing the guitar, and it made me miss Terrazas terribly.

Nathaniel looked at the weights and hesitated. "Technically, I should do another set of ten but . . ." He leaned in for a kiss. "I can think of more appealing ways to exercise."

Laughing, I kissed him back. "I'm not willing to face either of our doctors for you skipping PT. And ten is nothing."

"Fine." He picked up the weights—*One*—and nodded to my hand—*Two*. "What about you?"

Three. I flexed my fingers. *Four.* "I'm cleared. I had to do light stretching while the skin was healing." *Five.* "But Ana Teresa wasn't going to let me in a spacesuit until everything was back to nominal." *Six.* "So . . . I will just sit here and admire my husband."

Seven. He laughed. *Eight.* The dumbbells trembled slightly as he lowered them. "If you aren't otherwise occupied, there's some research I could use your help with." *Nine.*

"I am unscheduled. How can I help?" *Ten.*

"Well, Dr. York, there are some insertion points I have questions about." Nathaniel set the dumbbells aside and untied the arms of his flight suit from around his waist. Or rather, he frowned and fumbled with the fabric trying to get the simple knot undone.

"Do you need help?"

"I'm fine." He winced as if he could hear the snap in his own voice, but he didn't change his mind. Nathaniel untied the sleeves, shrugged the suit back up, and then looked down to work the zipper.

I bit my lips, watching him until I couldn't any more. I stood up and grabbed the dumbbells.

"I can get those." He looked up from the zipper.

"I know, but this gets us back to our room a little quicker." I set the dumbbells down on the rack. "I have a checklist that I need to run through. If you have nothing else scheduled."

"I'm happy to review any procedures you think we should go over." The way he looked at me lit every engine I had. As I turned to head to our cubicle, Nathaniel caught my hand. "We're in the new dome."

"Oh." I looked across the dome, through the "streets" to the south airlock, which had been a dead end and useful only for storage when I'd left. And a prison before that. There were so many more people here. I knew them all, but it had been so long since I'd seen them from a distance greater than the length of a module, that they almost felt like strangers. "Right. I knew that."

"I'm sure you did."

Hand in hand, we walked to the south airlock. All the boxes and bins that had been stored there had been removed from it. My gaze went to the hashmarks.

Aut viam inveniam aut faciam.

I stopped, turning in a circle in the middle of the airlock. Four meters in diameter. I tried to imagine the space filled with Kam, Rafael, Florence, and Leonard. Ninety-seven sols. I did not know how they managed in the small space, but my brain mapped it onto stories told by people in our synagogue. *I shall either find a way or make one.*

I dug in my pocket and pulled out my multi-tool. Don't ask me why this was suddenly urgent, but it was. I opened the awl and scratched on the wall opposite Leonard's text.

Az me muz, ken men.

"What?" Nathaniel tilted his head, mouthing the words. My husband doesn't speak Yiddish.

"If you have to, you can." The letters caught the light, undulled by an effort to erase them. "Aunt Esther used to say it when I was stuck on homework or, anything really."

He nodded, staring at the wall and then held out his hand. "May I?"

"Going to join me in defacing IAC property?" I handed him the awl.

"Project beautification." He stared at the ceiling for a moment, mouthing something silently, then stepped forward and put the awl to a spot to the right of mine and a little higher. His hand shook.

Sticking his tongue between his lips, he lifted his left hand and braced it under his wrist.

"Do you want me to—"

"Nope. If I have to, I can." His brows were drawn together as he concentrated on guiding the tip of the awl over the smooth metal. The lines wriggled in response to his tremors. His first letter was a nearly illegible malformed *n*.

He lifted the awl and set it down again, to the left of the letter and the context reshaped everything. That hadn't been a malformed *n* it was a perfectly shaped Hebrew מ.

My husband, the "terrible Jew," was writing a Hebrew phrase on the wall to add to my Yiddish one and Leonard's Latin. My heart swelled near to busting.

It took him longer than it had taken me and some of the letters were wiggly, but it was clear.

מקווה לנס, אבל אל תסמוך

He stepped back. "Hope for a miracle, but don't count on one."

"And you told me you were a terrible Jew."

"Dad had it carved on his toolbox." He fumbled while folding the awl and dropped it. "Shit."

I bent down to scoop it up. "It's perfect."

When I stood up, Nathaniel was looking at me with the goofy smile he gets sometimes, where his head tilts to the side a little and one corner of his mouth turns up. My whole face lit up in response. He stepped forward and I met him and we kissed, surrounded by words of perseverance.

Footsteps made us break apart as a couple of folks came down the corridor from the second dome. Completely casual, and not at all blushing, I followed Nathaniel down that corridor, toward the second dome, which still gleamed with the shine of new construction. Labels dotted the walls in the modules that had come from Earth, put there by people who would never see this place.

I imagined the frantic rush down the eighteen meters to safety. "Does the tunnel get its air from the main dome or the second?"

"Main." He grimaced, gesturing at a vent we were passing. "It made sense to link it to the established space so we could work in it."

After the accident, they would have had to transit the length of this in order for them to get to safety. And the airlock could only hold eight, maximum, so everyone would have had to wait as it cycled. I shivered and looked back down the length.

One of the folks had stopped in the airlock, looking at the wall. I saw them digging in their pocket. What phrase would they add?

Smiling, I turned away and stepped into the second dome.

Like on the Moon, this dome was broken into four stories, with two aboveground and two below. The top three floors had dorms with a maintenance level all the way at the bottom. The corridors cut through the middle to a central spiral staircase. Natural light cascaded down the stairwell, giving the middle of the space a glow. The Moon's dorms did not have anything like that. But they also had a monthlong day/night cycle.

"We're on the upper floor." Nathaniel led me up the stairs and the drag in his right foot was more apparent from below and behind. He held the handrail and lifted his knee higher to compensate. I was betting that Kam had made him practice on stairs a lot as part of his physical therapy.

"Would ground floor be easier?"

"We put light wells in to help people's circadian rhythms

adapt to Mars." Nathaniel continued up the stairs as if he had not heard me.

At the top of the stairs, we entered a common lounge surrounded by doors to individual dorm rooms. Some of them had nameplates on them. One had a painted wreath of white flowers. I could hear the sounds of a reunion coming from another door.

Ignoring that, I turned in a slow circle, taking in the rounded walls and bare floor. Someone had brought a pair of chairs up and set a packing crate between them. The small skylight overhead filled it with a radiant glow that made it feel more alive than any place on the *Goddard*.

Between a pair of doors, an improvised frame made from a packing crate held an embroidery of green trees backed by mountains under a blue sky with scattered clouds.

I walked closer to it, and the greenery seemed familiar and alien. "I didn't know Florence had finished that."

"She sent it down on the last flight for Catalina and Bolí's anniversary." He nodded at the door to the right of the frame. "That's their room. And this . . . is ours."

When I turned around, he was standing in front of the door with the wreath painted on it. I had been distracted by the flowers and hadn't noticed the carefully hand-lettered name in the middle: *The Doctors York*.

I brought my hands to my mouth to keep from crying. "Oh, Nathaniel."

"I hired Dawn to paint it." He stood awkwardly next to the door. "Part of my personal weight allotment on the next expedition. Not much. Just a couple of boxes of pigments."

"It's beautiful." I walked over to the door, wondering at the delicate little white flowers and the curving sprigs of greenery. "Thank you."

Nathaniel fished in his pocket. He pulled out a bundle of cloth and unfolded it. Inside lay our mezuzah from Earth. When we were packing, we hadn't even needed to have a discussion about *if* we would bring it, but my eyes still welled with tears at the sight of the small engraved wood case. The olive wood seemed even more precious on this planet without trees.

I slipped my hands under Nathaniel's so that we both held the mezuzah. "Baruch ata Adonai, Eloheinu melekh ha'olam, asher kid'shanu b'mitzvotav v'tzivanu likboa m'zuzah."

He turned to the door and paused. "Velcro. I worried that if I used pop rivets we wouldn't be able to get it off when we move."

"When we move?"

"Someday, there will be houses and apartments here." He aligned the mezuzah with a piece of Velcro that held it at an angle on the right side of the door.

Then he stepped back and together we said the closing words of the small ritual. "Baruch ata Adonai, Eloheinu melekh ha'olam, shehecheyanu v'kiy'manu v'higianu laz'man hazeh."

The final words had never resonated so deeply. *We praise You, Adonai our G-d, Sovereign of the universe, for giving us life, for sustaining us, and for enabling us to reach this moment.*

I leaned against my husband, looking at our new door—at our new home—and relished being alive, with him, on Mars.

Nathaniel kissed the top of my head. "I also need to give you your anniversary present."

"This isn't enough?"

His grin was shy and sneaky as he put his hand on the doorknob. "Take your shoes off and close your eyes."

"Okay?" Laughing, I did as he requested, setting my shoes by the wall, and then I closed my eyes. I felt his hands on my shoulder and behind my knees. Before I could register enough to protest, Nathaniel picked me up in a bridal carry. I tensed. "Nathaniel."

"Welcome home, Dr. York." He swung us through the door and set me down on a soft carpet. The door shut behind us. "You can open your eyes now."

I stood on a small area rug in a room glowing with light and color. In some ways this was a clone of the married couple dorms on the Moon. It was a wedge with a full-sized bed raised in a loft, with a fold-down table and cabinets underneath it.

But this one had a window.

Thick with multiple layers of glass, it was small and looked out in a tunnel through the rusty regolith that was piled around the outside of the dome. At the far end of that dim tube, a circle of the Martian landscape radiated sunlight. A swirl of dust drifted across the rocky terrain between us and the wall of Gale Crater.

Under the window, a large recycled can with a tomato plant grew on the desk. On one wall, he'd taped an eight-by-ten photo of the view from our old apartment, looking out at the trees in the courtyard.

I looked down at the rug again. It was a watery blue with flowers twining around a rich green border and no bigger than a bathmat, but it was glorious. Wiggling my toes, I sank deeper in the soft pile of the carpet.

"Happy anniversary." He stood behind me and slid his arms around my waist.

"Nathaniel." My throat was too full of my heart to be able to get more than his name past.

He kissed the side of my neck. "I remembered on the First Expedition that you wanted an apartment with a view of trees. This was the best I could do."

"It's perfect." I turned in his arms and began to reacquaint myself with my husband of twenty-one years.

I learned that our tiny room had the glory of two windows. At the head of the bed, a small oblong was centered in the low wall over a shelf. We lay tangled in the covers, one of which was a crocheted blanket that Myrtle had made, which we'd both selected to bring as part of our personal allotment. The rug had been a surprise, as had the photo of our apartment.

I lay on my side, curled against him with my right leg drawn up over his thigh. Outside, the sky was hinting at the deep blue of a Martian sunrise. Running my fingers through the pale hair on his chest, I watched the vein beat in the side of his neck. He slid his hand up my leg and lifted his head, peering down at my thigh.

His fingers traced the outline of the scar where Ana Teresa had taken a swatch of skin to use on my hand. "I'd wondered where that would be."

"It hurt more than the hand." I watched his fingers and the way they tremored. "Will you . . . will you tell me about the neuropathy?"

His head dropped back against the pillow. "It's nothing to worry about."

I caught his hand. I had practiced this conversation so many times in my head, but the reality of it was harder. "Nerve death doesn't sound like nothing."

"It sounds worse than it is." His fingers twitched in my hand. "It's only a tingling. Kind of like . . . it's kind of like the pins and needles you get when your leg goes to sleep. That's all. I've had it so long that I don't even think about it."

The tremors were new. His dragging right foot was new. "I read your medical report."

"Oh." He stared at the ceiling. "I wish you hadn't done that."

I pushed myself up to sit under the low ceiling of our little loft. "If I had just been me, I wouldn't have. Probably. But as a mission commander? With everything that was going on down here?"

His jaw clenched. The muscle at the corner stood out in clear definition. Nathaniel grimaced and nodded. "Okay. I can understand that. I still wish you had delegated that to someone else."

"Delegated? Is there someone—other than your *wife*—that you would have been comfortable with knowing?"

"I thought you were mission commander."

"I was both, Nathaniel. You know what that's like."

Wincing, he turned his head to look into the main part of our room. "Yeah . . . I do."

"Why didn't you tell me?" How many times would I ask this question tosol?

"There's nothing to be done." He sat up, adjusting the blankets across his lap. "And they said I was fit to fly, so . . . why worry you?"

"I'm your wife."

"Yes, but—but I knew this would make you fret and it's also not a problem."

"Progressive is a problem."

"See. This is why I didn't tell you. You're going to worry about it for no reason. And when we met, your anxiety was . . . I did everything I could to not worry you." He tried for a laugh. "Besides, you kick at night when you're fretting. It's still a small bed."

I let him have the laugh and leaned forward to kiss him. "I love you so much, but you have learned the wrong lessons." I took his hands and held both of them, looking at him. "Worrying is part of who I am. If you don't tell me what the real problem is, then I will invent ones in my head. Now . . . tell me about the neuropathy, please. How long have you known? What gives you trouble? What frightens you? Just . . . just trust me to manage my own worrying."

Nathaniel bit his lower lip and looked down, running his thumb over the scar on my left hand. "My right hand would go to sleep sometimes, since . . . well, I don't remember when it started. But after the poisoning—I mean the thallium on Earth—the pins and needles were pretty constant. And both hands. After the CO_2 . . . I have reduced sensation in my index and middle fingers on the left side. And across the entire right. And, well . . . you noticed my foot already, but that might get better."

His hair was rucked up and strands brushed the ceiling as he shifted his weight on the bed. "What am I afraid of?" His brows came together as he stared at our entwined hands. "I'm . . . It's already happened. I'm a disaster with a soldering gun. I can't draw a straight line to save my life. I can still direct and manage, but . . . but I'm afraid it will get worse. So. Now you know."

I lifted his left hand and kissed his ring finger. "Thank you for telling me."

"I'll set up a pallet on the floor so you don't kick me tonight."

Laughing, I leaned forward to kiss his warm, soft mouth. "Silly man. I did all that worrying on the *Goddard*." I would fret more, he wasn't wrong about that, but I'd left the panic behind on orbit. Whatever happened, we were together and we would find a way through it.

If you have to, you can.

I cleared my throat. "I mentioned that I had read your medical file. They also . . ." I had practiced this in my head on the *Goddard* and none of the sentences seemed to make it any better. "They also told me you were sterile."

His face slackened and his whole body seemed to go blank. Nathaniel's lips parted a little as if he were going to say something. Then he blinked a couple of times and shook his head.

"I'm so sorry." Bringing my hands together, all the anger that I had felt when they'd first told me sizzled through my muscles. I wanted to hit something with a violence that felt alien. "They should have told you."

"Why didn't they?"

"They thought if we knew that exceptions were being made, that we'd turn down the mission."

"Ah . . ." In that quiet exhalation, I could hear his understanding that they were afraid *I* would turn down the mission.

"I'm sorry."

He shook his head again and gave something that sounded almost like a laugh. "Well. Well, I guess that makes things easier." He laughed again, more genuinely this time, looking at a small drawer tucked under the shelf that stretched across the head of the bed. "All those condoms we don't need. We're rich!"

A laugh startled out of me. "You goof." I sat forward to kiss him and took my time with it. His lips parted, combining the warmth between us. I ran my hand up through his hair, shivering as his hand found the small of my back and traced circles there.

When I sat back, I was a little breathless. "You're not upset?"

"I mean . . ." Nathaniel ran his hand through his hair. "I

honestly don't know. We'd decided not to have children. I just . . . I just thought it was a choice."

"Yeah." I understood that all too well.

"And how about you?" He tilted his head, regarding me. "Are you going to tell me about being base administrator?"

For some reason, I flushed as if I'd done something wrong. "Leonard told you that he was going to ask?"

"Asked me if it was okay, in fact." The corner of his mouth twisted to the side as he looked at me. "I told him that he didn't need my permission."

I glared at the ceiling. "Well, that makes me even happier that I said no."

Nathaniel made a weird sound and when I looked down his mouth was hanging open. He shook his head. "Wha—why? You're finally getting recognized for your abilities and . . ." His brows came together and his hand tightened in the fabric of the blanket. "It's not because of me, is it?"

I shook my head, and I wasn't even lying. He was the catalyst but the change was for me. "I realized that I don't like being in charge. I watch Leonard, who came to Mars to be a geologist, and he never gets to go outside." I kept part of my reason un-voiced, because he would hear the wrong thing. I never wanted to be in a position where I had to choose between him and the mission. But that was for me and my heart, not for him. He would hear it as a sacrifice. It wasn't. "Most of Leonard's time is spent indoors doing paperwork. I want to fly."

"But—"

"And I'm a mathematician. Do you know the last time I cre-ated something new?" I sat back, propping myself up on my arms. "I don't think I've even thought about math as more than a utility since I was figuring out the equations for orbital tra-jectories over a decade ago. I miss it. So . . . so I told him no because being an administrator is not who I want to be. It's not how I want to spend my time."

"And how do you want to spend your time, Dr. York?"

I smiled slowly at my husband. "Well, Dr. York . . . how do you feel about a little stargazing?"

He answered me with action, slipping down to lie on the bed and I followed that gravity well down to a familiar warmth.

Nathaniel looked over his head at the window. "Wait." He flicked a switch I hadn't noticed set in the wall over the head-board and turned the lights out. "Look."

Past the tunnel of dirt, the sky came alight with stars. Nathaniel rolled on to his elbows, dipping his head to look out the window. His body was a moving darkness in the night. I saw the silhouette of his hand as he pointed. "That's Earth. And . . . the Moon."

The stars sparkled through my tears. Blue and red, silver and gold, danced against a deep purple. Amid them, low on the horizon to the west where the sun had set, there was a pair of stars. One pale blue, the other a small bright silver.

"That's why I picked this room." He leaned over and kissed my shoulder. "Do you remember when we used to go stargazing in my dad's cabin?"

I laughed, turning to lie down on the bed. "By which you mean sex? Yes, Dr. York, I do."

And then after that, the only stars I saw were the ones painted across the inside of my eyelids.

EPILOGUE

THIRD EXPEDITION LAUNCHES: TEENS TO BECOME MARTIANS

Special to The National Times

ARTEMIS BASE, the Moon, May 9, 1971—The International Aerospace Coalition's Third Mars Expedition commenced its journey today under the command of Sayf Ibn Al Nadim with the launch of the spacecraft *Astrulabi*. Named by its commander after the inventor of the astrolabe, the tenth-century Syrian astronomer Mariam Astrulabi, the *Astrulabi* aims to reach Mars in eight months.

Twenty teenagers are traveling with their parents as part of a study to see how their development continues in one-third gravity. Sixteen-year-old Dorothy Williams expressed her dedication by saying, "Someday I want to be a doctor, and a chance to help people learn more about human physiology on Mars is an amazing opportunity."

Director Stetson Parker of the IAC said, "The mission encapsulates a global effort, showcasing human ingenuity and collaboration." As the *Astrulabi* speeds toward Mars, it carries with it the collective aspirations of a planet eager to extend its reach beyond Earth's boundaries, marking a significant chapter in the history of space exploration.

Octm 51, Year 5, Wednesol-Landing + 446 sols

Leonard stands on a makeshift stage of tables in front of the audience of Martians. Everyone is crowded in the main dome, facing the mural Dawn painted. Folks stand shoulder to shoulder, spilling out of the large group area into the "streets."

I am standing on the floor, holding the book Leonard has entrusted me with. For the first time in more years than I can remember, I do not have to be "on." Sure, I've agreed to continue being the deputy administrator until the Third Expedition arrives, but this isn't my show. This is all about Leonard.

Leonard is in profile from where I stand but I can still see the brightness of his eyes. "You have made me deeply proud. We came here with a mission, to establish a habitat for humanity on a new planet. You have faced hardship, some of which—" His voice is strangled but he carries on. "Some of which was my fault. But you, my brave Martians, you have persevered. You have found a way or made one. I am grateful to have begun this journey as your commander. I am even more grateful to hand this role to someone I trust to keep you safe."

I tighten my grip on the book. Remembered butterflies cavort in my stomach.

"Now, you all know our next commander. He comes to us from Trinidad and has the unenviable distinction of having logged more time as CAPCOM than anyone else on the mission. That means he knows how to translate for every department we have. Sheldon! Come on up."

Sheldon Spender, who I had thought was white for an embarrassing number of years, is focused and calm and one of those fellows who seems to disappear into the background until you realize that he's been tracking every supply and knows where every bolt is stored. He climbs up onto the table next to Leonard.

"Commander Flannery, I stand ready to relieve you."

"I am ready to be relieved." Leonard holds out the logbook for the base. "Your habitat is in good repair and the personnel are as solid a group as one could ask."

"Thank you." Sheldon takes the logbook, and his Adam's apple bobs as he swallows hard. That is the only sign he gives of acknowledging the enormity of the task he is taking on. I know that feeling—the wondering about if I'm making a mistake or if I'll let down the people who have trusted me. But maybe Sheldon is lucky and doesn't have those fears.

Leonard reaches down to me and I put the book in his hand. That is my one task, done. I step to the side and slide into the first row of folks. Leonard straightens and hands the book to Sheldon. "I bestow on you the *Odyssey,* and I know it seems like something useless on Mars, but I promise you that opening it randomly and realizing that you aren't being molested by a Cyclops is very grounding."

Sheldon's grin reminds me of Parker at his most charming but without the shark teeth behind it. He takes the book, weighing it as if feeling a gravity beyond Mars. "Thank you. I shall try to remember that."

"Then I have no further duties."

The younger astronaut straightens his shoulders and sticks his hand out to shake. "I relieve you, commander."

"I—" Leonard's voice breaks and his jaw clenches for a second before he forges ahead. "I stand relieved."

I'm relieved for him. I hadn't understood what a hard road Leonard had needed to forge just to be here at all, much less as our commander. In the South we say "he meant well" and "he did the best he knew how" as a form of insult.

Leonard *had* meant well. He'd done the best he knew how to protect his crew, and those choices had caused harm. But they hadn't happened in a vacuum.

The fault ultimately lay in the people who had not listened to the very first problems with DeBeer. The ones who had said, "It'll be all right," and wanted the money that South Africa had brought more than they had wanted the well-being of their crew.

Leonard steps off the table and people surround him in a massive group hug. From the *Goddard,* we can hear the sound of cheering like rain upon the dome.

Leonard is done with his work as mission commander. Now he is the chief geologist of Mars.

The Martian landscape spreads below us in territory I've never seen before. For a moment, we go weightless as the hopper hits the top of its arc and begins to curve down to the survey site. I watch my altimeter, waiting for it to hit 2,100 meters before I hit the thrusters. Listen, I'm a pilot, and conserving fuel is a game for us.

Beside me, Leonard gasps. "Look at that ridge cut."

Aahana leans forward toward the window. "Is that a gully?"

I concentrate on my instruments. "Firing thrusters in five . . ." In my periphery, I see Leonard brace. "Four, three, two, one."

The thrusters respond to my touch and I ease them into power. In the beginning, it had always been a kick, but I've been flying the hopper so much that I've learned to ghost them into being so that our downward progress slows in a beautiful, imperceptible cancellation of momentum.

I slow us and carefully set us down on Mars.

On Mars.

"Contact light." Beyond the windows, the valley we've flown into stretches its walls toward the butterscotch sky.

"Shutdown." I pull my hands off the control stick and set it to neutral. "Engine stop."

Leonard is grinning so hard that it looks like his face hurts. He leans toward the windows the whole time as if he's going to skip the depress and dive right out onto the surface of Mars. He'd walked out to the hopper but that was across ground he'd been over when we landed.

This? This is a piece of Mars that no human has set foot on before. It is a valley with red walls, streaked with purple-grays. The wan sun casts blue shadows across the corners of the valley. In the distance, a dust devil cavorts in reddish swirls above the valley floor, which is rippled as if waves rolled along here.

"Hot damn. You were right. That's *definitely* a gully. Look at that gorgeous incised network of channels." Leonard thumps Aahana's Mars suit with the back of one hand, not tearing his gaze away from the view.

"Placing bets on downslope sediment deposits?" Her smile matches his.

I laugh, because their delight is infectious. "Y'all are adorable. I'll get you out there ASAP."

They don't skip a step of the checklist, but Leonard keeps pausing as the view catches his gaze. It doesn't really slow him down, though. In short order, we have the hopper secured, supplies ready to off-load, and the depress sequence underway. When the pressure gauge reads green, I stand at the hatch and undog it. "Thank you for flying with Martian Air. We hope you have enjoyed your journey with us."

I swing the hatch open, and a breeze pushes amber dust into the room. I inhale as if I could smell that sulfur funk in my suit.

"Leonard?" Stepping to the side, I wave toward the hatch. "Want to do the honors?"

"Oh!" He steps forward and stops. "Aahana, do you want to be first?"

She steps back. "I've already been the first at a lot of Martian sites."

I wink at him. "Same here. And you are the mission's chief geologist."

He blinks, biting his lips, and nods. Leonard ducks through the hatch and balances on the top of the ladder. He is a silhouette against the backdrop of Mars.

A few steps down the ladder, and then a final hop and Leonard is standing on Mars.

Over the comms, I hear the telltale sniffle of an astronaut whose nose is running. In a helmet, you can't wipe it. I catch Aahana's arm before she steps onto the ladder and nod toward

Leonard. Her eyes widen with understanding and she stops, giving him time to just be on the surface of Mars.

From our place in my ship, we watch him take a few steps forward and then bounce up so that he can sink to his knees. He leans forward and then picks up a stone. "Huh."

I let go of Aahana and she nods, heading toward the ladder. "What did you find?"

"A gneiss rock." He half turns and his smile could power the sun. "Literally."

From there on, the two of them do geology and I act as support personnel. On Mars.

Beneath a translucent dome, the pale green fuzz of living walls circles the greenhouse with layers of racks growing seedlings carefully selected for Mars. Arugula, mouse-ear cress, flax, tomatoes, and radishes are promises to our future. The translucent part of the dome comes down farther here than it does in the main habitat to maximize the amount of daylight the plants get. That translucent arc glows with the pale blue light of dawn.

It has been a long hard slog to get here, but we are finally going to hear the concert that Nicole promised us all when we landed. It had been put off, once because of our disaster and once because of Nicole's schedule. And now I stand at the front of the room helping Aahana and Sheldon prep for their first broadcast.

All of the chairs in our community have been carried in and arranged in rows facing the speakers. Florence looks up from one of the comms stations they'd dragged in here. "Copy, *Goddard*. We read you loud and clear." She laughs, shaking her head. "Listen, I'm still in my pajamas. Hm? Hell, yes, I brought pajamas. You didn't? You're telling me you're sleeping in that rough-ass crepe paper the IAC passes off as nightwear?"

As Florence chats, Dawn checks her watch, then opens her channel to Earth. "New White House, Bradbury. All is ready on this end." She glances at me, standing there, and says, a little pointedly, "Everyone is taking their seats now. Over."

I wave at Dawn. "Sorry. I'll get out of your way."

Another person might be jealous about stepping out of the spotlight. Me? I feel guilty. I know the pressure that Aahana is going to face stepping into this role. She looks calm and regal in a sari of burnished copper, crisscrossed with red and dotted with flecks of brilliant green that seems equal parts Mars and Earth. But one hand is tapping fingers against her thumb as if she's counting something.

I squeeze Aahana's other hand. "You'll do great."

She nods, drawing in a deep breath. "I'm running through the Mohs' hardness scale over and over."

I don't want to abandon her, but I know my role here and step to the side so I can clear the "stage." Some people are seated, others are gathered at the edges, chatting in small groups. Catalina is bending over a planter in a pale green linen sundress. Wilburt is in conversation with a group of other Jewish folks.

Sheldon faces the audience and his voice booms across the parabola of the dome. "Ladies and gentlemen, take your seats, please."

And that is my role now. I am part of the audience.

Silence fills the dome for a moment, before people start moving toward their chairs and resume their interrupted conversations. The makeshift HVAC is quieter than the other domes' because it is so large that it's housed in a storage tube outside, instead of in the machine room at the base of the dome, so I keep hearing snippets of people's chatter.

"... been looking forward to this for months ..."

"... would have sworn to God, I saw a blue box on the surface but ..."

"... saw two dust devils out on survey the other sol ..."

"... nothing there. Just the whirring of the wind ..."

"... a new niece? That's fantastic ..."

"... saving this for Elma." Nathaniel sits in the second row, with a hand on the chair between him and Leonard. He smiles apologetically up at Mavis. "We can talk about the specs for the cliff expansion later?"

"Sure thing." She gives him a little salute and saunters off.

I slide into the vacant chair and lean over to give Nathaniel a kiss. Then I glance at Leonard. "How's the hand?"

"Fine." He grimaces at the ridiculously oversized bandage on his index finger. "Why does Kam do this?"

"I think he's just cruel at heart."

Kam leans forward from the row behind us. "I represent that remark."

Sheldon and Aahana wait at the microphone at the front of the room and have nothing to do. Howard Tang has a camera pointed at them. Another member of the comms team has one of the other cameras aimed at the audience.

"One minute," Dawn says.

In eight minutes, Earth will see us. We won't see anyone from their concert hall, because we only have the ability to get live audio from them. The inequity of that isn't fixable. Not yet. Someday we will have enough satellites orbiting Mars and antennas large enough that we can get moving images from Earth. Now, I have only my memory and imagination to picture the concert goers back there. The people in tuxedos and gowns that could be worn just once. Clothes that were dependent on seasons. Jewelry heavy with metal and stones that did not need to fit into a weight allowance.

Florence says, "Mics are hot."

Aahana wets her lips. My heart speeds up for her, watching another lady astronaut in the spot where I've so often stood. Smiling, she seems calm and at ease as she watches Howard, who watches Dawn. He holds up his hand.

Five. Four. Three. Two. One.

He points at Sheldon, who grins at the camera and the people who fill the greenhouse. "Hello from Bradbury Base on Mars. My name is Sheldon Spender and I'm the habitat administrator. We have assembled all hundred Martians both on the planet and on orbit overhead to join you for this historic concert. In the future, we may have bandstands and concert halls here, but for the moment, we greet you from the greenhouse dome. We are grateful to President Wargin and Duke Ellington for making music for every person across our solar system."

Sheldon yields the microphone to Aahana, whose sari flourishes around her in the light gravity. She smiles at us and at the camera. "Of course, as we say these words, you are already listening to music composed to celebrate the expansion of humanity's home on Mars." I'd told her to imagine speaking to a single person she loves. She'd told me that she will talk to the cousin with whom she'd grown up after her parents died. "When you hear my voice, you will have just finished listening to this wonderful gift even as the first notes reach us. The distance in time makes the distance in space all the more apparent, but we are still united even with the asynchronous nature of this concert."

She passes the mic back to Sheldon, who keeps smiling the same easy smile. He'd told Leonard that he doesn't get nervous. I have no idea what that's like but I'm happy for him.

"What we want you to know is that we think about you all every sol. We're recording this concert to play again later so that the notes will continue to link us together. Thank you for this reminder that regardless of where we live now—Mars, the Moon, or our space stations—we come from many nations and from one place. Earth."

A moment later, Florence says, "And we're out. Mics are off."

Sheldon raises his voice a little, but it doesn't take much given how small the group is. "Okay, everyone, you can chat amongst yourselves until the broadcast from Earth reaches us."

Wilburt says, "I used to tell jokes about radios when I was on the Moon, but the reception was poor."

I laugh with everyone else. Aahana comes to the front row and sits down in the empty seat next to Jaidev, slipping her hand into his. He leans over and kisses her cheek, murmuring something in Hindi. She smiles, dipping her head with pleasure.

I lean forward. "Good job."

"All I did was say a few words."

I remember deferring praise the same way. "You did more than that."

And I was talking to my past self as much as to her.

The sound coming over the speakers changes and delivers the quiet rustle and murmur of a room full of people. Behind them, you can make out the random toots and honks of musicians warming up. More people will be in that room by several magnitudes than live on this entire planet.

An unfamiliar man's voice fills the dome. "Ladies and gentlemen, the president of the United States."

Cloth rustles as people in that distant place stand. I feel the urge myself and stifle it.

Nicole has taught me the power of an image. I know what they will see on Earth. If I stand, everyone else on Mars will stand and the image that they will show on Earth is of Mars honoring a single nation. We can't be that. We need to be for everyone, so I stay seated with my husband.

"Thank you." The richness of Nicole's voice is attenuated by the distance but her warmth remains. In the silence, fabric rustles as hundreds of far away people sit again.

"Good evening, everyone and good morning, Mars. Sorry about the time." Nicole gives a low chuckle. "But if it makes you feel better, our friends listening in Taiwan are experiencing the same time zone today. For those of our listeners who don't know, Mars's day is thirty-nine minutes longer than ours. I wish I had some of that extra time to get things done."

The polite laughter of the room merges with ours in the dome even though my sol doesn't feel thirty-nine minutes longer. I slip my hand into Nathaniel's. I will always, always need more time than I have.

"This evening, we are going to hear the debut performance of a new composition by Duke Ellington sung by the incomparable Ella Fitzgerald. This is the first interplanetary concert and the composition we'll be hearing is honoring your work." Her voice thickens as if she is on the edge of tears but that has to be my imagination because Nicole never cries. "I can't tell you how much I wish I were up there with you, so consider this music an umbilical connecting our homes. I hope you enjoy it."

Applause fills our space and I can imagine Nicole walking off the stage. I clap, missing her. A hush falls over the crowd on Mars, matching the active silence of the broadcast. A moment later, the audience on Earth applauds something we can't see which is probably Duke Ellington walking to the podium or perhaps Ella Fitzgerald. Or maybe both.

I have listened to so many live radio broadcasts of concerts on Earth and I have never put so much effort into imagining the room where the concert took place. I've listened to them while doing dishes or sitting in the living room with my parents on a lazy Sunday evening. And now on Mars.

The first notes cross the 149 million kilometers from Earth and twinkling piano notes bounce around the dome in a complicated 5/4 rhythm that is mathematically beautiful as the notes fold around themselves. Beneath the piano, a bass swirls like dancers across the floor.

Ella Fitzgerald croons into a space between the notes, weaving her voice into the pattern as if it has always been there.

Mars Maiden, in the vast expanse
Mars Maiden, my heart's caught in a trance
I made my approach and then revolved
But my big problem is still unsolved.

The music is beautiful but it doesn't conjure Mars in my mind. It represents a vision of Mars by someone who has never been here and likely never will be.

Mars Maiden, listen here, my dear
Your vibrations are coming in loud and clear.

How long will it take before musicians compose music on Mars for Martians? How long will it take before the embroidery that Florence does is replaced by equally beautiful but very different views of Mars? The music loops and soars on.

> *To help a wanderer, lost in space*
> *And with you, I'll find my rightful place*
> *Mars Maiden, Mars Maiden*
> *Lady of the Red.*

As I listen to music from another world, I squeeze Nathaniel's hand. It's amazing how much time can change the way you see something. Earth had been our home and it isn't anymore. This is my rightful place, here with Nathaniel and Leonard and Helen and Aahana and all the other Martians, building a future together. We aren't wanderers, lost in space.

We are home.

ACKNOWLEDGMENTS

Writing books is always hard. This one was particularly hard because I was writing it in what we've started calling "The Year of Five Deaths." I turned it in the week before my mom died, rougher than any book I've ever turned in, because I knew that if I didn't do it then, I wouldn't touch it for months. So, I want to thank my family, who helped me make time for writing during a really rough period. Also thanks to my agent, Seth Fishman, who is my constant advocate. My editor, Claire Eddy, who didn't complain about the extra work of getting a novel that was pretty messy. Eli Goldman, for going above and beyond. My assistants Jessi Honard, Marie Parks, and Sarah Sward kept my "tiny empire" functional when I was not.

With the Lady Astronaut novels, in particular, I rely on the kindness and expertise of so many people because there are a lot of subjects that need an expert's eye.

I had been having trouble finding the right structure for the novel. We were recording an episode of *Writing Excuses* about structure with Peng Shepherd, and she talked about how you could structure a story around an object, like a building, a clock, or a calendar. The book kind of unpacked itself in my head while we were recording because I realized that calendar touched everything I wanted to do with the book, because calendar and culture are so intertwined. As people become Martians, how will the different calendar affect them? I am happy I did it and also regretted that choice so many times. I have to give a big thank you to Max Fagin and Jesse Vincent for the help with the calendars. I'll talk about that more in the "About the History" section. Also on the calendar front, thanks to Rabbi Dr. Andrea Lobel for having conversations with me about how the Judaic calendar would interface with Mars. Rabbi Rachel Barenblat had great insights on being a Southern Jew. And Rachel Gutin provided much of Druzylla's commentary about dates in her notes on the novel. (They are Rachel B. and Rachel G. in the novel.) I need to do a HUGE thanks to Bailey Harrington who caught a ton of continuity errors with the calendar. FYI calendars are hard.

Thanks to Mahtab Narisiman for the little bit of Hindi. I asked her for a terrible pickup line and she gave me "You must be a thief, you've stolen my heart."

One of the mantras in my life that I gifted to the characters comes from Jen Coster: "Two things can be true." I keep having to remind myself of this.

For the environmental controls, I had a delightful conversation with Kipp Bradford about HVAC and repairs on Mars. That's where I got the CO_2 accident, salvaging the engines, and the heat sink. You can watch part of that conversation on my YouTube channel, and the full conversation is in the archives of my Patreon. Also providing excellent Mars knowledge, Dr. Tanya Harrison responded to numerous geology questions. The gullies that Leonard and Aahana discover come from her.

Cassie Alexander helped me with all of the burn stuff. You know you're a writer when you get excited by learning words like "deroof." On the other medical stuff, thanks go to Benjamin Kinney.

Years ago, I went on a #NASAsocial event and they talked about growing plants in space. One of the folks there was Dr. John Kiss, who was doing all sorts of interesting plant experiments. He gave me an hour of his time to understand what they would be growing and how it would grow. He also gave me this great list of plants that have already been trialed in simulated Martian regolith. You have no idea how much I wanted to use allllll of that.

Also on the food front, Vickie Kloeris gave me so much information about the problems of food on Mars. She was the NASA manager of first the shuttle and then the International

Space Station food systems. She also has a book called *Space Bites* that was not out in time for me to use as a resource but all of you can. The food is the part of the science that I probably handwave the most.

Many thanks to Jenna Ruggenberg and Lindsay Jones Marean for talking to me about Citizen Potawatomi Nation. I knew that I wanted to talk about the word "colony" and they helped me shape that conversation.

I'm always eternally grateful to the people who work in space who help me with these books. In particular, Cady Coleman, Kjell Lindgren, Yael Hochberg, and Cathy Watson. Adam Savage let me try on more than one of his spacesuits which was so, so helpful.

My beta readers for this one were Sorcha O'Brien, Francesca Kuehlers, Steve Ramage, Carol H. Mack, Kimberley Savill, Caroline Westra, Vicky Hsu, Deana Covel Whitney, C. L. Polk, and Rachel Gutin. The members of the Lady Astronaut club are always wonderful, but especial thanks go to Rhonda Rowland, Gabrielle Moticka, Ana Ortuzar, Rachel Gutin, Demetria Lam, Savy Meacham, and Alyshondra Meacham, who listened to me read the copy edit out loud amid much cursing as I found continuity errors. Speaking of reading aloud, my audiobook engineer Andrew Twiss has been with me for all of these books. He continually makes me sound better and catches continuity errors that everyone else misses. Plus, he's fun.

Thanks to everyone at Tor who cares about my books. I appreciate each of you. Claire Eddy, my editor; Eli Goldman and Julianna Kim, assistants to Claire; Jamie Stafford-Hill, my amazing cover designer; Desirae Friesen, my publicist; Emily Honer, my marketer; managing editor Rafal Gibek; Dakota Griffin, my production editor; production manager Jim Kapp; copyeditor Janine Barlow; and Lauren Hougen, my proofreader.

Also, thanks to my team at Kaye publicity: Katelynn Dreyer, Dana Kaye, Amanda LaConte, and Eleanor Imbody. Y'all rock.

Other folks to thank just for being great: Erin Roberts,

DongWon Song, Howard Tayler, Sandra Tayler, Dan Wells, Emma Reynolds, Marshall Carr Jr, Nathan Beittenmiller, Lisa Crotty, and Mary Tucker.

Finally, I want to really thank my husband, Robert. I always do in these, but he kept me steady more than usual. I literally could not have written this book without him.

ABOUT THE HISTORY

The farther we get from the Meteor strike in 1952, the more the Lady Astronaut Universe diverges from our own. Still, I am constantly using real history and science as models for events in the book. Because I am a giant nerd, I love learning about things, and I hope you do, too.

When Perseverance and Ingenuity arrived on Mars, they both carried microphones. You can hear the sound of Mars for the first time. Having a different atmosphere than Earth's, the speed of sound is also different. According to the paper "Sound Speed on Mars measured by the SuperCam Microphone on Perseverance," delivered at the fifty-third Lunar and Planetary Science Conference, "due to the unique properties of the carbon dioxide molecules at low pressure, Mars is the only terrestrial-planet atmosphere in the Solar System experiencing a change in speed of sound right in the middle of the audible bandwidth (20 Hz—20 kHz)." Basically, if you were listening to music on the surface of Mars, you'd hear the sopranos before the basses. I did not have an opportunity to use as much of this as I wanted to.

The atmosphere on Mars is the narrative gift that keeps giving. It makes landing on Mars hard. It's got just enough atmosphere to be a problem and not enough to be useful. In Elma's world, they are using a craft that comes in similar to a shuttle, with as much aerobraking as it can, then does a "swoop" maneuver to shift so it can use retro-rockets to control the descent.

I'll be honest, some of the reason the craft lands like this is that I did *not* check with a rocket engineer when I had Elma land at the end of *The Fated Sky*. I based that on Moon landings and Mars is very, very different. I worked with Max Fagin to come up with a plausible design that would work with what I'd already written.

All of the cargo drops are much more sensible and are based on real designs. The hopper is also based on a real proposed design.

The plans for Bradbury Base come from multiple sources, most of which I modeled after Moon bases. My reasoning is that the IAC would test things on the Moon and then modify them for Mars to speed up development time and reduce costs. As such, Bradbury Base's components are basically the same as Artemis Base, which is inspired by a 1989 inflatable dome design from NASA.

Because they are in Gale Crater, they have set down close enough to the crater rim to be able to tunnel into it. Ultimately, Bradbury Base will be part cliff dwellings and part buried habitats. Due to the radiation on Mars, living on the surface will never be a good idea.

Times and dates on Mars are weird and hard. So many regrets. There's the obvious thing that Mars's day is thirty-nine minutes longer than Earth and its year is almost twice as long as ours. This means that meshing the Earth calendar and the Mars calendar was already going to be annoying. Then I needed to layer on the Jewish calendar, the Islamic calendar, the Chinese calendar, and the Hindu calendar, and, and, and . . . It was a lot. Jesse Vincent listened to me complaining and fell down the rabbit hole of researching various systems for telling time on Mars.

We settled on the system designed by American astronomer I. M. Levitt. It divides the year into twelve months that are 56 or 55 sols. He's the one who had the idea to just append an "m" to the end of the months. The sol versus day was proposed much earlier and is in active use at the Jet Propulsion Laboratory for people who work with the Mars rovers. "Next sol" and "yestersol" evolved naturally in their conversations as a way to differentiate between talking about Earth or Mars. Check out Nagin Cox's TED Talk, "What time is it on Mars?"

So, in addition to all of that, the time lag from Earth to Mars affected so many things. Max Fagin then created this massive spreadsheet that tracks allllll of that. It even tracks Elma's period. Without him, I wouldn't have known about the communications blackout when the Earth goes behind the sun.

Throughout the book, I base newspaper articles on real ones from *The New York Times* and adjust events to match the conditions of my world. One of the excerpts that is unchanged is the one that heads chapter five, "Indian Schooling in US Is Assailed." In it is the phrase "the only good Bureau of Indian Affairs." This is a loaded phrase and I waffled about including it. It comes from a really horrific thing that General Philip Sheridan said in the 1880s. You can look it up. I'm not going to reprint it here. The original writer of the article knew that history and used it to slam the United States for its policy of forcibly removing children from their families.

When I talked to Lindsay Jones Marean about Opal, I wanted to know about cultural traditions she might have brought to Mars with her. Given when the character would have been born, she would have been taken from her family and raised in a residential school. Her name would have been changed. She would have been punished for speaking her own language. She would have been raised with "Anglo-American ideals" and not allowed to practice her own culture. Bounties were offered for students who tried to run away, and the schools had a very high rate of death by suicide. So what culture would she have brought to Mars? One made of childhood memories and forced assimilation.

Also among the real articles is the one at the start of chapter twenty-nine, "Kashmir Assembly to Get Bill Legalizing Abortion." This article is real and from 1970. The bill passed in 1971. I made some adjustments to include pressure from the Meteor, but otherwise this is just straight-up history. In 1970, Iceland was not the only country that would have allowed Ana Teresa to perform the abortion, but it met my needs for citizenship requirements in that period. Plus, I just like Iceland.

Mars suits would have similar constraints that the Apollo

suits did. Regolith is hard on spacesuits. It's very sharp. There are some cool designs out there. One place that I deviate is that I think Mars suits would be high-viz green to contrast with the regolith. The shuttle-era "pumpkin suits" were bright orange to help with search and rescue. Orange wouldn't have a high contrast on Mars, so I'm guessing they would go with green. That said, this only works because red-green color-blindness is currently a disqualifier for being an astronaut. A shout-out to Bailey Harrington who checked for me and proposed royal blue for future missions.

Speaking of spacesuits, the pull-up sleeve of fruit used to be standard in the Apollo suits. That anecdote about the cherry pull-up making an astronaut's foot look bloody apparently really happened. The bruising, delamination of fingernails, and shoulder problems are all things that happen to astronauts. There is one thing however, which is all my own—the fruit pull-up repair. One of the astronauts I showed this to said that there was a seriously unbelievable thing about it: "I don't believe, for a minute, that they wouldn't have already eaten the fruit pull-up."

The song "Mars Maiden" at the end is based on "Moon Maiden" by Duke Ellington, which was composed for the Apollo 11 mission. He sang it, and it was very much a song from the late 1960s. Worth a listen, but also why I had Ella Fitzgerald sing "Mars Maiden" instead.

BIBLIOGRAPHY

Chaikin, Andrew. *A Man on the Moon: The Voyages of the Apollo Astronauts.* New York: Penguin Books, 2007.

Coleman, Cady. *Sharing Space: An Astronaut's Guide to Mission, Wonder, and Making Change.* New York: Penguin Life, 2024.

Collins, Michael. *Carrying the Fire: An Astronaut's Journeys.* New York: Farrar, Straus and Giroux, 2009.

Etzioni, Amitai. *The Moon-Doggle: Domestic and International Implications of the Space Race.* New York: Doubleday and Company, Inc., 1964.

Hadfield, Chris. *An Astronaut's Guide to Life on Earth: What Going to Space Taught Me About Ingenuity, Determination, and Being Prepared for Anything.* New York: Back Bay Books, 2015.

Hardesty, Von. *Black Wings: Courageous Stories of African Americans in Aviation and Space History.* New York: HarperCollins, 2008.

Holt, Nathalia. *Rise of the Rocket Girls: The Women Who Propelled Us, from Missiles to the Moon to Mars.* New York: Little, Brown and Company, 2016.

Jessen, Gene Nora. *Sky Girls: The True Story of the First Women's Cross-Country Air Race.* Naperville, Illinois: Sourcebooks, 2018.

Kloeris, Vickie. *Space Bites: Reflections of a NASA Food Scientist.* Ballast Books, 2023.

Kurson, Robert. *Rocket Men: The Daring Odyssey of Apollo 8 and the Astronauts Who Made Man's First Journey to the Moon.* New York: Random House, 2018.

Nolen, Stephanie. *Promised the Moon: The Untold Story of the First Women in the Space Race.* New York: Basic Books, 2004.

Roach, Mary. *Packing for Mars: The Curious Science of Life in the Void.* New York: W. W. Norton & Company, 2011.

Scott, David Meerman and Richard Jurek. *Marketing the Moon: The Selling of the Apollo Lunar Program.* Cambridge: The MIT Press, 2014.

Shetterly, Margot Lee. *Hidden Figures: The American Dream and the Untold Story of the Black Women Mathematicians Who Helped Win the Space Race.* New York: William Morrow, 2016.

Sobel, Dava. *The Glass Universe: How the Ladies of the Harvard Observatory Took the Measure of the Stars.* New York: Penguin Books, 2017.

Teitel, Amy Shira. *Breaking the Chains of Gravity: The Story of Spaceflight before NASA.* New York: Bloomsbury Sigma, 2018.

von Braun, Dr. Wernher. *Project MARS: A Technical Tale.* Burlington, Ontario: Collector's Guide Publishing, Inc., 2006.

Weinersmith, Kelly and Zach Weinersmith. *A City on Mars: Can We Settle Space, Should We Settle Space, and Have We Really Thought This Through?* New York: Penguin Press, 2023.

NOW'S *YOUR* CHANCE TO BE A
Lady Astronaut

Adventure in Outer Space... thrills and excitement as space-ships soar from planet to planet! Here's how you can start now to be a Lady Astronaut! Be the first in your crowd! And then -- get the whole crowd to

FORM A
LADY ASTRONAUT CLUB!

DON'T WAIT!
use address below and
SEND A SASE TODAY!

This is to certify that

is a qualified member of
The Lady Astronaut Club

And solemnly swears to uphold the ideal of freedom for individuals — to advance cooperation between nations — and promote the cause of peace throughout the Universe.

A Lady Astronaut Club
Interplanetary Membership Card!

Lady Astronaut Club
PO Box 686
333 E Main Street
Lehi UT 84043
USA, EARTH

Learn more about the adventures of Dr. Elma York, the original Lady Astronaut! Plus, at live events show your Lady Astronaut Club card for additional membership perks! Don't delay!

maryrobinettekowal.com

ABOUT THE AUTHOR

Dani Lore

MARY ROBINETTE KOWAL is the author of the Hugo, Nebula, and Locus Award–winning alternate history novel *The Calculating Stars,* the first book in the Lady Astronaut series. She is also the author of the Glamourist Histories series, *Ghost Talkers,* and *The Spare Man.* She has received the Astounding Award for Best New Writer, four Hugo Awards, and the Nebula and Locus Awards. Her stories appear in *Asimov's Science Fiction, Uncanny,* and several Year's Best anthologies. Kowal has also worked as a professional puppeteer, is a member of the award-winning podcast *Writing Excuses,* and performs as a voice actor (SAG/AFTRA) recording fiction for authors including Seanan McGuire, Cory Doctorow, and Neal Stephenson. She lives with her husband, Rob; their dog, Guppy; and their talking cat, Elsie. Visit her online at maryrobinettekowal.com.